MORNING AT JALNA

MORNING AT JALNA

MAZO DE LA ROCHE

DUNDURN
TORONTO

Copy Editor: Jennifer McKnight
Design: Emma Dolan and Jesse Hooper
Printer: Webcom

Library and Archives Canada Cataloguing in Publication

De la Roche, Mazo, 1879-1961
    Morning at Jalna / Mazo de la Roche.

Issued also in electronic formats.
ISBN 978-1-55488-915-0

    I. Title.

PS8507.E43M67 2011   C813'.52   C2011-901924-8

1   2   3   4   5   15   14   13   12   11

We acknowledge the support of the **Canada Council for the Arts** and the **Ontario Arts Council** for our publishing program. We also acknowledge the financial support of the **Government of Canada** through the **Canada Book Fund** and **Livres Canada Books**, and the **Government of Ontario** through the **Ontario Book Publishing Tax Credit** and the **Ontario Media Development Corporation**.

Care has been taken to trace the ownership of copyright material used in this book. The author and the publisher welcome any information enabling them to rectify any references or credits in subsequent editions.

J. Kirk Howard, President

Printed and bound in Canada.
www.dundurn.com

Dundurn
3 Church Street, Suite 500
Toronto, Ontario, Canada
M5E 1M2

Gazelle Book Services Limited
White Cross Mills
High Town, Lancaster, England
LA1 4XS

Dundurn
2250 Military Road
Tonawanda, NY
U.S.A. 14150

To Jack and Tony Gray with my love

CONTENTS

I

THE HOME IN THE NEW COUNTRY

When the American Civil War broke out, this house Jalna, in Ontario, had been completed not many years before. The owner, Captain Whiteoak, and his family had been installed there since the birth of his second son. He and his Irish wife, Adeline Court, had come from India and romantically named the house after the military station to which his regiment there was assigned. Captain Whiteoak had been tired of the restraints of army life. He had longed for the freedom and space of the New World. Adeline Whiteoak always was eager for adventure. Now they felt themselves, if not actually pioneers, to be imbued with the spirit of pioneers, yet they had surrounded themselves with many of the amenities of the old land.

The house, a substantial one of a pleasing shade of brick, with green shutters and five tall chimneys, stood in a thousand acres of land only a few miles from Lake Ontario, the shores of which were deeply wooded and were the haunt of thousands of birds. The virgin soil was rich and prolific of its life-giving growth. Whatever was planted in it flourished with abandon.

The children of the Whiteoaks knew no life other than this free and healthy round of seasons. There were four of them — Augusta, Nicholas,

Ernest, and the last comer, the baby Philip. (His father had gone back on his earlier determination to be the only Philip in the family.) The parents were indulgent with them, though at times severe in discipline. Their father would give them orders, when they displeased him, in a stern military voice. Their mother would sometimes, in exasperation, beat them with her own hands, for she had a fiery temper. The daughter, Augusta, suffered discipline with dignified resignation; Nicholas, with a certain haughtiness; Ernest, with tears and promises to be good. Philip, the baby, scarcely knew what it was to be crossed, and if he were, lay down on the floor and kicked and screamed.

On this summer day, husband and wife were looking forward, with not unmixed pleasure, to a visit from an American couple from South Carolina.

"I can't understand," Philip was saying, "why you are so concerned over this visit. The Sinclairs must take us as they find us. We have nothing to be ashamed of in the way we live. There is no finer house or better-run estate in this province, I'll be bound."

"But think what they are used to," cried Adeline. "A huge plantation, with hundreds of slaves to wait on them — We don't know the first thing about real elegance. We should have an entire suite to offer them, instead of one paltry bedroom and a cubbyhole for Mrs. Sinclair's maid."

"The guestroom is not paltry. It's a fine room handsomely furnished. If they don't like it they can lump it."

"And how are you going to entertain Mr. Sinclair?" she demanded. "Escort him to view the turnip field? To inspect the twin calves?"

This conversation was interrupted by the noise of their two sons racing along the passage and clattering in their sturdy boots down the stairs. As Nicholas overtook Ernest, the little boy gave a shriek of pretended terror. Ordinarily this display of high spirits would have passed unnoticed by their parents but now Philip said, "They must not carry on like this after our visitors arrive."

"Don't worry," said Adeline. "I am sending the older children to the Busbys for three days. I arranged it with Mrs. Busby yesterday."

"Gussie knows how to behave herself," remarked Philip.

"She would miss her brothers. I want an atmosphere of complete peace when the Sinclairs arrive. In Lucy Sinclair's last letter she spoke of the sad state of her nerves."

"Are you aware," demanded Philip, "that the Busbys are completely on the side of the Yankees?"

"I have not told them," she said, "who our visitors are. Simply that they are friends we made on our last trip to England."

Philip was perturbed. "Elihu Busby would not like it. I'm certain of that."

"The Sinclairs are not visiting him." She spoke hotly. "Let him mind his own business."

"The children will tell."

"They'd better not," she exclaimed. She gathered her three eldest about her.

"You are to spend three days with the Busbys," she said.

"Hurrah," cried Nicholas. "I've always wanted a visit to their farm. Everybody works but they always have time for fun."

"Listen to me, children." Adeline spoke in a tone of portentous warning. "You are not on any account to mention that our guests are from the South and may be bringing one or two servants with them."

"Blackamoors!" exclaimed Nicholas. "I've never seen one and I'm dying to."

"Are they dangerous?" asked Ernest.

"Of course not, you little ninny," said his mother. "Remember to say that our guests are friends we met in England. I depend on you, Augusta."

"I'll remember," Augusta promised, in her low voice that would become contralto, "but sooner or later the Busbys will find out."

"Of course they will, but if they find out at once they'll probably be so disgusted they'll send you home again. Patsy will drive you to the Busbys'. Now go, and remember also your manners."

She left them.

"Manners, my eye," said Ernest. Augusta was shocked.

"Ernest, wherever did you hear that horrid expression?"

"I don't know."

"Well, you had better forget it. Come now and wash your face and brush your hair." She took him by the hand.

Patsy O'Flynn, the Irish servant from Adeline's old home who had accompanied the family to Canada, was waiting on the drive with a wagonette drawn by a sturdy piebald cob. His sharp features looked out from a fringe of sandy whiskers and unkempt hair.

"Come along, do," he urged the children, "for I've no time to be gallivanting the countryside, with the work of two men piled on to me."

Philip and Adeline had come into the porch to see their children depart. It was as if they were setting out on a journey, rather than going to spend a few days with a neighbour. The children were somewhat pampered. Captain Whiteoak himself carried their portmanteau, though Nicholas was a strong lad. Adeline took out her own handkerchief and wiped Ernest's pert little nose, though he had a clean handkerchief of his own, with the initial E on a corner, in the pocket of his blouse.

"See to it that his nose does not dribble," she admonished Augusta. Captain Whiteoak lifted Ernest into the wagonette. Their mother raised her handsome face and gave each of her children a hearty kiss.

"Whatever comes your way," she said, "accept it with the gracious calm shown by me." She said to the driver, "Patsy Joe, if you let that pony wander into the ditch and overturn the wagonette, as you did once before, I'll be the death of you."

The wagonette moved swiftly away. Nero, the great black Newfoundland dog, bounded alongside. Summer sunshine found its way through the densest trees and glittered on the rump of the piebald cob whose hooves made only a soft thud on the sandy loam of the road.

When the Busbys' rambling frame farmhouse appeared, Augusta said to Ernest, "Not a word now about blackamoors. Remember."

"Blackamoors, my eye!" said Ernest. There was no time to reprimand him. They all clambered out.

II

The Visitors

Lucy Sinclair remarked to her husband:

"That little fellow could be a perfect pest but so far he's rather sweet."

"Certainly he's very pretty," said Curtis Sinclair.

Both turned their weary eyes on little Philip Whiteoak who was struggling to build a house of toy bricks on the grass nearby. It was as much as he could do to place one brick on top of another but he heaped them with commanding concentration and pouted his baby lips in resolve.

"He favours his papa," said Lucy Sinclair.

"A typical Englishman." Her husband spoke half-admiringly, half in resentment. "A stubborn, self-opinionated type."

"These people," said she, "are our friends; it's heaven to be here."

"They are generosity itself," he agreed. "Whiteoak said to me this morning — 'You are to consider this your home — you and Mrs. Sinclair and your servants — till the war is over.'"

She took out a lace handkerchief and wiped her eyes. "What will be left to us?" she exclaimed with a sob.

The tiny boy left his building bricks and came to her. He patted her on the knee. "Poor lady," he said. "Don't cry."

She stroked his blond curls. "You little darling," she said, and added, "No, I won't cry. I'll be brave to please you."

Her husband laid his hand on her other knee. It was a singularly handsome hand. Always had she admired the thumb in particular. It was almost as long as a finger and perfectly rounded, the nail showing a half-moon. Her eyes moved from his hand to his pale elegant profile, and from his profile to his strong thickset body, with the pronounced hump on the back. He was a hunchback, and because of this affliction had not been able to remain in the South and fight for his country but had come to Canada with his delicate wife, hoping that he might do something to influence the fortunes of the South. In any case it was necessary to get Lucy out of the country. He was now impoverished yet still thought of himself as an independent Southern planter.

Shortly before the Civil War the Sinclairs had met the Whiteoaks in England where Philip and Adeline were on holiday. The meeting had quickly blossomed into friendship. Both couples were fascinated by the differences in the others — the Sinclairs typically Carolinian, the Whiteoaks English and Irish. The Whiteoaks had invited the Sinclairs to visit them in Canada but it was only now, and in such tragic circumstances, that the visit was paid.

They had arrived three days before. Everything to the Sinclairs was so strange, so Northern, yet so friendly, the Whiteoak family so healthy, so amiable. The days were warm but the nights cool. They slept in a great four-poster and under them a feather bed. They felt far removed from the ruin of their own home, from all that was familiar to them. They had brought with them three slaves, for they felt incapable of living without them. One was Lucy Sinclair's personal maid, an attractive mulatto. One was a cook, already quarrelling with the Whiteoaks' cook. The third was a man, a sturdy young Negro.

Lucy Sinclair remarked to her husband: "At any moment we shall be summoned to tea, a meal I could very well do without. Oh, this eternal tea-drinking!"

Her husband grunted in sympathy but said, "Control your voice, Lucy. Even that child appears to be listening to you."

The small Philip had his blue eyes fixed disapprovingly on them.

He looked about to cry. Lucy bent towards him as though admiring the house of blocks he was building.

She clapped her hands and exclaimed: "Pretty! Pretty!"

"Be thankful we're here, Lucy. Show the Whiteoaks that you appreciate their kindness. Here comes Philip. Eager, I suppose, for three cups of tea, scones, and blackberry jam. Smile, Lucy."

She did not need to be told that. The sight of the handsome blond Philip Whiteoak was enough to bring a pleased smile to any woman's face. He said:

"I hope you're feeling better, Mrs. Sinclair, and ready for a hearty tea. I'm told that it's waiting in the dining room."

He gave her an admiring look as she rose and shook out the folds of her skirt. He averted his eyes from Curtis Sinclair's disfigured back. At that moment a nursemaid came hurrying from the house, picked up the tiny boy, who gave a cry of protest, and carried him indoors.

They found Adeline Whiteoak and her three older children standing about the tea table: Augusta, with long black curls and a heavy fringe of hair over her high forehead — a reserved child, just nicely into her teens; Nicholas, next in age, an eager boy, with beautiful dark eyes and wavy hair. He looked fearless and proud, even bold, but was well-mannered. The blue-eyed, fair-haired Ernest was two years younger. Adeline appeared almost consciously to make a picturesque group with her children.

"My brood," she said, "all but the baby. They have been spending a few days with friends. I thought it a good idea, while you settled in, for I knew you must be very tired."

The Sinclairs greeted the three children with formal courtesy, most flattering to them. Nicholas drew himself up and looked manly. Ernest gave a pleased smile. Augusta, with downcast eyes, wore an expression of uncertainty. She could not decide whether or not she would like these slave owners. Certainly they were the guests of her papa, but in the house where she had been visiting she had heard things said against them. How beautiful the lady was and how elegantly dressed! Even though Augusta's eyes were downcast, she was conscious of all this.

"Thank God," exclaimed Lucy Sinclair, "I have no children to inherit the tragedy of our lives! That would be beyond bearing."

Her husband, to relieve the tension caused by her emotion, remarked: "I suppose all your children were born here at Jalna."

"No, indeed," said Philip. "Our daughter was born in India where my regiment was stationed. I sold my commission. We sailed to England and Ireland to visit our people and from there sailed for Canada."

It was not in Adeline Whiteoak's nature to be outdone in an exhibition of feeling. Now, the picture of a tragedy queen, she recalled that voyage.

"What a heartbreaking time it was!" she cried. "The goodbyes to my family in Ireland. We knew we might never see them again. There were my father and mother mourning — all my dear brothers. And then a terrible voyage. My Indian ayah died and we buried her at sea."

Here Philip broke in to say, "And I had the baby to dandle! That one," and he pointed to Augusta whose head drooped in shame. He went on, "This boy Nicholas was born in Quebec. Ernest was the first Whiteoak to be born in this house." He put his arm about the little boy's shoulders and Ernest looked proudly about the table at which all were now seating themselves.

Adeline poured tea and Lucy Sinclair remarked, "I've been admiring those handsome portraits of you and Captain Whiteoak."

"In his Hussars' uniform," said Adeline. "We had them done just before we sailed for Canada."

"In Ireland?" asked Lucy Sinclair.

Adeline nodded, avoiding Philip's eyes, but he said firmly, "No. They were painted in London by a very fashionable artist. Do you think they are good likenesses?"

Both the Sinclairs found the likenesses perfect. They gazed at them in admiration, then Lucy Sinclair said, "It breaks my heart to think what has probably happened to the portraits, going back for four generations, in my old home."

"You must not feel discouraged," said Philip, with his strong, comforting glance. "Things will take a turn for the better."

They were now seated at the table. Nicholas said suddenly, addressing the Sinclairs, "In the house where my brother and sister and I have been visiting, they think Mr. Lincoln is a splendid man."

"Do they indeed?" Curtis Sinclair said tranquilly.

"One of their sons is fighting with the Yankees," continued Nicholas. "They pray for him and Mr. Lincoln. Do you think that is wrong?"

"Nobody wants to hear your voice," said Philip sternly. "Eat your bread and butter."

Little Ernest spoke up. "Our friend Mr. Busby says Lincoln is a hero."

"One word more from either of you," said their father, "and you go."

The small boys subsided but appeared less crushed under the rebuke than did their sister.

"I hear," said Adeline Whiteoak, "that the Lincolns know nothing of good manners."

"Neither they nor their sons," said Mrs. Sinclair. "They are an uncouth quartet."

"Manners maketh man," spoke up little Ernest. "That's in my copy book."

"Children," said their mother, "you may be excused."

The three rose, each gave a little bow to the grownups and sedately left the room. Once outdoors they danced across the lawn in their excitement. It was so unusual to have visitors, especially visitors from America.

"They're having a civil war," said Nicholas.

"Does that mean they're fighting to be civilized?" asked little Ernest.

Augusta put an arm about him. "No, little silly," she said. "They are very elegant and well-mannered, Mr. and Mrs. Sinclair, I mean. But the Yankees won't let them keep their slaves in peace. So they are at war."

"There goes the man slave now," said Nicholas. "I'm going to speak to him."

"No, no," begged Augusta. "He might not like it."

He put aside her restraining hand. Gussie and Ernest remained aloof but Nicholas marched straight to the Negro.

"You like being in Canada?" he asked.

"Yaas, suh, it's fine here," said the man, his inscrutable eyes looking toward the treetops.

"Do you like to get away from the war?"

"Yaas, suh, it's good to get away from the war," answered the man.

Ernest had followed his brother. Now clinging to his arm he asked, in a small voice, "Did you like being a slave?"

"Yaas, suh, it was fine."

"But you're free, now that you're in Canada, aren't you?" persisted Nicholas.

"I haven't thought about it," said the Negro.

"What is your name?" asked Ernest.

"Jerry Cram."

Augusta called sternly to her brothers, "Boys! You were told not to ask questions. You'll get into trouble with Mamma. Do leave off and come for a walk."

The two boys came reluctantly. They saw the pretty young mulatto housemaid come out of the side door and linger near the Negro.

"She's not supposed to talk to him," said Augusta.

"How can she help it when she's in the same house with him?" Nicholas eyed the pair with curiosity.

"Is that flirting?" asked little Ernest.

"Wherever did you hear such talk, Ernest?" She took her small brother by the hand and led him firmly away.

Nicholas said, "I asked Mrs. Sinclair's lady's maid."

"What is a lady's maid?" interrupted Ernest.

"Little silly! A lady's maid dresses a lady, brushes her hair, sews on her buttons. This Annabelle gives Mrs. Sinclair's hair one hundred strokes with the brush every night. Have you noticed how her hair glistens? That's the brushing."

"Our mamma's hair is red," said Ernest. "She says she is glad none of us got it from her. Why, I wonder."

"It's considered a blemish," said Augusta.

"Why?"

"I don't know, but I suppose black or brown or golden are better."

"Gussie, I heard someone say to Mamma, 'Your beautiful hair, Mrs. Whiteoak.'"

"Who said that?"

"I think it was Mr. Wilmott."

"What did Mamma say?" asked Nicholas.

"She said — 'You old silly.'"

"That's just her way," said Nicholas. "She didn't mean it."

"Do you think she *liked* it?" asked Augusta, shocked.

"Certainly. Women love compliments. When you're grown up you'll love them."

"Indeed I shan't." She looked offended.

Two manly figures now emerged from the woods that bordered the very paths of the estate, giving it an air of primeval seclusion and grandeur. These were the figures of Elihu Busby, the neighbour in whose house the three children had been visiting. He had been born in Canada and was excessively patriotic, and proud of the fact. Compared with him his neighbours were newcomers and he expected them to look to him for guidance in the affairs of the country. One of his sons was fighting with the army of the North in the American Civil War and of this he was proud. He looked on slavery as an abomination.

The other manly figure was that of David Vaughan, another neighbour.

"I hear," said Busby, "that you have visitors."

"Yes," said Augusta. "They have come for a visit because we are peaceful here."

"Do come and meet them, Uncle David," put in Ernest, tugging at David Vaughan's sleeve. He was not related to the Whiteoaks but the young ones always addressed him so. "They are nice, Uncle David."

But David Vaughan and Elihu Busby showed no inclination to meet the Southerners.

"You will see little of us while they are in your house," said Busby. "You know what is our opinion of slavery."

Nicholas's eyes sparkled with mischief. He said:

"I guess they'll be staying a long while because they've brought three slaves with them."

At the word *slaves* the two men drew back in consternation.

"Slaves," repeated Busby. "*Here? At Jalna?*"

"Yes. And there is one of them now. That fat woman hanging clothes on the line."

The woman, middle-aged and very black, was at some little distance from them and appeared to be unaware that she was watched.

"Poor creature!" exclaimed Busby on a deep note. "What a fate!"

"The slaves could leave if they wanted," said Augusta. "But they appear to enjoy their servitude."

At this moment the negress let out a jolly peal of laughter, and called to someone in the basement kitchen.

"That's Cindy," said little Ernest. "She can make a lovely cake — called angel food. I shall ask her to make one tomorrow." And he darted off.

Augusta and Nicholas also continued their walk. With them out of earshot, Elihu Busby asked: "Is that negress married?"

"How should I know?" said Vaughan.

"Well — if she's not, she ought to be. It's disgraceful to have her in the house with those children. They're remarkably observant. They see everything. Especially that boy, Nicholas."

"He wouldn't be his mother's son if he weren't remarkable," said David Vaughan.

Elihu Busby gave him a sharp look, then said, "What I cannot understand is why Mrs. Whiteoak could bear to make friends with these slave owners and invite them to visit Jalna and bring slaves with them, in a time when their country is at civil war. I'm shocked that Captain Whiteoak should countenance it."

"They will soon know our opinion concerning it all," said David Vaughan. "For me, I will not enter their house while those people are under its roof." His sensitive lips quivered in his emotion.

The front door of the house opened and the figure of a woman appeared in the porch, on the white-painted pillars of which a lusty young Virginia creeper was already spreading its greenness. Adeline Whiteoak descended and came with a light step to where the two men stood.

"An admirable walk," said Busby, out of the side of his mouth. "She's graceful as a doe."

Vaughan made no reply. His deep-set eyes met hers in sombre accusation. She saw but refused to recognize it. She said:

"How glad I am you two have appeared! I was longing for this. You must come straight in and meet our guests from South Carolina. You'll find them perfectly delightful."

"I refuse to meet any slave owners," Busby said violently. "You must know that I am heart and soul with the North."

"I also," said Vaughan, in a low, tense voice.

"Ah, but you'll change your minds completely when you meet them. They are full of charm. And their voices! So soft and sweet."

"I'd as soon touch a cobra as shake hands with a slave owner," said Elihu Busby.

"Then you won't come in?" she asked, as though deeply surprised.

"You know that my son Wellington is fighting on the side of the North? These people are his enemies. We may get word at any hour that he's been killed."

David Vaughan asked — "Mrs. Whiteoak, have you read *Uncle Tom's Cabin*?"

"I have and I'm disgusted with Mrs. Stowe. She took particular cases and wrote of them as though they were universal. Mrs. Sinclair has never heard of such a brutal master as Legree."

"Why," pursued Busby, with contempt, "did these Sinclairs bring slaves with them?"

"Because the slaves begged to be brought. They worship the very ground their master and mistress walk on. Ah, 'tis beautiful to see them. These Southerners are the real aristocrats. They are waited on hand and foot. When I consider the rough haphazard service I get, I feel really sorry for myself."

"Mrs. Whiteoak," said Elihu Busby, "would you like to be waited on by slaves?"

"I should indeed."

"Then I'm thoroughly ashamed for you," broke in David Vaughan, greatly moved.

Elihu Busby began to laugh. "Don't believe her, David," he said. "She doesn't mean a word of it. She's just showing off."

"She is showing a side of her I had rather not see." Vaughan waved a dramatic arm in the direction of the three slaves gathered together in admiration around the baby, Philip. "Do these slave owners realize that they are now in a free country? That those miserable blacks can walk out at any moment and leave them to wait on themselves?"

The Sinclairs accompanied by their host now appeared on the porch. Adeline, with a triumphant smile, moved across the well-kept lawn to join them. Over her shoulder she threw a goodbye to the two neighbours.

"What a lovely walk that woman has!" repeated Busby.

She knew that they were gazing after her. She could feel it in her prideful bones. The long flounced skirt of her puce taffeta dress swept the grass. She bent to smell a tea rose that grew by the porch, before she mounted the steps.

Curtis Sinclair carried in his hand the latest copy of the *New York Tribune*. The news it brought was the basis for long military discussions between him and Philip Whiteoak.

Now the Carolinian had been telling of the route by which his party had arrived in Canada. They had taken ship at Charleston, passed through the blockade on a stormy night, and then made for Bermuda. "There we were able," he said, "to exchange our Confederate dollars for pounds sterling."

"And at a loss to us, you may be sure," chimed in his wife.

Curtis Sinclair went on, "There we managed to catch an English passenger ship which brought us safely to Montreal."

"What adventures!" Adeline fairly danced up the steps to the porch. "Adventure is the savour of life."

The Busbys and the Whiteoaks were naturally much affected as were all people in that part of the province bordering on the States. But these two families were aware, more than most, of an underground group of agents of the Confederacy sent into Canada with the object of making raids across the border and destroying Yankee shipping on the Great Lakes.

While Elihu Busby was so passionately on the side of the North, Philip Whiteoak had sympathy with the South, stimulated by the Sinclairs, though, as events progressed, he began to realize the hopelessness of their cause. As a soldier he understood the import of these events, and their meaning to Canada, much more clearly than did Elihu Busby.

III

THE TUTOR

Lucius Madigan was an Irishman who had come out to Canada to better himself, but he was fond of saying that he was worse off in this new country than he had been in the Old Land. He had come as tutor to the young Whiteoaks six months before. Twice during those months he had been absent on drinking bouts, but on his return he was so humble and looked so ill that he was forgiven. He was a graduate of Dublin University. He had travelled in Europe and both Philip and Adeline had great respect for his learning. In any case his time at Jalna would not be much longer, for the children were to go to boarding schools in England.

Madigan was naturally a contrary man. It was almost physically painful to him to agree with anyone on any subject. Yet he was always gentle with the children. He fascinated them by his contradictor opinions. He begged them to forgive him his faults because they were the only three in the world whose opinions he valued. Once Nicholas, when repeating, as his own, some iconoclastic opinion he had heard from the tutor, was given a sound cuff by his father.

Madigan was immensely attracted by Lucy Sinclair. She was an exotic type, new to him; her slow elegant movements with her hands fascinated him. He was a man who must have a female to put on a pedestal and worship, but if she disappointed him, his worship turned to scorn. A while ago it had been Amelia Busby — she preferred her second name to Abigail, her first — whom he had worshipped, but in some way she had offended him. Now her buxom figure, her loudly expressed views, were repellent to him. She had not valued him highly, because of his habit of drinking too much, but he was far cleverer than her brothers and she was both ashamed and sorry she had lost him.

In Lucy Sinclair he had found the perfect object for worship. If Curtis Sinclair was aware of this, he made no sign. Outwardly he was as tranquil, as charming as a Southern gentleman should be. "Ah, what a manner that man has!" Adeline exclaimed to Philip. He demanded:

"What's the matter with my manner?"

"It's the manner," she returned cryptically, "of a cavalry officer."

At the beginning of the American Civil War, Lucius Madigan was in concord with the North, that is to say, as nearly in concord as was possible for his nature to be. When he heard that Irishmen were in the Northern Army he said fervently, "Ah, those lads would fight for freedom!"

But when he saw the abhorrence in which Elihu Busby held the South his opinion changed. He thoroughly disliked Elihu Busby. Everything connected with Lucy Sinclair must be admired, or at the least defended, by him. Busby had an almost worshipping admiration for Lincoln. Lucius Madigan ridiculed him. "He is the type," he said, "who sits with his cronies in the little room behind the grocery shop, whittles a stick, and tells dirty stories."

He said this to the three young Whiteoaks when he met them that same afternoon in the woods. His last words made Augusta turn away her face, and he glimpsed the colour deepening on her cheek.

"My dear," he said contritely, "forgive my slip of the tongue. I should not have said that in front of you."

Nicholas winked at his sister, which made her embarrassment even more acute.

"Would you please repeat that, Mr. Madigan?" said little Ernest. "I didn't hear clearly."

The tutor ignored this remark and began to talk poetically of the beauty of the trees. Among their branches darted yellow finches, elegant little bluebirds and black and gold orioles. There was a clearing in the forest, carpeted with flowers. Augusta and Ernest began at once to pick them.

Nicholas said to Lucius Madigan, "If I were grown I shouldn't mind going to that war. The trouble is I shouldn't know which side to fight on. Our friends are all for the North, but our mother and father and you are for the South."

"I'm against all wars," said Madigan. "Life in Ireland was bad enough. I didn't come to this country to get embroiled in a cause that means nothing to me."

"But you have principles, haven't you?"

"Devil a one," said Madigan. "I had them once but they were swept away when I saw the peasants starving in Ireland."

Ernest came running to them, his hands full of flowers. "Mr. Madigan," he said, "wouldn't you like to free the slaves?"

"They're a spoilt lot," said Madigan. "If they were earning a living in Canada, they'd find out what it is to work."

"But still they're slaves," said Nicholas.

"Not since Lincoln's proclamation. They could leave in a body if they wanted, but they know when they are well off."

The Southerners and their black slaves fascinated the children. They could talk of nothing else. The boys sought to draw out the Negroes on the subject, but they would give no opinion. Their black faces were a mask. Augusta was herself too reserved to desire to probe the feelings of others.

Before the three reached the house they met their father and Mr. Sinclair. Philip was displaying, with a good deal of pride, the orchard he had planted after coming to Jalna. "I had saplings sent from England and already they have borne good crops for young trees. Such Cox's Pippins! I never have tasted any better flavoured."

"Pippins, eh?" said Sinclair. "I should like to taste a pippin."

"I have some good Canadian apples too. The little snow apples are really a treat. Red skin, white flesh, tender as a pear, with fine red veins. They'll not be ready till the late autumn, but you shall soon have an Early Transparent. Their sauce is excellent with roast duck — smooth as ointment. We know no such thing as blight; as for insect pests — the birds keep them down." Philip Whiteoak went on to talk with gusto of his various crops.

"How many labourers have you on the land?" asked Curtis Sinclair.

"Six. Good workers, all of them."

"I have more than a hundred in the cotton fields, but it needs all of them to do the work of half that number of white men. And there are their large families to clothe and feed."

"Good Lord! I never could afford that."

"It's all right if you sell your cotton, but the Yankees are spoiling that business with their blockade. They're the people who have made money and still are making it. They sold the slaves to us in the first place." He spoke with restrained bitterness.

"Yes, I know," said Philip, though he knew very little about it.

They walked on in silence for a space, then Curtis Sinclair said, "Captain Whiteoak, I think your sympathies are with the Confederacy."

"They are indeed."

"The Yankees have ruined my country. My father has large estates. Over seven hundred Negroes. A few of them have drifted away but the great majority remain. To be clothed and fed. All ages — old people — young children." He hesitated, then raised his fine eyes to his host's fresh-coloured face. He said, "Captain Whiteoak, I have certain plans in mind. I am committed to an enterprise which, we hope, will put a stop to the activities of the Yankees on the Great Lakes."

Philip opened his eyes wide. "I've never heard of such a thing," he said.

"It's quite true and I will tell you more about it later. What I wish to know now is whether you would object to some of the men who are engaged in this enterprise coming here to discuss matters with me. It would be less conspicuous than meeting in a hotel. If you have any objection to my using your hospitality in this way, say the word and my wife and I will depart."

"I'll be glad to have you meet your friends here." Philip spoke cautiously; he did not quite understand the possible complications of such a scheme.

"They are scarcely to be called friends," said Curtis Sinclair. "They don't want to see our country swallowed up by the Yankees."

Philip wondered what all this was about, but he was of a sanguine nature and being himself so secure he would have liked to see his friends in security. The two strolling men were now overtaken by the children and their tutor. Ernest was gnawing, with his white teeth, at a hard green apple. This Philip at once snatched from him and gave him a hearty whack on the behind.

"You know very well," he said, "that unripe fruit gives you a pain in the stomach. Do you want to keep our guests awake tonight with your howls?"

Ernest hung his head. "I forgot," he said.

He wanted to be again in favour. He pressed between the two men and slipped a hand into Philip's, then, after a moment, put the other hand in Sinclair's.

Nicholas said, "Gussie told Ernest not to eat it."

"I don't think he heard," she said.

"I continually do what I know I shouldn't," Madigan said. "I expect no better of my pupils."

"That's a bad way to talk in front of them," said their father.

"I'm sorry, sir, but if I set myself up on a pedestal, would they believe in me?"

Philip turned to his daughter. "Gussie, do you believe in Mr. Madigan?"

"How can I help," she asked, "with him under my nose all day long?"

"That's rude," said Philip. "Apologize at once."

"I refuse" — Madigan spoke with heat — "to be apologized to by anybody. I don't recognize rudeness. In fact, I approve of it."

"If I called you a liar," said Nicholas, "what would you say?"

"I'd say you are a clever boy to have found me out."

A diversion was caused by the appearance of Nero in search of them. He was a huge creature with black curly hair and a benign expression. This successor to the original Nero was himself growing old and heavy but was still active and ramped about the children in joy. They romped with him. They and Madigan fell behind.

"These young 'uns of mine," said Captain Whiteoak, "are getting no proper discipline. Thank goodness, they'll soon be going away to school."

"Better send them to France," said Curtis Sinclair. "That's where I was educated."

"You speak French then?"

"I do."

"I have a French Canadian working for me. He'd be delighted if you spoke to him in his native tongue. He is quite a good woodcarver."

They were now rejoined by the children and Nero, and all entered the house, which was suffused by the radiance of sunset. Philip went to the large bedroom, opening into the hall, which he shared with Adeline. He found her brushing her long hair. Always he admired her hair, which was rather more red than a glossy ripe chestnut. He did not tell her so, for she was vain enough already, but he asked, "What are you wearing for dinner?"

"This green brocade."

"Dressing for dinner," he said, resting his hands on the footboard of the painted leather bed that showed a gorgeous assembly of flowers and fruit, among which the mischievous faces of monkeys peered. This bed they had brought with them from India, also the gaily plumaged parrot that perched on the headboard. "This dressing for dinner," he repeated, for he was sure she had not heard him with all that hair over her ears, "is a confounded nuisance. Why should a country gentleman dress for dinner?"

She heard him and said, "Wouldn't it be nice if you came to dinner smelling of the stable? No — we do right to put our best foot foremost. The Sinclairs appreciate it. That lovely dress she wore last night she bought in Paris before the war. As for her other clothes, she tells me they are practically in rags — her shoes with holes in them."

"Why don't you give her a pair of yours?"

"Mine! Haven't you noticed how tiny her feet are?"

He hadn't noticed, he said.

She was delighted. She put both arms about his neck and kissed him. "You darling!" she cried.

He could not know why he had pleased her and he did not try to guess. She went on to say, "It is a great grief to Lucy that she has no children. She shed tears over it today, even though, as she says, they are ruined — their estates taken by the Yankees, so they would have nothing to leave their children."

"It's as well they have none," said Philip.

"You mean because of his deformity. But have you noticed what beautiful small hands he has?"

"Don't you get sweet on him, Adeline. I won't have it."

Philip removed his outer garments and, in his underclothes, planted himself in front of the marble-topped washing stand. The marble was glossy black but the large ewer, basin, soap dish, and slop bowl were cream-coloured with a design of rich crimson roses. Philip poured water into the basin, lathered well his hands with Adeline's Cashmere Bouquet soap, washed his face and neck. He emerged handsome and ruddy, and soon was dressed and prepared to go to the dining room.

Descending the stairway were their visitors, the Sinclairs, she holding up her velvet train. They proceeded to the dining room where windows stood open to the warm breeze. There was not on the table the variety of food to which these Southerners were used, but the Scotch broth, the roast duck with apple sauce, the new potatoes, the fresh garden peas, and asparagus were excellent. The raspberry tart, with thick Jersey cream, was pronounced delicious. The coffee the Sinclairs found atrocious but drank it with a smile.

Also present at this dinner were the Laceys. He was a retired British rear-admiral but was always called Admiral. Though their means were slender, their house small, they behaved as they felt became their station. Both were polite, though a little standoffish. Both were short, plump, blond, and had what might be called "pretty faces." They bore a striking resemblance to each other, though they were of no blood relationship. They had at the first been attracted by this resemblance and were pleased when their children were the image of them.

Philip Whiteoak had taken care to make certain, before he invited them, where lay the sympathies of the Laceys. After his first glass of wine Admiral Lacey said in a warm undertone to Lucy Sinclair, "As I live, madam, I've always detested the Yankees."

She answered, in her soft Southern tones, "Oh, Admiral, I could embrace you for that!"

Mrs. Lacey overheard. Her shock was reflected in the deeper pink of her face, her mouth which took on the form of an O. The Admiral beamed delightedly, without regard to his wife's feelings. He repeated, "Always detested 'em."

"They are getting rich out of this war, while we lose everything," said Lucy Sinclair.

Curtis Sinclair thought the talk should be changed to a lighter subject, for he feared that his wife was about to burst into tears. He therefore praised the roast duckling. "I must tell you," he said, "that, shortly before we left Richmond, Mrs. Sinclair paid seventy-five dollars for a turkey."

There were general comments of amazement, then Adeline cried, "How I should love to see Richmond! The very name captivates me. It's so romantic, so civilized, while here we are in the wilds."

"But you have everything," said Lucy Sinclair. "Beautiful furniture, exquisite linen, superb silver! I cannot tell you how surprised we were to find it so, for we had pictured log cabins — with Indians and wolves prowling about."

The Whiteoaks were uncertain whether to be pleased or not. Philip said, "You'd have to go far North or West to find such conditions."

Lucius Madigan remarked, from the far end of the table where he sat with his three pupils:

"If you want to see wildness, Mrs. Sinclair, you should go to Ireland."

"We have many soldiers of Irish antecedents in our Carolinian army," she said, "and they are the best fighters of all."

"My grandfather, the Marquis of Killiekeggan," said Adeline, "was a great fighter. In his day he fought seven duels."

"A *Marquis*," Lucy Sinclair breathed, wide-eyed. "Did you say your grandfather was a Marquis?"

"Indeed he was," said Adeline, "and a hard drinker, even for an Irish Marquis."

Nicholas spoke up. "It's a wonder that Mamma hadn't told you already about her grandfather, the Marquis. Usually she tells about him at the start."

Adeline might well have been angry. On the contrary she looked pleased and joined in the laughter.

Little Ernest felt that he had been long enough in obscurity and now remarked in his treble voice, "Before our visitors came we ate dinner at noon and supper at night. Why?"

"Because it's more stylish, silly," said Nicholas.

Adeline threw her sons a baleful glance. "Any more insolence from you two," she said, "and you leave the table."

Philip remarked tranquilly, "At Jalna we lead the life of country people. In fact, it is necessary in this strenuous part of the world."

Madigan appeared to be cherishing a secret joke. He shook with silent laughter, but no one paid any attention to him. Admiral Lacey told stories of the early days of his settling in Canada. He never tired of these reminiscences or of the sound of his own voice. Though he was strongly on the side of the South in the American Civil War he was of the opinion that they were managing their campaign badly and Curtis Sinclair agreed with him.

After dessert the three ladies and Augusta went to the drawing-room. The tutor and the two boys disappeared into the moonlit darkness of the lawn. The men left at table filled their glasses with port. Philip Whiteoak remarked, "I admire the restraint you show, Mr. Sinclair. I'm doubtful of my ability to hang on to myself as you do."

"It would be impossible to me," said Admiral Lacey. "I'd be furiously trying to do something about it."

"You mean," said Sinclair, "that you would not leave your country to its fate and escape to a foreign one."

The Admiral was a little embarrassed.

"You know your limitations, sir," he said with a glance at Curtis Sinclair's hump, "better than I do."

The Southerner's beautiful hand fingered the crystal stem of his wine glass.

"We of the South," said Sinclair, "have much to avenge. It's not enough to burn your house and leave your plantation a scorched ruin, as some are doing. There are those among us who want something more active than the mere destruction of our own property." He paused and looked enquiringly into the faces of the other two.

"You can be sure of our sympathy in anything you do," said Philip Whiteoak.

"With the exception of joining the Confederate army" — the Admiral spoke fiercely and drained his glass — "I will do anything I can to co-operate. But I am a poor man. I cannot give money."

"We are not without funds," said the Southerner haughtily.

He went on: "Last spring an officer of the Union army — a Colonel Dahigren — was killed in action. Our men found on his body an order from headquarters to sack and burn Richmond. We have not forgiven that, and never shall."

"Dastardly," declared Admiral Lacey. "As bad as Cromwell's Ironsides."

"Even worse," said Philip. "Now what do you plan to do?"

However, Curtis Sinclair retreated. He tapped nervously on the table with his fingers. He said, in a low voice, "It would take me some time to explain just what are our plans and I'm sure Mrs. Whiteoak will be expecting us in the drawing-room." It could be seen that, at the moment, he had nothing more to say. Shortly the three men joined the ladies.

It was noticeable to Philip Whiteoak that the atmosphere in that room was not of the happiest. Lucy Sinclair was sitting on a blue satin settee, the flounces of her Paris gown spread gracefully about her, the tip of one tiny slippered foot just showing. She was exclaiming on the beauty of some little ivory elephants from India, which Adeline had taken from a cabinet to show her. But Mrs. Lacey sat aloof, looking askance at the other two. Her husband, without a glance at her, went straight to Lucy Sinclair's side. Curtis Sinclair joined Adeline by the cabinet. Philip sat down beside Mrs. Lacey.

"Is it possible," she asked, in a tense whisper, "that all Southern women behave as flirtatiously?"

"Sh," he whispered back, "she will hear you."

"What are you two whispering about?" cried Mrs. Sinclair. "Not about me and the dear Admiral, I hope."

"I was thinking," said Mrs. Lacey, "that after all you say you have been through, I should expect you to be a little subdued."

"Ah," said Mrs. Sinclair, "if you had known me before, you would see a great difference in me. But it's my nature to be gay, and when I'm in such good company —"

There was a welcome interruption here, as the tutor and the three children came into the room through one of the French windows that opened on the terrace. The gentle summer breeze moved the curtains, and those inside the room could feel the pine-scented darkness of the night, barely lit by a few distant stars and a young moon rising above the ravine. A whippoorwill was repeating, with mournful ecstasy, his three insistent notes.

"Ernest," cried his mother, "you should be in your bed."

"I have come to say goodnight." The little boy spoke with polite self-possession and went to her.

She opened her arms wide, exclaiming, "Come and kiss me quick then and be off with you." She spoke in consciously Irish accents and made a consciously dramatic picture with her child, as though protecting him from all the dangers of this world.

"What lovely children!" Lucy Sinclair remarked to Admiral Lacey. "How I envy the parents! It's a sorrow to my husband and me that we have no children. How I could have loved a daughter!"

"I have two girls," the Admiral said proudly, "and one son. He is in the Royal Navy."

Adeline gave Ernest a resounding kiss. "Now," she said, "say your goodnights to all the company."

Nothing reluctant, Ernest embraced and kissed each one in turn. He wished he might stay a little longer in the drawing-room in the light of the chandelier. When he put his arms about Lucy, he said, "I can recite 'Bingen on the Rhine.'"

She smelled his sweet child's breath. She pressed him to her and said, "Will you recite it for me? I adore recitations." Mrs. Lacey, seeing the embrace, thought, "She pursues even little boys."

Ernest asked, "May I recite, Mamma?"

"You may," she answered grandly, "if you don't disgrace yourself by forgetting the words."

"I'll not forget," he promised with confidence. He moved to a position where he faced the company. He began, in his treble tones:

A soldier of the Legion lay dying in Algiers;
There was lack of woman's nursing, there was lack of woman's tears.

But a comrade was beside him, as his life-blood ebbed away,
And bent, with pitying glances, to hear what he might say.

And so on to the end without one mistake.

At the burst of applause, Ernest blushed and ran to sit by his mother.

"Who, in this part of the world, taught him to recite with such feeling and such distinctness?" asked Lucy Sinclair.

"Our rector's wife," said Adeline, "is very clever. She teaches them to recite and to play the piano."

"The piano," exclaimed Lucy. "Which of them plays the piano?"

It could be seen that Nicholas was the one. His downcast eyes, the pout of his lips, showed his embarrassment.

"Come now," urged Adeline, "play that pretty piece of Schubert's."

"No, Mamma" — he shook his head — "I can't."

"Why, you played it only the other day for my girls and me," cried Mrs. Lacey.

"That was different."

"Go to the piano at once, sir," commanded his father.

Nicholas rose and, with a hangdog air, sat down at the instrument. Without too many mistakes he played the piece through.

"What spirit — what finish!" exclaimed Lucy Sinclair.

"My wife should know," said her husband, "for she studied music in Europe."

"She must play for us," said Adeline.

"If there is one thing above another that I enjoy, it's a musical evening," declared the Admiral, who scarcely knew one tune from another.

"What I enjoy," said Mrs. Lacey, "are recitations."

"Ah, you should hear my daughter recite," Adeline said.

Nicholas had been well applauded for his performance and now returned to his tutor's side where he sat silent on a sofa just inside the door.

"Gussie," said Captain Whiteoak, "stand up and recite 'The Charge of the Light Brigade.'"

Unsmilingly and with girlish dignity Augusta rose and went to a suitable spot, not too near her audience, for her voice must be raised. In spite of her youth she was impressive, her sallow face intense, her black hair hanging in ordered ringlets to her waist. When she spoke the words "Half a league, half a league, half a league onward," she slightly waved her right hand and gazed into space, "Into the jaws of death rode the Six Hundred ..."

It was more than Lucy Sinclair could bear. She burst into tears. As he witnessed her emotion the Admiral's eyes also filled with tears. Adeline put an arm about Lucy and patted her back. Lucy sobbed:

"It was noble and heroic. You recited it beautifully, Gussie."

"I always want to cry when I hear that piece," said Adeline, "but it is hard for me to shed tears."

Lucius Madigan's voice, as though talking to himself, came from where he sat. "I can't understand," he said, "why such a tragic mistake should be celebrated. It is best forgotten."

"What would you have done if you'd been given that order?" asked Nicholas of the tutor.

"Run the other way as fast as I could," he answered without hesitation.

As he was an Irishman, this was considered to be funny. Everyone, with the exception of Lucy, laughed. She was wiping her eyes. Mrs. Lacey regarded her without sympathy. What right had she, an American, to work herself up over the Charge of the Light Brigade!

"I wish," said little Ernest, "that Mr. Madigan would sing one of his Irish songs."

"Ah, yes, do." Adeline spoke with rich emotion. "Though it breaks my heart to hear them." Always she spoke as though her poor torn heart were in Ireland, but in reality she had been glad to leave that country. Though she loved her family, she couldn't get on with her father. "Mrs. Sinclair will play your accompaniment, I'm sure. She plays so beautifully. Her fingers ripple over the keys like a brook over its pebbles."

Soon Madigan's cool Irish tenor voice charmed all in his rendering of "The Last Rose of Summer."

IV

NIGHT

When the guests had gone Philip Whiteoak and Curtis Sinclair went out into the velvet darkness of the summer night, for there was now no moon. They paced up and down in front of the house talking, talking. The door stood open and the lamplight from the hall fell on the figures of the two men when they passed. They were in striking contrast. Both were bareheaded and Philip Whiteoak was a head taller than the other. His fresh complexion, his bold handsome features, broad shoulders and flat back, his look of being accustomed to command, would make many another man wish he might be in Philip's shoes. He restrained his stride to suit the awkward walk of the southerner. Yet, in spite of the hump on his back, Sinclair was a figure of dignity. An arresting figure. A face subtle and sensitive.

When at last they turned into the house the Southerner held out his hand. "Goodnight, Captain Whiteoak," he said, "and thank you. I hope I shall do nothing to make you regret your kindness." They shook hands with warmth and Philip went straight to his own room.

He expected to find Adeline asleep but the moment he tiptoed into the room she sat up in bed. The candle nightlight on a table by the head of the bed barely revealed his stalwart figure.

"Whatever have you been up to?" she demanded. "What were you two men talking about?"

"Go to sleep." He spoke peremptorily.

"I will not go to sleep. I must know what all this talk is about."

"Why?" He came to her side.

"Because," she cried, "I am a woman and cannot rest till I know."

"Behave yourself and go to sleep," he said.

She caught his hand and pressed it to her cheek. "I'm burning with curiosity," she declared.

He gave her cheek a playful pinch.

"Good God," she cried, "can't you recognize that I am a woman of character, able to take part in any scheme that's afoot?"

Her parrot, roused by her raised voice, uttered loud protests in Hindustani, opened his beak, and showed his dark tongue.

"What possessed me to marry an Irishwoman I can't fathom," Philip said, and sat down on the bed beside her.

However, he was so full of Curtis Sinclair's plan that he could not restrain himself from imparting some of it to her. In fact it would be necessary for her to know. She was not an ordinary female to be put off with a few half-truths. She was a person to be reckoned with. Sometimes he almost wished she were of weaker fibre but, looking into her luminous eyes that had nothing wistful in them, seeing her proud and forward-looking profile, he could not wish her to be different. The snowy frill of her nightdress came up to her chin. He put his finger under her chin and remarked, "Well, here goes."

"Yes?" she breathed eagerly.

"Curtis Sinclair," he said, "is one of the organizers of an underground group — agents of the Southern Confederacy. They are being sent to Canada by President Jefferson Davis." Philip hesitated. He fingered his cravat. "I doubt if I should be telling you this, Adeline," he said.

"In any case, I'd get it out of Lucy," she retorted.

He went on, looking suddenly very serious, "These men are to conduct raids across the border with the object of destroying Northern shipping on the Great Lakes."

Adeline threw herself back on her plump down pillows, her body quivering with excitement.

"What a glorious revenge!" she cried.

"By Jove," he said, "you have a wicked grin."

"I feel wicked when I think of those despicable Yankees." Suddenly she too became serious. "What part are we to play in this?" she demanded. "For the Sinclairs must expect us to play a part, otherwise he would not have confided in you."

"Our part is to be a passive one," said Philip. "It simply is to allow Curtis Sinclair to receive certain members of this underground group under our roof and to give them orders."

"*I* will receive them." Again she sat up. "No one shall be able to say that I have not played my part."

"You have no part in this," he cried firmly. "All you have to do is to see nothing — say nothing."

"And all those brave men coming here! Never."

As she raised her voice, the parrot fluttered down from the head of her bed uttering noises of protest. He alighted at the foot, then walked the length of her body and, when he reached her head, pressed his feathered cheek to hers.

"Dear Boney," she murmured to him.

In Hindustani, the only language he knew, he muttered terms of endearment to her.

Philip began to undress. He said:

"Put that bird back on his perch. I refuse to get into bed with him."

Adeline rose and carried Boney to his cage. Through the bars he swore at Philip. "*Haramzada — Iflatoon!*"

Adeline, looking tall in her voluminous nightdress, went to the open window. "The lilac has almost finished its blooming," she said, "but oh, how heavenly the scent! Come and smell."

Together they sniffed the scent of the lilac and the sweet air of the virgin countryside. There was no sound other than the faint rustle of the leaves and the splash of the stream in the green depths of the ravine.

* * *

Upstairs in the Sinclairs' room the two Southerners had been discussing, first the evening that lay behind them, then the problems that lay ahead.

Lucy Sinclair exclaimed, "I am quite in love with these Whiteoaks. They are so natural, so spontaneous, and so handsome. Isn't her colouring exquisite? That auburn hair — that creamy complexion — those eyes! Thank God, I am a woman who can admire other women."

"Whiteoak is a very nice fellow." Curtis Sinclair said. "He is quite willing to let me use his house as headquarters. Of course, all will be done secretly. The men will come here only after dark. They will leave as quietly as they come. I think the neighbours will suspect nothing."

At this moment Lucy Sinclair's maid came into the room. "Ah've come," she said, "to brush yo' haar, missus. My goodness, it does need attention." She wielded the brush as she spoke, as though it were a weapon. Her face shone with benign purpose. When her mistress, wrapped in a satin peignoir, sank into a chair, she set to brushing the long, fair locks with soothing strokes.

"Are you getting on better with the other servants here, Annabelle?" asked Lucy Sinclair. "I hope you are always polite to them."

"Laws, missus, I'm all smiles when I speaks to them. All but that Irishman, Patsy, for I can't understand half what he says." Annabelle doubled up with laughter at the mere thought of Patsy.

Now Cindy, the Negress, entered, her arms full of freshly laundered clothes which she began to lay in bureau drawers, at the same time complaining loudly that she had been unable to get possession of the flat-irons before evening. "We'll all be in rags, missus," she said, in a mournful voice, "if we don' git some new clothes purty soon. Jus' you look at dis here shoe!" She held up a foot for inspection. The sole of her shoe was worn into a hole.

"Have patience," Lucy Sinclair soothed her. "We shall have new clothes when this horrible war is over. Then we shall go home, I hope."

The Negress raised her hands to heaven. "Ah pray to God, missus, it will be before winter comes, for they tell me it's bitter cold here and de snow up to your waist. Us niggers would suttainly die of cold."

Curtis Sinclair had been standing by the window with his back to the room. When the servants had left, he turned and asked his wife,

"Where do those two sleep?"

"In the small bedroom next this," she said. "And Jerry is tucked away somewhere in the basement."

"We should not have brought these three slaves with us," he said. "It's too much to expect of the Whiteoaks."

"Surely you would not want me to wait on myself!" There was a hysterical note in her voice. Twice she said this, her voice trembling.

"Of course not," he answered.

"And you must know that both women are in need of new clothes. Jerry too needs new clothes and shoes. All three are badly off for something new."

"They may go to the devil," he said calmly. "I have no money to spend on them." He took out his watch and began to wind it. She said nothing more.

V

A Call on Wilmott

The following morning Adeline set out on foot, accompanied by Nero, to call on James Wilmott, an Englishman who had come to Canada on the same ship as the Whiteoaks. He had bought a piece of land with a log house beside the winding river. He had made himself very comfortable in a primitive way. At the edge of the river a flat-bottomed boat was moored. On the little landing stage lay his fishing tackle. There was whispering among the rushes.

Usually Adeline, when she went to visit her neighbours, rode her favourite horse — but this was a secret call. She followed the grass path to the door and knocked. As she waited she felt the sense of mystery always associated with Wilmott. In the first place he had been so reticent concerning his past life. She had looked on him as a bachelor till, some time after he was settled in his new home, she had discovered, and he had confessed to her, that he had secretly left England to escape from a detested wife. He had impoverished himself to provide for her and her child.

When the wife had discovered his whereabouts and followed him, it had been Adeline Whiteoak who had put her off the scent.

Adeline could not think of that interview, almost twelve years ago, without a mischievous chuckle. Meeting the former Mrs. Wilmott, it had been easy to understand why her husband had fled from her.

Since that time Wilmott had lived in conscious happiness with his servant, companion, protégé, and pupil, a young partly French half-breed Indian called Tite. It was he who now opened the door to Adeline. In the years he had lived with Wilmott he had grown from a bronzed stripling to a muscular but still slender young man. He had that year passed his first examination in the study of law. Wilmott was proud of him, regarding him almost in the light of a son.

"Good morning to you, Tite," said Adeline. "Is Mr. Wilmott at home?"

"He is almost always at home," Tite said, with a dignified inclination of the head. "I will tell him you are here. He is at the moment sewing buttons on his best pants." Tite glided from the room and, in a few moments, Wilmott entered. Tite did not return.

"I'm sorry I have kept you waiting, Adeline." Wilmott spoke formally, as was his habit, but his deep-set grey eyes looked so intently into hers that she coloured a little. "It is not often that you come to see me," he added, and placed a chair for her.

She did not sit down but stood facing him.

"I come on an important mission," she said.

He was used to her exaggerations and waited composedly for her to go on. "Yes?" He spoke warily.

"Oh, don't be alarmed," she broke out. "I'm not asking you to *do* anything. I want only to have your sympathy in what Philip and I are undertaking."

"Philip and you?" he repeated surprised.

"Philip and I pull very well together," she declared, "when we are of one mind … But first tell me where do your sympathies lie in this Civil War of the Americans?"

"You know that I hate slavery."

"So do our guests from the South. But they inherited great plantations and hundreds of slaves. Those blacks were dependent on them. They were content and happy with their masters, but now the Yankee soldiers have invaded the South, pillaging, burning. Oh, 'twould break your heart to hear of the miseries those villains have brought into that happy country. Of course, you remember how your wife went through New England lecturing and stirring up hate for the South. And it was none of her business, was it?"

Wilmott did not want to be reminded of that woman. He retorted, "Surely this war is no business of ours."

Yet when Adeline poured out the plans of Curtis Sinclair, she moved him, as she knew she could. The very fact that his one-time wife had been active in stirring up hatred for the South was enough to rouse his sympathy for that troubled land.

As he hesitated, she caught his hand in hers, exclaiming, "Ah, James, how splendid you are!"

"But I have promised nothing," he warned. "And I hope you are not letting yourself be inveigled into some reckless act."

"Philip and I have no part in all this but to see nothing, say nothing. Nothing more than to lend shelter for meetings."

"Meetings?" He withdrew his hand and looked her sternly in the eyes.

"Now that I have won you over," she said, "you are to come to Jalna tonight and hear the details. You are going to enjoy this, James."

His voice trembled a little as he said, "You know, Adeline, that I will do anything for you." Yet he still held his look of sternness, for he lived a rather isolated life and, once his austere features lent themselves to any expression of mood, they were reluctant to change.

When Adeline was gone, the half-breed entered. He had been eaves-dropping and had heard every word, but his face showed nothing of this. He said: "I was hoping you'd tell me to make a cup of tea for the lady, Boss."

"You know very well, Tite," said Wilmott, "that I am not in the habit of entertaining ladies."

"But Mrs. Whiteoak is a great tea-drinker, Boss."

"That is nothing to us," Wilmott said curtly.

"I know that very well, Boss. But I thought she might like a cup of tea for the sake of her nerves. It must be strange to her to have slaves in the house."

"That is nothing to us," repeated Wilmott.

A silence followed, then Tite, with a sidelong look, asked, "Have you seen the slaves, Boss?"

"I have not. How many are there?"

"Three, Boss."

"Well!" Wilmott ejaculated. "Well — that seems rather a lot. Are they men or women?"

"One man and two women, Boss."

"Have you spoken with them?"

"I am always friendly with strangers, Boss. I have talked with them. The older woman is fat; for one thing she is heavy with child."

"Tck!" exclaimed Wilmott.

"Yes indeed, Boss."

"Is the man her husband?"

"No, Boss. She left her husband and three children in the South because she is so devoted to her mistress — just as I would leave my wife and my children, if I had them, to go with you."

"I should advise you," said Wilmott, "not to question these Negroes. Better keep away from them, Tite."

"I am a friendly man, Boss." The half-breed showed his white teeth in a smile. "Also I have no class-consciousness. I myself am of mixed blood. I am scarcely white. Yet a young white lady once told me that I had a mouth like a pomegranate flower. Do you think that was meant as a compliment, Boss?"

"Don't remind me of that affair, Tite," Wilmott said sternly.

"That was years ago, and I am of a more noble character now. You have heard of the noble red man, Boss?"

"I am glad to hear of your nobility," said Wilmott, wondering whether education had been good for Tite.

"The young woman slave" — Tite spoke in a judicial tone — "is a mulatto — the shade of café au lait. You see, I know a little French. She is a very pretty girl, Boss."

"I want you to keep strictly away from that young woman."

"Yes, indeed," said Tite with dignity. "Still, she is very pretty and her name is Annabelle. Her face is sensitive — a quality you don't find very often in women."

"Keep away from her," repeated Wilmott, "or you may get into trouble."

"Trouble with whom, sir?"

"Probably with the Negro man."

"Oh, no, Boss. Annabelle is miles above him. He is an ignorant fellow who knows not how to read or write, though he can do arithmetic in his head."

"How do you come by all this information, Tite?"

"I keep my eyes and ears open. That is what makes life interesting."

Tite drifted away. He fished in a shady pool of the stream which abounded in fish. He cleaned and cooked fish for the evening meal. He washed up. When dusk fell he took the narrow path to Jalna by which Adeline had come that morning.

The sounds and smells of night were stealing out, at first as though timidly, then taking possession of the darkness. The scent of virgin soil, of cedar, of pine, of the balm of Gilead tree, weighed sweetly on the night air. The twittering of small birds, the confidential croaking of frogs, the newly awakened chorus of the locusts, joined in the dismissal of day and the welcoming of night.

The half-breed did not consciously give himself to these pleasures. He absorbed them through his very pores — the soles of his feet, the skin of his dark face. Plainly this night walk was not aimless, for he turned abruptly from the path that led to Jalna, descended another path that would have been difficult to find, had he been less sensitive to the feel of the earth and the change in the air, as he followed the path down into the ravine. Down there a stream was moving swiftly, unseen but clearly heard in its nocturnal singing. It was spanned by a rustic bridge and walking across it was a large white owl whose hearing, even more acute than Tite's, detected the coming of the young man. It rose, with a heavy flutter of wings, into the shelter of a massive tree.

Tite gave a little laugh and, raising an imaginary bow, sent an imaginary arrow into the owl's white breast. As though in wonder, it uttered a loud "whoo-whoo." Tite now went and stood on the bridge listening. He had not long to wait. A dark figure stole out from the undergrowth. The young mulatto girl joined him silently on the bridge.

He took her hand and they stood so linked for a moment. Then he said, "You did well, Annabelle, not to keep me waiting. I am an impatient fellow and would have searched till I found you — and then —"

"What then?" she breathed.

"I can't tell you. I do things on impulse. Sometimes good. Sometimes bad."

In her soft voice Annabelle said: "Ah reckon you'se good, Tite."

"Why?" he laughed.

"You's so educated."

"That doesn't matter. We're happy together. As for my education — what chance has an Indian got? Any more than a Negro."

"Ah'm part white. My grandfather was a white man. My grand-mother was just his slave. But she was pretty."

"And so are you, Belle — pretty as a picture."

She moved closer to him. He could smell her warm dark flesh and cheap perfume.

"Tite," she whispered, "do you love de Lawd?"

He was startled but he asked, "Do you want me to love Him, Belle?"

"Ah certainly does. Ah'm religious. All us three — Jerry, Cindy, and me — enjoy a good meetin'. Next to a weddin' or a funeral."

Tite, after a moment's hesitation, said, in a voice that thrilled the emotional girl, "I too am religious."

"You ain't a Catholic, are you?"

"What made you think I might be?"

"Well, you said you was part French."

"What denomination do you belong to, Belle?"

"Ah'm a sort of Baptist. But I enjoy any sort of revival meetin'."

"So do I," Tite said fervently.

The girl said, in her soft thick accents, "There's over thirty of us coloured folk in these parts. There's a preacher among us. Cap'n Whiteoak, he's lent us a nice clean hayloft for meetin's. We're havin' one on Sunday. We'll sing and pray for the South, 'cause we want to go home again. Will you come to the meetin', Tite?"

"I'll be delighted," said Tite, imitating Wilmott's manner. He put his arm about the girl. Dusky cheek to cheek, they listened to the singing of the stream.

"Does religion mean more to you than love?" he asked, running his hand through her curls, for her hair was not woolly.

"Way more," she murmured.

He felt a little rebuffed. "Why?" he asked. "Surely a pretty girl longs for love."

"Ah likes the love of a man," came the answer, "but Ah clings to the love of de Lawd."

"So do I," said Tite fervently.

The following morning he raised his eyes from the fish he was scaling and announced to Wilmott, "I've got religion, Boss." His serious tone was scarcely matched by the expression of his eyes, for two fish-scales clung to his long lashes.

Wilmott looked down at him doubtfully. "What has brought that about?" he asked.

Tite winked the fish-scales from his eyelashes.

"I've felt the need of it for a long time, Boss," he said. "And when I was wandering solitary in the darkness, it struck me like a blinding light."

"I hope it will be good for you," Wilmott said without conviction.

"I'm sure it will, Boss. A man cannot live by fish alone."

"You had better go and tell this to Mr. Pink, the rector," said Wilmott.

"Can't you advise me, Boss?"

"I don't consider myself competent for that. Better go to the rector."

"But, Boss, I've never been baptized or confirmed. He'd likely want to do both to me."

"Do as you please," said Wilmott, and left him.

In spite of Wilmott's guardianship, Tite was accustomed to do as he pleased. Now it was his pleasure to seek out Mr. Pink, the rector of the small church that had been built by the Whiteoaks. It was but one of two country churches in Mr. Pink's spiritual care. Here, beside it, was the rectory, almost as large as the church. Mr. Pink was sitting in the porch enjoying his mid-morning pipe. At the half-breed's approach he gave him a friendly nod and said:

"You are Titus Sharrow, aren't you?"

"Yes, sir," Tite answered, in his gentle polite voice. "I have come to ask you a religious question."

The rector looked at him keenly. "Yes? Go ahead."

"Please tell me," said Tite, "whether unbelief is a sin."

"We all sin in that way, for none of us believes as completely as he should."

"How much do you believe, Mr. Rector?"

"I have never told that to any man."

"I am a beginner," said Tite. "You have told me all I need to know."

"Sit down," said Mr. Pink, "and I will explain further."

But Tite had drifted away.

VI

THE MEETING

Very soon the loft would be filled with this year's hay that now stood golden in the ten-o'clock sunshine. The floor of the loft had been swept clean and sprinkled from a watering can to lay the dust. A pulpit had been fashioned out of clean boards. On it lay a Bible. The window had been washed and over it a pink calico curtain was hung. The mulatto girl, Annabelle, was responsible for this. Once, in the South, she had been to a service in a church where there were stained-glass windows. Those windows, she thought, had given a holy feeling to all that took place inside the church. In the hayloft, the pink calico curtain was to lend this air of holiness. So Annabelle prayed. Indeed, as the sun shone through the curtain, a pinkish light was noticeable in the loft. It had been possible to borrow thirty kitchen chairs in the neighbourhood. If the congregation exceeded this number, the overflow were to sit at the back of the loft on a mound of last year's hay. From below came the mooing of a cow whose calf had been taken from her.

Thirty Negroes waited, with expectant faces, for the meeting to begin. Twenty were seated in chairs. The rest squatted on the hay, leaving the row of chairs at the front for the white visitors. These were Adeline and Philip, the two Sinclairs, Wilmott, David Vaughan and his wife,

Elihu Busby and wife. These two couples had come to encourage the blacks, to show their sympathy with the cause of emancipation. It was hard for them to sit at ease so near the Sinclairs. Their elegant airs were particularly distasteful to Elihu Busby. He wondered at their insolence in showing their slave-owning faces. Yet their three servants had begged them to come, polished their shoes, assisted them to dress for what was, to the Negroes, an important occasion.

The Negroes, of whom the gathering mainly consisted, had come by various routes to this sheltered part of the province of Ontario, where some had already found work and hoped to settle, while others strained toward the day when they might return to their own country. Among those who proposed remaining in Ontario were a couple who had left the devastated plantation of their master, taking with them whatever they had fancied. The man carried a heavy gold watch and chain. The woman, named Oleander, was arrayed in a crimson velvet dress with velvet flounces. She wore, on her woolly head, a pink satin bonnet tied in a large bow beneath her chin. Scarcely could Cindy restrain her contempt for this pair. But Annabelle was not aware of their existence. Hands clasped on breast, she waited in happy anticipation for the meeting to begin. Titus Sharrow, from the back of the loft, watched her.

Among the Negroes who had found refuge in this vicinity was one who had been a preacher in his native village. He was a man of forty with a deep and moving voice, a broad flat nose and humid bloodshot eyes. His thick-lipped mouth was flexible, his teeth fine.

He mounted the crude pulpit, bent his head a moment in prayer. Titus Sharrow, standing barely inside the loft, surveyed the scene with cynical interest.

The preacher gave out the name of a hymn. There were no hymn books but the Negroes knew it by heart. The fervour of their lusty voices made the cobwebs in the ceiling of the hayloft tremble. Months had passed, in some instances years, since they had been to a meeting. Now, in exultation, they poured out their feelings.

Following the hymn, the tribulations of Job were read by the preacher in a quiet voice. He gave a short address, welcoming all, thanking those who had assisted in making this meeting possible. He made no reference to the war between North and South.

Adeline was disappointed, for she had expected something emotional. The Busbys and the Vaughans were disappointed, for they had expected an impassioned outburst against slavery. The Negroes waited composedly for the praying.

Now, the preacher, after the singing of another revival hymn, left the pulpit and dropped to his knees on the floor. In his sonorous voice he began to pray, at first quietly, then becoming more fervent, less coherent, as he went on. A shudder of ravishment galvanized the Negro congregation. Kneeling they clasped imploring hands, raised eyes to the ceiling of the loft.

Now the preacher was uttering no more than broken phrases, "Oh, Lawd ... oh, Lawd ... Save us ... lead us ... out of the night ... save us!"

The Negroes rocked on their haunches, their faces wet with tears. Annabelle was sobbing without restraint. Suddenly the loft seemed unbearably hot to the whites.

It was more than Adeline could endure. To Philip's consternation she burst into tears. She leant forward in her chair, covering her face with her hands. The ribbon bow of her bonnet was loose. The bonnet all but fell off, disclosing her shining red hair. Lucy Sinclair put a consoling arm about her. On her other side Philip whispered, "Stop it ... control yourself! Adeline, do you hear me?" His face was scarlet. He gave her a pinch.

"Oh!" she said loudly, sat up and straightened her bonnet.

Wilmott's hand covered his lips to hide a smile of embarrassment.

The preacher rose to his feet and announced a hymn. It had as its refrain a jubilant "Hallelujah — we're saved!" Over and over this was reiterated. In exultation the Negroes jumped up and down, clapping their hands. They shouted, "Hallelujah — de Lawd has saved us!"

To escape from the hay-scented, sweat-scented atmosphere of the loft into the freshness of the outdoor air was a relief, especially to Philip. He made no reference to the scene Adeline had made in the loft till they were safely in their bedroom. Then he said, "I have never been so ashamed of you."

"Why?" she asked, in a gentle voice. She was examining her face in the mirror.

"Making an exhibition of yourself — just because a Negro preacher made an hysterical prayer."

"I found it very moving."

"I found it ridiculous. As for you — all our friends were staring at you in consternation."

"Were they?" She was not ill-pleased. She took off her bonnet and stroked a wandering lock into place.

He reminded her of his sister and her husband, the Dean, in the cathedral town of Penchester in Devon. "What would they have thought of such an exhibition?" he demanded.

Adeline retorted, "It would have done them good. It would have shown them that prayer can be taken seriously."

She threw her bonnet to the floor. "You criticize — you ridicule my deepest feelings. Why did you marry an Irish-woman? A phlegmatic Scotchwoman would be the right mate for you. Someone who would stare at you out of peeled-onion eyes, and say, 'Ay, lad, but you're a bonny fighter.'"

Her tear-stained face was flushed with anger.

Philip picked up the bonnet from the floor and set it on his own head. He tied the ribbon strings beneath his chin and gave her a flirtatious look. Adeline did not want to laugh. She was far too angry but she could not prevent herself. Laughter bubbled from her lips and rang out gaily. Philip looked so ridiculous in the bonnet that she simply had to laugh.

The sound of her laughter made the polite knock on the door inaudible. It was cautiously opened and there stood the three children. They had been sent to church and now, in their Sunday best, came to hear news of the Negro meeting, to which they would much sooner have gone. Church was to them an old story. Not that they were irreligious. Augusta and Ernest in particular held strong views on the subject. They were opposed to modern frivolity.

When the children saw their father wearing their mother's bonnet, saw Adeline's tear-dimmed eyes — apparently she had laughed till she cried — the boys were enraptured but Augusta was embarrassed.

"You should not rush in on your father and me," said Adeline. "Why didn't you knock?"

"We did knock, Mamma," they said in unison.

Philip turned to them with a stern expression but looked so ridiculous in the bonnet, with the satin bow under his chin, that the boys burst out laughing and Augusta looked more embarrassed.

"What are you laughing at?" Philip demanded of his sons. He had quite forgotten the bonnet.

"You, Papa," said Ernest.

Philip took him by the shoulder. "You'd make game of me, would you?"

Without flinching little Ernest answered, "You look so sweet in that bonnet, Papa."

Philip now saw his reflection in the looking glass. He too broke into laughter. He took off the bonnet and set it on Augusta's head. "Let's see," he said, "what sort of young lady Gussie will make."

"Quite impressive," Nicholas said.

Augusta saw nothing but amusement in the eyes of her parents. She hung her head and, as soon as she dared, took off the bonnet and laid it on the bed. The parrot flew down from his perch and began to peck at the bonnet as though in calculated destruction.

When the children were gone, Adeline said, in wonder, "How did I ever come by so plain a daughter?"

"Honestly, I hope."

"What do you mean?" Her eyes flashed.

"Well, there was that Rajah fellow, in India."

She was not ill-pleased. "Which Rajah?" she asked with an innocent air.

"The one who gave you the ruby ring."

"Ah, those were the days," she cried. "What colour — what romance!" She mused, studying her reflection in the mirror, while Philip took off his collar that was limp from the heat in the loft, and put on a clean one.

She remarked, "Nicholas is the only child who resembles me. Thank God he did not inherit my hair. I detest red-haired men."

"Your own father has red hair."

"A great part of the time I detest him."

The children had strolled through the open door on to the lawn. Their Sunday clothes lent them an air of sedateness, but beneath that air there flickered resentment.

"I can't see why," Nicholas complained, in his alto voice, "we were not allowed to go to the meeting in the loft. It would have been much better fun."

"Fun my eye," said Ernest.

Augusta spoke with some severity. "Boys, think what you are saying. We do not go to church for fun."

"Mr. Madigan does," said Nicholas.

"The more shame to him," said Augusta. "But I can't think quite so badly of him as that. He goes to church because it is his duty to go with us."

"Then why did he smile when we all called ourselves miserable sinners?" asked Nicholas.

"He may have been remembering his sins in Ireland and thinking how much better off he is in Canada."

Nicholas thrust his hands into his pockets and frowned. "I'll go to the next Negro meeting," he said, "or know the reason why."

"Me too," said Ernest. "I will go or know the reason why."

"The reason why," Augusta declared, "may be Papa's razor strop."

Her brothers were a little subdued by this remark. They brightened, however, when they saw Cindy, their favourite of the blacks, approaching. She was carrying the baby Philip, to whom she was devoted. To him Cindy was a source of delight. He would clasp her fat neck, press his flowerlike face to hers and rapturously lisp, "Nith Thindy."

"Nice Cindy, he calls me," she cried, "the little angel!"

The elder children regarded their little brother without enthusiasm. He was made too much of, they thought.

Augusta said sedately, "I suppose your meeting was a great success, Cindy."

"Success! Why, praise de Lawd, miss, that preacher had us all cryin' our eyes out."

"Did my mamma cry?" asked Ernest.

"She surely did, bless her heart."

The children were embarrassed.

"I guess she laughed till she cried," said Nicholas. "Sometimes she does that."

"If she laughed," said Cindy, "it was at Oleander, who came to de meetin' decked out in her old missus' fine clothes. She oughta be whipped, dat nigger. She surely is a scandal."

"Scandal, my eye," said Ernest.

VII

THE NIGHT PROWLERS

Dusk had fallen. It had passed into darkness, for the moon had not yet risen. It was a wonder that the three men could find their way to the house. Yet they had been well directed and one of them carried a lantern. Just inside the gate they had left the horse and buggy by which they had come. They walked quietly, speaking only in low tones. Their speech had the accents of the South.

Nero, the Newfoundland dog, had a keen ear. As the men approached he gave a deep growl and raised his majesty on the porch where he liked to sit on a warm evening. The light from the narrow stained-glass windows on either side of the front door fell on him.

The door opened and his mistress appeared. Swiftly she took him by the collar and dragged him into the hall, he lumbering along without protest but with a bark and growl at the approaching men.

When they saw that the door was shut they came into the porch, not stealthily but with the air of friends making an evening call. Though they did not knock, the door was opened to them by Adeline, who said, "Good evening to you," and gave them a smile that showed her white teeth, with a tiny corner broken off one of them.

The men bowed gravely, taking in her beauty with their travel-weary eyes, giving a glance to the lamp lit hall, with its graceful stairway. Nero had been shut in a small room at the back of the hall from where his low bubbling growl could be heard.

"Come right in," she invited them, and they entered the sitting room on the right of the front door.

It was lit by a lamp with a china shade, showing a design of red roses. This stood on a mahogany table where there was a framed photograph of the Whiteoaks taken in Quebec, soon after their arrival in Canada. They were shown as in a snowstorm which had been cleverly simulated by the photographer. The heavy curtains in this room had been drawn close. No breath of air stirred it.

"Thank you, ma'am," said one of the men.

"Sit you down," she said, "and I'll tell Mr. Sinclair you're here." She looked benignly at the men out of her dark eyes.

Again she was thanked. The three left alone drew sighs of relief and stretched their legs. They had travelled far under difficulties. Now they had arrived at their goal. In spite of weariness they were tense as they waited. They did not exchange a word.

Adeline fairly flew up the stairs.

Hanging over the banister was Nicholas.

"Listening — you rascal!" she hissed. "Go to your room."

"Who are the three men, Mamma?" He was altogether too self-possessed, too bold, she thought. But she had no time to waste on him. She hastened up the stairs, her voluminous skirt gathered up in her hand. She tapped on the door of the Sinclairs' room.

It was opened to her by her son Ernest.

Seeing her expression he said, in an apologetic voice, "I am only making a little call, Mamma." He looked so sweet standing there in his green velveteen jacket and lace collar that she could not resist taking him into her arms and planting a maternal kiss on his cheek.

"Come in — come in," Lucy Sinclair called.

"Where is Mr. Sinclair?" Adeline asked. She tried to speak calmly. "There are visitors for him."

"With your husband in the smoking room." Lucy Sinclair sought to control her excitement.

"I will run and tell him," cried Ernest. He flew along the passage to the small room at the end and back. "Mr. Sinclair will go down directly, Mamma. Shall I take the message?"

"No, no, it's high time you went to bed."

Adeline swept down the stairs and made a conspiratorial entrance into the sitting room. She was astonished to find Augusta and Nicholas in amiable conversation with the three callers. She could hear Curtis Sinclair descending from above. She waited till he appeared, then swept her children out of the room. She pushed them ahead of her through the open front door into the porch; Augusta moving slowly, with an offended air; Nicholas executing a caper and throwing a glance of defiance over his shoulder at Adeline.

"You'd give me a saucy look, would you?" she exclaimed and cuffed him on the ear.

Augusta's colour rose. "You have always told us, Mamma," she said, "to make strangers welcome."

"No insolence from you," said Adeline, "or you'll get what I gave Nick."

"Who are those men?" Nicholas demanded unabashed. "They look rough. Not at all like Mr. Sinclair."

"It is none of your business who they are."

"Do *you* know?" he asked, with a mischievous smile.

"Of course I know. But they are here on business connected with the Sinclairs' estate. In this time of war it is necessary to keep their movements secret. So you must be careful not to mention this visit to anyone."

Dutifully they promised and she glided away, with a conscious air of mystery.

"She is in her element," said Augusta, looking critically after her mother.

"You are trying to talk like Mr. Madigan," said Nicholas. He put his arm about her waist that was not yet corseted, and urged her down the steps and onto the driveway. "Let's dance," he said. "One, two, three, and a kick to the left. One, two, three, and a kick to the right."

Willingly, for the night air, the glimmering starlight, made her reckless, Augusta joined in this dancing progress. Their supple bodies linked, they danced, like charming marionettes, along the drive to the gate, her long black hair floating behind her. At the gate they came to a sudden stop, listening. They heard the approach of a horse's hooves, the rattle of buggy wheels. The horse was drawn up, as it neared the entrance. The children saw Titus Sharrow and the mulatto girl, Annabelle, alight. They saw him clasp her to him and give her a fervent kiss.

In shocked surprise Augusta would have fled, but Nicholas held her by the arm. "We've got to know what's going on," he whispered.

No whisper escaped the sensitive ears of the half-breed. In a bound he stood, half-menacing, half-apologetic, beside the brother and sister.

"You watching me?" he demanded.

Annabelle was hiding in some bushes.

"Yes," Nicholas said boldly. "We were trying to find out what you're up to."

Tite spoke softly.

"I was giving this poor horse a little exercise. Someone had tied him to the post by the gate and he was wild with the flies bothering him. So I took him for a little drive. It'd be best for you to say nothing about it. There are queer goings-on, you know." There was a veiled threat in Tite's soft voice.

Brother and sister turned back toward the house. They stared with curiosity at the closed curtains of the sitting room. "Gussie," said Nicholas, "what do you suppose they're doing in there?"

"Tite had no right to say there are queer goings-on," she cried.

"But who can those strange men be?"

"They've escaped from the war, I am certain, and are seeking refuge with us."

"One thing is clear," said Nicholas. "We must keep our eyes and ears open, and not repeat anything of what we have seen tonight to Ernest. He can't keep a secret, you know."

"I feel the weight of it here." And Gussie laid her hand on her chest.

When quietly they entered the hall, they were just in time to see their mother carrying a tray with glasses and a decanter of wine on it. They were astonished to see her bearing this into the sitting room, for she was not in the habit of carrying trays about.

"Why are you two loitering here?" she demanded. Then said, "Nicholas, go to the sideboard and fetch the biscuit box and be quick about it."

The tray in her hand, she waited for him, while Gussie surveyed the situation with disapproval.

"Mamma," said Nicholas, "do let me carry the tray for you."

She would not allow that, but he pressed through the door after her and passed the china biscuit-box. The Southerners regarded him distrustfully.

"This boy," Adeline said grandly, "is safe as a church. He would rather die than mention your coming." And she gave her son a threatening look.

When, a few minutes later, he rejoined Augusta, he was glowing with a sense of responsibility.

"Hurrah!" he cried. "I'm up to my neck in this."

"Nicholas," said Augusta, "I do wish you'd try to control yourself. You know how Mr. Pink preaches self-control. His last sermon was on that subject."

"Let him control himself and not be so long-winded," said Nicholas loftily.

Ernest appeared at the top of the stairs in his nightshirt which touched the floor and had a little starched frill around the neck.

"You had better come up," he said. "Mr. Madigan is lying on his bed singing and there is a bottle beside him."

Nicholas and Gussie bounded up the stairs.

An air of mystery pervaded. Try as Philip would to lead a normal life, it was impossible with all this secretive coming and going about him. He sometimes wished he had not allowed himself to get involved in this conspiracy. It might, he feared, cost him the friendship of at least two of his neighbours, if these secret meetings leaked out. Adeline was exhilarated. She wished for something more than the passive part she was playing. She was above eavesdropping at the keyhole of the sitting-room door to discover, if she could, what these men were really up to. She could not believe that Philip did not know all.

"Why don't you insist," she demanded, "on Curtis Sinclair making a clean breast of it? You have a right to know."

"One thing I'm certain of," said Philip, "is that I don't want to know more than I already know."

"How much do you know?" she shot at him.

He was not to be taken off guard. "I am lending my house," he said, "as a meeting place. That's the sum total of it."

"You're maddening," she cried. "I won't be treated so! Am I to carry refreshments to these rough men and never be told why they are here?"

"Ask Lucy Sinclair," he said. "She must know."

"I have asked her. She tells me that she has sworn by all she holds sacred to divulge nothing."

"You sound very theatrical," said Philip.

Bareheaded she travelled the narrow path to Wilmott's cottage. It was now August. Summer was past its most burning sun. Full-blown white clouds appeared from nowhere and cast their shadows on the green land. Sometimes the clouds darkened and sent down a shower. This had happened early that morning, so the path was now soggy wet under Adeline's feet. Burrs caught on her long skirt and hung there.

The path lay close beside the river for a short distance before it discovered Wilmott's small cottage. The river was the grey of a pigeon's breast, though now and again when the sun pushed the clouds aside the gentle greyness blazed into gentian blue. At one of these moments Adeline stood on the river's bank, lost in admiration of its blueness. But even while she admired, the canopy of cloud moved inexorably over the scene, not with the effect of gloom but rather as though in placid acceptance of the coming of fall. Those rushes called "cat tails" grew in a clump at the river's edge. Adeline thought she would ask Tite to gather some of them for her. There was a certain tall Chinese vase in the drawing-room at home in which they would be as pretty as a picture.

Now she saw on the river the flat-bottomed boat belonging to Wilmott, its oars gently moving in the silent water. In the boat were

Tite and the mulatto girl, Annabelle. She lounged in the stern trailing one hand in the water. "Like a lady of leisure," thought Adeline.

She called out, "I see you two! And I warn you, Tite Sharrow, to be careful what you're up to."

Tite lifted the oars, from which a delicate rain of clear drops slid back into the river. He called, in his soft voice, "I'm only taking Annabelle for a little boat ride. She'd never been in a boat."

"Does your mistress know you're doing this, Belle?" called out Adeline.

The girl burst out laughing. "Ah'll tell her, Miss Whiteoak. Don' you worry. Ah'll tell her."

As Adeline stood there she felt the moisture from the wet earth rise between her toes. Her shoes were sodden wet. She did not mind. In curiosity her eyes followed the boat as it moved mysteriously up the river between the misty green banks. The half-breed and the mulatto. What was between them? She must warn Lucy Sinclair and James Wilmott of the danger to Annabelle. Yet how boldly Annabelle had spoken — and shown all her white teeth in laughter! Doubtless she was a hussy.

Adeline herself was laughing as she followed the path to Wilmott's open door. She could glimpse him sitting at a table writing. He looked serene, absorbed in what he was doing. Yet he heard her laugh and raised his head. The sight of her, the sound of her laughter, made his pulse quicken.

"Good morning to you," she said.

He sprang to his feet. "Mrs. Whiteoak," he exclaimed.

"Am I not Adeline — James?"

"I try not to call you that," he said, "or to think of you as that."

"Yet," she smiled, "I don't feel in the least guilty when I think of you as James or call you James."

"It's different."

"But why different?"

"I belong to no one."

She considered this. Then — "I refuse to belong so completely to anyone that I cannot call a friend by his Christian name — especially such a solemn sweet name as James." She came into the room.

"Dear James," she said, "forgive me if I have interrupted your study. What is the book?"

"I have a habit," he said, "of copying into this notebook extracts from what I have read — bits that have particularly impressed me."

"How fascinating!" she cried. "May I see?" She bent over the page.

Wilmott tried not to look at her milk-white nape. No man could be expected to look at it and not desire to touch it. Adeline read, "'The uttered part of a man's life, let us always repeat, bears to the unuttered, unconscious part a small unknown proportion. He himself never knows it, much less do others.'"

"Thomas Carlyle," said Wilmott.

Adeline raised her head to give him an admiring look. "How clever you are!" she breathed.

"Do you agree with Carlyle?" Wilmott asked.

"It's quite beyond me." She spoke humbly. "But if you agree, I do also, James."

He gave an ironic chuckle. "That's news to me," he said.

Folding her arms across her chest she said, in the voice of a conspirator, "Things are coming to a head, James. Our plans are laid for a brilliant coup."

Wilmott closed the door into the kitchen.

"Don't worry about Tite," she laughed. "He's up the river with Annabelle."

"That young woman," said Wilmott, "has a good influence on Tite. He used to be something of a cynic in his superficial way. But now he studies the Scriptures. When they are together they speak only of religion, he tells me. In short, I think he has done some soul searching."

"My dear James," said Adeline. "You are so credulous."

"Credulous!" He was affronted.

"What I mean is, it's a good thing you have me to protect you." She took a turn about the room, her mind brimming with the plans afoot. So eager she was that the Sinclairs had confided all to her.

"As for protecting," said Wilmott, "I think it is you who need protection."

"Oh, I am enjoying myself," she said gaily. "I thrive on excitement. James, do you never get carried away by your feelings?"

"I'm afraid I do."

"Ah, I should like to see that."

"Adeline," he said almost harshly, "don't tempt me."

He went to the open door and looked out at the placid misty scene. He saw two men coming along the path from the road. They were tall, angular, purposeful men who asked abruptly, "Just where are we, mister? We've lost our way."

Wilmott directed them to the next village but they lingered, as though in curiosity.

"More of your friends from the South," Wilmott said to Adeline.

"No friends of mine. They're Yankees by their accent. They're here to spy on us. I must warn Mr. Sinclair of this. I will interview them myself." But when she went out they had disappeared. The wood, the lonely road had swallowed them. In spite of himself Wilmott felt perturbed. He accompanied Adeline a part of the way home. Nero, who had been occupied at the river's edge, had taken no notice of the men.

"A pretty watchdog you are!" Adeline said to him in scorn.

VIII

Up the River

It was a flat-bottomed boat, old and inclined to leak, yet Annabelle, sitting in the stern, her coffee-coloured hand with its pink palm trailing in the water, found it a wonderful experience to be gliding gently up the river with Titus Sharrow at the oars. The rowlocks were rusty and made a rasping noise as the oars moved in them, which accentuated rather than broke the misty silence. To Annabelle, Tite was a mysterious, almost supernatural being. His Indian forebears, he had told her, were masters of this vast country till the French had come and conquered them. Still, he had the blood of the conquering race also. He was free as air, while she was a slave and all her people had been slaves, brought by force out of Africa.

Never had she minded being a slave. She had been happy in her security. She had yearned towards the day when the Sinclairs would return to the South, and she and Cindy and Jerry with them. She pictured the plantation as it had been in the past, for she could not picture its devastation. She knew that Jerry wanted to return to the old life also, to marry her when that time came. But these placid imaginings of the future had been shattered by her growing love for Tite.

Cindy had warned her, "You be careful of yo'self, Belle. Ah don' trust dat Injun. He's got a wicked look in his eye and a no-good look in his smile.

His lips is too thin. It seems like he could bite better than he could kiss."

Cindy had never seen the sweet bend of his lips as he rested on the oars and gazed into Annabelle's pretty face, noted the curves of her seductive body. But Belle's mind was on things spiritual.

"Does yo' love de Lawd, Tite?" she asked.

"I do indeed," he said, "but not so well as I love you."

That was a shocking remark and she knew that she should be deeply shocked. Yet she was not shocked. On the contrary, a thrill of delight sent a tremor through her nerves. She could not keep back her happy laughter.

"Yo' surely is a wicked boy, Tite," she said.

"You must teach me to be good, Belle."

She had a vision of the two of them, as man and wife, in a cottage, perhaps on the bank of this same little river. She would teach him to be good and he would teach her to love, but never, never to forget her Lord.

They came upon a little clearing where surely someone had intended to build a house. There were even cut logs lying there but they were half hidden by brambles. The pair in the boat were astonished to see two men seated on one of the logs studying what looked like a map, spread out on their knees.

"I've seen those men before," said Tite. "They were asking questions in the village."

"Where do dey want to go, Tite?"

"I don't know but I guess they're friends of your Mister Sinclair."

"Dey certainly don' look like Massa's friends."

"You haven't got no massa now, Belle. You're a free woman."

"Not a nigger neither," she amended.

"You're as white — or whiter — than me, Belle." He drew in the oars, leant forward and laid his hand on her knee. "Put yours beside it," he said, "and see."

The touch of his hand went through her like fire. She laid her hand yearningly beside his.

"Hi, you in the boat," called out one of the men on the bank.

Tite turned towards him with dignity.

"Were you speaking to me, mister?"

"I was." The man got up from the log and came to the river bank. He said, "Can you tell me if there's a man named Sinclair living hereabouts?"

"He was visiting friends here," said Tite. "He may be gone, for all I know."

"He's a slave owner" — the man spoke with scorn. "He brought some slaves with him. Do you young folks happen to be two of them?"

"We might be," said Tite.

"Waal, you're free now. Do you know that?"

"Thanks for telling us," said Tite.

Annabelle was shaking with silent laughter. "What's the joke?" asked the man.

"This young fellah ain't a slave," she said. "He's an Injun."

The man grinned. "I ain't never seen an Injun and a mulatto sparkin' before."

"You've a lot to learn," said Tite.

Annabelle spoke boldly, "Ah guess you're a Yankee," she said.

"I certainly am," said the man, "and so's my friend here. We're refugees from the North. We don't want to fight. We don't want to be drafted into the army. There's lots like us comin' into Canada. We thought Mr. Sinclair might help us to find work."

"Then you're not agin the South?" Annabelle looked searchingly into the man's face.

"Do I want to fight my brothers?" he demanded. "No, I'm all for peace and prosperity."

The other man now came forward. "Can you tell us," he asked, "where Mr. Sinclair lives? We don't want to pester him but just to ask his advice."

"He's stayin' at a place called Jalna." Annabelle spoke with pride. "It's the finest place hereabout but not as fine as our plantations."

"Which direction does it lie in?" asked the man, as though unconcernedly.

She told him and the two men left, with a gruff thank you.

"You should not have told them, Belle," said Tite. "I don't like the looks of them."

"But they're not fighters," she cried. "Jus' poor refugees from the var."

"They look like murderers," said Tite.

He brought the boat to the shore, tied it to a fallen tree and scrambled out. "I must see where they go," he said. "You wait here, Belle."

"Be careful," she called after him; a rich proprietary feeling for him thrilled her being, causing her to watch his lithe figure with the benign concern of a dark angel, as he disappeared into the bush. Waterfowl, knowing little of fear, swam close to her. A blue heron stole colour from the sky as he flashed overhead. She could see his legs tucked under him, as though he never would consent to use them again but would fly on and on to the end of the world. Oh, that she and Tite could live all their lives on this river bank, loving each other, serving the Lord! A tiny house, of only one room, built of logs, would be enough. The thought of the coming winter, the snowdrifts, no longer frightened her. She would feel safe, with Tite always at her side. He had not yet spoken of marriage but he would. She was sure he would. She did not look ahead to the time when he would pass his final examinations, become a lawyer. She could not believe in such a possibility. It was quite beyond her. Always she pictured him as the agile half-breed, with French blood in his veins. No Negro could be so clever, so ready-tongued.

Now he came loping back to her.

"They're gone," he said, "but not in the direction of Jalna. By jingo, I believe they're Yankee spies."

"Ah'd be afraid if you wasn't here," said Annabelle.

"What about God? Won't he look after you?"

"He's got dis war on his hands. He won't have time for a poor girl like me."

Tite gave her a tender look. "Don't worry, Annabelle. I'll look after you." He scrambled into the boat.

"For how long?" she asked yearningly.

"For as long as you want me."

She drew a deep breath of joy. "Ah loves you, Tite," she said, and again trailed her hand blissfully in the river as the boat moved gently up stream.

The bank was blue with gentians and Michaelmas daisies. Goldenrod grew so tall that it was a secret place. Annabelle needed no persuasion to go with Tite into that flowery fastness. They sank to the grass and he put a coaxing arm about her waist. She laid her head on his shoulder, proud indeed that her hair was not woolly. Her languorous eyes were raised to his rounded brown neck.

"Don't be afraid," he whispered. His sinewy hand pressed her ribs.

A child's voice broke in on them. "I see you!" called out Ernest. He and the two elder children came crashing through the undergrowth.

"Having a picnic?" demanded Nicholas.

"Not yet," said Tite.

Nicholas looked accusingly at Annabelle. "You're needed at home," he said. "Cindy has just had a baby."

Annabelle sprang to her feet. "And me not thar to help!" she cried. "Oh, my goodness! Show me the path, chillen, and Ah'll run all the way. Was thar a doctor? Was thar a midwife?"

"There was only my mother," said Nicholas. "Our servants were too badly frightened." His handsome boy's face was flushed by excitement.

"Was you sent to fetch me?"

"No, I was told to take Ernest out of the way. He doesn't understand such things."

"Understand — my eye," said Ernest. He was so excited that he walked in a circle.

"Do you know the shortcut to Jalna?" Tite asked of Nicholas.

"I do. Come along, Annabelle. Let's see how fast you can run." He led the way, the mulatto running lightly after him.

"This baby," called Tite, "is born into a free country. What colour is it?"

"Black as the ace of spades," said Nicholas.

"I shall follow with Ernest," said Augusta. Her pale face was even paler than usual, though she had been running. She took Ernest firmly by the hand. The moist earth was soft beneath their feet. Slender larch trees and leafy undergrowth pressed close on the path, across which a mottled snake glided, pausing just long enough to spit out its yellow venom at them.

"If Nicholas were here," said Ernest, "he would kill it."

"We are supposed," said Augusta, "to love all God's creatures."

"Gussie, do you love Cindy's baby?"

"I daresay I shall."

"How did Nicholas know it was black?"

"Perhaps Mamma told him."

"Tell me, Gussie, how does a baby get born? Does it take a long while or does it come fast — *whoosh*, like that?" He made a violent gesture with his right arm.

Augusta held firmly to his left hand. She said, "You should try to keep your mind off such things till you are older."

"As old as you?"

"Much older. You must make the effort."

"I try to be brave," said Ernest, looking fearfully into the moist August undergrowth.

"You may not succeed in being brave but there is nothing to prevent your being good."

"Are we rewarded if we're good?"

"It is promised to us."

"Is Cindy being good or bad?"

"I do not know."

"Then you don't know if the baby is a reward or a punishment?"

"How can I tell what sort of life she has led?" They had now reached the open parkland that lay about Jalna. Augusta freed Ernest's hand and he darted ahead. Annabelle was nowhere in sight, but Nicholas and Lucius Madigan came to meet them.

The tutor said, "I suppose you have heard of the new arrival?"

"How black is the ace of spades?" asked Ernest.

"I am colour blind," said Madigan.

"Is that why you wear that bright green cravat?" asked Ernest.

Madigan fingered the cravat as though lovingly. "I wear this," he said, "in memory of dear old Ireland. Thank God, she's only a memory."

"Mr. Madigan," said Ernest, "can you tell me how long it takes to be born?"

Augusta fled.

"My parents," said Madigan, "had been married ten years when I came on the scene. So you may say it took me ten years to be born. But things move faster nowadays."

Nicholas was watching with curiosity the approach of three men along the drive, on either side of which Captain Whiteoak had planted young hemlocks and spruces that were flourishing and growing tall.

One of the men called out, "Is this where a gentleman named Elihu Busby lives?"

"No," answered Nicholas, "but I'll show you the direction."

"Why do you want to see him?" asked Ernest, always on the watch for information.

"We'd like to buy land and settle here," said the man.

Nicholas went with them to the gate and pointed out the way.

"Liars," said Madigan looking after the men. "They're spies."

Ernest was jubilant. "Just like the stories in the books," he said, and ran down the driveway after the men.

Lucius Madigan saw Mrs. Sinclair descending the steps from the porch. Her slow graceful movements filled him with a longing to serve her. However, she turned her face away from him. She was afraid he might mention the humiliating incident of the recent birth. Humiliating it had been to her because she had fled in panic to the latticed summer house hidden among trees. It had only been built that spring and was the haunt of bluebirds who made their nests and reared their young in it.

It was stout-hearted Adeline who had delivered the baby, had held it up by the feet and smacked it on the back till it had let out a yell. When young Doctor Ramsay arrived too late, she had met him with a derisive laugh. "I'm going to hire myself out as a midwife," she declared. "I can bring young 'uns into the world faster than you can. This one took only ten minutes."

The doctor looked the baby over.

"I'm glad to see that it's black. Does Cindy know who is the father?"

"My dear puritan," cried Adeline, "Cindy is an honest woman. She has a husband and three children in the South. All living with her mother."

"She should be ashamed of herself for deserting them," said the doctor.

"Ah, she's so devoted to her mistress! 'Tis a wonderful thing to have such devotion."

"What does she do to merit it?"

"If we only got what we merit, heaven help us," said Adeline.

* * *

Lucy Sinclair cast a gentle, almost pleading look at the tutor. "My husband and I," she said, "have drunk the cup of humiliation to its dregs. What has happened today is the last bitter drop, my husband says."

Something puritanical in the tutor was repelled by this frankness. He hastened to say, "But it wasn't his fault, dear lady, it wasn't his fault."

"Indeed it was not," she agreed.

Madigan bent to pick a little pink blossom from a scant rosebush that grew near the porch.

"'Tis the last rose of summer," she said in a poetic voice, but he was obliged to put his thumb in his mouth, for a thorn from the little rose had drawn blood.

She sniffed the blossom's scent. "The last rose," she murmured. "Oh, if you knew how I dread the winter in this climate. Is it very terrible?" She raised her large blue eyes to his face.

"Well," he said judicially, "I have spent only one winter here and I must say I found it less disagreeable than the chill fogs of Ireland. For one thing, Captain Whiteoak sees to it that the house is kept warm. Fires in all the principal rooms."

"If our plans are successful," she said, in a burst of candour, "we may be able to return home sooner than we expect."

"It will be happy for you," he said, "but a sad day for me — when you leave."

"It is very sweet of you to say that, Mr. Madigan. But I fear there will be nothing but sorrow in our return — if ever we can return."

"As for your plans," he said, burning with curiosity and a great desire to serve her, "I tremble for them, when I see strange men lurking about the grounds."

Her candour overcame her discretion. She spoke low.

"You must not worry about those men. They are Southerners who come to see my husband on — important business. Oh, you must understand. They are here consulting him concerning our great project. You are on our side, I know."

"Heart and soul, Mrs. Sinclair. But I must tell you this — there are other men lurking about. Yankee spies. They were here today enquiring for Mr. Busby's place."

She was shocked and dropped the rose from her trembling hand. Madigan picked it up and inhaled its late summer scent.

"If I knew a little of your plans I might better be able to put these spies off the trail."

"What would my husband say?"

"He should know that I am a friend to be trusted."

Lucy Sinclair's cheeks were flaming. She could not restrain her pride in these daredevils from the South. In a rush of words she told him that more than a hundred of them, in civilian clothes, were in this part of the province, under orders from the President of the Confederacy to do as much damage as possible to the Yankees across the border.

"They'll make raids," she said. "They'll set buildings afire. You, as an Irishman, will want to take part in all this, especially as you say you would like to help us."

"Dear Mrs. Sinclair," began Madigan, but he could not tell her of the feelings she roused in him. He put out a trembling hand and laid it on her shoulder. "I will do all I can," he went on, "but really there's little I can do, except to warn you of the danger." The scent that came from her elegant clothes, so unsuitable to this northern country life, intoxicated him. She felt her power and gave him her consciously sweet smile. "From the moment I heard you sing," she said, "I realized how different you are from the people here. Ireland must be a wonderfully romantic country."

"It is that," he said fervently, and for the moment forgot how glad he had been to get away from it.

A figure now came out of the house and walked determinedly towards them, the hump on his back evident.

"Good morning," he said coldly to the tutor, and to his wife, "I should like a word with you in private, my dear."

Madigan moved away with a frown. He felt insulted, yet helpless. He longed for a drink to make him forget his feeling of inferiority before that proud misshapen man.

Curtis Sinclair said angrily to his wife, "I will not have you flirting with Madigan. I should think you would have more sense. But, in spite of all our misfortunes, you appear as frivolous as ever."

"How little you understand me, Curtis," she cried. "Come with me to a more private place and I will tell you what my conversation with Mr. Madigan was about."

He followed her round to the back of the house where there was a grassy space and about it clothes lines from which white linen sheets and large tablecloths moved wetly in the August breeze. In the vegetable garden the asparagus stalks had grown into a forest of feathery turgescence, low down in which the grasshoppers gathered and sang. Vegetable marrows lay in shapely ripeness. Tomatoes ripened and, because they were so prolific, some of them dropped overripe from the vine and lay on the ground split open for hens to peck.

Beyond the vegetable garden there was an open space before the apple orchard was revealed, the trees having their branches propped, in the case of the early apples, against breaking because of the heavy crops. In this open space there were a few plum and pear trees, their fruit showing purple and gold among the leaves.

"Is this private enough?" asked Curtis Sinclair. He gave his wife a cold look that did not invite confidence.

"How lovely it is here!" she exclaimed. "It's hard to believe that winter is only a few months away. I dread it so." She shivered in anticipation.

"You will not be here," he said curtly. "What are you going to tell me about that Irishman?"

"Don't belittle him," she said. "He knows more than you think. He's a most unusual man and a scholar."

"I hope," Curtis Sinclair spoke with calculated severity, "that you're not making a fool of yourself by confiding in him. It would be dangerous."

"Oh, no," she said mildly. "On the contrary, he has been telling me something very disturbing. He says there are spies about."

"How the devil should he know? He has been told that these men who come to see me are men escaping the draft ... I believe you are carrying on a flirtation with him."

She began to cry. "No, no — I have no admiration for him at all. When we do meet, the children are always present."

"They weren't present just now."

"Oh, why are you so unkind? Everything is going well, isn't it?"

He spoke more gently and laid his small elegantly formed hand on her arm. "Everything is going fairly well," he said, "but I have much to irritate me. For instance, this escapade of Cindy's."

Now her tears were changed to laughter. "Having a baby an escapade! Oh, my dear, how funny you are!" She patted the hand on her arm. Her diamond rings glittered in the sunlight.

He was mollified. "Why did this Madigan think he saw spies?" he asked quietly.

"Strange men have come asking questions. He could tell they were Yankees."

"What questions?"

"For one thing — the way to the Busbys'. Nicholas has gone with them to show the way."

"They're too late." He gave a short laugh. "Everything is in order. Don't let anything that happens surprise you. Not even my sudden going away."

That really frightened her. "Oh, you can't, you can't," she cried. "It would be horrible to think of you in danger."

"I have as much right to be in danger as any man," he said.

"I know," she agreed quickly, fearing he would suspect she was thinking of his deformity, "but danger to other men means nothing to me."

They turned back to the house. The cry of a newborn infant came to them, the voices of the Negro women chattering excitedly.

"Damn Cindy," he said. "Why didn't she have her baby in one of the workmen's cottages instead of in the house? It is humiliating to me that Mrs. Whiteoak should have played the part of a midwife to one of our slaves."

"She's marvellous," said his wife. "Nothing daunts her. She's as proud of that piccaninny as if she had created it."

"Probably some Yankee soldier is its father."

"How can you say such a thing of Cindy! She's devoted to her fat black husband."

"Lots of women had no scruples," he said, then drew a deep sigh.

"However, that's neither here nor there. The affair on hand is what's important. Lucy — I may be obliged to go away for a short while."

She put her hand to her heart. "Not into danger, I hope," she breathed.

"I think not. I have a hundred and fifty stout fellows assembled at the border. We hope and expect to make raids on the Yankees — burn property across the line. In Chicago we have many Confederate sympathizers. They will move on Camp Douglas. Five thousand Southern soldiers are held there. Once they are freed, the entire force will march to Springfield, Illinois, and release seven thousand Confederates. Good God, Lucy, it's a stupendous undertaking. If it succeeds, we may save our country yet." His eyes shone in his emotion.

Lucy was trembling. She put out her hand against the trunk of a birch tree to steady herself. A fine misty rain was beginning to fall. A grey veil dimmed the August scene. The pigeons on the roof dissolved into the mist but their cooing was heard, as though the mist had been made manifest.

"See that you say not a word of this, Lucy," he said. "My life may depend on your caution."

"I would die rather than breathe a whisper of it, but — these spies. They fill me with terror."

"They are too late to stop us. Our plans are too well laid."

They turned smiling to meet Adeline Whiteoak who was coming out of the house with Nero, the Newfoundland dog, at her side. Her hand rested on his collar. He wore an expression of beaming self-confidence and benignity such as is seldom seen on the face of a human being.

IX

COUNTERPLOTS

Nicholas walked with the three Yankee strangers to the Busbys' homestead. While the Whiteoaks, the Vaughans, and the Laceys had come
from England to settle in Ontario, it was the grandfather of Elihu Busby
who had been given a grant of land when, as a United Empire Loyalist,
he had left his property in Pennsylvania after the American Revolution
and brought his young family by oxcart to the wilds of this province.
Life here had changed greatly in the past eighty years. Roads had been
made which linked every village to the next. A railway linked the villages
to the cities. Life was no longer the life of the pioneers. The fields were
cultivated and the farmers were mildly prosperous.

Elihu Busby had reared a large family. They were in some awe of him
but considered no people their betters. They combined an ardent loyalty
to the Queen with a look askance at English manners. They liked the
Whiteoaks but were often affronted by what they felt were their lofty
ways. They cherished an undying dislike of Americans and exaggerated
the importance of the property they had left behind, two generations
ago, in Pennsylvania. To their liberty-loving spirits the very thought of
slavery was hateful and they were heart and soul with the North against
the slave-owning South.

Their comfortable farmhouse was four miles from Jalna. Nicholas led the way along that road, giving guarded answers to the questions with which the spies plied him. He was sure that they were spies and he felt himself to be in the midst of portentous doings.

They found the Busby family gathered about the table enjoying a meal. The strangers were, with old-fashioned hospitality, invited to join them. They accepted, but Nicholas, who always was made welcome, said he was expected at home. Yet outside he lingered, hoping for he knew not what. His boyish imagination was fired by the conflict below the border. He longed for a part in some dangerous enterprise. All he could find to do was to collect little green apples fallen from a tree on the lawn and hurl them at the pointed gable of the house.

Amelia Busby came to him then. "You mustn't do that," she said. "You might break a window. Then my father would have something to say to you." But she gave Nicholas a friendly look and, in a moment, added, "I suppose Mr. Madigan has left you."

"What makes you suppose that?" he demanded.

"Oh, I don't know."

"He's always dissatisfied, if that's what you mean," said the boy. "But he won't leave. He is a fixture at Jalna till us young ones go away to school."

Amelia could not restrain herself from asking, "Does he ever speak of me?"

Nicholas hedged by muttering, "I should have said we young ones. It would have been more grammatical."

"He is particular about your grammar, eh?"

"Rigorous," said Nicholas loftily.

Amelia thought the boy insufferably conceited but she put up with him because she had to know about Madigan. So she repeated, "Does he ever speak of me?"

"Never," said Nicholas firmly. He hurled another green apple at the gable.

"Listen," said Amelia. "Will you please give him a message from me?"

"Very well," said Nicholas. "But make it short. I have a poor memory."

"Tell him," she spoke slowly, her high colour mounting, "tell him I'm sorry if I have offended him."

Nicholas stared. In spite of himself he was interested.

"I'd like you to tell me who are those strange men making themselves at home in your kitchen," he asked.

"I don't quite know," she said truthfully, "except that they are Yankees."

"The very name," he said, "makes my blood boil."

"But surely you are not for slavery?"

"These darkies *like* being slaves. Mr. Madigan says we all are slaves — to one habit or another."

"What a clever boy you are, Nicholas!"

He was forced to agree with her. As he ran home he went over their conversation in his mind and thought he had acquitted himself well.

He found Lucius Madigan in the summer house giving Ernest a lesson in geography from a globe of the world. "That little island is Ireland," he was saying, and pointing with a bony forefinger.

Ernest leant forward till his little nose almost touched the globe. "Why is Ireland so small?" he asked.

"It's due to oppression by the English," said Madigan.

"Our country is very large," Ernest said proudly.

"Its size is its affliction," retorted Madigan. "It's a great hollow frozen space."

"At the present moment," said Nicholas, "I'm sweating like a horse."

"Before many years" — Madigan spoke sombrely — "this country will be taken by the Americans."

"We have the North Pole," said Ernest. "The Americans can't take that from us."

"Wait and see," said Madigan.

Nicholas broke in with, "You'll never guess, sir, who I've been talking with, and about you too."

"Amelia Busby?" guessed Madigan.

"Right! And what do you guess she said?"

"That she loves me?" said the tutor with an assumed simper.

"Not quite. But she's sorry if she has hurt your feelings."

"No woman has the power to do that."

"Not even Mrs. Sinclair?" The boy's smile was not quite a grin.

"For that piece of impertinence," said Madigan, "you will do fifty lines. Begin where you left off last time."

"May I give Gussie her present first?"

"Her present?"

"Surely you know it's her birthday! I have a pet dove for her. It's hard to be punished on a family birthday."

"I'll let you off this time," said Madigan, "but in future control your desire to be flippant."

"What is flippant?" Ernest asked.

"Pert," said Madigan. "See that you guard against it."

"Pert, my eye," exclaimed Ernest, and tore off after his brother.

They found Augusta reclining in the shade of a little grove of white birches. She too was in white, to honour her birthday. Blissfully she fingered the gold locket that hung from a chain round her slender neck. She had not hoped to own anything so beautiful, not for years and years. But this morning her mamma had put it round her neck and her papa had lifted the mass of dark hair from her nape and had fastened the clasp. In one side of the locket there were plaited together two strands of hair — the fair hair of Philip, the auburn hair of Adeline, under glass.

The boys looked on reverently while Augusta opened the locket and disclosed these mementoes. She said, "You can see that there is hair in only one side. In the other side I shall have hair from your two heads and from Baby Philip's, plaited neatly together. Then my family will all be represented."

Ernest clapped his hands in delight. He lay down beside her so that he too might finger the locket. He looked so small lying there beside Gussie that her heart, suddenly susceptible to new emotions stirring in her, went out to him. She stroked his cheek and, turning her head, kissed him.

Nicholas, looking on jealously, said, "I suppose you're not interested in a present from me."

She perceived then that he held, tucked under his arm, a beautiful sleek dove whose head, above its pouting breast, kept turning from side to side.

"For me?" Gussie cried in delight.

Nicholas set the bird on her breast. It was not at all afraid and began to peck at the locket she wore.

"It's yours," said Nicholas, "and I have made a dovecote for it."

Ernest, who had sat up, put out his hand to stroke the dove's sleek plumage.

"It will not fly away," said Nicholas, "for there is a band on its leg and I have tied a ribbon to the band." He put the end of the ribbon in his sister's hand.

The three were supremely happy in the glowing August afternoon. As they reclined on the warm grass Augusta drew Ernest's head to her shoulder and stroked it. A kind of rapture surged up within her. Nicholas laid his head on her other shoulder. "Stroke me, too," he said.

Towards evening Lucius Madigan appeared in the room that served the children as a schoolroom. Augusta was memorizing a poem by chanting its lines over and over in a monotone. Nicholas was making a kite, while Ernest cut up strips of paper for its tail.

The tutor wore an expression half-pleased, half-apologetic, as he said, "Well, it's not my birthday but I have been given a present. Look."

There was no need to draw attention to his present, for it was a bulky sofa cushion of red and gold satin, with a tassel on each corner.

"I may tell you," Madigan said confidentially, "that I became so hot carrying it that I was tempted to leave it by the roadside."

The children stared in curiosity, while the dove walked daintily to the end of its tether.

"How beautiful!" said Augusta.

"I'll wager I know who gave it you," said Nicholas. "It was Amelia Busby."

Ernest jumped up. "Let me hold it, please," he said. "I want to know how heavy it is."

With the cushion in his arms he exclaimed, "It's quite light. I could carry it all that way and not be tired." Then he promptly dropped it to the floor.

As though exhausted Madigan sank down and laid his head on the cushion. "Now," he said, "we can all rest together in peace."

"You're a funny sort of teacher," said Augusta.

"I instruct you," Madigan said, "by example. If you will watch me you will discover without effort what you should not do — should not be."

"We were happy here," said Augusta, "till you came." She spoke in wonder rather than displeasure.

"It is my fate," said Madigan, "to bring unhappiness."

"Then why," asked Nicholas, "does Amelia Busby intend to marry you?"

Madigan clutched his hair, as though distraught. "Don't tell me," he exclaimed, "that she intends to marry me!"

"My mamma says" — Nicholas spoke didactically — "that when a woman begins to fuss over a man she means to marry him. Mamma says there's no escape for him."

"You are wise beyond your years," said the tutor. "Soon you will be instructing me, instead of I you."

Laughing he left them and carried the sofa cushion to his room on the top floor. Really he did not know what to do with it and his face sobered to a look of concern. There was no sofa in his room, so he laid it on a rather uncompromising cane-seated chair. Now he felt that the chair would be of no further use to him. He could not sit on that elegant cushion. He had a mind to carry it back to Amelia and tell her that there was no place in his life for such an article. He wished he had not shown it to the children. They would be certain to tell their mother. He had a mind to disappear that very night and leave the cushion behind him.

The children did tell their mother of this present from Amelia. They told of it in a spirit of mischief, but Adeline regarded it seriously. She would have liked to see Madigan settled comfortably in life and feared that when he left Jalna he would drift aimlessly from one indifferent position to another. She admired Madigan's learning. When speaking of him to outsiders, she exaggerated his scholarship to lofty intellectual attainment, but to the Sinclairs she called him "that good-for-nothing Irishman — God help him." His admiration for Lucy Sinclair was too obvious.

Adeline said, at the tea table, "I hear you've been given a handsome present by a young lady, Mr. Madigan."

"Ah, 'tis of no use to me," he said.

"Come now, don't say that. There's nothing more useful than a soft place to lay one's head. Isn't that so, Mr. Sinclair?"

"I have forgotten how to relax," he returned.

Nicholas put in, "This cushion is of red and gold satin, with a tassel at each corner."

Nicholas pronounced it *tossel*.

"Dear Mr. Madigan," cried Adeline, "as soon as you have finished your tea, you must bring it down to show us. I'm dying to see it. Aren't you, Lucy?"

"There is nothing that interests me more than fine needlework," she replied.

"There is nothing that interests me less," said Madigan.

"Ah, what an unfeeling remark!" cried Adeline, pouring him another cup of tea. "Really, this Irishman is hopeless. He gives quite a wrong impression of himself. In reality he has a tender heart and the sensibility of an —"

"Irish wolfhound," interrupted Philip. "Another cup of tea, please."

Lucius Madigan subsided into silent laughter. He was suddenly in high good humour. He had that day been paid his quarterly salary. This usually was the occasion of a few days' disappearance and a return to Jalna, pale, contrite and considerably lighter in pocket. But now instead his purse was untouched and he was the centre of romantic speculation. After tea he consented to bring down the cushion for inspection. All agreed that it was handsome. Philip put it on the sofa in the sitting-room and laid his blond head on it, to his daughter's embarrassment, for she was concerned that her parents should keep their dignity. The baby, Philip, was brought in for his bedtime romp and was tossed up by his father till he screamed with delight and wet himself.

Adeline drew Madigan into the hall and, standing impressively, with one hand on the newel-post, on the top of which a superb bunch of grapes was carved, she said, "Lucius, I have something important to say to you and I hope you'll take it to heart."

It was the first time she had addressed him by his Christian name and it brought tears to his eyes. He thought of himself as a poor lonely

Irishman sadly out of place in this virile pioneer country. He thought of his poor mother in County Cork and how he had not written a line to her in the last ten months.

"I take everything you say to heart, Mrs. Whiteoak." There were tears in his voice.

"Well, I say this," she went on. "You cannot do better than by marrying Amelia Busby."

"But —" he exclaimed, in panic.

"Listen. It is plain to see that she is badly smitten by you. She is a healthy young woman who will take every care of you. She is good-natured. She is wild to get married, which her sisters accomplished years ago."

"But I have no means. Nothing to marry on."

Adeline's persuasive voice sank almost to a whisper. "Don't let that worry you," she said. "Amelia is a woman of means. Her bachelor uncle left her a fine farm which she has rented. He left her also a small house in the town. You could move right into it. Amelia is going on for thirty and panting to settle down with a mate. She adores you. That's plain."

"But why — why?" stammered Madigan. "There is nothing about me to adore."

"You don't know your own value," said Adeline. "That's the trouble with the Irish. We are too modest. The English are so quietly self-assured. The Scotch so conceited. Take my advice, Lucius, and ask Amelia for her hand. She'll accept you, I'll be bound."

Madigan clasped his hands in front of him, tried to speak, failed, tried again and brought out, "There is one great obstacle to my marriage with a girl like Miss Busby."

"Don't tell me you're already married."

"Thank God, no," he said, "but I am a Catholic."

Adeline was astonished but not dismayed.

"Strange," she said, "that you did not tell me this at the first, but I suppose you feared that, if I knew, I would not engage you."

"That was my reason." The tutor looked into her eyes with defiance. "It was not that I was ashamed of having been brought up a Catholic, but I was desperate for a situation and I knew this was a strongly Protestant community."

"Then," she agreed sadly, "I'm afraid it's all up with this marriage."

Madigan's contrary nature asserted itself. "I don't see why," he said. "Religion of any sort means little to me. I have not been to confession in five years."

"Does your mother know this?" Adeline demanded.

"She does not."

"Poor woman — she has a wayward son."

"I love her dearly."

"I hope you write often to her."

Madigan twisted his fingers together. "Very seldom," he confessed. He was thankful when they were interrupted by Ernest. "Come quickly and see Nero," he said. "He's shaking hands with Papa."

They returned to the sitting room. There Nero was reared on his haunches, while Philip bent in front of him with outstretched hand. "Shake," he said. Nero eyed the hand reluctantly but after the order was repeated, this time in a cajoling tone, he laid his woolly paw in the inviting hand.

"What a lovely picture!" cried Lucy Sinclair. "What confidence — what affection between master and dog!"

Philip, smiling, went to the tea table and returned with a piece of iced cake, which he presented to Nero, who devoured it in one mouthful.

The soft cushion was forgotten by all but Adeline and Madigan. Every now and again she gave him an encouraging smile. When he returned to his bedroom he took the cushion with him, and there it haunted him. If he woke in the middle of the night the moonlight was sure to be shining on it. He had no use of his chair, for he would not sit on the cushion for fear of crushing it.

And that was not all. The very next day he was encountered by Amelia Busby in the ravine, where he had gone to find refuge. She presented him with a plate mounded with cream puffs which she herself had made. Two days later she gave him a linen handkerchief with his initials L.M. embroidered on the corner. Almost before he was aware of it, he had made an appointment with her to walk to the lake shore.

The weather was hot and humid. The road was rough and stony, but Amelia seemed not to mind what it did to her shoes or feet. Before long she had a blister on her heel, but her amorous glances never faltered. She showed all her white teeth in a possessive smile.

On the beach she demonstrated that she could skip stones better than he. She longed to take off her shoes and stockings and paddle in the cool green water, but modesty forbade her. The rowdy waves that came tumbling on the sand gave her a wild feeling. Her black locks were blown across her light blue eyes. Madigan had not before noticed how attractive she was.

Adeline invited her to supper at Jalna, at table placed her next to Madigan. Amelia was so embarrassed by the presence of the Sinclairs that she could not bring herself to open her mouth excepting to put food into it. After supper she and Madigan disappeared into the porch and she sat close to him on one of the two stout oak benches there.

In private, Philip remarked to Adeline, "That young woman is after Madigan, tooth and claw. He has no chance of escape. And you are aiding and abetting her. Don't deny it."

"I want to see the poor man comfortably settled in life by the time we take the children out of his hands. He'll never find another position as tutor."

"I have a poor opinion of him as such," said Philip. "For one thing, he drinks too much; for another, he has no discipline. You engaged him. I merely put up with him."

"There is one obstacle to this marriage," said Adeline. "Lucius is a Catholic."

Philip opened his eyes wide. "Elihu Busby will never countenance a mixed marriage," he said.

"He need not be told," declared Adeline. "Lucius is not a practising Catholic. He has not been inside any church save ours — not in years."

"My opinion of him has not risen," said Philip. "I should like to stop this, but — what's the use? The girl is out to capture him and capture him she will."

* * *

Philip was right. While all about them seethed with plotting and coun-
terplotting, Amelia Busby and Lucius Madigan became engaged. He
scarcely knew how it happened, but he felt a great peace that was akin
to happiness when the struggle was over and he was landed. Amelia's
family were on the whole glad of her impending departure. She was a
forceful character, always convinced that she was in the right.

She made her own wedding dress and the pair were married in the
Busbys' homestead by a Presbyterian minister.

Amelia did not attempt to conceal her triumph. She had captured
the man of her choice. No man in these parts, not even the rector, Mr.
Pink, could compare with him in learning. To be sure he was of melancholy bent but she had high spirits enough for the pair of them. She was
hopeful that he would (with her influence — for she felt nothing to be
beyond her) secure a professorship in a university.

They went to Niagara Falls on their honeymoon. There, in the roar
of the cataract, they strolled hand in hand. At night, his tongue loosed in
the dark intimacy of the hotel bedroom, he poured out the poetic long-
ings of his Celtic soul. She understood not the half of what he was saying
but she was a superb listener, her round light eyes wide open in the dark,
drinking in his imagined face, as her neat rosy ears drank in his words.

On their third and last night in Niagara, Madigan was moved to
confide in her all he knew of Curtis Sinclair's plans. Through scraps of
conversation overheard, through Lucy Sinclair's impulsive confidence,
he had learned more than anyone at Jalna suspected. Now, intoxicated by
abstinence from drink and indulgence in animal gratification, he poured
out all he knew. Amelia learned to her horror of planned raids across
the line, of fires to be set, of shipping destroyed. She was in sentiment,
in strength of character, her father's daughter. She hid her feelings, she
clasped Madigan close, till he slept.

She spent the first sleepless night of her life.

When morning came she knew just what to do. She slipped out
of bed, dressed herself without disturbing Madigan, and went out into
the little town. She knew where to find the small cottage that was the
headquarters of the Yankee spies, for she had been sitting in the room
knitting when they had told her father. He knew she was to be trusted.

She remained for some time in the cottage telling the men there of her discovery, but she did not disclose how it had been made. She was almost breathless from excitement, but they were fairly desperate and snatched at any clue. Also Amelia wore, like a garment, an air of wholesome reliability.

In her excitement she missed the way back to the hotel and the return took her longer than she had expected. Her amorous proclivity was in no way lessened by what Madigan had divulged. Almost she ran in her eagerness to return to him. She intended merely to tell him that she had been for an early morning stroll. She would never let him know the use to which she had put his nocturnal confidence. She had a feeling of power, and even of noble rectitude. She did not realize how deeply jealousy of Lucy Sinclair entered into her feelings.

She found the bedroom in the hotel in a state of disorder. Lucius Madigan had taken himself off and all his belongings with him, leaving no word of farewell.

X

A Variety of Scenes

While Amelia and Lucius Madigan were on their brief honeymoon, the amorous affair between the mulatto, Belle, and the half-breed, Titus Sharrow, was moving to its predestined close, to the satisfaction of both. For Belle was happy in the expectation of marriage with this lithe Lothario, and he was happy in the certainty that he would seduce her.

He spoke of the good state of his spirits one morning to Wilmott, as he carried his bacon and fried potatoes to him. Wilmott raised his eyes from last week's paper to look into the dignified but amiable countenance of his protégé.

"You look nice and cheerful this morning, Tite," he remarked.

"I feel happy, Boss," said Tite. "Even more so than usual. I cannot explain why but there it is. The sunshine is so yellow. The river so smooth. Yesterday I rode that old grey mare of the Whiteoaks down to the lake and it was as smooth as the river. I rode the mare out into the water till it reached her belly. She took a big drink and then turned her head to give me a look of gratitude. She was as grateful as a woman. Life is very interesting, isn't it, Boss?"

"I suppose life is as interesting as we make it, Tite."

"I have great curiosity, Boss," said Tite. "When the holidays are over

I shall go back to the study of law and find out still more about the right and wrong of things. You yourself have taught me a great deal, Boss."

"You will discover more from your books than I can tell you."

"Have you noticed, Boss, that I have become religious?"

"I have not noticed."

Tite looked downcast, but for a moment only, then he said, "I hoped you would notice that I am more humble than I was."

"I had not noticed."

Tite continued, "It is not easy for me to feel humble, Boss, because I have a proud nature, but I am learning to subdue it. I have a very good example in my little friend Annabelle. She teaches me to be humble and I teach her to value herself more highly."

"Tite" — Wilmott spoke solemnly — "I have warned you before and I warn you again to avoid any intimacy with that girl. It can only end in serious trouble for you both."

"But we are so happy together, Boss. We have much to learn from one another."

"I wish you would learn that I like to eat my breakfast in peace — with my newspaper."

"There is nothing more peaceful than a week-old newspaper, Boss. You know that everything read is over and done with. It seems to me it would be a good idea if all newspapers would be delivered only when they are a week old."

Wilmott, his mouth full of toast and bacon, uttered the one word — "Go!"

Tite, in good humour with all the world, sought the meeting place that he had chosen for his dalliance with Annabelle. This was a small open space in the heart of a dense green thicket. He and she had made meandering, scarce visible, paths to it from both Wilmott's house and Jalna. She came to it with singing heart, full of the love of God, and of drawing the wayward Tite into that blessed communion. On his part he scarcely heard what she said. Out of his narrow Indian eyes he saw the tempting curves of her youthful yet seductive body. This was the place, this was the day. She would forget the love of God in her ardour for him. A million leaves shut them in. Among this wilderness of leaves flitted orioles, scarlet tanagers, bluebirds and golden finches, without fear. The leaves were as glossy as in springtime, though in a few weeks they would be showing the bright panoply of the fall. When a few more weeks were added, they would be blown by the will of the wind, leaving the limbs of the trees naked. But now — what luxuriance, what madness of growth! And not only the trees. Vines and creepers used the trees as foothold for their adventuring. A wild grapevine, its tendrils clinging to a young alder, reached out to embrace a young maple. Clusters of little green grapes thrived in the course of its wandering. The vine was relentless, seeking to smother what gave it support.

What seclusion was here! Half-breed and mulatto sat clasped in each other's arms. Remote continents lay behind them.

"Tite, mah darlin'," sighed Annabelle, "ain't it wonnerful how de Lawd has brought us together? All the rest of mah days, Ah'll praise Him for that."

"Me too," said Tite, stroking her thigh. "I'll praise Him."

Trying to bring him to the point of proposing marriage, Annabelle said, "One of these days my massa will be sayin' we can go back to the South. What's to become of me then?" Her humid eyes sought to probe the mystery of his mind.

Tite answered, "I am familiar with philosophy and what it says to me is — enjoy what comes your way and leave all the rest in the hands of the gods."

"But, Tite, there's only one God."

"Don't be too sure of that," said the half-breed. "Mr. Wilmott talks of the gods, and he should know."

Annabelle drew a little away from him, shocked by the strangeness of this remark. But he was tired of waiting for her surrender. Roughly he clasped her to him.

"No — no!" She was suddenly in panic, yet she had no power against him.

His white teeth showed between his thin lips. He reared himself like a cobra prepared to strike.

But her cry had reached other ears. They were not the only ones who knew of this densely wooded retreat. Curtis Sinclair had reached it by the wayward path that led to it from Jalna. Here he was to have consulted secretly with one of his agents.

It would have been difficult for an onlooker to have decided which of the two men was the more infuriated by the encounter. Both were in a high state of tension. On Curtis Sinclair's part, the frustration of all his plans, on Titus Sharrow's sensuality.

He was the first to speak and shouted, "Leave us alone, mister! We don't want interference from you." He was so incensed in his frustration he scarcely knew what he was saying. Such an outburst was foreign to his nature.

Curtis Sinclair, on the other hand, was not accustomed to bridling his emotions, though in the past months he had had considerable practice in self-restraint. Now he let his outraged feelings as owner and protector of the mulatto have full play. Leaning on his stick he limped into the leafy privacy of the retreat and stood scowling down at the pair — the girl almost stunned by shock.

"How dare you!" he stormed, and directed a blow at Tite with his stick. The blow struck him on his aquiline nose. Blood trickled from it. Annabelle raised her voice in a shrill scream.

"Go back to your quarters," Curtis Sinclair stormed at her. "You deserve to be beaten. Don't let me see your face again!"

The girl scuttled out of sight into the thicket, while her master stood planted in possession of the place of assignation. Tite plucked a large leaf from the wild grapevine and wiped the blood from his mouth and chin.

"You'll be sorry for this, mister," he said composedly. "I could strike you back but I wouldn't fight a cripple."

"Be off," Sinclair said furiously. "I will tell your master of this, you may be certain."

Tite spoke with dignity. "No man is my master. My forefathers were the owners of this country. Us Indians call nobody our betters."

"Miserable loafer!" said Curtis Sinclair. "Make yourself scarce before I strike you again."

"I'm not afraid of you," said Tite. "Nor has Belle any reason to be afraid of you. She's no slave but a free woman. Some day the Indians of

Canada and the Negroes of your country will take possession and you white folks will be the slaves."

"I don't want this woman as a slave." Curtis Sinclair spoke with vehemence. "She may go where she chooses. Shift for herself."

He turned from the half-breed to meet two men who were slowly approaching along the path. Tite drifted away and was soon hidden in the density of the woods. He did not linger there but might have been seen moving in his swift gliding walk along the road to the homestead of Elihu Busby.

The serenity of the golden August weather was shattered by the return of Amelia to her father's house. He was almost overwhelmed by the startling and outrageous events which pressed in on him. Not an hour had passed since his deserted daughter had appeared at his door, when Titus Sharrow came, with a still bleeding nose, to tell of the strangers in the woods.

Elihu Busby was divided between rage at the treatment his daughter had had from Madigan and furious anger at Philip Whiteoak for giving hospitality to the Southerners. He had an interview with Titus Sharrow, whom he never had liked or trusted but whose story he was willing to believe, since it involved Curtis Sinclair. But all else paled beside the bitter fact of Madigan's desertion of Amelia. He tied his horse to the hitching post in front of Jalna which was topped by the iron head of a horse. He found Philip in the orchard. After a genial greeting to him, Philip said, "There's a fine crop of apples coming on here. I hope yours are doing as well."

"I grow only grain," said Busby. "Fruit doesn't pay." Then he burst out with, "There's a pretty kettle of fish in my house. If I could lay my hands on that tutor of yours I'd horsewhip him."

"Madigan?" exclaimed Philip, his blue eyes wide.

"Who else? He married my daughter and deserted her after three days — the scallywag."

"Where is he?"

"I wish I knew. Amelia has come home — a deserted wife."

"Well," said Philip, "I've never actually looked on him as a reliable man."

Elihu Busby gave him an infuriated look. "He's a scoundrel. And it was an unfortunate thing for my family when you brought him here."

"What do you want me to do?" asked Philip.

"Find out where he is, if you can. And another thing — watch that man Sinclair. He's up to no good. It seems to me, Captain Whiteoak, that you are collecting some queer characters at Jalna. Certainly it does not raise you in the esteem of the neighbourhood."

"I need no one's advice on that score," said Philip.

Not long after this he sought out Adeline where she was counting silver teaspoons. She greeted him with:

"There are three of the apostle spoons missing."

"There's more missing than spoons," he said.

"What then?"

"Madigan."

"What in heaven do you mean?"

"He's deserted his wife. Her father has just been here to inform me."

"Where is she?"

"At home with her luggage. You may imagine the state Elihu Busby is in."

"Oh, the poor man!" cried Adeline.

"Who? Busby?"

"No indeed. Lucius. He never wanted to marry. Ah, he should have remained with us."

"But," Philip said accusingly, "you urged him to marry Amelia. You can't deny it."

Adeline was wholehearted in admitting that she had been mistaken. "But I thought it was for his good," she said. "I could not guess how it would turn out."

"Neither did you take into consideration that the young ones will have no one to teach them."

"I will teach them," she declared. "And you will help."

Philip groaned. "I have not a great opinion of Madigan as a teacher," he said, "but he was better than I should be."

At this moment Nicholas came running into the room, a letter in his hand. "It's for you, Mamma," he said, his breath coming quick. "It's from Mr. Madigan. I guess he's telling all the news of his honeymoon. Shall I bring your paperknife?"

"Yes," said Adeline, "then make yourself scarce. I must have peace for perusing this letter."

"Should you like to have me read it to you?" The boy's face was bright with curiosity. "Mr. Madigan's handwriting is peculiar but I can read it with no trouble."

"And so can I," said Ernest, who had followed his brother into the room.

Adeline opened the letter but had difficulty in deciphering the erratic script. Before she was aware of it Nicholas was looking over her shoulder. He read aloud:

> Dear Mrs. Whiteoak,
> Pray don't think too badly of me but I find I cannot face the life that lies before me. I am on my way back to Ireland, probably on a cattle boat. I shall always be grateful for your kindness to me. Please give my affectionate regards to my dear pupils. I should like to leave my books to them.
> Yours respectfully,
> Lucius Madigan

When Nicholas had finished reading the letter Adeline gave him a smart slap. "Impudent boy," she said. "How dare you read my private letter!"

"It's not very private," said he. "Everyone knows Mr. Madigan disappeared and the only message he has sent was to us children."

"Philip," cried Adeline, "will you stand by and do nothing about the insolence of this rogue?"

Philip took a step towards Nicholas but the boy darted out of the room. "Come along," he called to Ernest. "Let's divide up the books!"

"Books, my eye," said Ernest. "I want his compass and his indelible pencil."

But when they arrived in Madigan's room Augusta was already there, a history of the sport of cock-fighting in her hand. "I have never seen this before," she said doubtfully. "Do you think it is suitable for us?"

"I had better be the judge of that." Nicholas took the book from her hand. "But how did you hear the news?"

"Everyone knows it," she said. "Even the blacks. Also I was standing in the passage when you read the letter. So I came straight up."

"Here is the compass," said Ernest triumphantly. "Now I shall know whether I am going north or south. I've always wondered. Gussie, will you take the cushion?"

The news of Madigan's desertion of Amelia had indeed spread like wildfire. However, there were five people at Jalna for whom it had little interest. These were the Sinclairs and their servants. Their thoughts were concentrated on what, to them, was a far more important event. This was the departure of Curtis Sinclair on the following day.

He and his wife were together in their bedroom, she in a state of tremulous excitement that she sought unsuccessfully to conceal. Her hands were shaking, her sensitive lips trembling.

"For heaven's sake," he said, "try to control yourself. It's not going to be pleasant for me to leave you in such a state."

"But I am so afraid for you. You are going into danger."

"I'm going into action — what I've been waiting for this long while." His sudden sweet smile lit his face. "Be happy for me, my dear. Remember the five thousand Confederate soldiers we're going to free at Camp Douglas. Others will join us. The accursed Yankees will get their fill of us. They can't hold us in the Union."

"If only we can secede — save our country."

"We will. Luck is with us. Right is with us." Then he added testily, "I wish you'd let me make my preparations in peace. It confuses me to have you buzzing about — always on the point of tears."

"I'll try," she said humbly.

The servant Jerry entered, carrying some freshly laundered shirts. "Ah've brought an extra pair of boots for you, massa," he said, "along with the shirts." He showed them, well polished.

"I don't think it's well to carry so much. One pair should be enough."

"These is your mos' comfortable ones, massa. Let me try them on you."

Curtis Sinclair seated himself and the Negro knelt at his feet, trying the effect of the boots on him. "Ah wish," said Jerry, "Ah might go with you, massa. Yo' ain't used to dressin' yo'self. Yo' need me to look after yo'."

"There will be something more important for you to do," said Curtis Sinclair. "I hope that before long your mistress will be able to join me. You will be needed to travel with her. Unless you want to remain in this country."

"De Lawd forbid." Jerry kneeling rolled his eyes ceiling ward. "Ah wants to go back to our plantation. So does Cindy. She wants to show her new baby to its pa. She ain't nebber heard news of him. He may be livin' and he may be dead."

"Well, we shall soon know everything," said his master. "In the meantime hold yourself in readiness to take charge when I send for you."

When the Negro had gone, Curtis Sinclair walked up and down the room in some agitation, while his wife kept her troubled eyes on him, trying to discover all that was in his mysterious mind. The truth was that he was so occupied by the campaign in hand that he had little thought for domestic problems. At last he went to a drawer and, taking out an envelope containing bank notes, put some of them into her hand. He said:

"This money is for your expenses when I send for you. I would to God it were more."

Lucy stared at it almost in consternation. She was so unused to any responsibility. "Wh-what shall I do with it now?" she stammered.

He snatched it in some irritation from her, put it in a leather wallet and returned it to the drawer. "Leave it there," he said, "till the time comes, then give it into Jerry's keeping. He's to be trusted. As for those two women, I don't care a tinker's curse whether they return with us or remain in Canada. Cindy has complicated travelling by producing a baby. I doubt whether her husband begot it. Annabelle is probably with child by that rascally half-breed."

"No, no, I won't believe that," she cried. "Belle is a religious girl. She's cried her eyes out over your anger. I mean when you caught them spooning by the river."

"I gave him a bloody nose," said Curtis Sinclair with satisfaction.

"These Indians are so revengeful. I am really afraid of what he may do."

"He can do nothing to harm me."

A shadow of suspense brooded over the house all that day. The following morning the Southerner and his host set out, mounted on spirited horses which seemed as eager to be gone as Curtis Sinclair. "I cannot attempt to thank you and Captain Whiteoak for what you have done for me and mine," he had said to Adeline. "I never shall be able to repay you, but I hope that, in happier times, you will come to visit us in the South. We have the name of being a hospitable people, but nothing could surpass the hospitality of Jalna."

"We have enjoyed every moment of your visit," declared Adeline.

The two wives stood together in the porch watching the departure. Their arms were about each other and they smiled as they waved a good-bye. Yet a strange foreboding enveloped them. It seemed to rise out of the very earth which suddenly had taken the aspect of autumnal resignation. Grass and trees looked less green. A few leaves were fallen and a gusty wind shook the branches, as though eager to tear off the fragile armour of summer and expose their limbs to the onslaught of the equinox.

When the horsemen were halfway to the gate a figure in a blue cotton dress darted from between the trees and on to the drive. It was Annabelle. She fairly flung herself at her master's stirrup and, clasping his spurred boot in her hands, raised her streaming eyes to his face.

"Forgive me — forgive me, massa," she sobbed. "Ah didn't mean no harm. Ah don' wanna be left behind when you all go home!"

Philip Whiteoak laid a soothing hand on the neck of Curtis Sinclair's restive horse and looked down with distaste into the distorted face of the girl.

"I won't have any half-breed babies about," Sinclair said harshly.

"No — no — dere won't be none," Annabelle sobbed, desperately clinging to his stirrup. He asked:

"Where is that fellow?"

"Ah don' know. He's gone away."

"See him once more and you'll be left behind!"

"Is yo' goin' to sell me, massa?" she wailed.

"I cannot sell you in Canada and no one would want you as a present." He urged his horse forward. The pair trotted to the gate, held open by Jerry.

"Good luck, massa!" he called out. He stood watching them disappear down the road.

It was nightfall when Philip returned. Adeline drew him into their bedroom and closed the door.

"What news?" she demanded.

While she spoke excitedly, Philip answered with deliberation. "Sinclair was met," he said, "by confederates. He is full of hope but, thinking it over, it seems to me a risky business. He will cross the border into the States tonight. Then his campaign begins. How is Lucy?"

"She's bearing up well," said Adeline, "but she's very wrought up. Upon my word, I shall be thankful when we settle down into our own life once more."

He was surprised. "I thought you enjoyed the Sinclairs' visit."

"So I have, but I'm a little tired of Lucy's melancholy. She's not always congenial. Also I'm tired of those blacks who are here, there and everywhere."

Philip told her of the encounter with Annabelle on the driveway. "Why do women insist on being miserable?" he exclaimed. "There's that negress. There's Lucy Sinclair. There's Amelia Busby. All determined to be miserable. It's extraordinary."

"Not in the least," said Adeline. "In every instance it's the men who make them miserable. As for me, I'm at my wits' end to keep any sort of order now that Lucius Madigan is gone. God knows he was not much of a disciplinarian but better than none."

"You have yourself to blame for Madigan's marriage."

"I had thought it would be easy to find a tutor to replace him but it seems impossible. Just look at that trio. They are completely out of hand."

They peered out through the vine-embowered window and saw

Augusta dressed in white pacing the lawn with one of Madigan's books in her hand. She was declaiming from it.

> Ah, Love, but a day,
> And the world has changed!
> The sun's away,
> And the bird estranged;
> The wind has dropped,
> And the sky's deranged:
> Summer has stopped!

Nicholas, the picture of boyish vitality and witless concentration, was walking on a pair of stilts, made for him by Jerry. His dark hair hung in thick waves, almost into his eyes.

Ernest was aloof; holding the tutor's compass before him, he sang, "Always I've wondered if I was going north or south or east or west. Now I know! I'm going in a circle."

A maid passed, carrying the baby Philip who was having a whole-hearted tantrum.

"'Twould break a mother's heart," mourned Adeline, "to see her children so fey."

"Well, after all," said Philip, "they are half Irish."

XI

News from the South

Life at Jalna settled down to waiting for news of Curtis Sinclair. The weather was dim and, in the mornings, misty. By late afternoon a smoky sunlight gilded the trunks of the pines. The crops of the farmland and orchard were garnered. The children, free of restraint, roamed the estate like young vagabonds, carrying picnics into the woods, riding on the farm horses, or being taken, as a great adventure, to the lake shore to bathe. That shore, bordered by trees, stretched remote and beautiful all the way to Niagara. Life at Jalna was in a state of suspense, waiting for some impending change; it was not clear what it was to be. The two women, Cindy and Annabelle, did nothing to assist their mistress to any state approaching tranquility. Always were they fussing over her, making Southern dishes to tempt her appetite, carrying eggnog laced with sherry to her. They were the centre of continuous quarrels in the kitchen, for they thought nothing was of an importance comparable with her well-being. They continually asked her questions about their master, questions which she would have given much to be able to answer. How soon would Massa send for them? How would they travel back to their homeland? Would he soon send the money needed to buy them new clothes for the journey? Oh, how badly off they were for new shoes! Cindy's baby had grown apace. Clothes for it had been provided from the outgrown clothes of the Whiteoak children. The tiny Philip sought to play with it, as with a toy. Once, when he saw it being suckled at Cindy's bursting black breast, he had tugged to dislodge it and himself have a share. Laughing, Cindy took the nipple from her little one's mouth and, heaving Philip on to her lap, offered it to him. Golden head took the place of woolly black head. The piccaninny was so replete that it made no protest. The two women screamed with laughter.

Annabelle had almost completely recovered from her infatuation for Tite Sharrow. After the encounter with Curtis Sinclair, he had disappeared. It was supposed he had gone on a visit to relations who lived on an Indian reserve, but again it was said that he had been seen in the company of Yankee spies. It was certain that Wilmott did not know his whereabouts and was inclined to think he would not mind if he never laid eyes on him again, so disgusted was he by Tite's pursuit of Annabelle. Annabelle herself had returned, heart-sore but not heart-broken, to the shelter of her love of God. For earthly love she now turned to the devotion of Jerry in whose company she felt a security she never had experienced with Tite. In these days, laughter and tears were so imminent, each to each, that sometimes she wept in the midst of laughter, and laughed even while the tears were falling.

The three Negroes and the black baby took such possession of the basement at Jalna that frequent quarrels reached a climax in which the Whiteoaks' cook, after receiving her monthly wage, simply disappeared without notice. She was a strong-willed country woman and Adeline depended on her. Without the cook, she wondered how this complicated household could be maintained. Life was altogether too complicated, Adeline told Philip.

"The house no longer belongs to us," she said. "Those blacks are everywhere. They are dirty in their habits. As for order, I've never in all my life met a woman so untidy as Lucy Sinclair. She goes trailing about in her pink peignoir, with her hair streaming, looking like a dishevelled tragedy queen."

"She's awfully pretty," said Philip.

He could scarcely have made a more unfortunate remark. Adeline's eyes blazed. She retorted:

"And well she might be, for she never raises a finger to do anything but titivate. As for me, I'm entirely run off my feet. Up and down stairs all day long, trying to keep order, and every other person in the house making disorder."

"Come and sit on my knee," said Philip.

Adeline gave him a look of fury.

"Nothing that goes on in this house affects you," she stormed. "The cook may leave. The kitchen may be taken over by blacks. Your children may become little savages — it does not matter to you, so long as things go well on the farm and in the stables."

"What do you want me to do?" he asked. "Give the boys a taste of my razor strop?"

"Gussie is no more manageable than they. Today she informed me that she *cuts* the tangles out of her hair, rather than take the trouble to *comb* them out. Nicholas spends hours with the blacks. I cannot believe a word Ernest says. Even the baby, Philip, throws his pap on the floor if there is not enough sugar in it to please him."

Philip made noises suitable to an outraged father. "I shall attend to them all," he said heavily.

Silence fell between them while both brooded on the fact that home was not what it had been. Much as they liked the Sinclairs they could not deny that they wished this prolonged visit were at an end.

Philip said in a low tone, "Sometimes I wonder whether this venture of the Confederates can succeed. There are strong forces against it."

"But their plans are so well laid," cried Adeline. "They're bound to succeed."

Light footsteps could be heard running along the gravel sweep. The voice of Nicholas called, "Papa, are you there?"

Philip went to meet him.

"Mr. Busby is here," said the boy breathlessly. "He wants to see you. He has news for Mrs. Sinclair."

Elihu Busby now appeared. It was his first visit since the coming of the Southerners. He said, not attempting to hide his triumph, "Well, I guess your slave-owning friend has come to the end of his tether, Captain Whiteoak. He's met his Waterloo."

"What's this?" demanded Philip.

Nicholas, now as bold as brass, with his father beside him, demanded in the self-same tone, "Aye — what's this?"

Elihu Busby answered, "Simply that this Sinclair was captured by Union soldiers as soon as he crossed the border. He's been put in irons, I believe, and I don't doubt that he'll be hanged."

"My God!" said Philip. "This is awful. Some villain has betrayed him."

"He's a dangerous man." Elihu Busby looked his satisfaction as he added, "They've done well to capture him. I've said all along that he was up to no good here. I've said all along that you and your wife have laid yourself open to suspicion in housing him and his."

"Suspicion," shouted Philip. "It's no business of Lincoln or his gang what we in this country do. We're British subjects and have naught to fear from them."

"Well," said Busby, "I just thought I'd let you know what has happened to your fine gentleman from the South."

"You're right," said Philip. "The Southerners are gentlemen."

"They're defeated," Busby said, as if laying down the law. "Those hotbeds of cruelty, their plantations, are laid waste. Their miserable slaves are free."

"I'll wager," said Philip, "that those slaves are happier and as well cared for as the farm hands that work for you."

"Thank God," snorted Busby, "no man has ever called me master."

"They've doubtless called you by worse names," said Philip calmly.

He watched the angry Busby mount his horse and ride away. He turned then to speak to his son but Nicholas had slipped away, eager to bear the news of Curtis Sinclair's disaster. Philip shouted thrice for him before he appeared.

"Have you told what has happened?" Philip demanded of him.

Nicholas hung his head.

"You have?"

"Yes, sir."

"You young rascal! Come indoors with me."

Nicholas went, with fast-beating heart. The punishment he received was severe. He could not restrain a cry or two, which being heard by the parrot, Boney, he raised his nasal voice in a stream of curses in Hindustani. He hung head downward from his perch flapping his bright-coloured wings, and showed his dark tongue in fury. "*Haramzada! Haramzada! Iflatoon!*" he screamed. Then added four newly acquired English words, taught him by it was impossible to discover whom. "I hate Captain Whiteoak!" he screamed.

Up from the basement kitchen came a still more piercing scream, followed by despairing wails. Cindy and Annabelle joined their voices in wailing.

Down from the attic flew Adeline, her face deathly pale. She was met by Philip.

"What in the name of God has happened?" she cried. She looked ready to faint. Philip put his arm about her, led her into the drawing-room and shut the door behind them.

"I have had bad news," he said.

"From Ireland?" she asked, for she somehow associated bad news with that country.

"No. From the United States. The Yankees have captured Curtis Sinclair. Busby came to gloat over it. He says they will likely hang him."

"Merciful heaven!" cried Adeline. "Oh, the poor man! Is that what the clamour is about? We must not let Lucy know. 'Twould be the death of her."

"I have just been giving young Nicholas a hiding," said Philip. "He overheard and did not waste a minute in running to tell the blacks."

"The young villain — if I set eyes on him I'll give him another." At that very moment she saw him, as he passed the open French windows, his face flushed and tear-stained.

Philip restrained her. "He's had enough," he said. "What you must do is to go straight to Lucy. Tell her that Curtis is lucky to be alive. She must not hear of hanging. There she comes down the stairs now."

Lucy Sinclair's agitated voice was heard above the wailing from the basement.

"Captain Whiteoak! Adeline! Something terrible has happened. Oh, what shall I do?"

"Go to her, Adeline," said Philip. "It's your place to go to her."

"I can't — I can't! You must go."

For answer he took her by the shoulders and pushed her into the hall. The two women met at the foot of the stairs. Adeline opened wide her arms and gathered Lucy to her breast. "My poor shorn lamb," she moaned, "my poor plucked duckling! Oh, those villainous Yankees! Before many months they will be invading this country and will carry off all the women and put the men to the sword!"

At those words Lucy Sinclair collapsed fainting in the arms of Adeline who half helped her into the library and laid her on the sofa there. Simultaneously Cindy and Annabelle tore up the stairs from the basement, with Jerry close behind. All three threw themselves at Philip's feet. They wailed in unison, "Save our massa, Cap'n Whiteoak! They's gonna hang him sure."

Philip now took command. To the Negroes he said, "If you have any regard for your mistress, stop your howling." To Adeline, "Bring brandy for Mrs. Sinclair, while I dispatch a man to fetch the doctor." His authoritative voice brought a certain calm. After a small glass of brandy Lucy Sinclair regained consciousness. Adeline held a bottle of smelling-salts to her nostrils, reiterating, "There, there, now," as to a child.

But consciousness brought hysteria. Nothing could restrain the Negroes from joining their voices to that of their mistress. Philip was almost at his wits' end. He paced up and down in front of the house waiting for the doctor. When Dr. Ramsay came he administered a sleeping draught. Lucy Sinclair was enfolded in the comfort of oblivion.

When the doctor and Philip found themselves alone together Philip said, "This is a tragic business, Dr. Ramsay. I am very much afraid that the Yankees will execute our friend Sinclair, confiscate his estate, and leave his poor wife penniless.

"The best thing for you to do, in my opinion," said the doctor, "is to get rid of her and her servants, as soon as you can. All the countryside look on Jalna as a centre of Confederate plotting. The Yankees are going to be top dog. We live next door to them. On my part, I'm against slavery, as you know."

"So am I," said Philip. "But I hope I am at liberty to choose my friends."

The two men were in the porch, seated on one of two massive oak benches. Adeline now appeared in the open door. Her hair, of a copperish red, had become loosened, and had fallen over one shoulder. Her luminous dark eyes looked out from a pale face. Dr. Ramsay hid his admiration behind a frown.

"It's rideeculous for you, Mrs. Whiteoak," he said, "to wear such a tragic face because of the troubles of these people. 'Twill always be so. What does our greatest poet say?

Man's inhumanity to man
Makes countless thousands mourn.

"My advice is — pack the Southerners back to their own country where they'll be taken care of. Otherwise you will injure your own health."

"Did you hear those blacks howling?" asked Philip. "Strange! They are quiet now."

"They are quiet," said Adeline, with great calmness, "because I have dosed them."

"*Dosed them!*" exclaimed the doctor. "With what?"

"Laudanum."

"Good God!" cried Dr. Ramsay. "Where are they?"

"In the little room at the end of the hall. Stretched out on the floor."

And there they were revealed, snoring in the heaviest slumber. Dr. Ramsay knelt by each in turn, felt the pulse of each, lifted an eyelid of each, then rose to his feet with a sigh of relief. "You may thank God, Mrs. Whiteoak," he said, "that you did not kill them, for you certainly dosed them heavily. How did you come by this laudanum?"

"I bought it from the chemist for Patsy O'Flynn's toothache," she answered simply. "It quieted the tooth and it quieted these poor darkies." She looked with satisfaction at the recumbent forms.

Indeed the silence in the house was startling, after the violence of the grief which preceded it. Dr. Ramsay promised to return in a couple of hours. Philip and Adeline stood in the porch, watching him as he rode away. "We're lucky," said Philip, "to have such a good doctor in this out-of-the-way place."

"If only," cried Adeline, "doctors would not put on that superior, high and mighty tone! Now I feel superior to no one, yet, while he quieted only one fragile woman, I quieted three rackety blacks and made nothing of it."

"I shall make myself scarce," said Philip, "when they all wake up."

At that moment the baby, Philip, toddled down the hall. Philip senior sat down and put his youngest on his knee. He allowed the little one to listen to the ticking of his massive gold watch, the heavy chain of which hung across his flowered waistcoat.

"Tick-tock, tick-tock," said the baby.

"My favourite child," declared Philip. "I see him as the future master of Jalna."

"Not for many long years, I hope," said Adeline gazing at him with sudden fondness.

"Come and sit on my other knee," he said.

And she did.

While these things took place in the house, the three older children had hidden themselves in the wood. The bond among them was so close, possibly because of the scarcity of friends of their own age, that when one of them was in disgrace, they all felt themselves to be in disgrace. Equally they shared the burden of it, even though but one bore the stripes.

Nicholas lay breast downward beneath the low-spreading branches of a magnificent beech. Ernest had stretched his slender length beside him in the self-same attitude. Augusta sat, her hands folded in her lap, brooding over her brothers. Ernest said:

"Do you suppose we shall ever be happy again?"

"I doubt it," said Augusta. "We may be less unhappy but it's quite a different thing to be happy."

"I had to tell what had happened to Mr. Sinclair," said Nicholas. "Elihu Busby had brought the news. The blacks were bound to hear it. I thought I should be the one to tell them."

"I think that perhaps Papa wanted to be the one," said Augusta.

"Anyhow," said Nicholas, "he was in a towering rage. Should you like to see my bruises?"

"No." She turned her head away. "It would not do you any good and would turn my stomach."

"It wouldn't turn mine," Ernest said. "I'd like to see them. I guess they're no worse than some I've had."

"You've had nothing equal to this." Nicholas sat up with a groan.

Ernest too sat up and moved closer to him. Nicholas stripped off his fine white shirt, with the fluted collar, and drew his underpants from his buttocks. "Whew!" cried Ernest. He was so impressed, so almost exhilarated by what he saw, that he rolled over twice and again ejaculated, "Whew!"

"Oh, Gussie." He could scarcely articulate for excitement. "You ought to see! Really you ought to see."

Augusta took one glance out of the sides of her eyes. She said, "If Papa were to come this way and see you so nearly undressed he'd give you another whacking."

"For some reason," said Ernest, "I feel less unhappy."

Augusta gave him a critical look. "It's rather heartless to feel less unhappy when you see welts on somebody else."

"Well," said Nicholas, "I like to show them."

"It's just as wrong," Augusta said, "to boast of beatings as to boast of getting prizes."

"I got a prize for my pony at the fall fair last year." Nicholas spoke through the shirt he was pulling over his head.

"I got a prize," said Ernest proudly, "for taking a dose of castor oil."

"What would you have got if you had refused to take it?" asked Augusta.

Ernest felt insulted by this question. He scrambled to his feet and walked a short distance away. When he returned he was eating beechnuts. Augusta firmly took them from him. "You're a naughty boy," she said. "Those nuts will not be fit to eat till we've had frost."

"Even then," Nicholas put in, "they'll give him bellyache and he'll keep me awake half the night crying."

Ernest turned his back on them. "I'm going home," he said. "I want my dinner."

The two older children watched his small figure disappear along the path, flanked by delicate white birch trees. Twice he looked back at them and the second time waved a hand.

"He didn't stay unhappy for long," remarked Nicholas.

"He's hungry," said Augusta. "It makes such a difference."

"I suppose," said Nicholas, "that Mr. Sinclair will never be hungry again. Not if he knows he is going to be hanged."

"I wish," Augusta's voice trembled a little, "I wish that Mr. Madigan were here."

"Why?"

"Oh, I don't know, except that he makes light of serious things. It takes the weight off you." She lifted her heavy hair from her forehead and drew a deep sigh. "It's well to be young like Ernest," she added. "He can be unhappy and happy again in short order."

"If he had had the hiding I got," said Nicholas, "he'd have howled the rest of the day."

"But he is delicate." She spoke with a gentle folding of her hands. "We must remember that."

"Yet he thinks well of himself," said Nicholas, "and he can be very sarcastic. Think how he will say 'My eye!' with a sneering look."

"That's something that must be stopped." She looked disapprovingly after the small figure being swallowed by the leafiness of the wood.

But, after a few moments, he came tearing back to them. "I'm afraid to go alone," he gasped. "I keep thinking of Mr. Sinclair. Do you suppose they've hung him yet?"

"*Hanged* is correct," said Augusta.

"I know," he agreed, then repeated, "Do you suppose they've hung him yet?"

"You are incorrigible," said Augusta, rising and taking him by the hand. "I will go with you. What are you eating?"

"Wintergreen berries. Farther along they are as thick as blackberries."

Augusta promptly took them from him.

She turned then to Nicholas. "Fasten your collar," she said. "There's someone coming."

"It's Guy Lacey," said Nicholas. "He's home on leave from the Royal Navy. Doesn't he look fine in his uniform?"

The handsome slender young officer now called out to them, "Hello, you there! Do you remember me?"

In unison they murmured that they did. They were a little shy but he was self-possessed, a travelled man of the world. "How you've grown!" he exclaimed. "I should hardly have recognized you."

He laid his hand on Ernest's head. "This fellow was a very small codger then."

"There are four of us now," said Nicholas. "There's the baby — Philip."

"A baby, eh?"

"Well, he's on his feet."

"I hear you have guests from Carolina. I'd like to meet them. We of the Royal Navy have great sympathy for the South. I hear that France is putting a finger in the pie. Certainly Washington could not have done what he did without help from the French. But all this, I guess, is Greek to you young people."

"We have heard a great deal," Nicholas said proudly.

"You're lucky," said Guy Lacey, "to be living in this lovely spot." His eyes ranged from the hazy blue of the sky, glimpsed between the gently moving, leaf-laden boughs of the forest trees, where birds flitted, calling sweetly to each other, and lively red squirrels and chipmunks peered down in fearless curiosity at the young people below.

"Yes, you're lucky," continued Guy Lacey, "to live here. It's like the garden of Eden and you, Gussie, are a romantic-looking Eve. I hope you don't mind my calling you Gussie, the way I used to?"

"Oh, no," she murmured, her pale cheeks burning in embarrassment.

"We boys," said Nicholas, "are Cain and Abel. I'm Cain and I'm going to murder this young fellow." He put his arms about Ernest and bore him to the ground where they lay laughing.

Guy Lacey said, "There's a burr in your hair, Gussie. Did you know? Do you mind if I take it out?" With a sailor's assurance, he took the long black tress in his hand and gently removed the burr. "What silky hair!" he exclaimed, and smiled into her eyes.

Augusta was so embarrassed that she turned to the two boys who now were on their feet, Nicholas's tear-stained cheeks still recording his punishment. "You two young 'uns," said Guy Lacey, "should go into the Royal Navy. It's a good life." With a little bow to Augusta he strode away.

"Royal Navy, my eye," said Ernest.

Slowly Augusta followed her brothers homeward. The long lock of hair, from which Guy Lacey had taken the burr, hung over her shoulder. She raised it in her hand and looked at it in wonder. It no longer seemed quite to belong to her. Shyly she pressed it to her lips and kissed it.

Slowly the three children entered the quiet house. Once inside, Augusta flew up the stairs to see if all went well with her dove. From the moment when first she possessed it, she had loved it, but now for some reason she could not divine, she loved it even more.

Nicholas lingered in the hall, awaiting with humility the meeting with his father. Ernest noticed that the door of the small room at the end of the hall was closed. This was unusual and at once he ran lightly to it to investigate. He opened the door and peeped in. What he saw was Cindy, Annabelle, and Jerry stretched motionless on the floor. He banged the door shut and, with a shriek, ran back through the hall.

"The blacks are dead!" he screamed. "Every one of them! Dead of broken hearts!"

At his cries Adeline came out of her room. When he saw her he scampered straight to her arms. She lifted him and he clung to her still screaming. He wrapped himself about her, absorbing the comfort of her body.

XII

REWARD

In the days that followed the news of Curtis Sinclair's capture by the federal forces, tension at Jalna was almost unbearable. Not one beneath that roof was unaffected. For the first time since the building of the house Philip shrank from returning to it, but spent his days in the fields or stables. He visited a number of fall fairs, taking Nicholas and Ernest with him. Adeline was glad to know they were out of the way, for she was short-tempered and found the managing of her household and the comforting of Lucy Sinclair almost more than she could cope with. In truth Lucy refused to be comforted, had frequent fits of hysteria and at night terrible dreams in which, with awful clarity, she witnessed the execution of her husband. The Negroes incurred the anger of Doctor Ramsay, for when she lost her self-control, they lost what little self-control was theirs and loudly wailed with her. It was not unusual for Adeline to find the three of them in the bedroom with Lucy, all four weeping in unison. At all hours the blacks prayed, "Oh, Lawd, save our massa!" Yet, even while they prayed, they were convinced that he was a dead man. They forgot his occasional severity and dwelt on his kindness till he became, in their eyes, a saint and a martyr.

Three of the household were less affected than the others by the tragedy of Sinclair's fate. These were — first the piccaninny, which Cindy had named Albert, after the Prince Consort, of whom she had heard for the first time, since coming to Jalna. This infant throve amazingly, his time divided between guzzling at his mother's breast, and dark primitive slumber. The second was the blond youngest Whiteoak who was struggling with all his might to escape from babyhood. He attempted to run and, falling, scrambled to his feet without tears. What did make him weep was to be picked up and carried when he wanted to walk, or, worse still, to be set on the chamber pot. He had few words and appeared to feel that these would be sufficient to carry him through life, for he took no trouble to add to his vocabulary.

The third member of the household somewhat aloof from the melancholy speculations concerning the fate of Curtis Sinclair was Augusta. There was a dreamlike quality about her in these days. Often she appeared to be lost in thought, yet it would have been impossible for her to tell what her meditations concerned. One object of her thoughts was the memory of her meeting in the wood with Guy Lacey. To her he embodied all that was wonderful and exciting in young manhood. She wandered alone in the woodland with the tenuous hope of meeting him, yet when once she saw him coming she hid among some alders till he passed. Once she walked into the sitting room where he was talking with Adeline. He had been sent by his mother to enquire after the health of Lucy Sinclair. Mrs. Lacey, from resenting Lucy's flirtatious ways, had come to be deeply sorry for her. She had sent a blancmange and a pot of grape jelly to tempt her. When Augusta saw Guy Lacey, who had brought these delicacies, she was overcome as by a blinding apparition and, in panic, fled from the room.

Later Adeline said to her, "I was ashamed, Gussie, to see you so mannerless in front of Guy Lacey. You scuttled off like a frightened hare."

Gussie just stared.

"Why did you do it?" demanded Adeline.

"I — I don't know," stammered Gussie.

"Why, when I was your age," said Adeline, "the boys were fighting over me."

"Duels? With pistols?"

"Mercy, no. Fists and hair-pulling."

Gussie stared in wonder, then drifted away. Over her shoulder she said, "I shouldn't like that."

Later Adeline remarked to Philip, "I don't know how we came by such a daughter."

"She'll likely be the comfort of our old age," said Philip complacently.

"She may be the comfort of your old age but I don't intend to live past my prime."

"Red-haired people are notoriously long-lived," he said.

Giving herself a glance in the mirror, Adeline remarked, "Thank heaven, none of my children inherited my hair."

"I agree with you for once," said Philip.

"Contemptible Englishman!" she cried. "Why did you pursue me?"

"I was under the impression that you pursued me."

This might have ended in a quarrel had they not seen the slender form of Tite Sharrow glide along the hall. "He cannot have knocked," said Philip. "I'll have something to say to him."

"Perhaps he has heard news of Curtis Sinclair." Adeline pressed ahead of Philip to meet the half-breed.

"I'm sorry to intrude," he said, "but I was told in the kitchen that I might find Madame Sinclair here." He spoke with Indian dignity and what he considered to be French courtliness.

"Why should you wish to speak to her?" demanded Adeline.

"I have news for her," Tite said with gravity.

"Is her husband dead?" Adeline spoke in a hushed, fearful voice.

"He may be," said Tite, "but I do not think so. I have here a letter from him, in his own handwriting. It came through a secret agency with which I am connected."

"I don't believe a word of this story of yours," said Philip. "Give me the letter."

Tite shook his head. "No, Boss. I promised, on the honour of my ancestors, not to give this letter to any but Madame Sinclair, but I will show it to you." He moved a pace away, took an envelope from his breast pocket and held it warily in front of him for the Whiteoaks to see.

"It's Sinclair's handwriting," Philip exclaimed. "By Jove, it is!"

Tite returned the letter to his pocket. "You see, Boss, I speak the truth and nothing but the truth," he said.

"I have kept in close contact with the Government of Upper Canada," said Philip impressively. "I have read every newspaper I can lay my hands on, but I have discovered no reference to Mr. Sinclair."

Tite said, with something like a sneer, "Perhaps the gentleman is not so important as we think he is, Boss."

A strange procession now descended the stairway. It was led by Lucy Sinclair, in a trailing dress of black cashmere which appeared too heavy for this mild autumn weather. But then, she was always cold in these days and Cindy, who followed her, was carrying a huge plaid shawl with deep fringe. Close behind was Annabelle, holding in her arms an earthenware bottle filled with hot water. Close on her heels came Jerry, bearing a tray with a pot of coffee, a tiny decanter of brandy, and an ornately cut glass bottle of smelling salts. Also on the tray was a silver muffin dish.

The Whiteoaks gazed upward at the descending procession in apprehension. Tite's eyes were on Belle. Jerry rolled his humid black orbs in hate at Tite.

"Ah, dear Captain Whiteoak and Adeline," said Lucy Sinclair in a weak voice, "I am ashamed to bring all this confusion into your house but — I am so ill — so heartbroken."

Philip put out his hand to help her down the remaining steps. Tite came boldly forward and held up the envelope for her to see. Seeming about to faint, she gasped, "His writing! His very own writing!"

She snatched the letter from the half-breed and held it to her breast. Then, turning to Philip, she said:

"I can't read it, Captain Whiteoak. I dare not. Please tell me what it says." She put the letter into his hand, then supported herself against the carved newel-post while he tore it open. It consisted of only a few lines. Philip read:

I have been captured along with Vallandigham. I understand that Lincoln is going to send us through the Northern Army's lines down to Richmond. Do not

worry about me. I shall turn up again. My love to all.
As ever
Your
Curtis

With remarkable resilience she gathered herself together and, assisted by Philip, descended the remaining stairs, followed by the blacks, and went into the sitting room.

"This should be a heavy load off your mind, Mrs. Sinclair," Philip said.

Clasping the letter to her, she said, in a controlled voice, "It is! But when I think of my husband in the power of that beast Lincoln — that baboon — I could die of rage."

"Try not to let your mind dwell on that." Philip's deep voice soothed her. "Think only that he is alive."

She raised her large blue eyes to his face. "Shall I ever see him again?"

"Of course you will," he said heartily, though he felt far from certain. He patted her gently on the back.

Her three servants had followed close behind her and stood like decorative ebony statues about her. They could be heard to breathe but otherwise seemed scarcely alive, such was their power of obliterating themselves. Through the window Titus Sharrow was moving darkly among the trees like some lithe forest animal. With every gust of wind, showers of bright-coloured leaves were blown to the ground, yet scarcely were they missed, so dense was the foliage.

Adeline, after bursting into tears of joy at the good news and embracing Lucy Sinclair, had hastened to the basement kitchen to order fresh tea for everybody. Three times had she pulled the bell-cord in the dining-room but there had been no response. The household was disorganized. The tea-kettle, which was always on the boil, was sending up a dense spiral of steam, the lid was literally jumping from the pressure. Adeline put six heaping teaspoonfuls of Indian tea into a silver teapot on the top of which was a plump silver bird. She went to the larder for milk. Two large pans of Jersey milk stood on a shelf waiting to be skimmed. She dipped a cup into one of them and filled a jug. It looked so good that she took a mouthful, leaving her mobile upper lip decorated by a creamy moustache. She was unconscious of this and carried the tray up to the sitting-room, quite pleased with herself.

Philip eyed her with disapproval. "Lick your lip," he said. "You've been drinking out of the jug."

"I never touched the jug," she denied, facing him like a big unrepentant child.

The sight of her released the tension of Lucy Sinclair's nerves. She laughed, for the first time since her husband's departure. At the sight of her worn face suddenly alight, at the sound of her laughter, a transformation took place in the three slaves. They gave way to joyous laughter. Jerry slapped his thigh and exclaimed:

"Massa's alive! Massa's safe in the South!"

The women, Cindy and Belle, joined in this jubilation.

Outside, the dark shape of Tite Sharrow moved subtly among the trees. Only when he had seen Philip leave the house, seen the three blacks in a confab in the vegetable garden, heard Adeline in her bedroom sing "I dreamt that I dwelt in marble halls," somewhat off-key, did he venture to return to the presence of Lucy Sinclair.

He stood looking down at her as she lay with closed eyes on the sofa, the curtains drawn against the yellow September sunlight. So stealthily had he entered that she heard nothing. She knew nothing of the thoughts awakened in him by the sight of her lying there, thoughts dimly adumbrated by old tales he had been told of helpless white women taken captive by his Indian forebears.

Now, like a cloak, he put on his best French manner.

"Madame," he said.

Her blue eyes flew open.

"Madame," he repeated.

"Who are you?" She spoke as though at the next moment she would cry out for help.

"I am the one who brought you the good news," he said gently.

"Yes. I remember." She sat up, her eyes looking with desperate earnestness into his. "How did you get possession of the letter? May I see the man you had it from?"

"Madame, I had it from many men. I risked my life to get it. It was for your sake because my heart is overflowing with compassion for you. I am only a poor student, working my way through college, but I am of noble blood, from both French and Indian ancestors. There is a saving Noblesse Oblige. I try always to remember that."

Lucy Sinclair said accusingly, "You made my little Annabelle love you. She has been very unhappy."

"Annabelle taught me to love the Lord," he said. "She loved me the way a shepherd loves a poor lost sheep he is bringing into the fold. I am very poor."

"What do you want me to do?" Lucy Sinclair asked, with a suddenly decisive manner.

"I have thought," said Tite gently, "that you might like to give me a reward. Something — not too small — to help me through college."

New vigour had flowed into the veins of Lucy Sinclair since the coming of the letter. She rose to her feet. "Where is Jerry?" she asked. "He knows where my money is kept."

Tite's face, usually inscrutable, now perceptibly fell. "It would be better," he said, even more gently, "not to send for Jerry. But do not trouble yourself, Madame, I will do without the reward. It is enough for me that your heart is less heavy."

"You shall have your reward." She spoke with vehemence. "I will myself bring it. Wait here."

The house was now quiet. The children had gone with their mother, in the phaeton, to carry pumpkins, ears of corn, clusters of purple grapes, white asters, and pale-blue Michaelmas daisies to the church for the Harvest Festival. Augusta's dove, being under the impression that spring was approaching, uttered continuous gurgling cooing sounds. These amorous cooings so stimulated the fancy of the parrot, Boney, that he puffed himself to twice his normal size, turned round and round on his perch and rolled his eyes in a madness of lust. The front door stood open. Through it coloured leaves had been blown and lay on the rug.

New hope gave new strength to Lucy Sinclair. She climbed the stairs with less effort than it had cost her to mount them for weeks. In her bedroom she found the wallet her husband had left her, with banknotes for travelling expenses. Several times she had counted this money but the result was never twice the same. She glanced at herself in the looking-glass. There was reflected a face no longer wan and weary from anxiety, but bright with a new hope. She hastened down the stairs. In the sitting room Titus Sharrow awaited her. He stood up very straight, aloof yet watchful.

He gave a little bow.

"Madame," he said.

Her hands trembled so that she could not properly count the banknotes. One fluttered to the floor. Tite picked it up and looked at it doubtfully. "This is Confederate money," he said.

"But it's perfectly reliable," she answered. "How much would please you? Of course, if I gave you the whole amount it could not repay you for the relief you have given me."

"I do not like to accept more than you can spare, Madame." His greedy eyes were on the wallet which bore in gold-embossed letters the initials C.S.

She put it into his hand.

"Count," she said. "I can't."

His deft greedy fingers ran through the notes.

"There seem," he said, "to be more than six hundred dollars."

"Take two hundred and I wish I could give you more."

He returned the somewhat thinner wallet to her. With a deeper bow than usual, his slanting eyes downcast, he said, "*Mille remerciements*, Madame." With her he was determinedly French.

"If you are able to bring me any further news of Mr. Sinclair," she said, "I shall be most grateful." She smiled a little and suddenly looked pretty, with the appealing prettiness of a girl.

Tite Sharrow, drifting rather than walking from the house, came suddenly on Jerry, or the Negro came purposefully on him. With dignity Tite sought to avoid him. This heavily built black man was not one with whom Tite would be willing to be involved in a quarrel. Not that Tite was a coward but he preferred peaceful ways of settling disputes or rivalries.

Now Jerry, with an incredibly swift movement, whipped out a knife.

"See this," he growled in his thick voice. "Ah'm gonna run this right into yo' guts, if yo' don' keep away from mah gal Belle."

"Nigger!" said Tite.

"Yo' better be careful if yo' don' wan' yo innards ripped out," Jerry yelled, forgetful of his nearness to the house.

Philip Whiteoak appeared, as it were from nowhere, and placed his stalwart body between them. Like figures of the night dispersed by the sun god they drew away.

"No more of this," he said, "or I'll knock your heads together. There's trouble enough without your getting into a fight."

"Boss," said Titus Sharrow, "I am a peaceful man. I don't want a fight with one of my own race. I am above tussling with a nigger."

"This won' be no tussle," growled Jerry. "This will be the end of you. De Lawd is on mah side."

"The Lord don't think well of you," said Tite. "If He did you'd not be a slave."

Philip Whiteoak said, "Get along with you, Tite. Hand over that knife, Jerry."

Jerry sullenly parted with the knife. Philip felt its edge with distaste. "This is a nasty weapon," he said. "We don't use knives in this country. If you want to fight, go at it with fists."

Philip watched the two young men disappear, Jerry ambling, Tite gliding; Jerry ebony-faced, Tite dusky as the twilight; Jerry lumpish, Tite lithe. Philip was accustomed to the Indians of the East and thought that helped him to understand Tite. A clever rascal. About Negroes he thought there was little to understand. Animals. Possibly quite useful on a plantation, but not the sort of animal an Englishman would want underfoot in his own house.

He stood watching a pair of red squirrels scampering among the branches of an ancient oak, from the short thick trunk of which massive branches spread. It was also a tree of great height and had produced a vast number of leaves that still were glossy and green. The squirrels were collecting acorns for their winter store but stopped every now and again to chase each other. "Empty-headed little rascals," Philip said aloud.

He did not see Elihu Busby till he stood beside him.

"Fine old oak," remarked Busby.

"Yes. It's been standing here for hundreds of years, I suppose. I'm very fond of it. It branches out so low that my youngsters have no trouble in climbing it."

"Surely Gussie doesn't climb trees."

"She certainly does. Why not?"

"Well, I always look on you as a conventional British father who would insist on his daughters behaving like little ladies."

"Do you really?"

There was a silence which Philip looked capable of continuing for a long time. However, Elihu Busby had sought him out with a purpose.

"I want to say" — he brought it out doggedly — "that I'm sorry for my harshness towards those Southerners. It must have seemed even unfriendly towards you. But I felt strongly on the subject of slavery and I felt bitter about the way my poor daughter had been treated by that rascally tutor of yours."

"Have you changed your mind?" asked Philip.

"Not in the least. But I've always been on good terms with you folks. My wife seems to blame me for things being different. I know I spoke harshly about the South. My sympathies are strong for the Yankees."

"You've always seemed proud," said Philip, "that your forebears were United Empire Loyalists and that they came to Canada after the Revolution. If you're so fond of the Yankees, you must be sorry that your people ever left the States."

Elihu Busby's colour rose. He found it hard to be calm. "I would not live in that country," he said, "not if they gave me back all the valuable property my folks left behind there."

Philip gave him a bland inscrutable look.

"I took it hard," said Elihu Busby, "that Jalna should be a centre of plotting by these slave owners. I was glad when I heard that that man Sinclair had been captured before he'd had time to carry out his accursed schemes. I'd have been glad to hear that Lincoln had hanged him."

"I don't see why you're telling me what I already know," said Philip.

"Because I want you to understand that I'm sorry for that poor little woman. I hear she's a gentle soul. She's in an awful position stranded here with those miserable slaves of hers. I can tell you I've lain awake nights worrying over her and being sorry I said the things I did."

"By Jove!" ejaculated Philip Whiteoak.

Elihu Busby expanded. "I've wanted to do something to show that I have only kindly feelings towards her. This morning my chance came. That letter from her husband was intercepted and brought to me to read."

"Nice teamwork," said Philip.

"I had guessed it to be a letter of farewell written when he was condemned to be hanged, but when I discovered the good news, I thought I'd bring it straight to her myself."

Philip's bright blue eyes rested on Elihu Busby with no expression whatever.

The deliberate voice went on. "However, when I got here I felt sort of shy about coming in. Mrs. Whiteoak has avoided me for months."

"I hadn't noticed," said Philip.

"The trouble with you," said Elihu Busby, "is that you don't take a proper interest in the affairs of this young country. A man like you could be a real power for good but you concentrate on your own affairs. You're more interested in your Jersey cows than in the fate of those poor helpless slaves."

"Their fate is none of my business."

"Do you or do you not think Lincoln is a great man?"

"I never give him a second thought."

"Do you *ever* think, Captain Whiteoak?"

"Not if I can avoid it. I leave that to my wife."

"It would be easy to quarrel with you, sir. But I didn't come here to quarrel. I came to deliver a letter to Mrs. Sinclair. On the way I met Titus Sharrow and gave it to him with instructions to put it into the lady's hand. Now I want to know whether he did this."

"He did indeed."

"That's good. I gave him a York shilling for delivering it. I consider he was well paid, so don't let him wheedle anything more out of you."

"No, indeed," said Philip.

"I guess Mrs. Sinclair is overjoyed by the news."

"She is indeed — and so are the slaves overjoyed."

"Perhaps you will tell her that it was through me she got the letter?"

"I'll see to that," said Philip laconically.

They parted. At the same time the half-breed returned to Wilmott's house, along the winding moist green path.

Tite was in good spirits and remarked as he entered, "I hope you're as glad to see me, Boss, as I am glad to be back."

"I am indeed," said Wilmott, "for you left a confounded mess here. Nothing in order — every pot and pan dirty — no kindling for lighting the fire. Where have you been?"

"I have been visiting my grandmother, Boss. I should have come sooner but I found her very sick, with no one to wait on her. Then, as I was coming back, I met Mr. Busby who confided to me that he had a letter for Madame Sinclair, telling her that her husband is still alive. Mr. Busby was afraid to bring the letter to her...."

"Why?" interrupted Wilmott.

"I do not know, Boss, but he was afraid. He gave me a York shilling to deliver it for him." Tite drew the coin from his pocket and looked at it pensively. He said, "It is not much but enough to buy me a good notebook for my lectures which will soon begin. I think I had better lay it here on the clock shelf for safe keeping. Then I will make your lunch. I'm afraid you don't eat enough when I'm not here."

Wilmott's voice cracked with self-pity. "I have not had one decent meal," he said.

Very soon the rattle of dishes being washed came from the kitchen, and after that the smell of sausages frying and the aroma of coffee. Tite spread a clean cloth on the table and laid places for two. Wilmott drew up a chair, his mobile face expressing both annoyance and hunger. "This is an enormous meal you've given me," he said, eyeing the six sausages and the mound of fried potatoes.

"The sausages are pure pork, which are the only good ones," said Tite, "and the potatoes are this season's. Let me help you to some of these ripe tomatoes that I lifted from the tomato patch at Jalna as I passed. Let me pour you a cup of coffee. The cream is thick as pudding, Boss."

Wilmott's sense of well-being returned. There was no doubt that Tite spoilt him, as he, in spite of suspicions, tolerated Tite. Now the half-breed remarked, "I have a very interesting life, Boss. Every day something curious happens to me. I am never dull. I always find something to do. Right after lunch I am going to pluck the fat goose I see hanging in the kitchen."

Some time later he came to Wilmott carrying the goose. He held it close to Wilmott's nose.

"Would you say, Boss," he enquired, "that this goose smells high?"

Wilmott sniffed, then shouted, "Take it away! It's horrible."

Tite sniffed the carcass, it almost appeared, with relish.

"It is," he said, "pretty high."

"Take it away and bury it," ordered Wilmott.

Yet when, a little later, he came into the kitchen, Tite was sitting on a low stool plucking the goose. "It would be a pity, Boss," he explained, "to waste these fine feathers. As for the stink, it's surprising how one can get used to it."

"I can't," said Wilmott and slammed the door.

In a short while the two were seated amicably in the flat-bottomed boat that always was tied waiting at the little wharf. Tite leisurely rowed, while Wilmott lounged on an old faded cushion in the stern. He was trolling with bits of the goose for bait. The river was glassy smooth. The ripples left by the boat were enough to rock the painted leaves of the willows that floated there. A mysterious birdsong thrilled the air but the little singers were unseen. They congregated among the fading foliage to presage their perilous migration to the South. But the blue jays and other birds that were to remain here spread their wings and swept in unconcern above the river, casting their reflections on a glassy surface which before long would become ice.

"I still am thinking," said Tite, "of what an interesting life I lead, Boss. Something unexpected happens to me almost every day. Though I may have problems they are always somehow solved for me. Do you find it so, Boss?"

"I ask no better life," said Wilmott.

XIII

DEPARTURE

From the hour of receiving the letter from Curtis Sinclair, Lucy was almost visibly quivering in a state of high excitement. She could not settle down to anything, not even to make any real preparation for the journey southward which she looked on as imminent. She would command Cindy and Belle to lay out all her dresses, her flounced petticoats, lace-trimmed chemises and nightgowns, that they might be put in order, but when she beheld this array of finery she became utterly confused and bade the women put it out of her sight. She constantly worried about money and would count over and over what she had left, quite forgetting the sum she had given Tite Sharrow. She slept badly and would wake sobbing from nightmares in which she saw her husband with the halter round his neck. Cindy now slept on a mattress on the floor in Lucy's room. When the sound of her mistress's grief woke her, the Negress would join in her lamentations. Belle, in the next room, would be roused and the loud talk, the noisy weeping of the slaves would wake the children. Adeline and Philip, in their room on the ground floor, would not be woken, but Nero, who slept on the mat outside their door, would stalk up the stairs and look in on the visitors with dark disapproval. He would utter a deep-throated "woof" of protest and then return downstairs.

The life of the three elder children was strangely coloured by the unsettled state of the household. Now they were under very little supervision. They did what their erratic wills prompted them to do. They wore what clothes they chose, ate when and what they chose. They (that is to say, Augusta and Nicholas) had invented a game, a kind of serial play, in which they had the roles of Elizabethan adventurers, discoverers of new lands, sometimes pirates. Nicholas was known as Sir Francis Drake, sometimes as Sir Walter Raleigh, but Augusta was faithful to the role of Sir Richard Grenville. There being no special character for Ernest to play, he was made to represent all the coloured peoples of the strange lands discovered, or even the Spaniards of the Armada. He threw himself into these various parts with the greatest enthusiasm, executing war dances or bartering his lands for a few beads, or being converted to Christianity, as was demanded of him.

Now Sir Richard Grenville was captured by the Spaniards. He, in the person of Augusta, stood upon the deck of their flagship. "Old Sir Richard caught at last!" Nicholas quoted in his best manner:

And they praised him to his face with their courtly
foreign grace …

Reverting to ordinary speech he said to Ernest:
"You are the Spaniards. Go ahead and praise him."
Promptly Ernest declaimed, "You done well, Musha."
"Listen to him," Nicholas said in an aside to an imaginary audience. "You *done* well! That's not the way a stately Spaniard would speak."
"He'd speak broken English, wouldn't he?" Ernest defended himself.
"You *done* well isn't broken English. It's just bad grammar. Besides, no Spaniard would say Musha. Musha's French. A Spaniard would say Señor."
"Señor, my eye," Ernest said crossly. He felt that he was too often criticized.
During this altercation Sir Richard had stood noble and aloof on the deck of the Spanish galleon.

Now Ernest brought out with clarity (he knew that if he did not give satisfaction in his parts they might be taken from him) "You did well, noble Señor."

At last Sir Richard was able to continue.

> I have fought for Queen and country like a gallant man
> and true;
>
> I have only done my duty as a man is bound to do.
> With a joyful spirit I, Sir Richard Grenville, die.

With these words Augusta fell at full length on the floor. Her long black hair lay spread on the Axminster carpet. Ernest examined her prostrate form with some concern.

"She's dead," he announced.

"You silly little duffer." Nicholas regarded his junior with scorn. "She's just acting Sir Richard properly. Now it's up to you to lower his body 'with honour down into the deep.'"

Ernest manfully laid hold of Augusta. He gasped: "Where is the deep?"

"At the edge of the carpet. Heave ho, lads!"

Augusta lay with her hands crossed on her breast. Try as Ernest would he could not lower her into the sea. His face flushed with the effort. His mouth trembled. In a sudden burst of temper he shouted, "I can't do it! I can't — and I'm damned if I'll try!"

Up from the deep rose Augusta. She took him firmly by the hand and led him away, into her own room.

"Give him a good smack!" Nicholas called after her.

Inside her bedroom Augusta closed the door.

"Why will you persist in using bad language?" she asked.

"I don't know."

"Is it because you like bad words?"

"No."

"Who did you hear saying he'd be damned?"

"Mamma."

Augusta looked thoughtful. "Grown-up ladies sometimes use language that is not suitable when they're excited. But that is no reason for a small boy to use it."

"I wasn't a small boy when I said it. I was a Spaniard."

"But you can't deny," said Gussie, keeping her face stern, "that you have a leaning towards bad language?"

"Mr. Madigan said it was better to deny everything."

"Ernest."

"Yes, Gussie."

"Do you consider that Mr. Madigan is a better man than our rector, Mr. Pink?"

"I'd rather listen to Mr. Madigan's talk."

"Talk is not preaching. Sermons are not talk. They are meant to be listened to solemnly."

Nicholas now came pounding on the door. He called out, "It's stopped raining! I'm off for a walk. Coming?" They heard him rattling down the stairs.

"Ernest," said Gussie, "do you promise to try hard not to use bad language?"

"I promise," he said fervently.

She flew down the stairs to join Nicholas. Before Ernest followed her he went into the room once occupied by Lucius Madigan. He opened the smallest drawer in the chest of drawers and peeped in at a little pile of linen handkerchiefs. Each had an M embroidered in the corner. He had been told not to touch these, but he now decided to take one, because his nose was dribbling a little as it had a way of doing. He examined the initial in the corner. If it was turned upside down the M became W, his own initial. He carried the handkerchief into Augusta's room and dosed it liberally with scent from a bottle Mrs. Lacey had given her on her birthday. He could hear Nicholas calling to him from outdoors. He ran lightly down the stairs. The tiny Philip was toddling through the hall, dragging a small toy horse on wheels. He at once toddled to Ernest.

"Me go too," he begged.

"No. You're too little. I'm going for a walk."

"Me walkee too. Me big boy."

"Big boy, my eye!" said Ernest.

But the little one insisted, clinging to Ernest. "Take Baby too," he begged, his pink hands surprisingly strong.

"I'm damned if I will."

Realizing the language he had been using, Ernest clapped his hand over his mouth and ran out of the house.

Little Philip stared after him a moment, then raised his infant voice and shouted, "Lucee! Lucee!" He began laboriously to mount the stairs.

Lucy Sinclair ran down to gather him into her arms and carry him up to her room. The truth was that she doted on this tiny boy and did everything in her power to spoil him. Yet so sweet was his nature that in spite of all he retained his endearing ways. Of all people in the house, the one he liked best was the piccaninny, Albert. The very sight of Albert was enough to send him into happy laughter. He would rapturously hug Albert, press his flowerlike face to the chubby black face. If Albert cried, he would put on an act of crying also.

He loved the supreme disorder of Lucy Sinclair's room where he was allowed to handle all he chose, where he hid under the bed when his nurse came in search of him. This nurse was a bouncing country girl, constantly at odds with the three Negroes. She had other duties besides looking after little Philip, whom she often neglected. Yet it angered her to see how he preferred the blacks to her, and she sometimes gave him a smart slap when he showed this preference. She would do this right in front of the Negroes, who would burst into abuse of her and even strive to take him by force from her.

This girl, Bessie, was now in search of him. When Philip heard her in the passage, calling his name, he delayed not a moment in scrambling under Lucy Sinclair's bed. Bessie now appeared in the open doorway.

She had no manners and blurted out: "Have you seen anything of Philip?"

"I have not seen him," answered Lucy pleasantly.

"I'll wager," said the girl, "he's followed them other young 'uns out-doors. He's no sense and they've no sense. They'll all be as wet as rats."

When she had left, Philip crept from under the bed, ran to Lucy and hugged her. Well he understood that she had lied to protect him. "Lucee

— Lucee," he repeated, hugging her. "Give Baby toffee." She popped a toffee drop into his mouth and he ran to the window to see Bessie going in search of him.

Now Jerry came into the room. "Ah've been thinkin' about all that money Massa left," he said. "Don't you want me to count it over, Missus, and see if it's all dere?"

He made straight for the drawer where the wallet was kept. Lucy cried out, "It's all there! I counted it yesterday!"

But she could not stop him. He took out the wallet.

"Missus," he cried horrorstruck, "dere's two hundred dollars gone! Oh, my Lawd — it's been stole!"

"Don't make such an outcry," she begged. Then added calmly, "I gave it to Tite Sharrow for bringing the letter."

Jerry broke into noisy weeping. "Lawd ha' mussy! What's gonna happen nex'? We nebber gonna git home!"

"We shall have plenty of money," said Lucy.

"Oh, dat Injun," shouted Jerry. "Why didn't I rip him up wid mah knife! Ah'll do it yet — you just wait!"

Little Philip toddled to Jerry. "Don't cry, man," he said. "Take Baby walkee." He clapped his hands in anticipation.

"A very good idea," said Lucy. "That nurse of his is searching for him and he doesn't want her to find him — do you, sweetheart?" She fondled the little one.

"Oh, how Ah hate dat Bessie! She's mean to dis li'l' boy. We won't let her catch us, will we, Baby?"

Jerry snatched him up and shortly might be seen marching in the direction of the stables with the child on his shoulder, Philip grasping a handful of Jerry's kinky hair.

Lucy Sinclair tried in vain to achieve order in her belongings. She felt that at any moment she might be sent for to join her husband. The greater the energy put into the preparations for departure, the greater the confusion. Cindy and Belle constantly washed, ironed, mended, carried bundles upstairs and downstairs, packed and unpacked portmanteaux, increasing day by day the dire confusion. Quarrels in the kitchen became so frequent, so noisy, that they could not be ignored. Cindy was subject to attacks of weeping, for she was becoming convinced that her family in the South had been murdered by the Yankees or that her husband had taken himself a new wife. Jerry was doggedly urging Annabelle to marry him, and she as stubbornly putting off the day. To put it mildly, things were at sixes and sevens at Jalna.

Like a thunderbolt, word came from Curtis Sinclair that his wife was to join him. He wrote from his father's plantation. She and her servants would be met at the border by a reliable escort who would have money for travelling expenses. The jubilation that followed brought sheer chaos in its train. Then Adeline took matters in hand. With promptness and exactitude she supervised the packing, set Cindy and Belle to washing and ironing Lucy Sinclair's intricate and much embroidered lingerie. The basement reeked with the smell of steaming suds, the rub-a-dub of the washboard. Their backs bent over the washtub, their knuckles fairly skinned from rubbing over the corrugated surface of the washboard, they lifted their voices in songs of rejoicing. Lucy Sinclair gave, in spite of Philip's protests, extravagant presents to all the family. To Adeline a string of pearls. To Augusta a moonstone ring which she insisted the young girl should be allowed to wear at once. To Nicholas a gold watch and chain. To Ernest a gold pen. To baby Philip a pin set with turquoise, to hold his bib in place. She lay awake for hours trying to decide on a present for Captain Whiteoak. Finally she offered him a ring belonging to Curtis Sinclair set with a splendid carbuncle.

"No, no, my dear Mrs. Sinclair, I cannot accept this. In the first place it is much too grand for me. As you see, I wear only a seal ring with my family's crest. It belonged to my father. In the second place, your husband will probably demand it of you as soon as you join him."

"He would be delighted if he knew I gave it to you."

"I doubt that."

"Then I will tell him it has been lost."

But Philip would accept no present. To Adeline he remarked, "Lucy is a little liar. But then, I suspect all women lie to their husbands."

When the excitement of leave-taking was at its height, Annabelle suddenly decided that she was willing to marry Jerry at once and would like to travel southward as his wife; would feel safer travelling as a married woman, for she had heard terrifying reports of Yankee soldiers' attacks on girls. She wanted the ceremony to be performed by the Negro preacher, who still continued to hold meetings regularly. Scarcely a week passed without the addition of a few more Negroes to the group, stragglers who came, it seemed, from nowhere but always were made welcome. Elihu Busby did much to assist them to find a roof to cover them and work for their support. He was generous with his money.

It was arranged that the marriage should take place after the mid-week prayer meeting. Adeline Whiteoak gave the bride a white muslin dress with a wide plaid sash. She wore a straw bonnet covered with red and yellow flowers. Jerry, for the first time in his life, wore a white starched collar so high that it caused him real suffering. Yet he was a proud man wearing it. The Negro women present wore bright-coloured shawls or, failing these, red blankets over their shoulders. This was the first wedding in their midst. They demonstrated their joy in it by vociferously singing the hymns, by stamping of feet and clapping of hands. Later they were given a supper by the Whiteoaks.

To Philip and Adeline these last days of the long visit from their Southern guests were a trial. It seemed that the day of departure would never arrive. But finally the morning dawned, clear and joyously windy. Philip was to drive Lucy Sinclair, her servants, and luggage to the railway station where they were to be met by a Mr. Tilford, a Carolinian who had lived for many years in New England. He was a man of influence, a man to be depended on to escort Lucy to where she would be met by relatives.

As the wagonette stood before the door on the gravel sweep, Adeline, with her children about her, waved goodbye from the porch. She had put on the pearl necklace given her by Lucy Sinclair and, though it was not in accord with the everyday dress she wore, it expressed her lively appreciation of the gift. Gussie held aloft her hand that wore the moonstone ring. Nicholas stood upright with the gold watch in the pocket of his jacket, its chain across his chest. Ernest made as though to write on the air a message with the gold pen. Baby Philip threw kisses which caused Lucy to shed tears.

"Goodbye!"

"Goodbye!"

The loving words echoed among the falling leaves.

When the Whiteoaks had been newly settled at Jalna, Philip's sister in Devon had sent out to them a married couple named Coveyduck, as gardener and cook. This comfortable couple had been the domestic mainstay of the house for years, but they were persuaded to go to Manitoba, where relations of theirs were, as they wrote, making more money than could be made in Ontario, leading in every way a better life. Now suddenly, on the very day of Lucy Sinclair's departure, they appeared at Jalna and asked if they might be given their old situations. Such a felicitous surprise it was that Adeline hugged Mrs. Coveyduck to her in rapture, and slapped Coveyduck on the back. It was a summer-like day. Adeline kissed each of her children and carried little Philip to the basement kitchen. Mrs. Coveyduck had not before seen him. "Oh, what a little luv!" she exclaimed. She held out her arms to him. "Will 'ee come to me, luv?"

Philip would go to anyone regardless of colour or unfamiliarity. At once he took possession of Mrs. Coveyduck. She and her husband were thankful to be again at Jalna. They had had quite enough of the rigours of Western life. They had lost their fresh complexions, looked thinner and older. But they were full of energy and scarcely was their tin trunk unpacked when they set to work to restore order. Time and again Mrs. Coveyduck exclaimed that never, never had she seen a kitchen and pantries so dirty. Indeed, she would not be satisfied till she had, with Bessie's help, housecleaned from attic to basement. Adeline could scarcely bear to wait for Philip's return that she might tell him the crowning event of that wonderful day — like a conjurer produce the Coveyducks. All day she went about the house singing, sometimes on the tune, more frequently off it.

By early evening Adeline began to feel anxious lest Philip might have had an accident. Why was he so late in returning? The children waited by the gate to welcome him. The days were growing shorter. Soon it was dark. An owl began to hoot. A chilly wind whistled among the dying leaves.

Adeline was about to go to the gate to discover why the children lingered so long. Really they deserved to be punished. That little Ernest would be catching one of his colds.

Then suddenly she heard them running and, right on their heels, the sound of horses' hooves. Nicholas was first to appear. He was almost beside himself with excitement.

"They're coming!" he shouted.

"Your father?"

"All of them!" he shouted. "They're back!"

Now, out of the twilight, appeared horses and wagonette. It was crowded as when it had set out that morning. Jerry jumped out and stood at the horses' heads. They were restive, anxious for their evening meal. Philip alighted.

"What has happened?" cried Adeline.

"Nothing."

"Nothing! Then why are you back?"

"We were not met. The stationmaster held the train while I went through every carriage enquiring. There was another train in six hours. We had a good meal at the hotel. You can imagine Mrs. Sinclair's disappointment. We met the second train. No better luck. So I had to bring them back. I don't know what the devil to think." He stared ruefully into Adeline's distraught face.

During this recital, Jerry stood, an ebony statue, at the horses' heads. Cindy and Belle, worn out by emotion, slumped inside their shawls. The piccaninny slept. It was Lucy Sinclair who caught and held Adeline's fascinated gaze. Lucy, who was inclined to snuggle luxuriously, indolently, among cushions, now sat bolt upright. The cushions had been provided, but she, a stark figure of tragedy, was as cut from stone. When Philip handed her out of the wagonette she moved rigidly past him, mounted the steps on to the porch and, out of pale set lips, said to Adeline:

"I shall never see Mr. Sinclair again. He is dead, I'm convinced of that."

Adeline tried to embrace her but her arms hung helpless at her side.

Her face was the picture of consternation. The vision that possessed her mind was the Coveyducks and the blacks contending for supremacy in the basement. Her tongue clove to the roof of her mouth. When Cindy and Belle bundled themselves out of the wagonette she could only say to them:

"Put your mistress to bed. Carry a tray to her."

Lucy Sinclair and her women disappeared into the house. The statue that was Jerry now spoke.

"That thar Annabelle is mah bride," he said, "an' I ain't nebber been to bed wid her."

With a flourish of his hand, Philip ordered Jerry — "Get into that wagonette and drive to the stables. Tell the groom to feed and bed down the horses."

The children, open-mouthed, were drinking in all this. Now Ernest spoke.

"Bed, my eye," he said. But whether he referred to Belle and Jerry or to the horses, nobody knew. In fact the remark passed unnoticed.

But what Nicholas said did not.

With a look of deep concern he asked his mother, "Now that *she's* back, must we return our presents?"

That artless question loosed the spell that held Adeline speechless. "Miserable boy!" she cried. "Worthless, ungrateful rascal! Thinking of nobody but yourself!"

"I think of all of us who got presents," Nicholas answered boldly.

She ran down the steps towards him but he darted out of reach. "Philip," she cried, "catch him! Give him a sound beating."

"It was only a natural question," said Philip. "But, as things have turned out, I think I should offer to return the presents. Mrs. Sinclair will need all her resources."

Adeline fairly tore the string of pearls from round her neck and threw them at him. "Take them — take them! Leave me with nothing to repay me for these long months of patient self-sacrifice — nothing but an ache in me back and a pain in me stomach!" As always in moments of emotional stress, she assumed an Irish accent.

Philip deftly caught the pearls.

"Faith," she cried, "if anyone has suffered in this visitation, 'tis meself!"

"For God's sake, behave like a lady — if you can!" Philip implored.

"That's right," she hissed, "insult me in front of my poor little children!" Tears trickled down her pale cheeks.

Nicholas spoke up. "Papa, must I return the watch?"

"It's the decent thing to do."

His eyes filled with tears, the boy took the watch from his pocket and surrendered it to his father. Augusta slowly drew the moonstone ring from her slender white finger and, with dignified submission, laid it on Philip's palm. Ernest had disappeared into the shrubbery but now returned.

"What about that gold pen?" demanded Philip, fixing a stern eye on him.

"I'm sorry, Papa," said Ernest, "but I've lost it."

"Already?"

"Yes, Papa."

"Come here," said his mother.

Adeline opened wide her arms to her child and he ran into them.

What this family scene would have developed into was never known, because Mrs. Coveyduck, very red and flustered, now appeared. Without preliminary she announced, "Coveyduck and me — we think we'd better be going."

"Oh, this is the last straw," declared Adeline.

"I'm sorry for 'ee, madam," said the cook, "but Coveyduck and me — we're not used to working with darkies. Already they're making a fine mess in the kitchen I've just cleaned. That new married pair are claiming the basement bedroom I'm just making ready for me and my 'usband. It's more than human flesh and blood can bear. Those darkies be a murderous lot, if you ask me."

Little Philip now toddled into the porch, calling out, "Cubbyduck! Cubbyduck!" He threw himself on her, clasping her knees.

Adeline spoke with dignity. "Baby welcomes you. We all welcome you. The blacks will be here only a short while ..."

Mrs. Coveyduck said mournfully, "They tell me their massa is dead."

"No, no, he is just delayed by a meeting with Mr. Lincoln. In the meantime you and your husband may use the bedroom in the attic. It's a long climb for you from the basement, but it will be for only a little while, as I have said. Try to bear with the blacks. If you knew how tired I am you'd not desert me."

The Coveyducks were persuaded to remain. The Negroes again took possession of the basement. Lucy Sinclair moved like one in a melancholy trance. When Philip sought to return the pearl necklet, the gold watch and chain, the moonstone ring, she at first refused them but was persuaded. With the first spark of her former mettle she said, with vehemence, that when she was sent for, if ever, she would restore them to Adeline and the children.

Some days later, when she had recovered from the exhaustion of the fruitless journey, she told Philip that she had decided to sell Jerry and Belle. They were a healthy, active young couple and should bring a good price. Did Philip know of anyone here in Canada who would be likely to offer her a good price? She had not yet grasped the fact that emancipation had taken place.

Ten days passed. Fall weather was threatening the last of the flowers. A flock of bluebirds about to migrate gathered in the garden. They sang their pretty songs, they showed, without peacock pride, their heavenly colour.

Philip Whiteoak tried, by every means possible, to get news of Curtis Sinclair. He considered the possibility of buying a small house for Lucy and her retinue. Certainly things could not go on as they were. There was a limit to what a man could endure. He would sit brooding — wondering what to do next.

Then the unexpected happened. From the railway station, in a hired carriage, appeared Mr. Tilford. He was a man of influence. He had come, armed with passes, plentifully supplied with money, to conduct Lucy Sinclair to Charleston. He was an old friend, a connection by marriage of her family. He had little time to spare. The southbound party must leave the following day.

XIV

THE VISIT OVER

An almost feverish excitement swept through Jalna like a forest fire, with the coming of Mr. Tilford. It spread from basement to attic, from barn and stables to the two cottages occupied by farm labourers. Everybody knew of his coming and that the lovely Southern lady would, early next morning, leave for her perilous journey, to meet her strange husband. All the neighbourhood knew of her leaving. All agreed that the journey was perilous. All agreed that the husband she was rejoining had something strange about him. Yet Mr. Tilford viewed the situation with fatalistic calm. He had little to say about Lucy Sinclair's terrible disappointment in not being met on her first attempt to return to the South. He had little to say about the ruin of the plantations. It was obvious that he himself was not financially ruined. He was a shrewd business man — still youngish, with a future far from dark ahead of him. His mother was a Northerner and it had been through her relatives that he had gone into the cotton trade with England. He did not in his talk with the Whiteoaks show any violent partisanship. He knew so much and the Whiteoaks and Lucy Sinclair so truly little of the intricacies of the situation in the States that he preferred to skirt the edges rather than attempt to plunge into the depths.

Lucy Sinclair had gone to her room to make final preparations, which consisted in putting her hair in curlers, packing small things in a small dressing case and taking them out again, ordering her maids to do certain services for her and then expressing amazement that they had so done. As for Cindy and Belle, it seemed doubtful if they would close their eyes in sleep that night.

They would have sat up half the night talking, but it was necessary for Mr. Tilford to get rest. At midnight he was shown to his room, walking steadily, clear-headed in spite of all the Scotch whisky he had consumed. As for the Whiteoaks, they felt that they had a new grasp of the situation in the United States, the possible results of the civil war in that country, and its probable future. They lay awake a long while talking. At last there was silence from Philip to whom Adeline had put a question of (she considered) extraordinary importance. She repeated it on an imperative note. Now there came from him a bubbling snore. She was angry — outraged. "Insensate pig," she tried to hiss, but could make no sound beyond a whimper. She doubled her fist and tried to strike him, but when the blow landed it was no more than a pat.

She was brought back to consciousness by a knock on the door. It was Mrs. Coveyduck with early-morning tea. It was seven o'clock. Outside the window a turkey-cock gobbled his pleasure in this Indian summer morning, and spread his splendid tail for the admiration of his several wives who trailed their long feet on the dew-soaked lawn. Philip and Adeline sat up in bed and attacked the tea and thinly cut homemade bread, spread with freshly churned unsalted butter. The Coveyducks were again in charge.

Another knock came on the door. This time it was no more than a tap. Still, the tapper had the courage of his need and he came straight in. It was Ernest in his little white nightshirt, with a frill round the neck.

"Well, young man," said Philip, "and why are you barging in here, so early in the morning?"

"I've a splinter in my heel," said Ernest, and at once began to get into bed with his parents.

"The tea!" cried Adeline. "Be careful of the teapot."

"Get in on your mother's side," ordered Philip.

Ernest crept in beside Adeline. "I've brought a needle with me. Gussie can't get the splinter out. She said to come to you. She was near fainting. May I have tea?"

Adeline held the teacup to his lips. "Ah," he gurgled in ecstasy, and helped himself to a piece of bread and butter.

"Isn't this lovely?" he said.

"What? Having a splinter in your heel?"

"Having early tea with you."

Philip put in, "Be quick about it. Then I'll take the splinter out."

All too soon the tea had been drunk, the bread and butter eaten. Ernest's pink heel was exposed. Philip attacked the splinter with the needle. Ernest screamed.

"Come, come, be a soldier," said Philip.

"It hurts too much — I can't bear it!"

Philip said, "You'll find in life that the more you struggle, the worse you'll get hurt. Be still! Ah, there's the splinter — look!" He held it up on the needle. "A small thing to howl about, eh?"

Ernest was in ecstasy. He ran upstairs, taking the splinter to show Gussie. From then on the morning sped with incredible swiftness. A substantial breakfast was set out in the dining room, but Lucy Sinclair was unable to eat for excitement. Yet she had enjoyed the first untroubled sleep she had known since the news of her husband's capture. Fortunately Adeline had a substantial hamper packed for the travellers. Lucy Sinclair was dressed with care and had an air of real elegance, somewhat incongruous considering the journey she was to undertake. Like one in a dream she said her goodbyes.

Mr. Tilford kissed Adeline's hand. "Goodbye, dear lady," he said. "May we meet again under happier circumstances." He added, in a lower tone, "You must not for a moment worry about Mrs. Sinclair. I will see to it that she and her servants reach their destination in safety. Also remember that I have ample funds for every contingency."

"Ample funds!" The children overheard those words and, when the horses and carriages had moved away, they gathered about Adeline.

"Mamma," Nicholas asked, in an ingratiating tone, "did Mrs. Sinclair return our presents?"

"Grasping, greedy boy!" cried Adeline. "How can you think of presents at such a moment as this? Certainly she did not return them."

"Then we have nothing," said Nicholas, "for all our trouble. Even Ernest has lost his gold pen."

"It may turn up," said Ernest.

Augusta gave him a long look out of her large serious eyes.

Philip had accompanied the travellers to the railway station.

How different was this setting out compared to the previous one! Then, emotionally uplifted, Adeline and her children had waved goodbye from the porch. Thrown kisses, held up their beautiful gifts to show their pleasure in them. Then, confident that all would be well, they had awaited Philip's return. Now Mr. Tilford had taken everything into his own hands. Philip would be a spectator. Yet Adeline would scarcely have been surprised if the entire party had returned with him.

Although she had warned Mrs. Coveyduck that this might be possible, Mrs. Coveyduck had thrown herself with passion into the obliterating of all traces of the foreigners (so she called them). She and Bessie scrubbed, polished, swept, dusted, threw wide the windows to let the gusty wind blow away "the smell of the darkies," which she declared lurked in every corner.

Philip drove up the drive and reined in his horses in front of the porch sooner than Adeline would have believed possible. Coveyduck, thickset and cheerful, was awaiting him there. Philip sprang out of the wagonette and the three children scrambled in, to drive to the stable.

"Don't be long," Adeline called out. "Cook is making a boiled pudding with custard sauce!"

"Hurrah!" shouted the boys.

Philip ran up the steps to Adeline's side. He gave her a hearty embrace. "They've gone," he said. "The train was on time, for a wonder. Everything was done in order."

"Are we actually by ourselves again?" she asked, looking at him as at one returned from a long and perilous journey. "Is this house actually ours?"

"We are — and it is," he said, and added, "Thank God!"

He snatched up his youngest and sat him on his shoulder.

"Off we go," he said, and galloped prancing along the hall.

* * *

There was an unbelievably holiday feeling. Clean sheets were blowing wetly on the clotheslines. The pudding was merrily bubbling in the pot. Twin Jersey calves were born in the stable. Mulberries were lying darkly on the lawn. Yet, though effort was involved in these activities — the sheets had had to be washed, the pudding concocted, the cow had laboured to produce the calves, the tree had struggled against storm and drought to produce the mulberries, Philip and Adeline had been through stress and strain during the long visit from the Sinclairs — yet, on this day of Indian summer, all might have been spontaneous and without effort, so happy were all living creatures at Jalna.

Augusta said, "It seems to me that this would be a good day for a picnic."

"I was just going to remark," said Ernest, "that this would be a good day for a picnic."

"A lovely thought," said Adeline. "We'll have a picnic by the lake and go in bathing. I'll pack a hamper with good things to eat. We'll invite James Wilmott and the Laceys. Will that suit you, Philip?"

"It's just what I need," said Philip, "a picnic by the lake."

"I was going to remark," said Ernest, "that what I need is a picnic by the lake."

Philip fixed him with a cold blue stare. "We can do without any remarks from you," he said.

"He pushes into everything," said Nicholas, "as if he were the most important person in the house."

Ernest hung his head. Yet he was not subdued for long. Soon he was taking part, as well as he could, in preparations for the picnic. There was much running up and down stairs with bathing suits; much panting up and down, from and to the basement, on the part of Mrs. Coveyduck and Bessie with provisions. Messengers were dispatched by Philip with invitations for the Laceys and James Wilmott.

Wilmott appeared, wearing a light-coloured jacket, tight trousers, large dark cravat, and wide-brimmed straw hat. He carried a basket containing fillets of salmon that had been stored in his ice-house — on ice cut from "his own river," as he called it. All the way from the sea these salmon came to spawn in the river, so he said. He deplored the fact that every year there were fewer of them.

The Laceys too came happily to the picnic — the parents, the two little daughters who were the age of Nicholas and Ernest, and their son, Guy, who was still on leave from the Royal Navy. The sight of him was as thrilling to Augusta as the sight of the azure lake that sent its countless gleaming ripples to the edge of the sandy beach, on which a flock of sandpipers strutted without fear of the picnickers, till Nero routed them with boastful barks. Curly-pated, woolly footed, he romped up and down the beach. There was nothing he enjoyed more than this annual picnic by the lake.

Baby Philip also was of the party. It was his first sight of the lake and he stood thunderstruck by its immensity. He had not known that any body of water could be so large. He, every night at bedtime, was put into his own tin bath. It was painted blue, like the lake, and to his mind was large enough for any purpose.

Now his father picked him up and made as though to throw him into the water.

The little one in fear clutched the lapel of Philip's jacket. "No — no!" he whimpered.

Nicholas and Ernest came to see the fun.

"Papa," said Ernest, "would you really throw him in?"

"Of course I should," shouted Philip. "Hoopla, out you go!"

Augusta had had enough of such teasing. "Papa," she said firmly, "please give Baby to me. If he is frightened he is sure to wet himself."

In haste Philip tossed the little one into her arms. He said sternly, "That's a very bad habit and he should be broken of it."

"Males," Augusta said sedately, "are more addicted to wetting than females."

Philip had no answer to that. He stared truculently at his daughter out of his rather prominent blue eyes and then strode off to throw sticks into the lake for Nero to retrieve.

It was decided to have a dip in the lake before supper. This Mrs. Lacey and her husband would not take part in, but retiring behind some shrubs with her little daughters, she put them into flannel nightgowns and drawers gathered at the knee, to serve as bathing dresses. Philip and Adeline wore navy blue outfits, his somewhat tight, for it had been made some years ago; hers with a sailor collar and full skirt reaching to the knee, both collar and skirt trimmed with rows of white braid. Nicholas and Ernest had proper bathing suits of grey flannel with red belts of which they were very proud, even though they were not quite comfortable. Augusta had, with the help of Lucy Sinclair, made herself a bathing costume of light blue serge, the skirt rather short, the sleeves reaching only halfway to the elbow. With this she wore long white cotton stockings and shoes with elastic sides. It was the first time this garment had been worn.

Augusta emerged from the bushes feeling very self-conscious. She wondered whether she were indeed decently covered. She envied Adeline her self-possession, even while she disapproved of her flaunting of herself in front of Admiral Lacey and his son.

Everybody now turned to see Augusta. The two small boys had just been ducked by Philip and ran dripping out of the lake.

"Look at Gussie!"

"Hello, Gussie!"

"Do you think you're a mermaid, Gussie?"

They shouted at her, dancing up and down, half-mad with spirits.

Admiral Lacey said patronizingly, "You look very nice, m'dear. Quite *comme il faut*, eh, Guy?" But he had eyes only for Adeline.

Guy Lacey had made friends with Baby Philip and held him in his arms. But the little fellow wanted to go to Augusta. "Gu-gussie," he stammered, marvelling at the strangeness of everyone's appearance. This was a new world to him.

Augusta took him into her arms. In an odd way she felt that his small familiar body would be a shield for the inadequacy of her bathing dress. He clasped her tight.

Guy Lacey's appearance was even more embarrassing to Augusta than was her own. It was all very well for her father and brothers to romp on the beach in semi-nakedness, but — this young man whom she was accustomed to meet in uniform!

"Come on in," said Guy.

"Yes," called out Adeline. "Go on in, Gussie."

Adeline took possession of her youngest. Guy took Gussie firmly by the hand. They walked sedately, as though for a ceremony, into the bright water of the lake. Gussie felt that she should make some conversation. The trouble was she could think of nothing to say excepting, "The lake is very large." When those words had passed her lips, she saw them in her imagination as a sentence at the top of a page in a copy book. "The lake is very large." Write carefully, children. No blots, please. Then she saw a primer, a first reader, with a lesson that began: "The lake is very large. I see the lake. It is as big as the sea." She could not stop herself from saying, in her clear voice which, when she was grown up, would be contralto, "It is as big as the sea."

Guy Lacey gave his light easy laugh. "Have you ever seen the sea, Gussie?"

"Not to remember. When I was a baby I went in a sailing ship from India to England — then came to Canada." She was proud of having travelled so far, but Guy Lacey only said, "This lake is tame compared to the sea."

"Is it?" she breathed, her eyes on the dim blue horizon; then added, "Is the sea colder than this?"

"Do you find the water cold?" he asked solicitously. "Then the thing to do is — *duck*."

"Duck?" she repeated.

"Yes. I'll count three. Then we'll both duck."

"Do!" she giggled, and so unusual it was for Augusta to giggle that instantly she looked serious.

Guy was counting. "One — two — three — *duck!*"

Down they went, he now gripping her two hands. They were engulfed, half-drowned it seemed, in the immensity of the lake. She held her breath.

Then it was down again and up into the balmy air, her long tresses — Guy thought of her hair as "tresses" — streaming over her shoulders.

"Why, Gussie," he exclaimed laughing, "you look just like a mermaid — that lovely black hair — those alluring eyes." His white teeth gleamed in his wet face. He had a lock of yellow hair plastered on his forehead.

They danced up and down, holding hands. Gussie was no longer cold. Her blood raced through her veins. She felt wild, reckless, as she had never felt before.

"Hoopla!" shouted Philip, and bore down upon them.

He was followed by the two boys, Guy's little sisters and Adeline. A battle of splashing ensued. The small boys sought to duck Guy but it was he who ducked them. Adeline delighted in this sort of wild play. None of the young people was so boisterous as Philip and she. Those remaining on the shore were well occupied. Admiral Lacey was in charge of Baby Philip who, from the safety of the Admiral's arms, watched his family apparently about to drown and, being safe himself, enjoyed the spectacle. He clasped his hands over his round little stomach and laughed in glee. Every few moments Admiral Lacey would shout to his daughters:

"Be careful, girlies!"

Or to his son, "Watch over your sisters, Guy!"

Not one of them paid the slightest attention to him or indeed heard him.

Mrs. Lacey was well occupied in unpacking the picnic hamper and laying the table for tea. The cloth was spread on the fine clean sand and, considering the haste of the arrangements, there was a generous supply of ham sandwiches, hardboiled eggs, cucumbers in vinegar, and plain fruit cake.

James Wilmott had not brought a bathing suit but was occupied in building a fire for the boiling of a pot of water to cook corn and make the tea. He was an expert at this, choosing stones of the right shape to support the large black pot. But his chief concern was the salmon he had himself donated. As the sun sank toward the horizon the breeze fell and the air became deliciously warm. The bathers felt that they could remain in the lake all night. But Wilmott was anxious about the salmon. He had made a miniature cellar among the shrubs to keep it cool. Every so often he took it out and sniffed it. It retained the freshness of its odour. Nevertheless he was anxious.

He went to Mrs. Lacey and said, "I am of the opinion that the salmon should be eaten. It cannot stand this heat without spoiling."

Mrs. Lacey, her face crimson, asked, "Has the pot boiled?"

"It has boiled."

"Then I shall put in the corn." One by one she dropped the symmetrical ears of corn into the bubbling pot. She called to her husband:

"Tell the children to come at once. They have been too long in the water as it is." To Wilmott she remarked, "I'm surprised that Mrs. Whiteoak allows little Ernest to remain so long in the lake. He is a delicate boy and might easily get his death."

Wilmott said gruffly, "Mrs. Whiteoak has no more sense than a child."

Mrs. Lacey was delighted to hear him speak disparagingly of Adeline because she had been under the impression that he almost too warmly admired her. Mrs. Lacey found James Wilmott now more congenial to her than she had thought possible. Again she called out to her husband, "Order Guy to bring in his sisters at once."

Admiral Lacey set Baby Philip on the sand, cupped his own hands about his mouth and shouted, "Ship ahoy! Ethel! Violet! Come ashore! Your mamma orders!"

"Supper," shouted Wilmott, with a scornful look in Adeline's direction.

The bathers now emerged dripping. They sought suitable retreats for drying and dressing themselves among the scrubby cedars. Philip and Guy together, the three young girls, each with her own towel and modesty, Nicholas only half drying himself before he pulled on his tight ankle-length trousers, his undervest, his cambric shirt, his jacket trimmed with silk braid. Already his hair was drying into charming waves about his ears and neck. "Really such hair is wasted on a boy," Mrs. Lacey observed to Adeline, who had just appeared in a flannel wrapper, with Ernest by the hand. The little boy was delicate, and for fear he might take cold she had given him a brisk rub down and wrapped him in a plaid shawl. He was in high feather and danced along, the fringe of the shawl trailing after him.

The party seated themselves on the sand about the tea-cloth. They were hungry and could scarcely bear to wait for the first course. This was the steaming hot corn on the cob, to be eaten with salt, pepper, and plenty of butter. Wilmott carried the pot round the festive cloth and laid a glistening ear of corn, with its pearl-like kernels, on the plate of each.

The only two who were left out were Baby Philip and Nero. Adeline had her little one on her lap and now and again fed him enormous spoonfuls of bread and milk with brown sugar.

"How angelic Baby has been!" said Mrs. Lacey. "He's never cried once."

"I'm ravenous," declared Ernest, and at that Adeline espied the ear of corn on his plate. She nipped it up and laid it in front of Nicholas. "Ernest must not eat corn," she said. "It gives him a terrible bellyache."

"But I'm hungry!"

Mrs. Lacey looked offended by the word bellyache.

"What can I eat?" Ernest's lip trembled, yet he knew his mother did right in taking the ear of corn from him.

Wilmott rose with alacrity. "You shall have the first helping of salmon," he said, and strode to where he had buried the crock containing it. The crock felt delightfully cool when he unearthed it. The salmon looked tempting when he uncovered it. Ernest's eyes shone when the firm pink slice of the fish was laid on his plate.

"Are you going to say thanks?" asked Adeline.

"Thank you very much, sir," Ernest said, his hunger mounting. He was greedy for the first bite but scarcely was it in his mouth when he spat it back on to his plate.

Every eye was on him.

"Whatever is wrong?" demanded Wilmott.

He picked up the plate and sniffed the fish.

"It stinks," said Ernest.

Philip and Adeline fixed stern glances on their son.

"How dare you spit out a special present?" she asked with severity. A kernel of corn hung on her red underlip.

"How dare you say it stank?" demanded Philip.

Ernest began to cry. "Leave the table," ordered Philip.

"Oh, I say!" exclaimed Guy Lacey. "The poor little beggar!"

"This is none of our business," said his father.

Mrs. Lacey said to her daughters, "Ethel — Violet — don't stare."

Wilmott rose with dignity. He emptied the salmon from Ernest's plate back into the crock, rose and stalked away with it across the sand.

Nero who all this while had been gazing hungrily at the party about the table and avidly sniffing the scent of the salmon, now slunk after Wilmott with an air so patently criminal in its intent that only the picnickers' absorption in their own doings prevented his being detected.

When Wilmott had buried the salmon deep, rinsed the crock that had contained it in the purifying water of the lake, he returned to the table. Philip at once proffered a plate heaped with ham sandwiches.

"Have some, old man," he said. "They're first-rate. Have some cucumber. Too bad about the salmon but those things will happen. I remember a picnic in India —"

Adeline interrupted, "Stop, Philip! You're not to tell about that picnic. You're worse than that little viper Ernest."

Wilmott asked, "Is Ernest to have nothing to eat?"

"Supperless to bed. That's his medicine," said Philip.

Guy Lacey dropped a sandwich into his own pocket.

Meantime the outcast walked lonely along the beach. He felt ill-used, outraged. He was as furiously angry as was possible to his gentle nature. He talked to himself in a growling voice. "I was expected to swallow that stinking fish, wasn't I? I wish every one of them had been made to swallow a big mouthful of it. 'Specially Mamma and Papa. Nobody cares if I'm sick. Nobody cares if I'm hungry. They can have their old picnic. I don't want any of it. I'll not eat anything for a week — I'm damned if I will."

Now the sun was a glowing crimson ball casting its fiery causeway athwart the placid lake. A flock of gulls sailed by, close to shore. The sound of little waves lapping on the sand only made the silence more serene. Ernest ceased his dogged plodding and stared in wonder at the clouds of pink and amethyst which drifted with the sun in his setting.

Ernest began to feel more peaceful. A thrill of something — was it joy in the lonely beauty of the evening sky? — ran through his nerves. Now he heard the voice of Gussie calling him. "Ernest! Ernest! We're going!"

He had a mind to hide among the scrubby trees that grew dense and mysterious along the shore. But they were too dense, too mysterious. He could see, out of the sides of his eyes, Gussie coming hurriedly towards him. "Ernest! Listen, dear! We're going!"

She had called him *dear*! He would show her what they had done to him. He laid himself flat on the sand and began to cry.

Now she was bending over him. "You can't stay here, you know. Patsy O'Flynn has the horses ready. You don't want to be left here alone, do you?"

She assisted him to his feet. Suddenly he felt weak and wobbly. In his excitement he had eaten almost no lunch. One day, not long ago, he had heard his mother say of someone, "Poor man, he is old before his time!" Now this remark came back to him and he thought, "Old before my time. That's what I am."

The others of the party did not notice him when he came back with Augusta. They were occupied in collecting their belongings and clambering into the wagonette and the Laceys' phaeton which were now waiting at the bottom of the road. Wilmott had ridden his old black mare that somehow had a funereal look. He had not yet recovered from the way his gift of salmon had turned out. Yet most of the others were in high spirits.

"Where is Nero?" shouted Philip. "Nicholas, go and find Nero and be quick about it."

Nicholas ran along the beach calling to Nero. It was not long before he returned, dragging him by the collar. "Nero'd dug up the salmon," he announced, "and eaten it!"

Out of his woolly black face Nero gave a roguish look.

"Merciful heaven!" cried Adeline. "It will be the death of him!"

"I'm afraid I did not bury it deep enough," Wilmott said contritely.

"Nothing can kill that dog," said Philip.

He gave Nero a clout, then bundled him into the wagonette beside Nicholas and Ernest.

"He ought to follow the horses," said Adeline.

"Too much effort after that meal. It would be the death of him." Philip was growing impatient. "Come, come, everybody. Into your seat, Adeline. Is the baby asleep? Goodbye, Wilmott — better luck next time."

Wilmott, on his mare, was the first to leave. He called back, "I warn you not to invite me to the next picnic. I am guaranteed a spoil-sport. Happy dreams, Nero!"

Guy Lacey came to the side of the wagonette. He remembered the ham sandwich he had hidden in his pocket for Ernest. Surreptitiously he took it out. Furtively he offered it to the little boy. But before Ernest could get his hands on it, Nero had intercepted and, in one mouthful, bolted it.

Nicholas laughed. "I hope it will make his breath better," he said, "for just now it's disgusting."

"Hard luck, old fellow," said Guy, patting Ernest's knee. "I'll bet you're ravenous."

Mrs. Lacey was in a state of anxiety about her daughters.

"Hurry, Guy," she called. "I'm so worried over the sunburn your sisters have got. It serves me right for allowing them to go into the sun without hats. These delicate complexions require constant care."

"Thank goodness," said Adeline, "I don't need to trouble about Gussie's complexion, for she's sallow as any Spaniard." Mrs. Lacey cast a sympathetic look at Gussie.

The pleasure vehicles moved up the road, away from the sound of the wavelets. The road lay thick in dust. Evening closed in with great suddenness. There was as yet no moon. Darkness rose from the earth to meet darkness from the sky.

XV

The Golden Pen

The house was extraordinarily dim and quiet when the family entered it after the picnic. Usually, at this hour, it was the scene of bewildering activity — Lucy Sinclair dressing for the evening meal, her servants engaged in argument with the cook over the preparation of her special dishes; Jerry seated at the kitchen table devouring what pleased his palate; the two boys running up and down the stairs defying the order to go to bed; the baby Philip crying as he found himself alone in the dark; Adeline and Philip seeking, not very patiently, to create order out of chaos; Nero and Boney, the parrot, adding their voices to the confusion; people calling for hot water; people calling for oil lamps; shutters and doors banging to keep out the evening air.

But now how different!

The picnic party were met at the door by Bessie, a tidy, clean-aproned Bessie, with a smile on her face instead of a frown, who took little Philip gently in her arms.

"It's late for his bath, ma'am," she said to Adeline. "Do you think I might just wipe his face and hands and knees with a sponge and pop him into bed?"

"You may," agreed Adeline. "We all are tired. What a lovely long day! What peace in the house!"

Bessie beamed. "That there Mrs. Coveyduck," she said, "is a marvel. Everything goes as smooth as silk with us now that she's back and them niggers is gone. She has a nice hot meal waiting for you."

"Goodness, I'm not hungry."

But when Adeline came to the dining room, saw the table invitingly laid beneath the light of the chandelier, she changed her mind and decided that she was very hungry. The tureen of vegetable soup sent up a delicious odour. After the soup came an omelette, light as a feather, and after the omelette an apple tart, smothered in Devonshire cream which Mrs. Coveyduck well knew how to make.

Philip and Adeline, Augusta and Nicholas, sat in comfortable relaxation about the table. Agreeable, charming as Lucy Sinclair had been, there was no doubt that her presence had been a weight. Philip never had found Curtis Sinclair congenial to him. Now he looked about the table at his family with satisfaction. However, he missed someone.

"Where is Ernest?" he asked.

Augusta spoke up, with an accusing look at him.

"Papa, you said Ernest was to go supperless to bed."

"Ah, so I did. Now I forget why." He took a mouthful of the crisp crust of homemade bread.

"It was because he spat out Mr. Wilmott's fish and said it stank."

This remark struck Nicholas as being excruciatingly funny. He bent almost double in laughter.

"Do you want to follow your brother to bed?" asked Philip.

That sobered Nicholas. The meal proceeded in serenity and good appetite. Both Philip and Adeline remarked on Guy Lacey's charm and good sense. It was a pity, they said, that his leave was so soon to be over. Augusta said nothing but, as soon as she could, stole up to her own room. It was dark and the smell of fall came in on the dew-drenched air. She struck a match and lighted a candle on the dressing table, which had a flounce of glazed chintz round it. Her reflection showed in the mirror, so strangely intimate that it was like another girl in the room with her — a girl who, Guy Lacey had said, was like a mermaid, with her long black hair and

alluring eyes. Were those his exact words? She could scarcely remember —
she had been so confused. And leaping up and down with him in the lake
had trebled the confusion and the delight. She looked deep into the large
dark eyes of the girl in the mirror, trying to solve their mystery. Often she
had heard her mother's eyes admired, called luminous, gay. She had seen
the golden lights in their brownness, seen how they could change with her
mood. But these eyes of her own were always the same — sombre, like the
eyes of some melancholy Spaniard, Adeline had once remarked.

Her attention was diverted from her reflection in the mirror to the
hunched figure of her dove that had spent the day in his cage, alone,
unnoticed. Contrite, she opened the door of the cage and spoke to him.

"Oh, my lovely dove! My little love — my dove."

Never before had she used such endearments to him. Tonight they
came naturally to her lips. Everything was different tonight. Over and
over she said loving words to him. But he was feeling his neglect. His
head that had been under his wing was indeed uncovered, but it was
some little time before he shook himself and hopped down from his
perch and then to her shoulder. There again he shook himself and made
a loving noise, deep down in his burnished throat. Delicate undulating
movements vibrated through his body.

"My little love — my dove," murmured Augusta. "My love hath
dove's eyes." She was tired after the long day and dropped to the floor
and sat there.

Three leaves from the Virginia creeper had blown into the room and
lay trembling a little on the floor. Augusta felt strangely happy. But her
peace was broken by the sound of a sob from the room next hers. She was
sure it was Ernest who was crying.

There was hazy moonlight in the boys' room. It fell across the bed,
on which she could make out the figure of Ernest, curled up in a little
bundle of misery.

She came and sat on the side of the bed. His hand reached out to her
groping. "Is it you, Gussie?" he whispered.

"Yes," she answered calmly. "I heard you crying. Are you hungry?"

"Hungry? No." His voice came thick with sobs. "I'm not the least bit
hungry, but — oh, Gussie, I've done something bad."

She drew the sheet down to uncover his tear-stained face. "Yes, Ernest, what is it? Tell Gussie."

"Is that the dove?" he asked.

"Yes. He's been alone for hours. Now he's so happy that I am back."

The dove cooed in his throat.

Ernest was easily diverted, even from real unhappiness. Now he sat up in bed, then knelt up to stroke the dove. "How nice he is! I'm sure he knows me and likes me better than he likes Nicholas. Do you think he likes me, Gussie?"

"Tell me what you have done," she said.

"You won't tell Papa?"

"Have I ever carried tales?"

"No. But this is the worst thing yet."

"Is it about the gold pen?"

He threw himself back on the bed and pulled the bedclothes over his head. "How did you guess?" came in a strangled voice.

"I saw you go into the shrubbery. I saw you come back."

"I couldn't help myself, Gussie."

"Where have you hidden the pen?"

"Oh, I have it safe enough."

In the dim moonlight she could just see his face, a girl's face, pink and delicate, with the forget-me-not blue eyes and the rumpled fair hair, but the mouth was the mouth of a boy, sensitive and delicately arrogant.

She said, "Do you realize, Ernest, that it was stealing?"

He wriggled beneath the bedclothes. "But the pen is really mine, Gussie," he said.

"Then why were you crying?"

He could not answer.

She went on, "Mamma and Nicholas and I had given back our presents — the pearl necklet, the watch and chain, the ring. They weren't ours any longer. Neither is the pen yours. It was stealing to take it."

"I know — I know," he moaned.

"In England, not very many years ago," she said, "there were more than a hundred crimes a person could be hanged for —"

"Even a boy?" he faltered.

"Yes — even a boy. A boy could be hanged for stealing a sheep, and a gold pen is worth more than a sheep."

"Did you say a hundred crimes?" he quavered.

"More than a hundred. Mr. Madigan told us."

Ernest now tried to obliterate himself in the bedclothes. Gussie could barely make out what he said. "Then," he said, "I could have been hanged every day in the week. Oh, Gussie, tell me what to do!"

She patted him on the back. "We must find a way," she said comfortingly.

Now his flushed little face appeared over the edge of the sheet. "Please don't tell Papa," he begged. "I don't want to be thrashed."

"Why did you start all this tonight?" she asked.

"I was so lonely and now I'm so hungry."

"Roll over on your face and press your fists into your tummy. That will help."

He did. Then he said, "It seems to make me hungrier."

"Now, listen," said Augusta. "You must stay quietly here and I will go to the kitchen and get you something to eat."

"Don't leave me alone!" Ernest's voice was no more than a wail. He tried to make himself even younger than he was.

"Come, then." Gussie spoke in resignation.

Ernest scrambled out of bed with surprising alacrity.

"I suppose you know," said Gussie, "that I should not be doing this. It's breaking rules, you know."

"How would you feel if you found me dead of starvation in the morning?"

"You would not die from missing one meal. It is not the first time this has happened to you."

"But it's the first time I'd such a weight on my conscience. Is your conscience in your stomach, Gussie?"

"You are always so ready to talk," she answered wearily. "I want to get this thing over — so come along and don't make a sound." She returned the dove to its cage.

The sudden transition from fear and loneliness to security and the comfort of Gussie's presence not only filled Ernest with gladness but gave him a pleasing sense of adventure. It was the first time that he had gone down to the basement at this hour. He clung tightly to Augusta's hand and they fairly held their breaths. Philip was in the sitting room reading the weekly newspaper. They could hear the rustling of it as he turned the pages. Nero was with him and came to the door and looked out at them and whined.

"Come back here, sir." Philip spoke with his pipe between his teeth.

The children stole silently through the hall, past the door of the bedroom inside which they could hear their mother softly and not very musically singing. Certainly she would not hear them creeping past. They descended the stairs into the basement. Here it was pleasantly warm. The moonlight lay in shining rectangles on the freshly washed brick floor and discovered a golden gleam in the copper utensils hanging on the walls. The Coveyducks and Bessie were long ago in bed, tired out after their efforts to obliterate all traces of the Negroes.

As the children crept down the basement stairs Ernest whispered, "Just like thieves in the night, aren't we?"

Scarcely were the words past his lips when he realized how terribly well they applied to himself. It was fortunate that he was on the bottom step, otherwise in his dismay he might have lost his balance. As it was he clapped his hand over his mouth and rolled his eyes up towards Augusta's face to see if she had noticed.

If she had, she made no comment but led the way into the larder. It was possible by the light of the moon to see the large pans of Jersey milk, the loaves of bread, and many tempting edibles, tempting especially to one as hungry as Ernest. Augusta discovered a candle and matches. She lighted the candle and held the candlestick aloft, so that it shed its light on the shelves.

"Bread and milk?" she invited.

But he had seen the slab of apple pie, the bowl of Devonshire cream. "Oh, Gussie, *please*, some of that," he begged. Without comment she cut a large helping for him, laid it on a china plate with a chip out of it, then mounded it with cream. Like a priestess in some Gothic ceremony, she led the way back to the kitchen and set plate and candle on the clean-scrubbed table. He slid on to a chair and she put a spoon in his hand.

"If your feet are as cold as mine are," she said, "you'd like a hot drink."

His mouth was too full for speech but he made eyes of gratitude, and pointed with his spoon to the teapot. In this kitchen the teakettle was always on the boil. Gussie stirred the coals under it and when the exact moment of bubbling came she had the teapot ready with plenty of tea in it.

She seated herself beside Ernest and poured a cup of strong Indian tea for each. The first mouthful brought tears to his eyes it was so hot. But he was so happy — just the two of them together and he not the odd one as so often he was!

He said, "Nicholas will wonder where I am. He will wish he might be in my place, won't he?"

"I don't know who would choose to be in your place," said Augusta.

That remark subdued him, though only briefly. The pleasure of the late feast, the two cups of strong tea, had an exhilarating effect. He was still hungry.

Gravely she considered his plea for a second piece of the pie. He was delicate. The second piece might be too much for his digestion. Still — he had eaten little since breakfast. She rose. "I'll risk it," she said.

Ernest remembered a proverb he had heard from Lucius Madigan. Now he brought it out. "Might as well be hanged for a sheep as a lamb," he said.

Augusta looked at him in despair. "Can't you keep your mind off bad things?"

He hung his head. He was speechless a moment, then he said, "I guess bad things come natural to me."

"You look innocent," said Augusta, "and that's a danger. Anyhow, I'll risk giving you more pie."

She did and they both had more tea. He looked at her in love and gratitude. On their way through the hall, Ernest fairly skipped in his happiness.

"It's been a jolly good evening, hasn't it, Gussie? I guess it's worth a crime or two to have such fun."

Would he never show sense? Augusta in exasperation took him by the ear and led him to the stairs. He uttered a squeak of protest. The door of the sitting room, already ajar, was pushed open and Philip and Nero stood there.

"What's this?" demanded Philip.

"I made Ernest some tea," said Augusta.

"Why are you holding him by the ear?"

"To keep him quiet while we passed your door, Papa."

"Upon my word, a strange way of keeping a boy quiet, eh, Ernest?"

In two strides Philip was beside them. He took Ernest under the arms, lifted him till their faces were on a level, then kissed him.

"Good night," he said, "and now off you go." He bent over Gussie and touched her forehead with his small blond moustache that ended in waxed points. One of these points pricked her on the forehead. "Good girl, Gussie," he said. He stood with one arm upraised to the hanging oil lamp, waiting till they reached the top of the stairs before turning it out. The light fell softly on his sunburnt fair face, his blue eyes raised toward his children, his hair worn rather long and bleached to straw colour by the picnic sun. Gussie hesitated a moment, looking back at him. It was not often that she felt drawn in affection towards her sire. More often she regarded him dubiously or with a certain apprehension. But now she saw him looking young — young and fair and kindly to his children.

As the hall below was lost in darkness, Augusta and Ernest reached the boys' bedroom. Nicholas was in bed fast asleep. He had tried to keep awake for them but had not been able to.

"If only he knew," giggled Ernest, "of all I've done, wouldn't he be envious?"

"You have a queer way of looking at things," said Augusta. "Have you said your prayers?"

He nodded an affirmative and scrambled into bed. Well, it was not quite a lie. She had not asked if he had said his prayers *tonight*. He would say them snug in bed beside Nicholas, that is, if he could keep awake. Nero had decided that he would like to sleep on the bed with the boys. He scrambled in at their feet, making the mattress groan with his weight.

"Goodnight," Augusta said and blew out the candle.

She went softly out of the room.

How quiet — how frighteningly quiet and dark it was when she had gone! Ernest snuggled against Nicholas's back and pressed his ice-cold feet under Nero. Nero uttered a protesting groan and Nicholas began to gabble in his sleep. Ernest tried to remember his prayers but could not for the life of him remember how they began. Well — he would say the hind part and arrive so much sooner at the end. He murmured:

> If I should die before I wake,
> I pray the Lord my soul to take.
> In my little bed I lie,
> Heavenly Father, hear my cry —
> Lord, protect me through the night
> And keep me safe till morning light.

He was not sure that he had said it properly. Still, it would do. The apple pie, the cream, the strong tea, lay comfortably in his stomach. His mind was at peace, for he knew what he had to do.

The sound of a whistle came from the hall below. Nero well knew that summons was for him. With a groan he tumbled off the bed and lumbered down the stairs. At the same time Ernest fell fast asleep.

Augusta, in her room, sat by the open window. Her elbow on the sill, she rested her head on her hand. The dove sat drowsy on her shoulder. It had been safe to open the shutters because, while she was with him, he would not fly out, and if he did he would return, as he had done time and again.

She raised her hair from her forehead to let the night air cool it. She had been told, ever since she was little, that night air was bad. It was bad for all ailments and could even cause sickness in the healthy. But there was something in the night which was more in concord with her spirit than was the day. The hemlocks and spruces along the drive were now dense and mysterious. She could picture a horseman, in velvet cloak, wearing a plumed helmet, galloping along the drive. He drew in his horse beneath her window. He raised his arm and she could see the glint of his breastplate beneath his cloak. He lowered his visor and she could see that his face was the face of Guy Lacey. Her head drooped and she closed her eyes.

"My dove — my lovely dove," she whispered, and the dove made little moaning noises.

"Thou hast dove's eyes," she whispered, and the dove pressed his breast to her cheek in an ecstasy of companionship.

When again she opened her eyes, the horseman had vanished. Was that the beat of hooves she heard in the distance? No — it was the sound of the stream, down in the ravine, passing in the cool darkness beneath the rustic bridge. In the mystery of the lawn the young white birch tree stood naked, its narrow golden leaves on the grass like a cast-off garment.

Augusta's head drooped to the windowsill. The dove, finding it difficult to keep his foothold on her shoulder, moved to the back of her neck. A breeze ruffled her hair. She realized that she was tired and for a while she slept.

When she woke she saw the candle burning low. She thought of the two boys snug in bed. Quickly she drew off her clothes and found her nightdress folded under her pillow. Before putting it on she carried the candle in front of the looking-glass and gazed pensively at her naked reflection in the glass. Why did it interest her so greatly, she wondered. *Whoo-whoo!* cried an owl from the ravine. The dove had been shut in his cage, but at the cry of the owl he raised his head from under his wing and gave an enquiring look towards the ravine.

It seemed no time till the misty morning sunlight shone through the scented boughs of the pines into the room. The days were growing shorter. This, she realized, was a Sunday morning. There would be breakfast, with perhaps ripe pears on the table — one's best clothes — and then church.

She poured water out of the ewer into the basin, where it fell tinkling with a chill sound. She could hear the boys quarrelling in their room as to whether or not Ernest's ears should be washed.

"There is sand in your ears. I can see it," came in Nicholas's voice.

"My ears are cleaner than yours," said Ernest. "They are the cleanest ears in the family."

"Go and tell that to Mamma."

"All right — I will."

"What a little liar you are!"

Gussie hurried down the stairs. For some reason she felt light and gay.

Philip and Adeline were already at table eating oatmeal porridge. This had been cooked a solid two hours by Mrs. Coveyduck, till it was of a creamy consistency. A large bowl full of it was placed in front of Philip and he had just given himself a second helping when Augusta entered. She dutifully kissed both parents and, with a look askance at the porridge, said, "Just a tiny bit for me, Papa, please."

"What's the matter with you?" demanded Philip.

"Nothing, except that I'm not fond of porridge."

"You'd have a better colour if you ate more porridge. Look at your mother's complexion."

"That's the Irish climate," said Augusta. "This climate dries you up. Mrs. Coveyduck told me so." She drew back from the dish of porridge Philip set in front of her. "Oh, Papa," she protested.

"Eat it up," he ordered.

Just then the two boys romped into the room.

"Boys!" exclaimed Adeline. "Is that the way to come to breakfast on a Sunday morning?"

"Go straight out," ordered Philip, "and come in properly or you'll get no breakfast."

Subdued, the two slunk out and entered again with decorum.

Adeline said, "If my brothers had come rioting to table at my home in Ireland, my father would have thrown them out on their heads and they would have had no morsel of food." She sighed deeply, then went on, "Ah, what beautiful manners has my father! The courtesy, the amiability of an Irish gentleman! 'Tis my regret that he does not live nearby for a constant example to you."

This remark, for some reason, appeared to strike Philip as funny. He laughed silently for some moments. It was fortunate that Mrs. Coveyduck placed a platter of poached eggs on toast in front of him at this juncture.

"I'll wager," he said to Ernest, "that you're hungry for your breakfast. Eat your porridge and you may have a poached egg."

"I am not hungry," said the little boy. "I'd rather go to church than eat."

"Good Lord!" Philip laid down his knife and fork and stared in dismay at his son. "He'll be wanting to take holy orders next."

Nicholas said, "He's been talking in that pious way ever since we got up."

"Part of the time," returned Ernest, "we were talking about my ears."

"He has sand in them," said Nicholas.

After breakfast Adeline had a critical look at both her sons — made Ernest wash his ears and herself attacked the tangles in Nicholas's thick wavy hair, which he simply smoothed by running a hairbrush over it.

At last the family were ready for church, and very elegant they looked, Adeline in an immense hooped skirt that caused her to take up room for two in the barouche. Philip drove the spanking pair of bays. The two little boys, in velvet jackets and hats with tassels, were in the driver's seat with him. Nero ran alongside, Augusta, her long black hair floating, sat with her mother.

The church stood on a small but noticeable eminence and was surrounded by trees that had, during the last three days, become almost bare. Above arched the sky of an amazing blueness, like a southern sea. Against it sailed a great flock of passenger pigeons, as over a sea. Nicholas raised an imaginary gun in his arms, fired imaginary shots.

"I brought down three," he announced.

Ernest ordinarily would have imitated his brother but instead he walked with dignity up the path toward the church. His Sunday shoes squeaked a little, which pleased him.

A slender young man in naval uniform strode along the path and joined Gussie. Adeline greeted him gaily. She was waiting for Philip who had gone to put the horses and Nero in the shed behind the church. Adeline stood in the churchyard on the plot retained by Philip for the family. It was level and grassy. Not a grave yet. Her mind lightly touched the thought, as something inconceivable, that someday, years distant, the hump of a grave would rise there.

The church bell was ringing.

Augusta found herself walking along the aisle with Guy Lacey. The bell had ceased and now James Wilmott was playing a processional hymn on the organ, she and Guy moving in time with it. His naval cap was carried on his arm, his head was bent a little towards her. She felt almost giddy with the splendour of the moment.

Now her parents and the two small boys were close behind. Guy had disappeared into the Lacey pew. Augusta knelt; the wide brim of her hat, the silky black locks of her hair were a retreat for her. She was neither happy nor sad, but like a dreamer who feels himself to be far removed from reality and asks for nothing but to remain in the magic crystal of his dream.

The sonorous voice of Mr. Pink was now heard. Ernest's little face, with its sunburned nose, was raised to the face of the rector. He drank in the words.

"I acknowledge my transgressions, and my sin is ever before me."

"Hide Thy face from my sins, and blot out all mine iniquities."

"The sacrifices of God are a broken spirit: a broken and a contrite heart, O God, thou wilt not despise."

Adeline looked down complacently at the bent shoulders of this little son. She whispered, "Take your hand out of your pocket." She took the hand comfortingly in hers.

The service proceeded.

When it came the time for collecting the offertory Philip slipped out from the pew and joined Thomas Brawn, the miller. They moved up and down the aisles presenting the alms dishes at each pew. Philip watched the members of his own family each lay his contribution on the alms dish. When it came to Ernest, he ceremoniously laid the gold pen there. He then folded his arms with a Napoleonic gesture, and looked his sire squarely in the eye.

Philip and Thomas Brawn marched to the chancel steps and presented the offerings to Mr. Pink.

Mr. Pink grew even pinker than was usual, as he stared, scarcely able to believe his eyes, at the gold pen on the alms dish. Indeed he might have been called Mr. Scarlet at that moment without exaggeration.

Philip Whiteoak's expression was imperturbable. He looked as though it were quite the usual thing to see a gold pen on the alms dish. He looked as though nothing that might appear on the alms dish would surprise him. When he returned to his seat he cast a repressive look at Nicholas, who was shaking with stifled laughter. On their side of the church there was a stir of wonder. On the other side, there was a straining to see what the wonder was about. The Laceys sat on that side and Augusta was thankful that Guy had not witnessed Ernest's act. She felt ready to faint from embarrassment.

She could not, however, escape him. In the small crush in the vestibule she felt his breath on her ear.

"What was all the stir about?" he whispered.

"Something on the collection plate," she was forced to answer.

"Did you put it there?"

They were now in the open air, beautifully clear with a sparkle as of blue lustre.

She drew away. "Me? No."

"Then it was a joke of young Ernest's." He caught the little boy by the arm and whispered to him, "Ernest, did you put one of your pants buttons on the plate?"

Ernest gave a skip of pure joy and relief from the burden that had oppressed him. "Pants button, my eye" he said.

When the Whiteoaks reached home, Philip took his son Ernest by the hand and led him into the library.

"Now he's for it," said Nicholas.

"Gussie," said Adeline, "tell me what all this is about? I will not be left out of things."

"Papa will tell you," Gussie said, and dashed up the stairs.

Nicholas had his ear to the keyhole of the library door. "I don't hear any whacks yet," he announced.

"Can you hear what's being said?" asked Adeline.

Nicholas darted out of the way as the door of the library opened. At the same moment Bessie beat on the gong, which had been brought from India, to summon the family to the midday Sunday dinner.

Philip and Ernest emerged, hand in hand.

It was only a morning or two later when Guy Lacey came to Jalna to say goodbye, for his ship was shortly due to sail from Halifax.

Adeline called her daughter. "Augusta! Gussie, come down and say goodbye to Guy Lacey! I see him walking along the drive."

"Please, Mamma, I'd rather not," called back Augusta.

"Why on earth not? He'll expect it. He quite admires you, you know."

"I'd rather not. Tell him I'm ill."

"Nonsense. Come right down."

Augusta slowly descended the stairs. Adeline looked her over. "Whatever is wrong with you?" she exclaimed. "You're as pale as a witch. Bite your lips."

Obediently Augusta bit her lips, bringing a reluctant red into them. Guy Lacey was at the door. Adeline threw it open to his knock.

"Good morning to you," she said, in her warm welcoming voice. "Come in, do! Ah, 'tis sad news to hear that you are sailing. Now where are you sailing for?"

"Ireland, Mrs. Whiteoak."

"Ireland! Ah, to think of it! To dream of it! Gussie, dear — Guy tells me he is sailing for Ireland. Don't you envy him?" She turned her eyes to the stairway where Gussie had stood, but the young girl had vanished.

"Forgive her," Adeline said resignedly. "She is not well this morning. The truth is, she has only just heard of your leaving and it has upset her."

"Will you give her my kindest regards," said Guy, "and tell her I'm sorry to have missed seeing her?"

"When may we expect you on your next leave?"

"In about two years."

Shortly he went to the stables to find Philip, whistling cheerily as he went. Adeline flew up the stairs to Gussie's room. She found her stretched on the bed, her face hidden in the pillows. Adeline took her by the shoulder and turned her over.

"Aren't you ashamed of yourself?" Adeline asked in a voice high with anger. "Running off and hiding when a handsome young man comes to call? Have I taught you nothing of manners? Has your father disciplined you to behold you coming to an end like this? You're nothing but a shy gawky country girl! Guy Lacey thinks you are, for he told me so."

That was too much for Gussie. She gave a cry of pain, rolled over and again hid her face. Adeline was moved to pity. She said, "Well, maybe I am mistaken. Guy may have not spoken so roughly. He may only have said you are shy. Upon my word, I've had so much trouble, it's affected me memory. Yes — now I come to think of it — he said a shy sweet country girl."

Tears of thankfulness ran from Gussie's large eyes on to her clenched hands. "I'm so glad," she whispered.

"The trouble with you, Gussie," said Adeline, "is that you are too sensitive. I know just how it is, for I'm over sensitive myself. Now get up and tidy yourself, and we'll collect the two boys and go a-nutting."

The boys were listening outside the door. As Ernest overheard the last words he could not restrain a "hurrah" of pleasure, for to go nutting was almost as good as a picnic by the lake. There were beechnuts, hazelnuts, butternuts — to say nothing of the last of the wild blackberries. Small wonder that Ernest ejaculated "Hurrah!"

Adeline threw open the door. "Who said 'Hurrah?'" she demanded.

Ernest hung his head.

Nicholas said, "I did."

"What have I done," cried Adeline, "that I should have brought such young vipers into the world! There on her bed lies my only daughter — no more than a child — yet ready to carry on a secret love affair with a naval officer! Here is one son listening at a keyhole, while another looks me in the face and lies!"

"I'm sorry, Mamma," said Ernest.

"I'm sorry too," said Nicholas.

Augusta murmured that she was sorry. But the idea of a clandestine love affair pleased her. She rose from her bed, tidied her hair, and joined Adeline and the boys. They could hear Baby Philip struggling to climb the stairs — grunting, panting, making infant sounds of triumph.

"And that one," continued Adeline, "is the worst of the lot. Coming, my pet!"

In truth she was so happy she did not know what to do next to express her pleasure in life.

XVI

EVENTS OF THE FALL

Wilmott could not choose between the threatening storminess of the November sky and the calm of the little river that was the colour of a moonstone. The low-growing bushes by the shore still showed the green of cedar and the scarlet hips of wild rose, the glossy red cranberries. A blue heron flew low above the river, its blueness reflected there.

Wilmott said aloud: "'The heron, when she soareth high, sheweth winds.'"

The voice of Titus Sharrow came from among cranberry bushes. He said, "That is very nice poetry, Boss. I'm something of a poet myself, so I am able to judge."

Wilmott had seen some childish verses by Titus, written in a school exercise book. "You have written some quite pretty rhymes, Tite," he said kindly. "Very nice indeed."

Tite came to him and drew a newspaper cutting from his pocket. There was polite rebuke in his voice. "The editor of this newspaper liked these well enough to print them, Boss," he said. "Would you care to read them?"

Astonished, Wilmott read the verses. They were unashamedly sentimental, signed with Tite's own name.

"Congratulations," said Wilmott. "I'm sure everyone hereabout will be surprised and pleased to find that we have a poet in our midst."

There was something patronizing in what Wilmott said, something a little amused. Tite responded with, "I have decided against the study of law, because I am sure I shall never succeed in that profession. I have decided to be a poet. Later on, in the winter, I expect to write a book."

Wilmott himself had written a novel which never had seen the light of the printing press. He felt a kind of grim pity for this cocksure half-breed.

"Be cautious, Tite," he said. "You would be attempting something that has defeated many men cleverer than you. It is one thing to have a few verses published in a local newspaper; it is quite a different thing to find your writings between the covers of a book."

"Boss."

"Yes, Tite."

"I was born for success."

"What makes you think that?"

"Well, in the first place, when I was a scholar at the Indian Reserve school, I was not only the best-looking but I was the smartest. The teacher was not young but I soon found out that she was in love with me. She gave me higher marks than I deserved because she could not help herself."

"Everything has conspired to make you conceited, Tite, but you are not so remarkable as you think you are."

"I think that you are remarkable, Boss, and all these years we have been together I have tried to make myself like you."

Wilmott stared at him in amazement.

"Do you think I have succeeded, Boss?"

"Well, you say you were born for success."

"Do you think we are alike, Boss?"

"The point is," said Wilmott, "that I was born for failure."

"You make me laugh, Boss, and I hope you will forgive me for laughing."

"What is funny about failure?"

"Boss, you own this pretty little cottage, a boat, four suits of clothes, five pairs of shoes, a gun and a lot of other things. You never work. I model myself on you."

"I worked hard in England. I saved what I could."

"What do you value most in life, Boss?"

"That's easy to answer — solitude."

"Then why have you kept me about, Boss?"

"I've asked myself that question."

"I can answer the question, Boss. It's because you're a lonely man. I myself am a lonely man. The great are always lonely. Lord Byron was a lonely man. You have a book of his poems and a book of his life. I have read both and I think he was a great poet, beloved by women. I am just the same. Women long to have me for a lover. Do you remember Miss Daisy Vaughan who visited Jalna when the little boy Ernest was a baby and I was a very young man?"

"I've no desire to hear that story," Wilmott said testily.

Tite went on, as though he had not been interrupted. "That young lady became lost in the forest. It was I who found her and claimed the reward. But first I spent a little while in the forest with her. She was very nice and she loved me dearly. She could not help loving me. It is always the same. High and low, they cannot keep from loving me. The latest was Annabelle. She thought she loved God but it was *me* she loved. She could not marry me, so she gave herself to the Negro, Jerry. I should not marry. I am a poet, I long for solitude — like you, Boss."

"I don't know what you are trying to tell me," Wilmott said, still more testily.

Tite answered patiently, "I'm talking about Lord Byron and you and me, Boss."

Wilmott turned to walk away but Tite planted himself in front of him.

"Boss," he said.

"What?"

"You said to me once that I am like a son to you."

"Sons sometimes talk like fools."

"I am sorry if I have offended you, Boss, because I love you better than anyone else on earth, even better than my grandmother, who is the daughter of an Indian chief. On my French side I am also of noble blood."

"So you have told me, time and again," said Wilmott drily. "You are of noble blood and you are a poet."

"With the winter coming on, Boss, we both of us need a woman to look after us — a good-natured, pretty, and hardworking young woman like Annabelle. We could have leisure for writing poetry. She could carry wood, clean fish, and cook. It would cost you very little."

"Explain," said Wilmott.

"I have a letter from Annabelle here in my pocket, Boss. She hadn't been at home long, before she found out that Jerry had been married before the war, had a wife and two children. So she left him and is back in Canada looking after the children of a couple who have moved here from the South. She is still anxious about my soul, Boss, and aims to come and work for us. A fine writer like you —"

"My God!" interrupted Wilmott. "Leave me out of this, Tite. You may be a poet but I lay no claim to being a writer of any sort."

"You can't be left out," said Tite. "Because you are a great man. You must be waited on." His narrow dark eyes looked compellingly into Wilmott's. "Do you remember how sick I was last winter and how you had to wait on me? And you yourself were not well. What a fine thing it would be, if you and I had a healthy young woman to wait on us! Belle is healthy. She is strong. She loves me. She admires you. Also she is a religious girl."

"Where would she live?"

"Right here, Boss, with us."

"We should be the scandal of the neighbourhood. I can't tolerate such a thing."

"People can get used to anything, I find. You are greatly respected."

"Hmph!"

"Think how happy we could be! We have our cottage — we have our river — we should have our hand-maiden. Boss, she is used to being a slave. She asks for nothing better. Do, please, let her come."

"Never." Wilmott turned away.

"You will not agree?"

"Never."

Tite became deeply thoughtful. The only sound that came to them was the resigned movement of the river as it surrendered itself to the waiting embrace of the lake and the icy threat of winter.

Tite spoke, in a peculiarly seductive tone. "Boss," he said, "for your sake I am willing to marry the woman."

"This is the most ridiculous thing I've ever heard," said Wilmott. "You have made extravagant remarks before but nothing to equal this. Would you marry a slave?"

"Belle is no longer a slave. I've heard you remark, Boss, that none of us is free."

Said Wilmott, "You have boasted of your noble blood. Yet — here you are, proposing to marry a mulatto."

"Belle is not black, or brown, or even yellow," Tite said proudly. "She has the eyes of a white woman."

"I hadn't noticed," said Wilmott.

"Her father," continued Tite, "was a Virginian gentleman."

"All this is so unreal," said Wilmott, "I haven't the patience to listen to it."

"But it would not be unreal, if you were to wake on a winter morning and hear the crackle of a freshly made fire and smell cornmeal muffins baking. Do you remember how you were forced to call me three times this very morning, Boss, and at last throw your boot against my door? And even when I did get up, I burned the toast and cooked the eggs too long. It would be so different with Annabelle here."

Wilmott thought of the oncoming winter. He weakened, yet he said, "I can't allow it."

"But why, Boss? Give me one good reason."

"You would be living in sin, as the preacher put it."

"Belle and I are religious young people. We would go straight to my grandmother on the Indian Reserve. The minister at the little church there would perform the ceremony. It would be simple but legal. It would be very different from Belle's marriage to Jerry, for he was already a married man — married and as black as sin."

"Tite," said Wilmott, "I will not agree to this queer union till I have consulted with my neighbours the Whiteoaks."

"I think that is a wise decision," said Tite.

During this conversation, Tite became momentarily more dignified, even judicial. He gazed at the glimmering river, at the sky that was neither silver nor gold but a blending of both; at the blue heron casting her reflection on the river.

Oddly enough Adeline Whiteoak agreed that it might add to Wilmott's comfort to have a wife of Tite's in the house with him. Often, she declared, she had been anxious about the neglect Wilmott had suffered during the winters when Tite's studies took him into the town.

"It is madness," she said, "for that fellow to imagine he can ever become a lawyer. You did wrong, James, to encourage him."

"He's clever, you know," said Wilmott. "I am often surprised by his understanding. He's loyal, too, in his own peculiar way. In the many years he's lived with me, I've grown very fond of him. I planned some future for him that would be better than a marriage with a cast-off mulatto."

Adeline spoke with decision. "In my opinion, Belle is far too good for him. She's sweet-tempered. She's religious. She adores Tite. When she told me that her infatuation for him was over — never for a moment did I believe her. She'll be a good influence on him."

"He no longer wants to be a lawyer," said Wilmott. "He intends to be a poet like Byron — he says. He's had verses published in the local paper."

Adeline was impressed. "Really? I'd like to read them."

"They're pretty bad," said Wilmott. Yet he could see that Tite had greatly risen in her opinion.

It was afternoon. Adeline wore a green velvet tea gown that enhanced the pearl-like lustre of her skin, the ruddy chestnut gleam of her hair which Philip called plain red, and there was firelight from silver birch logs to play on the diamonds, emeralds, and the one magnificent ruby of her rings. So many rings were in bad taste for a woman in this raw new country,

Wilmott thought. Yet, he reflected, Adeline was of no particular country. She drew her background about her like a cloak. The ruby ring had been given her by a Rajah, and this, on Adeline's finger, seemed natural.

Now she looked out at the first snowflakes, swarming, like bees from a hive, beyond the window. Some clung to the pane, as though they would enter the room. Others swirled again upward towards the grey sky. They danced on the air, in a gay allegro movement, deceptive, courting the belief that no dirge was to follow.

"James," said Adeline, "are you happy in your life?"

"As happy," he answered, "as it is in me to be."

"Don't you ever become restive?"

"Restive! Me? Oh, I passed through all that in England. Here, I'm content as a cow out at pasture."

"A cow," she laughed. "*You* a cow? Oh, James!"

He gave his reluctant smile. "I chew my cud. Reflect a little on the meaning of things, and consider how lucky I am to be here. Surely you are not restive."

"Would you despise me if I say I am?"

"You know very well that I could not possibly despise you, but — I sometimes wonder at you."

"Why?"

"Well, you have everything — beauty —"

She laughed in derision. "Beauty? I've lost all I had."

He half rose. "When you say such things it's time for me to go."

She laid a restraining hand on him. "I've had a letter from Lucy Sinclair," she said.

"Don't tell me you are envying her."

"How you read my thoughts! Thank heaven Philip is not like you. We should be at daggers drawn."

"I look on Mrs. Sinclair," he said, "as a very shallow woman."

"You are quite mistaken, James."

"I always am — where women are concerned."

"Lucy is courageous." Adeline's voice vibrated with the fervour of her admiration. "She endured terrible things and seldom complained. Now, at last, I have had a letter from her."

"So you have said."

"In the restricted life I lead, it is necessary for me to repeat myself, else I should have nothing to say."

"I'm sorry, Mrs. Whiteoak."

"Mrs. Whiteoak!" she cried. "This is the last straw! To think that after all these years of friendship, I should be no more than Mrs. Whiteoak to you!"

Wilmott bit his nail in discomfiture.

"To think," she went on, "that after all my many vicissitudes —"

This brought a smile to Wilmott's sensitive lips. "*Your vicissitudes*, my dear. But, feel as sorry for yourself as you will, everybody envies you. You lead a delightful life."

"But it is monotonous. You can't deny that it is monotonous."

"Better monotony than the changes that the Sinclairs have endured. Did Mrs. Sinclair tell you what is the condition of their plantation?"

"Ruin, James, ruin. But Curtis Sinclair has bought a fine house in Charleston, or what is left of Charleston. They beg us to visit them when conditions are more favourable." She gave a start as the scampering of feet and shrieks of children came from above.

"Listen to them," she said. "It's a horrid game they play. Old Witch they call it."

"Who takes the part of the Witch?"

"Gussie — and she's even worse than the boys."

"Dear me," said Wilmott, "I thought Gussie was much too dignified for such a game."

"She is at a ridiculous stage. Sometimes a wild child. Sometimes a prim miss. Sometimes shy. Sometimes forward … Listen to that! Even our youngest is into it."

It was true. Baby Philip was noisiest of all.

Adeline sprang up. From the bottom of the stairs she called, "Children! Come straight down here!"

Reluctantly they trailed down the stairway, Augusta leading the youngest.

"You are driving me," said their mother, "into nervous frustration. Oh, how I miss that nice Mr. Madigan! We had peace in the house when he was here."

"It is the first time I've heard you say that, Mamma," said Nicholas. "Always you said he had no discipline whatever."

"You may thank your stars, my lad," Adeline brought out in solemn tones, "that Mr. Wilmott is here or I would show you what discipline can be."

"Discipline, my eye," said Ernest.

Adeline let herself go in something approaching a scream. "Merciful heaven!" she cried. "Have I lived to see the day when I should get such sauce from a child of mine!"

"Apologize quickly, Ernest," implored Gussie.

"Sorry," said the little boy. "I didn't mean nothing."

An observer might well have thought that Adeline was about to faint were it not for her excellent colour. Now she spoke in a deep tone of sorrow.

"Bad language and bad grammar," she mourned. "Whatever am I to do with him?"

"It's nothing," said Wilmott, "but association with the illiterate. He will soon forget."

Baby Philip, seeing that Ernest was in disgrace, doubled up his little fist and hit him, but Ernest was not even aware of the blow.

"It is a puzzle to me," said Adeline, "how these wretched children are to acquire an education in this wild country."

"Is it wilder than Ireland, Mamma?" asked Nicholas.

"Ireland," returned Adeline, "is the oldest Christian country in Europe. It was from Ireland that Joseph of Arimathea went to England as missionary to the barbarians of that country."

When the children had drifted away Adeline said:

"I have engaged Elihu Busby's daughter, Amelia, the one who was deserted by her husband, Lucius Madigan, to come as governess to my children till next spring. Then we shall take the two eldest to school in England."

"Why don't you send Nicholas to Upper Canada College?" asked Wilmott. "It has a quite passable reputation."

Adeline chuckled. "Because I'm dying for a change."

"This is extraordinary," said Wilmott. "I had thought you were content at Jalna since your houseful of visitors has gone."

"Everybody likes a change," said she.

"Everybody but me," said Wilmott.

"Lucky you!"

"Unlucky me — when you are away."

He gave her a look half-quizzical, half-tender. It was seldom that he made a remark approaching the affectionate, and she sunned herself in it. "Poor pioneer wife that I am!" she ejaculated.

"There is one nice thing about you, James," she added. "You understand what I mean, though I only half say it."

"I'm glad there is at least one nice thing about me." He now used his most distant voice.

Adeline suddenly rose and struck a somewhat flamboyant pose.

"Do you see anything remarkable about me?" she asked.

"There is nothing about you that is not remarkable, but what strikes me at the moment is that you are wearing one of those new-fangled bustles."

She laughed, and demanded through her laughter, "Do you like it, James?"

"I find nothing to like or dislike about a bustle," he said.

"But do you think it becomes me?"

He countered with another question.

"Does Philip like it?"

"No."

"Then neither do I."

Adeline pushed out her underlip in a pout which Wilmott found more attractive than the smiles of other women, but he thought the bustle was disfiguring.

Steps were coming down the stairs. The four children appeared, Gussie leading the little Philip.

"What? Are you back?" cried Adeline.

"A lovely present for you, Mamma," said Nicholas. "We were investigating Mrs. Sinclair's bedroom and we found these tied up in a neckerchief with a note saying 'To be returned to my dear friends' — but she forgot, do you see?"

"My pearl necklace," Adeline cried, snatching it.

"My watch and chain," said Nicholas, appropriating them.

"My moonstone ring!" Gussie put it on her slim white finger and held it up to catch the light.

"Me's pin," said Baby Philip, feeling it on the front of his pinafore.

"What about me?" quavered Ernest. "What about me and my gold pen?"

"Never mind, my angel." Adeline clasped him to her. "I will give you Papa's best pen."

XVII

THE IVORY PEN

"Where is my ivory pen?" roared Philip, from the library. "Has anybody seen my pen?"

Ernest upstairs giggled, then clapped his hand over his mouth. He waited for his mother to reply. She did. "Your ivory pen, Philip?" she called back. "Your best ivory pen?"

"You know very well," he roared, "that I have only one ivory pen. I want to know who took it."

"Did you by chance give it to anyone?" she asked, with a wink at the children.

"I want to know where it is," he shouted. He was now at the bottom of the stairs. "I'd not be such a fool as to give it to anyone."

"Perhaps Mrs. Sinclair took it."

"I had it yesterday. Somebody in this house took it and I pity him." His eyes ran over the group at the top of the stairs, coming to rest on Ernest.

"I'll tell you what," said Adeline, her voice full of sweetness. "We'll all go down and help you search for it. Come, children."

They trooped down the stairs. At the bottom she said to Philip, "Have you thought of the possibility of Nero's having taken it? He might have looked on it as mere bone and chewed it up."

"Nero would not have taken it off my writing table."

Nero, from his place on the bearskin rug, rolled up an innocent eye. He yawned, as though to prove that no morsels of ivory clung to his teeth. Never, he intimated, would he offer any criticism of the family, but it was necessary for him to defend himself.

Ernest squatted, looking into Nero's mouth, again stretched in a yawn. "I see no signs of a pen," he said.

Nicholas also squatted in front of Nero. He said, "His tongue certainly would be bloody."

Nero now rolled over on his back, as though posing his body for inspection.

"His feelings are hurt," said Augusta.

"He is innocent," said Philip, "but someone has meddled with my things and I'm going to find out who it is."

"The best thing to do," said his wife, "is for all of us to search together. Come, children." They began to ransack the room. Augusta was of an age to be critical of her parents. She asked herself, "Why should they go on like this?" Listlessly, knowing there was no hope of discovering the pen — she had seen it in Ernest's room — she peered into corners. To Nicholas it was great fun. He began to open the drawers of the bureau bookcase and examine their contents.

"I have an idea," exploded Philip.

"Have you really?" answered Gussie. She intended to be polite but Philip did not like the remark. His eyes became prominent. "What is there peculiar in my having an idea?" he demanded.

"It depends on the idea," she said, but she trembled a little at his expression.

"Ideas are more often mine," said Ernest.

"If I hear anything more from you," said his father, "I'll put you across my knee."

Philip went on, now addressing Adeline, "What I think is that Boney has stolen my pen."

In great good humour Adeline led the way to the bedroom shared by Philip and her. Boney was in his cage hanging head downward from his swing. He gave a malevolent look at Philip. "I hate Captain Whiteoak," he enunciated clearly.

"Of course you do," said Philip, "you old devil, and that's why you've stolen my pen."

All began to search the room while Boney, head down, cackled derisively. On Adeline's dressing table Ernest found a bit of treacle toffee wrapped in paper. He put it in his pocket.

Finally Philip said, "I can't waste any more time. I must use my old pen. One thing is certain, I will not have any more birds in this house." He stalked out. At the door he turned. "If one of you children should find the pen," he said, "you'll get a reward."

"Now is your chance," Adeline said to Ernest, "to get a nice reward."

"I prefer the pen," he said.

However, the more he thought about his moral responsibility, the less happy he was. With the lump of treacle toffee in his cheek he lay on the sofa in the schoolroom considering his position. He had not stolen the ivory pen. His Mamma had stolen it — then given it to him. Yet once she had told him that what belonged to husband belonged to wife also. Children for instance. If Mamma had not stolen the pen, who had? Yet Gussie had once told him that to receive stolen goods was as bad as stealing.

Gussie now came into the room. He asked her, "What should I do with the pen, Gussie?"

She answered firmly, "Give it back."

"To Papa?"

"Certainly."

"But he would be hard on me. Oh, Gussie, I don't like to be whacked." Tears filled his eyes.

"Then give it to Mamma."

"But I can't bear to part with it."

Gussie came and looked at him. Her eyelashes were a black fringe on her long pale eyelids. She had fastened a small sofa cushion under her skirt at the back to represent a bustle. "Do you like it?" she asked.

"It's lovely."

She turned her profile to him, that he might the better view the bustle.

"It may be a bit too big," she said.

"The bigger the better."

Gussie looked at him with disapproval.

"How can you know? You have never seen a bustle in your life till Mamma's."

"I like them big," he persisted. "And I like hoops big and I like waists small."

"Oh, Ernest," suddenly she broke out, "I wish I were pretty."

He was astonished. "I thought you were," he said. "I thought all girls were pretty."

"No, indeed," she said. "Now *you* are pretty. I heard Mrs. Sinclair say to Mamma that you should have been a girl, that you are too pretty for a boy."

Nicholas had that moment come in. He heard what Gussie said and he danced about the room chanting, "Oh, what a pretty little boy, and what a jolly good licking he's going to get when Papa finds out about the pen!"

Ernest took the pen from under him and gazed at it proudly. "I'm not going to give it up," he said. Augusta swept across the room to his side, the bustle prominent. "You'll never be happy," she said, "while the pen is in your possession."

"Why?" he demanded, in a trembling voice.

"Because you have a conscience. Nicholas," she went on, "has no conscience. He will be able to enjoy wrong things without ever thinking — are they right or wrong? But you will have to keep your conscience clear."

It pleased Ernest to hear himself so analyzed. He could not always understand Gussie but she had a way of talking almost as good as Mr. Pink's. "That is why it is strange," she went on, "that you should so often do bad things."

"I try not to," he said.

"You must try still harder, now that Mrs. Madigan is coming to live here and to teach us."

"How can she be Mrs. Madigan?" asked Nicholas.

"Because she married him."

"Then why didn't she go off to Ireland with him?"

For a moment Gussie was shaken by silent laughter. Then she whispered, "Because he ran off and left her."

"Why?"

"Because he hated her."

"But married people can't behave like that. They've got to stay together and have children," said Nicholas.

"Not the Irish."

"But Mamma is Irish," said Nicholas. "Is she likely to run away?"

"It wouldn't surprise me," said Augusta.

Mrs. Madigan came to Jalna that afternoon bringing two portmanteaux and a bonnet box with her. She did not wear a bustle and looked askance at Adeline's. As she had been a school mistress before marriage she felt quite capable of instructing the young Whiteoaks and keeping them in order. Her brief marriage with Lucius Madigan had made a deep impression on her. She hoped and occasionally prayed, in a cool Presbyterian way, that he would return to her.

"Do you think it would be seemly," Adeline asked of Philip, "to put her in the bedroom that was occupied by Lucius?"

"It would be the next best thing to having him, I should say," he grinned.

So it was arranged, but the children did not want her on the attic floor with them. When she appeared there, looking buxom and abnormally clean, the three gathered about her doorway, with looks more forbidding than welcoming.

"This room," said Augusta, "is generally occupied by my dove."

"A dove and a parrot in one house," exclaimed Mrs. Madigan. "Well, I never! And flying loose! Don't you find that they're rather dirty?"

"We don't mind dirt," said Nicholas.

"We like it," said Ernest, wiping his nose on his sleeve.

Mrs. Madigan gave him a sharp tap on the wrist. "Disgusting boy!" She spoke with severity. "I'm astonished at you."

"He's been told, time and again," said Augusta, "but he forgets."

"He'll not forget when I've been here a little while." There was something really threatening in her high-coloured face.

After a little she spoke again. "Don't allow that bird in my room in future," she said to Augusta. "It smells."

"Mr. Madigan smelt," said Ernest, and he hastened to add, "My Mamma said so."

"He couldn't," she almost screamed. "It's impossible!"

"He scarcely ever washed," said Nicholas.

"This bed is lumpy. He said so," put in Ernest.

"I scarcely think," said Gussie, "that Mr. Madigan would have wanted you to sleep here."

"I am his wife," the governess declared firmly.

"Are you sure?" asked Ernest.

The little boy lacked the knowledge that might have made him question the legality of the union. He simply thought that it was queer. But Mrs. Madigan was incensed. "Leave this room at once, all of you, and don't come near it again till I invite you."

Lessons began the following morning and Mrs. Madigan declared that never in her life had she met with such ignorance. "Mr. Madigan really taught us nothing but Latin and poetry," said Augusta.

"It's what you call a classical education," added Nicholas.

"And what good will such an education be to you in this country, I'd like to know?" asked Mrs. Madigan, her eyes piercing him like gimlets. "What you need to know is how many cords there are in a woodpile, how much a month you must pay a hired man if he earns three shillings a day. Also many important dates."

"I know the date when Columbus discovered America," said Ernest. "Ten sixty-six."

"Wrong!"

"Mr. Madigan said so."

"Ernest is wrong," said Nicholas, eagerly. "Ten sixty-six is the date of the first Grand National."

"Miss Busby," began Augusta.

"Mrs. Madigan," the governess corrected proudly.

Augusta gave a polite little bow. "Mrs. Madigan," she said, "do you consider that Shakespeare was the author of his plays?"

"If he wasn't I'd like to know who was."

"I can tell you," said Ernest. "It was Charles Lever."

Mrs. Madigan was so irritated by this that she slapped him. It was a shock to all three children. They had not expected such an indignity from this woman. Though she had been a neighbour they had seen very little of her. She had appeared to them as a good-natured, rather stupid woman. Now she was in the house with them, in a position of authority.

"That will teach you," she said, "to treat me with respect."

The slapped cheek turned from pink to red. Ernest, after the first drawing back, sat very straight and regarded her with dignity. Mrs. Madigan treated the other two with almost too much geniality, as though to show them what it was to be in her good graces. But they did not respond. They were conceited, stand-offish children, she reported at home.

Clean sheets and blankets had been put on the bed she was to occupy. The carpet sweeper had been run over the floor. As Bessie was about to remove the few clothes that Lucius Madigan had left behind him, the governess said peremptorily, "You may leave my husband's clothes here. I will take charge of them."

When Bessie repeated this remark to Mrs. Coveyduck, she scarcely concealed and indeed did not try to conceal her mirth. "It hardly seems respectable," she said. "And her not married a week."

The children stood about the doorway of this bedroom when they had seen Amelia Madigan trudge off in the direction of her home. She scarcely could bear to wait to report on the day's doings and how she had put young Ernest in his place.

"Do you suppose," Augusta asked her brothers, "that she wishes he were back?"

"Of course she does," said Nicholas. "She's dying to have him back."

"I wish," said Ernest, "he would suddenly come back — right into that bed — and slap her face for her."

"Shall you tell Mamma and Papa," asked Nicholas, "what she did to you?"

"No," said Ernest. "I'll get even with her in my own way."

His two elders looked on him with wonder, as he dragged the bulky bolster from the bed, turned back the bedclothes and laid the bolster under them. He made the bolster comfortable.

"Oh, Ernest," exclaimed Gussie. "It looks almost too natural. I'm afraid it will frighten the wits out of the poor creature."

"It's not natural enough," said Nicholas. "Do you remember how once he went to bed tight, with his clothes on, and took his pipe with him? He set fire to the bed and that roused him. He put out the fire and asked us not to tell of him and we didn't and he never told of us."

"He was a fine, noble man," said Ernest.

"We appreciate him more, now that he's gone," said Gussie. She then opened the door of the clothes cupboard and discovered an old tweed jacket of Madigan's, a battered felt hat, and a strong-smelling pipe.

Now the children wrapped the jacket round the topmost end of the bolster, drawing the blankets close. They topped the effigy with the battered hat and laid the pipe on the pillow. For a while they stood transfixed by admiration — then, hearing footsteps on the stairs, they ran to Gussie's room. The dove flew straight to her, alighting on her head. To him no perch in the world was so desirable as this silky black head.

With fast-beating hearts the children waited.

They were prepared for something but certainly they were not prepared for the screams of terror given by Mrs. Madigan. These screams came from powerful lungs. She might well have been a singer in Wagnerian opera. They heard her running down the stairs. She ran with such speed that they would scarcely have been surprised if she had landed with one leap in the downstairs hall.

The children stared at one another in consternation.

"We builded better than we knew," said Gussie.

"She seems frightened," said Ernest. They saw, through the window, how she was running in the direction of her home. He added, "She's in the hell of a stew."

"If you think," said Augusta, "that you are admired for the bad language you use, you're mistaken."

"Gussie and I could use worse language if we chose," said Nicholas, "but we have too much sense."

"Let's hear just a little of it," said Ernest. "You might go first, Gussie."

But all three now had the same impulse — to investigate Lucius Madigan's bed. It was just as they had left it. Mrs. Madigan had not discovered the hoax. Carefully they put everything in order.

An hour later they were sent for to come down to the sitting room. It was growing dark and a bright fire sparkled on the hearth. Adeline and Philip sat like two judges. Nero lay on the bearskin rug. The heat of the fire was so great that it made him pant. He would then rise and take himself to a cooler spot, but as soon as he ceased panting he would return to the rug. Adeline was crocheting a tea cozy. Philip was playing cat's cradle with his youngest who was seated on his knee. As the three elder children entered he demanded, in his most army officer's tone:

"What's this I hear about your governess?"

"Actually," said Gussie, "we don't know what you've heard."

"What do you mean by that, miss?" he asked with severity.

"We could answer better if we knew," she said.

"You mean you could make up fabrications to suit the occasion," said Adeline.

"What I want is the plain truth," said Philip. "What did you do to her?"

"I think it upset her pretending her husband was back."

"After all my trouble of engaging her," put in Adeline, "she's gone off without notice and sent a man for her bags."

"What if she's taken your ivory pen, Papa?" asked Ernest.

"No impertinence from you, young man," said his father.

"Ernest," said Adeline, "come and hold my wool."

He went at once happily, feeling that they two were in league together. If there was one indoor pastime above another that he enjoyed, it was holding wool to be wound or stringing beads, and he did both very well indeed.

"Me too!" said the tiny Philip. "Me 'old 'ool too!" He struggled to get down from his father's knee.

"He says he wants to hold wool too," said Ernest.

"I can't teach him anything," said Philip senior. "When I was his age I could play a first-rate game of dominoes." He set the little one on the floor.

"You still can play quite well," Nicholas said kindly.

His father stretched out an arm as though to fell him where he stood, but changed his mind, folded his arms across his broad chest, and stared gloomily into the fire. He said to Adeline, "I was against your engaging Amelia Busby —"

"Amelia Madigan," corrected Augusta.

"It was no sort of marriage," he went on. "The woman strikes me as illiterate. Madigan could never have put up with her."

"She can both read and write," said Augusta.

"Before she was married she had taught school," said Adeline.

Philip groaned. "I could not put up with that woman about the house," he said. "I have enough to put up with as it is."

"You are very seldom about the house, Papa," said Nicholas.

"I am a busy man," Philip declared. "I oversee the sowing and reaping of crops. The setting out of orchards. The breeding of horses, cattle, and sheep. I am the first one out of bed in the morning and the last to retire at night. With the winter coming on I shall have much more leisure."

"Every season has its disadvantages," said Augusta.

"It is a great mistake," said Philip, "for any child here to think that, just because I appear good-natured and easygoing, I will tolerate any impertinence." He threw a pine log on the fire with such force that sparks flew in all directions and Nero leapt on the sofa for safety.

Darkness came like a black curtain outside the window but indoors it was defeated by the springing firelight, by the vivid colouring of the family. To shut out the darkness completely Bessie now came in and drew the curtains. Seeing her the baby Philip well knew it was his bedtime and crept underneath the sofa where Nero lay, to hide himself. Usually his father would have protected him but now he said with a frown:

"Carry him off, Bessie. It's already past his bedtime. He's getting completely out of hand."

Dragged from his retreat, the little fellow held up beseeching arms. "Awnt to tiss evbody," he begged. He pursed his scarlet lips in readiness.

"He says he wants to kiss everybody," translated Ernest, eager to show off.

"When I want you to tell me what Philip says I'll ask you," said their father.

"But he speaks so badly," faltered Ernest.

"He speaks as plainly as you do and at least knows when to hold his tongue."

Philip senior rose with a groan, as though suffering from lumbago, and went to his desk, where lay a box of cigarettes, and took one. He had lately begun to smoke these in preference to pipe or cigar, but to Adeline they appeared unmanly.

She whispered to Ernest, "You did wrong, my dear, in keeping the ivory pen."

"Is that what's annoying him?" he whispered back, with a look askance at his papa.

"Yes. He won't be happy till he gets it." She gave her husband a loving glance, as though in proof of her understanding of him.

"You see that smoke coming from his nostrils?" she whispered, her lips close to Ernest's pink ear.

"Yes, Mamma."

"That's rage. Smouldering rage — ready to blaze up. We shall have no peaceful times at Jalna till you restore the ivory pen."

"Very well, I will," he assented, shouldering the burden of the pen, just as though she had had nothing to do with it, which was what she intended.

Ernest pondered for some time over the best way of restoring the pen, and decided that nothing could be better than the manner in which he had restored the gold pen. He wondered what had become of it and decided that it had been sold for the benefit of the missionary society for which the collection on that Sunday had been taken.

Tomorrow it was Sunday again, the first Sunday in December.

The falling of the wind that had blown throughout the month of November, the sudden stillness, the swift drop in temperature, announced the arrival of winter. Above all, enveloping all, was a heavy snowfall. Off and on there had been snow flurries but nothing like this. All the night long large snowflakes fell, slowly, tranquilly, without ceasing, as though they were conscious that there was plenty of time for what they planned to do. This plainly was to obliterate every landmark from the countryside — to smother hedges, fences, and gates, to leave no trace of paths, to render the most stalwart of trees no more than nesting places for the snowflakes. Boughs bent with the weight of them. Every gatepost was majestically crowned.

The stillness was remarkable. The sky leaned low. The earth appeared to give up the ghost.

Philip had been preparing for this. Sharp at ten-thirty the large family sleigh was brought to the front door by a stableman. It shone like a piano. Bear skins hung from the back and others were folded neatly on the seats, ready to cover the knees of the ensconced family. The pair of bays were fairly snorting and pawing the snow in their eagerness to be off, excited by the ringing jangle of the strings of bells that were attached to their harness. Above their shoulders hung a silver bell whose melodious notes were in contrast to the wild jangle of the harness bells.

The horses could barely be restrained while the family settled themselves in the sleigh. Baby Philip was held in Bessie's arms at a window to see them off. He threw kisses to them as they moved away and they threw kisses back. His father saluted him with the whip, on which there was a bow of red ribbon. He wore a wedge-shaped cap of beaver. Adeline was in a sealskin sack, and a small sealskin toque showed her gleaming hair to advantage, rivalling the ruddy tones of the sealskin. Augusta looked quite a young lady in a red velvet jacket trimmed with the same fur. When entering the church, the boys pulled off their woolly caps and their hair stood defiantly on end. Augusta gave each an admonishing look.

Ernest sat between his parents. One hand was in the pocket of his jacket, his eyes were fixed on his prayer book of which he was very proud, as his aunt had sent it him from England one Christmas. He could scarcely bear to wait for the collecting of the offertory. A sense of goodness and peace possessed him. Life stretched before him as a succession of happy Sundays, with now and again a birthday or Christmas thrown in.

This pen which he now fingered was not only of fine ivory but was delicately carved in a design of lilies and their graceful leaves. It was remarkable that so much could have been put into so small a space.

Ernest was lost in thought when Philip left the pew and joined Brawn, the miller. He then appeared with the alms dish for the contributions from his family. Adeline, Gussie and Nicholas laid their donations on the dish and glanced toward Ernest with a certain expectancy.

From his pocket he took the ivory pen and placed it with a flourish in the centre. He then raised his eyes to his father's face, half-timidly but certain that this was an act of renunciation.

Philip's eyebrows shot up, but he did not for a moment hesitate. Briskly he took the pen from the alms dish and stuck it above his ear. Like a clerk in a dry goods shop he marched up the aisle while the organ broke into the voluntary. He stood, self-contained, stalwart, at the chancel steps, with the ivory pen behind his ear. Returning to his pew he gave a roguish wink at Ernest.

XVIII

A Night Visitor

In a strange way this fall, this Christmas time, this winter, seemed to Augusta a new experience. It was almost as though she had been born again. She no longer felt a child as formerly. She did not consciously think about Guy Lacey but he glimmered in and out of her thoughts like a bright thread in the pattern of a tapestry. For the first time in her young life, she wondered what that life would be. Friends never asked her, as they asked Nicholas, what profession he would choose. "The Army, of course," he would answer, "and after I retire, a farm in Canada." If anybody asked the same question of Ernest, he would say, "I shall stay at home always with Papa and Mamma." Everybody took it for granted that she, being a girl, would marry and go to the home of her husband. What would it be like, she wondered, to be the wife of a naval officer and have no proper home?

It had been arranged, some months ago, that the two eldest children would be taken that fall to England and placed in schools there, while the two youngest would remain in Canada, under reliable care. This, however, could not be done, because no reliable person was at hand. Mrs. Coveyduck was out of the question, as already she was unable to control little Philip; and Ernest was so forward that he required someone capable of teaching him. "A pity," said their father, "that the Irishman and the Busby girl turned out so badly."

Ernest declared, standing very straight, that if Gussie and Nicholas went to school in England, he also would like to go, but he was told that it was too expensive to send three children off at once, that he must wait his turn.

"When shall I go?" he asked.

"In a couple of years."

"But I'll be lonely without Gussie and Nicholas. I'll have no one to play with."

"You will have your little brother," Adeline answered, giving him an absent-minded look, for her mind was on her preparations.

"I wish Mr. Madigan would come home," said Ernest.

"*Home?*" repeated Adeline.

"He often called this house home."

"I expect he's at home now with his mother in Ireland."

"Poor man." Suddenly Ernest looked experienced, like a little old man.

Strangely enough, Augusta and Nicholas seemed content to leave him at Jalna. She gave him careful instructions for the care of her dove. Nicholas told him about the feeding of his pet rabbits. He listened with pretended docility, but he wondered how they would feel if they were to be left at home while he went off on a jaunt to England. Inside he was seething with impotent emotions.

Mrs. Lacey, who taught her own daughters, gave the young Whiteoaks some lessons. These were not a success. In certain ways they appalled her by their ignorance. In other ways they shocked her by what they knew. This was the result of Madigan's teaching. Yet they looked on him as superior in every way to those who, since his going, had tried to force book learning into their heads.

Mrs. Madigan was such a joke to them that they screamed with laughter at the mere thought of her.

There were times when Augusta was just another child with her brothers. At other times she kept aloof from them, trying in a confused way to find the path towards womanhood. She was such a contrast to her mother that they found little companionship in each other. What seemed only ridiculous to Adeline was likely to appear pathetic to Augusta. What might throw Adeline into a fine rage would pass unnoticed by Augusta. What would appear formidable to the daughter would seem trivial to the mother. Augusta had a yearning for solitude. Adeline loved companionship. The image of Guy Lacey often came to disturb Augusta's sleep. He would appear out of the darkness, bright and smiling in his naval uniform. She would lie entranced, waiting for him to speak, but he would disappear as silently as he had come.

She had another visitor and this one very real. It was Lucius Madigan, who came up the stairs one winter night to the schoolroom where the three young Whiteoaks were sitting in a pretence at doing lessons. Adeline and Philip had gone to Quebec for a visit.

Madigan appeared at the door and smiled at them.

It was so natural to see him there that for a moment they had not the wit to feel surprise. He had come out of their brief past to astonish them.

"What a lovely sight!" he exclaimed. "Working hard at your lessons! Oh, my dears, I could embrace you all." He held out his arms, as though to enfold them.

Ernest was the first to recover. He rose and ran to Madigan. "We were given snowshoes for Christmas," he said. "Want to see them?"

"There's nothing I'd like better," said Madigan.

The little boy ran off to fetch them.

Nicholas said, "It was better when you were here, Lucius."

Augusta corrected him. "You are not to call Mr. Madigan by his Christian name."

"I used to sometimes, didn't I, Lucius?"

"Yes, and I like it," said Madigan.

He advanced into the room and sat down at the table with them. He looked as he had used to when getting over a spree. His eyes rested on Augusta. "You look different somehow, Gussie," he said. "Do you feel different?"

"She's just the same," said Nicholas. "Bossy."

Augusta raised her long-lidded eyes to Madigan's face. "I remember things in a different way," she said.

"You begin to realize that you have a past," said Madigan. "It's a sad moment, Gussie. But never let your past haunt you. That's a terrible thing." He ran his hands through his hair making it stand up as though in fright.

"Are you going to see Mrs. Madigan?" Nicholas put the question boldly.

"Yes, I'm going to see my mother, Mrs. Madigan, as soon as I have money to pay my passage," answered Madigan.

"I meant your wife," said Nicholas.

"My God," cried the Irishman, "does that Busby girl call herself Mrs. Madigan?" He looked distraught.

This sent the young Whiteoaks into peals of laughter. Ernest had returned with the snowshoes. Then each made a characteristic remark.

Nicholas said, "She came to tutor us but we quickly got rid of her."

"Not before she'd slapped Ernest's face," said Augusta.

"If you like," said Ernest, "I'll show you how I made up her bed, with your coat and hat and pipe in it. That frightened her away."

"That coat is what I came for," said Madigan. "It has my savings sewn up in the lining and, by God, I need money." He looked searchingly into the children's faces. "I hope no one has meddled with the lining," he said.

"At least we are honest," said Augusta.

Ernest plumped the snowshoes on the table on top of the lesson books. Madigan examined them with sincere interest. "How I should love to see you on these!" he said, a light coming into his tired eyes. The children had not realized before this that his presence meant so much to them.

"How did you know our parents are away?" Augusta asked.

"I enquired in the village," Madigan answered humbly. "But I'm not going to stay. As soon as I have recovered my bit of money I'll be off."

"I wish we might go with you," said Nicholas.

"And leave this paradise?" exclaimed Madigan. "If you will take my advice you'll grow up here and never, never travel. If I had stayed in Ireland, I'd be a less miserable man today."

"Gussie and I are to go to school in England next spring," said Nicholas, "but this young fellow" — and he gave a patronizing tap to Ernest's head — "is to remain at Jalna with his baby brother."

"I won't! I won't!" Ernest jerked his head away from the patronizing tap and spoke loudly. "I'll run away first."

Madigan looked his most melancholy. "I can't think of anything worse than school in England," he said, "unless it is school in Ireland. I went to one."

"Our father says we'll learn all sorts of things."

"You will learn how to bear daily beatings with stoicism — that is, after the first term, when you'll cry yourself to sleep every night."

"Why would they beat us?" Nicholas asked without flinching.

"For the fun of it," said Madigan. "The big boys beat the small boys for the fun of seeing them suffer."

"But a girl would not be beaten," said Gussie.

"There are worse things than physical pain," said Madigan. "On my part I minded the beatings less than the moral humiliations."

"Please tell us about it," said Ernest. "I love to hear about suffering."

Madigan said, "I am not hungry but I have a terrible thirst on me. Do you think your papa might have left a drop of whisky in the decanter on the sideboard? But, for God's sake, don't let the servants hear you, because if that Busby woman discovers I'm here she'll be trying to meet me."

"Her father and brothers would like to meet you," said Augusta.

For a moment Madigan looked subdued, then he asked, "Have you still the dove with you?"

"He is the joy of my life," said Augusta primly.

Nicholas ran down the two flights of stairs, the upper serviceably covered in linoleum, the lower carpeted in red Wilton. Shortly he reappeared carrying a decanter half-full of Scotch whisky and a tumbler. Madigan poured himself a drink. "It does me more good neat," he said.

He drank it down.

"You used the word 'joy,' Gussie," he said. "As for me I have ceased to feel that emotion, but I'm happy to think a dove can give you joy. What about you, Nicholas? Has anything the power to give you joy?"

"Snowshoeing," said Nicholas. "When I'm on my snowshoes in the woods I'm full of joy."

"And you, Ernest?"

"It makes me joyful to have you here again," said the little boy.

Madigan's eyes filled with tears. His hand that held the tumbler trembled. The house was silent, cloaked in snow. Augusta's hands, elegantly shaped and of a pure pallor, lay clasped on the table before her.

Madigan continued, "Do not let your parents send you away to school. You will be half-dead from homesickness. You will be ill-treated and miserable."

"What can we do?" asked Augusta.

Madigan had downed his second drink. He looked into the amber shape of the decanter and said, "If I were in your place I should run away."

Augusta's eyes rested on the snow-blanketed windowpane. She murmured, "How can we?"

"I advise you," said Madigan, "to put on these delightful snowshoes and disappear into the woods. Never come back." His elbow rested on the table, his head rested on his hand. He looked desperately tired.

"Have another drink," suggested Nicholas.

Madigan refused with dignity. "I must keep my brain clear," he said. "I must find my savings. I must be away from here by daylight tomorrow." He rose, a little unsteadily, and moved towards his former bedroom, the children following him. Augusta went slowly, her head bent, her hair falling about her pale cheeks, as though she were musing on distant things. Nicholas marched along steadily, as though he were able to cope with whatever came his way. Ernest, gentle but dogged, followed last.

"I'm sorry," Augusta said to Madigan, "but my dove sleeps here. I can't have him in the room with me because he will perch on my pillow."

"I don't mind," said Madigan. "But you must tell me his name so I may talk to him."

"I give him a new name each season," said Augusta. "But the names are secret, so that only he and I know them."

"Once," said Ernest, "I heard you call him Mortimer."

"Mortimer is Guy Lacey's middle name." Nicholas gave a teasing laugh. "What a name for a dove!"

The dove settled more comfortably on his perch. Augusta went to him and stroked his silky back.

The boys pressed close after Madigan as he took his coat from the peg. When he turned it inside out they saw that the lining had been cut. Madigan put his finger inside, but there was nothing there. He gave a rueful look. "By jingo, I remember," he said. "I took that money myself — for the honeymoon with that Busby girl."

Ernest corrected him. "Mrs. Lucius Madigan."

Madigan clenched his hands. "Do you want me to cuff you?" he demanded.

"She slapped my face," said Ernest.

"That is not allowed," said Augusta. "If any chastising is to be done, it is done by your parents."

"They like doing it," added Ernest.

Madigan sat down on the side of the bed. "I must rest," he said. "Tomorrow I shall be up at sunrise. I must escape before the servants discover me." He looked into the face of each child in turn. "Never shall I forget you." His voice trembled and his eyes filled with tears. He sank on to the feather bed and almost immediately fell asleep.

Augusta brought a thick quilt called a "comforter," and spread it over him. The three stood looking down at him in solicitude. Outside, the wind beat the snowflakes against the pane, enfolding the house in a deep slumberous silence, broken only by the falsetto snore of Lucius Madigan.

Augusta went to her own room and from the sill of the snow-plastered window brought what appeared to be four russet apples, brown and rather wrinkled. She gave one to each of her young brothers, then laid one with a benign gesture in the curve of the sleeper's hand.

XIX

Doings of the Whiteoak Children

In the morning he was gone and no one in the house, with the exception of the children, knew of his visit. He had not left even a footprint in the snow, for the wind had obliterated them.

Yet his deserted wife, by some means, heard that he had been seen in the neighbourhood and ploughed her way through the drifts to Jalna to enquire after him. Her long heavy skirt was caked with snow, even to the knees. She marched into the room where the children were drawing maps and demanded:

"Has anyone here seen my husband?"

"He spent all his savings on his honeymoon," said Ernest, licking his crayon for colouring Ireland green.

She strode into the room and stood over him. "How dare you insult me?" She looked all teeth, blazing cheeks and round angry eyes.

"Ernest didn't mean to insult you," said Augusta. She bent her head above her map and her silky black hair fell over her face.

"All he had from Gussie was a russet apple," said Nicholas. "And we're not even sure he ate that."

"Yes, he did," said Ernest. "I know, because I found the seeds in his bed."

"Then he spent the night here! When did he leave?" The frustrated woman strode up and down in her fury, clots of snow falling off her.

"Miss Busby —" began Nicholas.

"Mrs. Madigan," she corrected, fairly spitting the words out, while her colour deepened, if that were possible.

Nicholas continued, "It looked like a little brown apple, but actually it was a medlar. You don't eat them till they're rotten."

"This is very confusing for Mrs. Madigan," Augusta said politely and with dignity. "We have only one medlar tree and this is the first year it has borne fruit."

Ernest went on as though he were giving a lesson, "Each medlar has five hard seeds. I found them in Mr. Madigan's bed. Should you like to see them?"

Her answer was to wheel, march out of the room, and down the stairs. Nero, who never had liked her, now appeared and, taking the hem of her skirt in his teeth, escorted her to the front door. Two floors up the children ran to the window to see her go.

Scarcely had she disappeared in the falling snow when there came the sweet jangle of sleigh bells and Philip and Adeline arrived, a day sooner than was expected. The children tore down the stairs to meet them. Adeline, glowingly handsome in her sealskin sack and cap, gathered all three into her arms but, when her youngest was carried to her, put them aside to embrace him.

In the days that followed, they were a happy family, in the fastness of midwinter. But such tranquility could not last — not with undisciplined children having too much time on their hands.

"You're a graceless trio," declared Adeline, eyeing her three eldest and holding baby Philip close, as though he were her one treasure. "If I, in my young days, had shown as little sense, my father would have turned me out of doors, to wander with the gypsies."

"What fun!" said Nicholas.

"Why do you always say 'my father,' rather than 'my mother?'" asked Augusta.

"Because," said Adeline, "I resemble my father."

The children pondered on this, trying to make sense out of it, but could not.

The rescue from illiteracy came from Wilmott. "When your young ones go to school in England, they will be jeered at for little ignoramuses, Adeline," he said.

"But why? I don't understand." Really she felt insulted. "Nicholas can play quite nicely on the piano, Gussie and Ernest both can recite poetry."

"What about mathematics?"

"I have got on without them," she answered proudly.

"You would get on if you were completely illiterate." It was seldom he spoke with such lack of restraint. Now to cover up the slip he hastened to add, "I was going to offer to give them lessons for the rest of the winter if you are agreeable to the idea."

"Oh, James, how heavenly that would be!" Before he could stop her she threw both arms about his neck.

He drew away but not before the sweet scent of her brought a moment's delight to his nostrils. "I should scarcely call it heavenly," he said stiffly, "and I fancy the children will not, but I will try to make it interesting, if you will let them come to my place. Five times a week from nine till twelve."

And so it was arranged.

Now it was that the snowshoes which had been given the children at Christmas came into full use.

It was a winter of great feathery drifts, that in shadow had a bluish tone stolen from the blue skies. At night the moon in its splendour subdued all earthly things. In time to reach Wilmott's cottage by nine, allowing for a little loitering on the way, the children set out. They put on their moccasins when they first got up, over two pairs of thick woollen stockings, that is to say one pair of stockings and one pair of socks. Outside they tied on their snowshoes.

In the weeks since Christmas they had become accustomed to these. No longer did the snowshoes feel clumsy or get tangled up with each other, but moved lightly across the snow, leaving prints like the shadows of birds. Often at that hour in the morning it was bitterly cold, but the children did not mind. Their stomachs were warmed by oatmeal porridge that had cooked for two hours. On their heads the boys had red woollen toques with bobbing tassels, but Augusta wore a hood of the same colour with a red silk bow beneath her pointed chin. On their backs were strapped satchels holding their books.

Long before it was time to set out for Wilmott's cottage Nero stationed himself in the porch, his eager eyes fixed on the front door. He too had had a bowl of porridge, to say nothing of bacon rinds and scraps of toast and marmalade and a dish of tea. He felt replete, yet all agog for the walk. Nothing could restrain him. Before the children were anywhere near Wilmott's door, he was there, scratching on it to be let in.

Invariably the door was opened by Tite Sharrow. Wilmott was seated at a small table and gave the young scholars a tranquil "good morning." They clumped in their snowshoes straight through to the kitchen, Nero stopping on the way to give himself a tremendous shake. He then settled down in front of the stove to pull out the clots of snow from the dense black curls that covered him.

Wilmott took these lessons seriously. He found the minds of his pupils an interesting contrast. He found they knew more than he gave them credit for. The Irishman had, in his erratic way, taught them a great deal. In spite of their advantages they were not such good students as was the half-breed, Titus Sharrow. He had a power of concentration which they lacked. He took such pride in what he had learned, yet sometimes Wilmott wondered if he had, in any degree, changed from the young barbarian he had first known. While the lessons were in progress Tite usually stood in the doorway leading to the kitchen, his arms folded, his intent eyes fixed first on one face, then on another. Usually he preserved a decorous silence, but when Wilmott's enthusiasm or wit was suddenly pointed by the telling phrase, Tite would double over in silent laughter and slap his thigh.

Nero would become so overheated that he would gather himself up with a groan, move to a cooler spot and cast himself down with another groan. But soon he would return to the heat of the stove.

Early in the year the young mulatto woman Annabelle had found her way back to Jalna and been made welcome by Adeline and the cook, Mrs.

Coveyduck. She had tales to tell of devastation in the South that fairly wrung the hearts of these two. Where their feelings were at variance was in their attitude towards the proposed marriage between Tite and Annabelle. To Adeline it was an unmixed blessing — a good-natured healthy young woman to serve Wilmott, to keep the cottage clean and to keep Tite satisfied. What would happen to Wilmott if Tite went to the West, as sometimes he threatened to do! "He'll never stay there," said Philip. "A lazy dog like Tite. In the West they work."

As for Mrs. Coveyduck, she never had trusted Tite and thought Annabelle far too good for him. The airs he gave himself were infuriating to her. Yet when she found that Annabelle loved Tite and that nothing would dissuade her, she knitted a "cloud," as they called it, in light blue wool, to keep her warm on her honeymoon, and mittens of the same colour.

But there was no proper honeymoon. Adeline had said to Wilmott: "James, I think you are the man to give Annabelle away. I am arranging the ceremony. It will be a bit of fun to brighten this long wintertime."

"Fun!" he had repeated. "I don't call getting married fun. And if I must give anyone away it will be Tite."

That made her laugh. She was exhilarated by the thought that Wilmott would acquire an industrious and docile servant, at no wage beyond her keep. She brought two goose-feather pillows to the little room off Wilmott's kitchen which Belle and Tite were to occupy. On top of the pillows she laid two frilled pillow shams on which were outlined in red stitching the words: *I Slept and Dreamt that Life was Beauty. I Woke and Found that Life was Duty.*

When Tite saw these he was as deeply impressed as even Adeline could have wished.

"Boss," he said, "always have I desired elegance and now I have it. Annabelle and I shall sleep and dream of beauty. You, Boss, will wake with the smell of bacon and potatoes frying, making a cheerful tickling in your nostrils...." Tite was thoughtful for a space, while Wilmott ostentatiously buried himself in a book.

"May I know what you are reading, Boss?" Tite asked.

"The marriage service," answered Wilmott. "I want to know what you are going to promise."

Tite asked, as though shocked, "Do you forget the marriage ceremony, Boss?"

"I forget," Wilmott said tersely.

"I think it will be best," Tite said, "for Belle and me to go to the Indian Reserve and be married by the minister there. My grandmother would be very happy to meet the bride and we could visit her for a few days and meet other members of her tribe. It will be educational for Belle and a great occasion for my grandmother."

Wilmott was relieved by this suggestion. The less he saw of the newlyweds the better pleased he would be. Sometimes he regretted that he had given permission for the pair to move into his cottage. He was so snug there but he was lonely in the long winter evenings. He missed Tite's lively presence — there was no doubt about that.

Therefore when, with a jingle of sleigh bells and a small blizzard, the young couple appeared one early evening at his door, he made them welcome. He had not before noticed, or had forgotten, how pretty Belle was. In fact they were a charming young couple. They established themselves without fuss in the little room off the kitchen. As Tite had foretold, Wilmott woke in the morning with the delicious smell of hot muffins in his nostrils. Never had he tasted such coffee as Belle made. Never had he realized that chicken could be so richly and yet tenderly cooked. And the young wife was as quiet as a mouse about the cottage. She wore carpet slippers. Never did she raise her voice. Tite also was quieter, more thoughtful for Wilmott's comfort. Little did Wilmott guess the hilarity which took possession of the mulatto and the half-breed when his presence was removed, when he went to a neighbouring house for dinner or to spend the evening. Tite and Belle would sing, dance, and shout. They would chase each other through the cottage without restraint. They would fairly raise the roof.

As the winter drew on Wilmott allowed Tite to take a hand in the teaching of the children. He discovered that Tite had an amazing talent for interesting the young Whiteoaks in their studies. He felt that here was a born teacher. At the same time he would not be sorry when the children left for England and school. He enjoyed having them as pupils, yet they took up altogether too much of his day. The children themselves had never been so happy. They had a warm affection for Wilmott. They found an exciting teacher in Tite. When Annabelle appeared each mid-morning carrying a tray on which were a pot of cocoa and a dish of hot buttered corn cake, they beamed their happiness. The boys did not look forward. They lived in the present. But Augusta awaited the spring as a time of wonderful happenings.

The season of Lent brought still heavier snowfalls. Snowshoeing was a delight, especially when the sun, gaining heat as spring approached, soft-ened the surface of the snow and, when the icy cold of night enveloped the land, a firm glittering crust was formed. What glorious fun to slide down their favourite hillside, squatting on their snowshoes!

On Good Friday Wilmott left the teaching to Tite. Wilmott was assisting the rector with the Easter music and was spending the day between church and rectory. The children had been invited, with Wilmott's consent, to spend the day at the cottage. Belle had prepared a feast for the midday dinner. She and Tite waited at table with mock formality, but soon the formality had disappeared and the five were seated together, eating lemon pie, eating nuts and raisins, and drinking blackcurrant cordial. Tite smoked one of Wilmott's cigars. Now and again, stretched on the sofa, he uttered a whoop of uncontrollable animal spirits.

Presently Annabelle grew serious. "This is a real solemn day," she said. "The day of Our Lawd's Crucifixion. We'd ought to be thinkin' of dat and not jes playin'."

"What can we do to make us feel solemn?" asked Ernest.

"Think of Mrs. Madigan," suggested Nicholas.

"She just makes me feel sick," said Ernest.

Annabelle sat, with eyes rolled ceilingward, in silence for a space, then she said, "Ah know what we could do. Act a religious play. I saw one at home long time ago — before the war. We could show the mob wan-tin' to crucify Our Lord. We could show the Crucifixion — not really — jes pretend, Ah mean —" and she gave a reassuring pat to Ernest's shoulder — "then we could have the glory of the Resurrection."

"Explain," said Augusta. "It would be a lovely thing to do."

As Belle unfolded the plan of acting the sacred events, all five occupants of the room became equal — the three young Whiteoaks, the lithe half-breed, the freed slave. She indeed was the instructor. The others hung speechless on her words till Tite exclaimed:

"I will take the part of a soldier."

"Do you feel that you can do it properly?" Augusta asked.

"Just watch me," he said fervently.

Exalted, Annabelle stared admiringly at Augusta. "Little Missus," she said, "you sure ought to be the Madonna, 'cause you have the right face and the beautiful hair."

Tite stared at Gussie, as though he had never before seen her clearly.

"What shall I be?" came from Ernest.

"You gonna be our Lawd," said Belle.

"And me?" demanded Nicholas. "Somebody horrible, please."

"Pilate," at once said Belle. "I guess Tite and me will jes' have to be the mob."

"Right," agreed Nicholas. "Let's get things moving while there's time."

They cleared the room for the play — all but Tite who went to the woodshed and returned carrying two pieces of scantling nailed together in the form of a cross. This he laid on the floor.

"You'll not really crucify me?" Ernest, in spite of the fact that he had been chosen for the part of Jesus, was beginning to be a little frightened.

"We not gonna tech a hair of yo' dear little head," promised Annabelle, and put her arm about him. She brought a piece of white linen and wrapped him in it.

"He should be naked," said Tite.

Ernest's modesty was revolted by this. Annabelle exclaimed, "No, no. He look jes' fine the way he is." She laid her blue scarf about Augusta's shoulders and brushed her long hair. Belle was in her element. She placed each child to the best effect. Nicholas washed his hands in a basin of water and said loudly, "I find no fault in this man."

Tite shouted "Crucify him!" and leaped about Ernest in what resembled an Indian war dance. He picked up Ernest and laid him on the cross. Augusta knelt at his feet, shedding real tears. Nicholas forgot he

was Pilate and joined Tite in dancing and uttering wild yells. Belle forgot she was civilized and leaped up and down, her head almost striking
the ceiling, while she screamed, "Save us, Lawd!" Ernest lay on the cross,
his little pink hands clenching and unclenching in imagined pain. Nero
barked with all his strength. The situation was entirely out of control.

The room was stuffing hot. No one in it perceived the faces at the
window. It was not until there came a thunderous knock on the door
(Tite had bolted it) that it was thrown open and Wilmott, Adeline, and
Philip were disclosed on the threshold. After the din in the room the
silence that fell was frightening.

XX

Punishment

The silence was broken by Wilmott who said — in a voice no one in the room had heard before — "I'm ashamed of you. Ashamed of every one of you."

Philip boomed, "It's an orgy. Nothing less than an orgy."

"What would have been the end to it," Adeline said, "if we had not come on the scene, I hate to think." She added, in a voice quivering with curiosity, "But I wish I knew. I wish I knew."

Tite kept his head. He stood up, very dignified and straight. He said, "We did get a little excited, but" — he waved an inviting hand — "if you, lady and gentlemen, will sit down, we'll act out the play and you'll see that we meant no harm."

Annabelle was crying without restraint.

When the door had been opened Nero had shot out into the snow. Now he was scratching on the door to come in again.

Wilmott said, "The first thing for you young people to do is to tidy up."

"Ernest," said Philip, "take off that white thing. Gussie and Nicholas, get ready to come home."

"Shall we put on our snowshoes?" they asked.

"Let me explain," said Tite.

"I want no explanations from you." Philip's frown would have made most young men quail but Tite's face was impassive. He said, addressing Wilmott, "You know me, Boss, and you know I would do nothing to disgrace you. What we were acting was a religious play. We were carried away by our feelings. It's a beautiful thing, Boss, to be carried away by religious inspiration."

"Take Annabelle to her room," Wilmott said tersely. He stood with folded arms as Tite led the weeping mulatto away. "I'm terribly sorry this has happened," he added to Adeline.

"It goes to show how little the dark races can control themselves. Now if I had been here I should have taken them in hand and made the play truly religious." Her eyes shone. She looked down in wonder at the cross on which her small son had been stretched.

"You probably would have been jumping and screaming with the best of them," said Philip in an undertone.

It was seldom that the children were taken out at night in the big red sleigh with the buffalo robes. But now they were tucked snugly into the back seat, the fur rug up to their chins, their flushed cheeks tingling in the icy air, their ears filled with the splintered music of the sleigh bells. The night was so clear that every sound, every sight, became brilliantly intensified. The moon rose up into the blueness of the sky, casting the shadows of the trees in splendour on the snow, turning the manes of the horses into flying metal.

Adeline delighted in the dashing over the smooth road, the boundless glittering solitude. "Can't we go home the long way by the church, Philip? I do adore sleigh riding on a night like this. It's as though we owned the earth."

So they went the long way, but Nero went the short way and was waiting on the porch for them when they jingled up the drive between the rows of snow-laden spruces and hemlocks. Adeline and the children went indoors (Ernest ready to drop from sleepiness) but Philip took the horses and sleigh to the stables.

When he returned on foot, his long strides crunching the snow, moonlight still flooded the land, the moon in its majestic power reducing the earth to no more than its footstool. Inside the hall Philip listened. He could hear his family moving about in the sitting room. Ernest was saying, "Mamma, I'm hungry," in a whiny voice, and her reply, "And so am I. It takes a sleigh ride to give one an appetite." She had so enjoyed this that she had forgotten the disgraceful scene at the cottage and beamed at her children. All divested themselves of their wraps and when she sank into a chair and Nicholas knelt at her feet to draw off her fur-lined boots, Ernest climbed on to her lap and repeated, "Mamma, I'm hungry." Nero picked up one of the snow boots, gave it a thorough shaking, and carried it under the sofa.

In a sonorous voice Philip remarked from the doorway, "So — this is the way you young'uns are being punished. Well, you won't feel so pert when I've done with you."

Adeline chimed in with, "And you'll feel still less pert when I've done with you." She pushed Ernest off her lap, and reached out to give Nicholas a slap.

He evaded it and said, "We were not really to blame. It was Tite and Belle. She'd seen something like it in the South."

"You should not have taken part in such a performance," answered Philip. "That couple are a bad example to you. Very well, you're off — the three of you — to England in the spring — to schools which will discipline you as you've never before been disciplined."

The thought of being left at home while Augusta and Nicholas went to England had been almost unbearable to Ernest. Now the news that he was to accompany them to a terrifying English school was even worse. As always when he was upset, Ernest's stomach clamoured for food. He whined, "I'm hungry."

"To bed! All of you," ordered their father.

"Thank you for a lovely sleigh ride," said Ernest.

"That sleigh ride," said Philip, "was to please your mother. You just happened to be there." He smiled into his blond moustache. "You may count yourselves lucky that you're not to be thrashed till the morning."

Three pairs of mournful eyes looked into his.

"We're to be thrashed in the morning?" quavered Nicholas.

"Before or after breakfast?" asked Ernest.

Philip considered. "Before breakfast," he said. "Razor strop."

"What about Gussie?" asked Nicholas.

"Her mother will deal with her."

"I'd rather you did," said Augusta, sedately.

"*What?* You'd rather I did?"

"Yes, Papa."

"You hear that, Adeline?"

Adeline looked smug. "You see," she said, "they really stand in awe of me."

"Might I," asked Ernest, "have one little dry crust of bread?"

Philip sprang up, went through the wide doorway to the dining room, and returned with the biscuit jar which was in the shape of a wooden barrel with silver bands. "Take these," he said, "and eat them in your rooms. Then straight to bed."

He dragged Nero from under the sofa and rescued Adeline's snow boot from him. "A buckle is missing," he said, and spoke sternly to Nero who immediately spat it out.

Augusta took it to her mother, asking at the same time, "Would you mind telling me what my punishment is to be, mamma?"

"A dose of rhubarb powder," grinned Adeline. "Twill be both punishment and cure, for it has an abominable taste and will likely save you from a bilious attack."

"But why should I have a bilious attack?"

"You know as well as I do how excitement affects your liver."

The two small boys were already on their way upstairs with the biscuits and now Augusta followed them. She wanted nothing to eat, the horrid vision of the rhubarb powder hovered before her. She felt ill.

Her room was deluged by moonlight. She closed the door behind her. She gave herself up to the silence and the moonlight. She was experiencing one of her lonely times. She seemed to belong to no one, no place. Not even to Jalna. Yet the thought of going away frightened her. If only she could fly away with her dove and be lost — the two of them — in some ancient and beautiful land! But, though she felt light spiritually, she was more conscious of her body than ever before. Her arms and legs felt heavy, her head strangely light. She felt a strange dizzy resentment towards the way her parents treated her. Their half-jocular sternness, their refusal to consider her as almost grown up. If Guy Lacey were here, she thought, he would protect me.

XXI

The Plan

The weather changed that very night. A boisterous wind, with the promise of spring in it, galloped across the land. The three young Whiteoaks
had no snowshoes for the morning walk to Wilmott's, so they were
obliged to wear galoshes and trudge through deep snow. Everything,
they thought, was against them. They were a sombre trio. Sombre too
was Wilmott and darkly tragic was Tite. Annabelle did not appear with
the mid-morning cocoa. Wilmott dismissed the children early. It was
Easter Saturday.

On the way home they heard the cawing of crows. The black-winged
birds swept across the windy sky like pirates across a storm-tossed sea.
"Caw-caw-caw," they shouted as though in challenge to the sleeping
earth. Like flails their wings beat the sky.

"It's slushy," said Nicholas. "We couldn't wear our snowshoes even if
we had them."

"There will be no more snowshoeing this year," said Augusta.

Ernest asked, "Do you suppose Mr. Wilmott is going to keep our
snowshoes for himself and Tite and Belle?"

"Quite likely," said Augusta.

She trudged doggedly on through the slushy snow. She clasped her bare hands, red from cold, together, as though in prayer. She said, "Life has become very dreary."

"Do you think it will become better or worse?" asked Nicholas.

"Worse," she replied.

"Still more dreary?" asked Nicholas.

"Still more dreary," she replied.

"Dreary, my eye!" said Ernest.

A spatter of ice-cold rain fell.

"Papa did not lay a hand on me," said Ernest. "I told him I have a cold coming on." Then with a sly look at Nicholas, he asked, "Did the razor strop hurt?"

"Shut up!" shouted Nicholas and gave Ernest a push that landed him flat on his behind in an icy puddle.

From where he sat, Ernest gave a teasing look at his sister. "How did you like the rhubarb powder, Gussie? Was it hard to get down?" Ernest would never have spoken so to Augusta, had he not been sitting in that icy slush and feeling so miserable.

Augusta turned away her head. "I'm going to bring it up," she moaned and ran into a dense thicket of cedars.

"Now you've done it," said Nicholas and he gave Ernest a smack on the head.

It did not hurt because of the woollen toque he wore, but it terribly hurt his feelings and he sat where he was in the icy slush for some little time after the others had disappeared among the trees. The flock of crows again passed overhead, cawing, it seemed, in derision of him. "Cawcaw-yah-yah-yah!" they screamed. Again a spatter of icy raindrops fell, as though from their wings.

Ernest gathered himself together and trudged homeward. It seemed that he would never arrive. He did not much care if he never arrived. He had a mind to lie down in the snow and be frozen to death. His family would be sorry then. They would cry — even his father. Ernest pictured the scene with satisfaction. The sufferings of Gussie and Nicholas were as nothing compared with his. What were a few whacks with a razor strop or a dose of rhubarb powder compared with his sufferings?

It was a rule of the house that galoshes should be left in the porch unless the side entrance was used. But Ernest walked straight in, leaving snow clots on the rug. Little Philip ran to meet him. It was surprising how, in the past months, he had developed from a baby into a small boy. In spite of his light blue dress, trimmed with braid, in spite of his long hair that hung in golden clusters to his shoulders, he looked and moved like a boy.

"Me go too," he said, attempting to follow Ernest up the stairs.

"No," said Ernest. "You can't come."

"Why?"

"Because I'm sick."

"Sick?" repeated little Philip. "Why?"

"Why is anyone sick?" said Ernest. "I shall likely die, and you won't care. Nobody'll care."

The little fellow took this to be a huge joke. He chuckled, then laughed with all his might.

"I ain't tik," he said through his laughter.

"What an ignorant way of speaking!" exclaimed Ernest. "*I ain't tik!* I suppose you mean you're not sick. Well, why don't you say what you mean? That's what I'd like to know." He hung on the banister looking down with contempt at his baby brother.

Adeline called from her bedroom. "What do I hear? Someone being unkind to his poor little brother? Up to your room, sir, and change into dry things."

Ernest dragged himself up the stairs but he did not change his wet clothes. He just threw himself on the bed and fell asleep.

He lay in bed for the next three weeks suffering from a severe attack of tonsillitis. During those weeks winter departed in a roar of floods and a flourish of snowstorms. Spring weather came in unseasonably warm. By the time Ernest was convalescent, the trees had clothed themselves in garments of rosy young buds, dandelions had appeared on the lawn, and chirping, grunting, bleating young creatures in poultry house and barn. Ernest could hear the gurgling of the stream as it threw off its bonds of winter. Nicholas, when he came to do his lessons in their bedroom after tea, could talk of nothing but fishing — what kinds of bait for different sorts of fish — where the best fish were to be found. Nicholas was supposed to come to the bedroom to be company for Ernest, but he did not do his homework. He talked of fishing and sailing a boat.

One Saturday in May Nicholas and Augusta were taken for a sail by Tite Sharrow. Tite had bought or had somehow acquired a small sailing boat. Without permission from anyone he took Augusta and Nicholas sailing on the sparkling expanse of the lake. They rowed down the river from Wilmott's cottage, Tite at the oars, till they reached the lake. There, on its solitary wooded shore, they found the small boathouse where the sailing boat was sheltered. Tite, with the help of the two young Whiteoaks, drew it across the stony beach and set it dancing on the wavelets. He raised the sail. The May breeze played with it.

"Have you ever enjoyed a sail?" asked Tite.

"You know very well we have not," answered Augusta. "But there's nothing we'd like better."

"Do take us sailing, Tite," begged Nicholas.

"Would your father allow it?"

"We need not tell him," said Nicholas. "Or our Mamma either. They have been severe with us, ever since the Good Friday party. We have no reason for being good."

Tite held the boat steady while brother and sister clambered in. He said, "Freedom is the best thing in life, if you know how to enjoy it."

Augusta, raising her face to the breeze, asked, "Why did you get married, Tite? Now you must always think of Belle."

"Do you mean Belle hinders me?" he said.

"Well, you're no longer free, are you?"

Tite showed his white teeth in an enigmatic smile. "Since I married Belle," he said, "I have even more freedom. When I go away, she looks after my boss for me. When I am at home, she waits on us both. She does all the work. She is accustomed to being a slave. Freedom is of no use to her. With me it is different. I am descended from Indian braves and from a nobly born French explorer. I must be free or die."

"And so must we," said Nicholas, sniffing the spring wind. "Isn't that so, Gussie?"

The small sailing boat, like a creature alive, sported over the waves, which increased in size as they ventured farther out on the lake. The early green verdure of the shore was one with the bluish-green waters. Water birds flew close to the land. Land birds tried their exulting wings at the lake's edge.

All was motion. Everywhere was a fluid intermingling of the elements. Augusta felt that never before had she known what true happiness was. It was, she thought, freedom to go where you chose, when you chose. Her eyes sought the faces of her two companions. That odd smile, that so inscrutable smile, never left Tite's lips. On the brow of Nicholas there was a frown of concentration as he bent all his powers on watching Tite at the sail. Yet there was a deep serenity on his face. Augusta said to him, "What if we never went back? Remember what Mr. Madigan said about running away."

"It's a good idea," said Nicholas. After a little he remarked to Tite, "I wish we had a light sailing boat like this. It's just what we need."

"Why don't you ask your Mamma to buy you one?"

"Why do you say Mamma?" asked Nicholas. "It is Papa who does the buying."

"But it is the wife who persuades," said Tite.

"Does Belle persuade you?"

"We have no money," said Tite.

"But how can you buy without money?"

"There are other ways." And he added, with easy satisfaction, "I know them all."

Augusta threw back her head, drank in the wild sweetness of the spring day, and remarked, "We are thinking — my brother and I — of leaving home."

It was impossible to surprise Tite. Now he looked as though this was no more than he had expected. But he asked, "What would you live on, my little lady, and where would you live?"

Augusta answered, without hesitation, "We have friends. Mr. and Mrs. Sinclair. They have invited us to come to them at any time and to stay as long as we wish in Charleston. You see, Tite, our parents intend to take us to boarding school in England."

"And we don't want to go," put in Nicholas.

"Young sir," said Tite "you would receive a beautiful education in England — better than in any other place in all the world. It was in England that my boss got his education and no one in all this country has an education to match it. I wish I had your chance."

"We don't want to be educated," persisted Nicholas. "We want to be free."

"And to have strange adventures," added Augusta.

"In the English schools," said Nicholas, "we'd be looked on as barbarians. We'd be bullied. Even our little brother would be bullied."

"Take my advice" — Tite's narrow eyes rested speculatively on the two faces so eagerly turned to him — "get all the book-learning you can. It is something solid to hang on to. You can listen to the talk of other folks — the way they chatter — and all the while you reflect on how much more you know than they know. Reflection is a very nice pastime, miss" — he addressed Augusta in particular — "there is no better way of spending your time. Your face, miss, shows that you were made for reflection."

"*And* adventure," said Augusta.

"*And* adventure," added Tite. "But look, the wind has veered. We must come about."

For a time they were occupied with the sail. Nicholas was especially good at manipulating them. After a time they were becalmed, and as they lounged in the small boat Augusta was moved to tell Tite of her plan. It was the first Nicholas had heard of it. Nevertheless he listened without turning a hair. Indeed an observer looking on might have thought he had concocted the whole scheme, so self-possessed was he.

When Augusta and Nicholas returned home after the sail they entered the side door, which was usual, tiptoed past their mother's room, from which came the sound of her voice telling a story to little Philip to keep him quiet while she coaxed the tangles out of his sunny hair. She interrupted her story to say, "This hair of yours, my little one, is like pure gold."

Philip had lately reached the stage of feeling himself to be an individual, one with feelings different from those of his family or of anyone else in the world. Now he said, "No."

"You silly little creature!" cried Adeline. "How can you know what colour your hair is? I tell you it's pure gold and you're the image of your papa who is the only man hereabout worth looking at."

"No," said Philip.

"Sit still," cried Adeline, "or you'll get smacked!"

"No," said Philip.

"Are you going to obey?"

"No."

Now there came the sound of a smart slap. Philip was set on his feet and at once ran loudly crying into the hall. When he saw Augusta and Nicholas trying to escape up the stairs his crying changed to laughter and he sturdily joined them, taking a hand of each.

"Gussie — Nicky," he said ingratiatingly.

"Shall we let him come?" asked Nicholas.

Augusta nodded, and clinging to their hands he climbed the stairs. They could hear Adeline calling, "Philip — Philip — come here and let Mamma put a clean dress on you!"

"No," said Philip.

They discovered Ernest on the second flight of stairs. He was playing his secret game. This was played with a few discarded chessmen, some scraps of paper, and coloured stones. He would write directions for the chessmen, move them from one step to another, at the same time making remarks such as — "Live long, O King" — or "Now is my Solitary Fate" or "Call the Wolves to their Tea." Augusta and Nicholas had a respect for this game. Never had they tried to understand it but they realized the comfort it had been to Ernest while he was ill. He gave them a wary look, as they guided little Philip past him, up the stairs, taking care not to disturb his solitary pleasure.

It was not long before he joined them in Augusta's room. Even they noticed how pale was his face and that he wore a red flannel bandage round his throat, from which came a pleasant odour of eucalyptus ointment.

Ernest said, "I heard talk when I was on the stairs."

"What about?" asked Nicholas.

"You should have been occupied with your game," said Augusta.

"I can play it and listen too," he said.

"What did you hear?" Nicholas asked peremptorily.

Ernest looked knowing. "Something about running away," he said, balancing on his toes.

Little Philip too looked knowing. "Me wun away," he said.

"Now everybody knows," exclaimed Nicholas crossly.

Ernest said, "If you run away I'll go too." He made a heroic stand. "I'll run to the ends of the earth with you."

Nicholas asked, "What do you know about running away?"

"I know that Mr. Madigan advised us to."

Augusta looked deeply thoughtful. She said, "I think we had better tell Ernest. He can keep a secret, as we know by his secret play. Also he will be useful for carrying supplies and to manage the boat."

Nicholas was still unconvinced. "Ernest's too little," he said.

Baby Philip pushed out his chest. "Me's big," he said.

Adeline's voice came up from below, calling Philip.

Augusta, weary she did not know why, had laid her pale cheek on the table and closed her eyes. Now her eyes flew open, she rose and picked up Philip. "You must go to Mamma," she said and carried him down the stairs. He liked the way Augusta cradled him in her arms. The face she bent over him appeared to him for the first time as a comforting face. He ceased to try to be a boy and resigned himself for the moment to babyhood. A flood of tenderness passed from him, through her arms and into all her veins. Her heart beat heavily and she paused halfway down the stairs wondering if she could go on.

Again came Adeline's voice calling to Philip.

"I'm bringing him, Mamma," Augusta called back. She handed him over. Adeline said, "This is the most disobedient child I've had. By the time he's seven he'll need a man to control him." Philip put both arms round her neck and planted a moist kiss on her mouth.

Slowly Augusta mounted the stairs.

She found Ernest making a list of the things they would need to take on the journey. "Just look at him," exclaimed Nicholas. "We've only just given him permission to come with us, and already he's taken the thing into his own hands."

"I'm good at making lists," said Ernest. "Look." He displayed a sheet of foolscap, on which two items were clearly written. Augusta read:

Eucalyptus
Rhubarb Powder

She demanded, "What are these for?"

Ernest answered, "You know I never leave home without eucalyptus...." He hesitated, then went on, "The rhubarb powder is for you ... in case ... you are bilious."

Augusta firmly crossed out that item. She said, "We shall need a blanket and a waterproof sheet —"

Ernest put in, "My compass and a notebook for the ship's log —"

"A lantern," said Nicholas, "and plenty of grub."

Ernest wrote, then clapped his hands. "What fun it is!" he laughed.

"It's a serious business," said Augusta. She insisted that their "homework" should be done, but every spare moment was given to the list and to plans for the journey. Augusta's plan was to cross the lake, take a train on the American side. They would sell the boat to the Americans and so obtain money for their railway fare.

"Where shall we get money to pay Tite for the boat?" asked Nicholas. Augusta was the leader, there was no question about that. "And we're not sure that he will sell it, are we?"

"Tite will sell anything," she answered. "We'll pay him for the boat with the presents the Sinclairs gave us. My ring and your watch, Nicholas."

While these sacrifices were being contemplated Ernest occupied himself by rubbing ointment on his throat. He hummed a little tune. He had nothing but imagination and courage to contribute to the expenses of the long journey. It was he who proposed taking Augusta's dove with them. He said, "We could release him like Noah did the dove and he would fly home and bring a message from us to say we had run away and were well and happy."

Nicholas felt this to be a good idea, but Augusta needed some persuading. Secretly she hoped that if the dove fared well on the voyage, she might take him all the way. Yet, if she had to send him adrift, as from an ark, she knew he would find his way back and once there Mrs. Coveyduck would care for him. Twice the dove had escaped and returned safely to Jalna.

That night she could not sleep for the plans, the fancies beating on her brain. Next morning the sweetest spring wind she ever had encountered rattled the shutters of her room, tossed the branches, tossed her hair, brought a wild pigeon to her window to say cooing love-words to her dove.

The suspicion dawned on her. Was the dove possibly a lady? Such a thought had never before entered her mind. Half-dressed she flew downstairs to her parents' room. She tapped on the door, which was opened by Adeline wearing a new pink and white dressing gown. Philip was putting lather on his face.

"Mamma," began Augusta, "do you think ..."

"Gussie," began Adeline, "do you think ..." but she had the stronger voice, and continued — "do you think I should wear pink? Answer me."

"No," Gussie replied truthfully.

Adeline began at once to take off the dressing gown. "I knew it!" she cried. "Yet the man in the shop persuaded me! With my hair, he said, 'twould look elegant!"

"And so it does," said Philip. "Gussie is only envious. Isn't that so, Gussie?"

"Yes, Papa." And she went on, "I really came to ask an important question."

"Out with it," said Philip, applying the razor to his chin.

"Do you think it possible," Gussie went on, "that my dove may be a lady?" She swallowed and then got out, "It has a caller. He is most persistent."

"Nothing is more probable," said Philip. "Don't let the fellow in."

"Do you think he is what Mrs. Coveyduck calls a *follower?*" asked Gussie.

"I do," said Philip.

"You are the silliest girl I've ever known," said Adeline. "And the only thing for you to do is to turn your dove outdoors to join the wild birds. That's what she wants."

Augusta went slowly along the hall. Before she reached the stairs Adeline called, "Come back here, Gussie!" And when Augusta reached her mother's bedroom, Adeline exclaimed, "Kiss me! Kiss me quick!"

The embrace took but a moment. Augusta was left with the feel of that warm vibrant body clasping her. There was little tenderness in the kiss. Rather it was the expression of a physical desire to dominate or, possibly, if Augusta had understood, a yearning to be protected from the world by the arms of her children.

That day the bargain was struck with Tite. It was to be kept secret for all time. Augusta's ring, Nicholas's watch, were handed over to Tite. The children now were owners of a good little sailing boat. Tite, during the next week, gave them lessons on how to sail it. Every afternoon they were late for tea. Wilmott had an attack of lumbago and was glad when Tite offered to go with the children to the summerhouse at Jalna and there give them lessons in mathematics. But the time was spent on the lake sailing the boat. In the solitary boathouse were stored the provisions for the voyage. Secretly these things had been carried there and hidden. So dense was the undergrowth of the woodland, so secret were the paths made by Tite and the children, that they were able to carry on their plans without hindrance or detection. Like members of forgotten tribes, they stole through the forest paths, carrying their booty.

"Shall we ever see home again?" Ernest asked one evening, when their preparations were completed.

"When we have made our fortunes," said Nicholas grandly, "we'll come home and bring presents for everybody."

XXII

Voyage

"We should," said Augusta, "eat a hearty breakfast to start us off well on our journey."

The boys agreed, but when they sat down to table they had little appetite. Philip was just finishing his ham and eggs. He held up a sun-burnt cheek to be kissed. It was extraordinary that he seemed to notice nothing odd about the children. Adeline was not yet out of bed.

"Well," Philip said cheerfully, as the three seated themselves, "glad to be off to school, as usual?"

"Rather gladder than usual," Augusta answered cryptically.

Philip seldom went to the trouble, the mental effort of analyzing the remarks made by his offspring, but this struck him as odd, worth looking into.

"Why?" he demanded.

Ernest took it on himself to answer. "Because," he said, "we are to begin the study of Euclid."

Philip stared. Then, "You little horrors!" he said.

This set Nicholas laughing. Philip was in great good humour and laughed with them. He now remarked to Ernest: "I see that your cold is better."

"Yes," Ernest answered proudly. "But I'm taking my red flannel neck-band and my bottle of eucalyptus with me, in case I feel a cold coming on."

Nicholas kicked him sharply under the table.

"Ouch!" exclaimed Ernest.

Philip said to Nicholas, "You may leave the table."

Nicholas left and ran down the basement stairs to the kitchen where the smallest member of the family, seated in his high chair, was eating his porridge. Nicholas patted him on the back. "Goodbye," he said. "I may not see you again till you're grown-up."

"Bye-bye!" Little Philip waved his spoon, then threw it on the floor.

Mrs. Coveyduck turned Nicholas out of the kitchen. "Do let your little brother be," she said. "He was as good as gold till you came. You always bring trouble."

The three adventurers gathered in the hall. They could hear the sewing machine humming briskly in the sitting room where the seamstress was already at work. Under cover of this they slipped out through the side door, ran along the path towards Wilmott's cottage, but soon turned off into the secret path that led to the boathouse. The wood was lively with the music of singing birds.

As they ran through the mossy greenness Ernest saw that there were tears on Augusta's cheeks.

"Why are you crying, Gussie?" he asked.

"Life is so sad." Her eyes looked large and mournful.

The little boy was puzzled. "What do you mean, life is so sad, Gussie? You make me feel sad too."

She could not answer.

"Perhaps we'd better stay at home a bit longer."

Nicholas, in the forefront, said, "If you're going to start whining, Ernest, you may go back."

That had the desired effect. Ernest strode out manfully. When he cast a sidelong glance at Gussie tears were no longer to be seen. He slipped his hand into hers.

Tite was waiting. Their supplies were already stowed in the boat as it lay beside the little wharf.

"All is ready," said Tite. "And it is high time you left because the boss is himself again. He expects to teach you this morning and has the books laid out in preparation. The next thing to happen will be that I shall be sent out to look for you. Ah, here is Annabelle. You had better be off before a search party is sent to look for you."

"Shall you be one of the search party, Tite?" asked Augusta.

"I shall be the leader," said Tite. A smile played over his thin lips.

"And where shall you lead them?" asked Nicholas.

"I shall lead them astray," answered Tite.

"What fun!" said Ernest.

"It is evil." Belle spoke up suddenly. "May de Lawd forgive us for what we are doin'. It's evil we're doin'."

"Evil, my eye!" said Ernest, jumping up and down in his excitement.

These children were used to being waited on. They stood passive while Tite carefully arranged their supplies already in the sailing boat which lightly danced on the sun-bright wavelets, as though eager to be off. Each little wave hastened to the shore, eager to find something to play with, were it only a tiny shell or a blade of grass. A throng of silvery minnows which had been spawned that morning darted with newborn assurance in a sunny pool.

Now Tite gave a deferential hand to Augusta to assist her into the boat. On her wrist she carried the dove, tethered by a ribbon tied to its leg. For the first time Belle saw the dove. She cried loudly in her distress. "Oh, Missy, don' take dat poor li'l bird. He don' want to go out in a boat! It will sho'ly kill him."

"He must not be allowed to mourn for me," said Augusta.

"Leave him with me! I promise to care for him!" Annabelle burst into tears.

"You would advertise the fact," said Tite, "that you knew of the voyage. Don't be a fool." He gave a push to the boat. He said to Annabelle, "Come, make yourself useful and dry your tears."

The two, side by side, pushed the boat. They ran out into the lake pushing with all their might. The dove sat quietly on Augusta's wrist, staring out of its round jewel-like eyes. Ernest sat at the rudder. Nicholas controlled the sail. The boat lay lifeless except as it was pushed. Nicholas's eyes were raised to the sail. Ernest's hands gripped the tiller. Gussie and the dove sat motionless as though dreaming.

Presently a shudder passed through the boat. The sail gave a gentle sound as though speaking. Then all was alive. The boat began its dance on the wavelets. The sail tugged at the boy's hand.

"They're off! They're off!" shouted Annabelle as though in jubilation, but soon she was in tears again, wringing her hands and wailing, "What will become of them!"

She was not the only one to regard the departure with concern. Nero now appeared, crashing through the underbrush, his eyes rolling. Bubbles from his shiny black nostrils showed how hard he breathed. He pawed his way to the boat's side.

"He will upset us!" cried Gussie.

But Tite was close behind him. Up to his armpits Tite pursued Nero. He caught him by the collar. It seemed that Nero would choke to death as Tite dragged on his collar. Then out of the breezy sky a wind blew into the sail, swelling it, turning lazy movements into swift purposeful motion. Almost it took the children's breath to see Tite and Nero left behind — two small figures struggling in the water — to see Belle wringing her hands far away.

"We're off! We're off!" shouted Nicholas.

"Goodbye to all!" sang out Augusta.

"I'm at the helm! I have my compass!" cried Ernest.

Even the dove flapped his wings and uttered noises of excitement.

The little boat was dancing on the blue-green waves that chattered and gurgled beneath her. Then there was the flapping noise of the sail that strained as though it would free itself from the mast. A flock of gulls hovered for a short while near them, screaming in greed as Augusta threw a piece of bread to them. But the children had not the lake to themselves. There in the distance was a large schooner. On it Augusta turned the spyglass that had been given her on her birthday by Mrs. Lacey. It had once belonged to Guy Lacey and next to the dove Augusta regarded it as her greatest treasure. Indeed, even more than the dove, it held the highest place in her affections. Now she held the spyglass to her eye, as the breeze blew back her long hair.

After a time the boathouse and the figures beside it were no more to be seen. The schooner was no more to be seen. The gulls were left behind. Ernest looked out on the vast expanse of the lake. "Do we go right across?" he asked a little fearfully.

"Right over to the American side," answered Augusta.

Faster and faster moved the boat, as though straining to reach the very source of spring. The wind was favourable, the sun warm, the breeze cool. Augusta had emerged as the commander. There was new life, new authority in her. She had provisions for her crew. She knew where she was going. She was free. The two boys depended on her utterly. Nicholas felt that all the stories of adventure he had read had led to this greatest of all. Ernest was heart and soul with the joy of freedom — no more lessons — no more restraint.

"Gussie," he said, with his eyes on the hamper, "I'm hungry."

Nicholas laughed outright at the thought of the hamper packed with good things. "I'm starving," he said.

Gussie lifted the clean white napkin from the pile of sandwiches and put one into each boy's hand, gave each a mug of coffee.

"This is such fun," said Ernest. "Why was Belle crying?"

XXIII

THE SEARCH

The morning was so fresh, so charged with Maytime vigour, so vibrating with the outpouring of a thousand songbirds, that Adeline could not help singing her favourite song. "'I dreamt that I dwelt in marble halls,'" she sang in her clear, though not very tuneful soprano, "'With vassals and serfs by my side.'"

She was dusting the contents of the cabinets of curios from India and was under the impression that she handled them with more delicacy and care than any maid could do. Yet when the dark figure of Titus Sharrow appeared in an open French window she was so startled that she dropped an exquisitely carved ivory monkey that fell with a small clatter to the floor. From appearing as a statuesque figure of dark foreboding, Tite instantly turned into one of lithe agility. He picked up the monkey and gazed at it with admiration before putting it into Adeline's outstretched hand and giving her a profound bow. He said, in his best French style, "Your song was very beautiful, Madame. I am glad to have heard even a little of it."

"You are a foolish boy," she said, returning the monkey to the cabinet, but she was pleased by a compliment from this clever half-breed. There were not many to pay her compliments in this remote place.

She now gave him an enquiring glance, to which he gently replied: "I have been sent by my boss to enquire about your children."

"My children?" She stared in astonishment.

"They have not come to us as usual for lessons this morning. My boss has recovered from his lumbago and is anxious to go on with the lessons. I too am anxious ..." Tite spoke with such deliberation that Adeline was impatient.

"The young rascals," she said, "they have loitered on the way. You will find them if you search."

"I have searched, Madame. It is eleven o'clock. Even the dog Nero is anxious. He whines and rolls his eyes, as though he would tell something."

"They are playing truant," said Adeline.

She herself took the path to Wilmott's cottage and was joined by Nero. With a businesslike air he led her along the path. She noticed that his curly black coat was damp. What a dog he was! In for a swim in the river at that hour — and he no longer young! But she enjoyed the walk and every now and again raised her voice and shouted the names of her children. "Gussie! Nick! Ernest!"

She found Wilmott sitting outside his door on a bench in the sun.

"Don't get up." She greeted him with gladness. "Oh, James, how splendid to see you well again! But you do look a bit peaky." He was indeed a contrast to Adeline, whose health and vitality matched the spring morning. "These Canadian winters," she said, "they leave one deflated."

"The truth is," said Wilmott, "that I am overfed. Since Annabelle's coming my table has groaned beneath the richness of pastry and hot bread. I tell her she's killing me with kindness, poor soul."

"But you do like having her here, don't you, James?"

"I hope I'm grateful," he said.

"But why do you call her 'poor soul?'"

Adeline had seated herself on the bench beside him. She had lowered her voice.

He whispered back, "I am sometimes afraid that Tite is not kind to her ... I have heard her crying."

"I will have a word with him," said Adeline. "But now he is in search of the children. They're playing truant."

"Who can blame them on such a day?" sighed Wilmott.

"What are you longing to escape from?" laughed Adeline.

"Myself."

"Ah, that's the way people feel after lumbago. You will be quite different after another day or two." She sprang up and went to the river's edge. She cupped her hands about her lips and shouted, "Gussie! Nicholas! Ernest! Where are you? You're going to catch it from your father when you come home!" Returning to Wilmott she said, "He really doesn't know they're playing truant."

Strong and clear as was Adeline's voice, no shout of hers reached the ears of the three runaways. By the time afternoon came and Philip returned from the farmlands, Adeline was very angry and not a little alarmed. Philip told her not to worry. The youngsters had gone on an exploring expedition, he said. The spring had got into their blood, he said. They would be home before dark and by Jove he would warm the boys' seats for them. Enquiry revealed that they had been given nothing in the way of a picnic by Mrs. Coveyduck. Surely something untoward had happened.

As evening fell Philip ordered Tite Sharrow to organize a search party. Tite knew every inch of the woodland along the river and much of the forest beyond. There was a full moon and the tranquil May evening was revealed in its mystery and enticement. Every tree wore its cloak of strangeness. The moonlight did not reveal the birds' nests hidden in their boughs.

Philip went with the search party. It was strange to see the dark forms of the men, in seemingly grotesque attitudes, brought to life by the light of the lanterns they carried. Their talk was full of foreboding — of bears that had been seen in the neighbourhood — of the howl of wolves heard in the last winter. Philip's great fear was the river that flowed down from distant hills, past Wilmott's cottage, to lose itself in the lake. He told Wilmott of this fear but mentioned nothing of it to Adeline. She showed her mettle by joining the men of the neighbourhood in the search. They urged her to remain at home with other women for company, but she scorned to do this. "Me stay at home," she cried, "while my three young ones are in danger! Not while I have a leg to stand on!" And use her two lithe legs to carry her about with the men, she did, and every now and again raised her voice and shouted her children's names. Twice during the night the search party were given refreshments at one of the farms. When the moon had sunk there still were lights stirring in the darkness, voices calling.

The nights were short. At daybreak three men were gathered in the living room of Wilmott's cottage making plans for the further search. These were Philip, Wilmott, and Tite Sharrow. Annabelle had brought them a tray heavy with ham sandwiches, freshly baked hot bread, and a huge pot of coffee. But the hot bread was burnt and the coffee such that Wilmott apologized for it. "The poor girl," he said, "is at her wits' end. She's really ill from anxiety."

"It's you I worry about," said Philip. "Here you are up all the night — just getting over an attack of lumbago. As for the coffee — I've tasted worse."

"Not at the table of my boss," Tite said, rising. "I will carry it straight out to Annabelle and she shall make a fresh pot for you." He carried the coffee pot to the kitchen.

A moment later they heard Belle crying, then Tite's low voice. Wilmott said, "The poor girl seems to feel that she is in some way to blame for the disappearance of the children."

Philip sprang up and went to the kitchen.

"Annabelle," he said, "it is nonsense for you to take blame to yourself for what has happened, unless — do you know anything you haven't told?"

She sank to her knees sobbing. "Oh, Lawd forgive me! Oh, Massa Whiteoak, forgive me!"

Philip turned to Tite. "What does she mean?"

Tite gently raised the young woman to her feet. He said, "Belle is so religious, sir, that she blames herself for everything that's happened since the world began."

"Have you anything to tell me, Belle?" asked Philip.

Tite was supporting her in his arms. "Speak, Belle," he said softly. "Tell this gentleman all you know."

"Ah knows nothin'." She spoke with passionate insistence. "Ah knows nothin', God help me."

Back at the table with the re-heated coffee, Philip said to Wilmott, "That's a strange couple you have here. One wonders what their off-spring may be."

Wilmott, after a swig of scalding coffee, said, "God forbid that there should be any."

Philip said, "As for my poor children — as soon as daylight comes, we must drag the river for them."

"I am convinced," said Wilmott, "that they are not drowned. We shall find them in the forest."

They did, however, drag the river, which was in its springtime full-ness. They even searched the stream which wound its way through Jalna but found no trace of the three runaways. The work of the farms was put aside in the search. All neighbours were drawn into it.

It became known that Philip Whiteoak had offered a reward of one thousand dollars for information leading to the discovery of the where-abouts of his children.

Nobody was so tireless in the search as Titus Sharrow. Into the depths of the woods he led his search party. Following the main road from the village, searchers went as far as the lake, from which a light wind was blowing, but so rough and densely wooded was the shore that they found no hope there. Wilmott's rowing boat was tied securely to its little wharf.

One very interested spectator of these activities was Nero. With a look of the greatest sagacity he peered into every thicket, dug a tenta-tive grave in every hollow, barked loudly at every stranger. He came carrying the strip of red flannel from Ernest's throat and laid it at Adeline's feet. When she saw what it was she fell to the ground in a flood of tears.

The day passed with no word of the runaways. The night came, dark and windy. Morning came, grey and windy. The police, the militia of the province were notified. At noonday it was twilight. Out of that twilight appeared Augusta's dove. It flew, white and ghostly, to the roof just about her bedroom window and perched there cooing mournfully. Adeline was the first to see it and to her it seemed to say, "Gussie's gone … Gussie's gone.…"

XXIV

The Runaways

Although the children had spent all their lives within a few miles of the lake they knew little of its moods. Twice during the summer there was a family picnic on its shore, with the added pleasure of bathing; and, when darkness came, a huge bonfire. Once, during the winter, well bundled against the cold, they were taken in a sleigh to see the great ice hummocks formed by the lashing of the waves. When a storm shocked the lake to fury the pounding of waves on the beach could be heard even at Jalna. These booming reverberations were exhilarating to the children. Sometimes the boys pretended that Jalna was a beleaguered place and that hordes of wild Indians were marching on them, with beating of tom-toms and threatening yells. But Augusta withdrew herself at these times and would hide in the summer house with her own vague imaginings. Sometimes the three would take a long walk in the woods, where the roaring of the lake became one with the soughing of the branches.

But now they were on the sunny bosom of that inland sea, heading straight south for the American shore. So favourable was the wind that any manipulation of the single sail was not needed. The little craft and its three adventurers were simply being wafted across to the beckoning States. Augusta had brought with her a map showing the very port for which they were headed. With this spread on her knees, her head bent over it, she studied the distance they must traverse and tried to reckon how long it would take them. They would have no difficulty, she thought, in selling the boat, for it was newly painted and the sail was as white as the dove. That bird seemed happy in his new situation. Now his beloved Gussie was ever close by his side, feeding him tidbits, gently cooing to him. Tethered as he was he strutted across the bottom of the boat and drank from the tin basin set there for him. Yet, Gussie asked herself, was he *really* he? She could not forget the visitor who had appeared without warning and behaved obviously as a suitor.

While Augusta had her map, her notebook, for she intended to keep a log, a complete record of the journey by water and by land, Ernest carried her spyglass and his compass. Already he had a proprietary air towards the spyglass and she almost regretted that she had let him carry it. Yet he was very careful of it. He was a gentle little boy and he had been ill. Through the spyglass he looked back at the Canadian shore, so heavily wooded that it appeared as one great forest, excepting in a spot where a cluster of houses, a church spire, marked a village. Yet nothing looked familiar. The three were explorers in a new universe.

Each time when Ernest examined the view through the spyglass, he consulted the compass and, now and again, would move the tiller. He allowed neither Augusta nor Nicholas to have any part in these activities. They were his own concern and gave him prestige in that company. As always, when he was excited, he was hungry. Even before the time came for a proper meal he begged for a sandwich, then another and still another. Then they all became hungry. Augusta laid the white cloth, with which Belle had provided them, on the lid of the hamper, and there the appetizing food was spread. They could only guess the time of day, for they had no watch.

Nicholas was happy and full of confidence. The immensity of the lake was a joyful challenge to him. He thought he knew all he needed to know to circumnavigate the world, if need be. The children finished the meal with slabs of raisin cake and cold tea. They were replete and of a sudden very drowsy. Ernest indeed fell fast asleep sitting up, with one hand on the tiller. Nicholas was the next to give in. He sat gazing at the exquisite colours of the sunset, his face tinted by its radiance, till he could no longer hold his large dark eyes open. Yet he fought against sleep.

Augusta said, "I will keep watch, Nicholas, till daybreak. Then I will call you. There must always be an officer on duty." She helped Ernest, from his place in the stern, to stretch out on the bottom of the boat, and lashed the tiller with a rope. She took Nicholas's place while he curled up beside Ernest. She laid a rug over them. She reassured the dove by stroking his pale plumage. She settled herself to watch through the night.

Now she was alone with her many responsibilities. Yet, in spite of them, she felt gloriously free. Straight as a die the boat seemed to speed southward towards the American shore. There were no lights of land in sight but a great moon rose and flooded the lake with its brilliance. The little waves were capped with silver. The sail was silver. The dove was a silver bird, immobile, his silver beak sunk on his silver breast.

Augusta could not allow her eyes to rest for long on the figures of her two young brothers lying in attitudes of complete abandon on the bottom of the boat. They looked so helpless and were, she felt, so dependent on her. Still she was not afraid. She set herself to counting the stars which, when the moon began to sink, showed themselves more luminous.

She saw, after a time, lights moving on the lake. They were the lights of a steamship which appeared to be bearing down on them. So close it came that Augusta could hear the engines and the churning of the great wheel. The steamship came overpoweringly near — then miraculously passed. But behind rose the waves of its wake, rocking the small boat so violently that it seemed likely to overturn. Still the two boys slept peacefully. Then by gentle degrees the rocking of the dinghy ceased. Peace and starlight enfolded the lake. Augusta's head dropped to her knees. She slept.

The dove and the three children slept so quietly, so tranquilly, the white sail so steadily received the wind and, with tiller lashed, moved the boat that it might have been guided by some supernatural agency. It might have been thought that the four occupants were under a spell from which only the light of day would wake them.

The sun had not yet risen but there were wafted on the horizon a group of apricot and gold cloudlets which had caught the first colour from the advancing sun. Their colour was cast on the sail of the little boat and on the faces of the two boys, drawing them out of the world of fantasy. The dove woke and spread his wings, as though ready for flight. He uttered cooing sounds.

So long had Gussie slept, with her head on her knees, that when the cooing of the dove woke her she at first felt powerless to move. Slowly she raised her head and, facing the east, received the first red shaft of the rising sun. She heard Ernest's voice.

"Gussie!"

"Yes, Ernest."

"Have you been sleeping?"

"I dozed."

Nicholas sat bolt upright. "You said you'd be on the watch."

"Nothing happened."

"I'm hungry," said Ernest.

They all were hungry.

The boat sped forward in the rosy radiance of sunrise. The waves — for they now had risen from playful ripples — were as though touched by fire. The sail tautened as it gathered speed from the light wind. The clouds became white and, like white-robed angels, moved away from the east and cast their shadows on the lake. Then the lake looked strange and somehow forbidding.

"I'm hungry," repeated Ernest, giving these clouds a slightly apprehensive look.

"You must not eat till you have washed," Augusta told him, "and you too, Nicholas, must wash."

Ernest spread out two small grimy hands. "I'm not dirty," he said, and giggled.

"I'm not dirty either," said Nicholas, showing his still grimier hands. His face was even dirtier.

"Wash yourselves," ordered Augusta, throwing soap, a washcloth, and a towel in their direction.

They obeyed, leaning so far over the side that she warned, "Be careful or you'll fall overboard!" The boys giggled, as though in rebellion. They lost the soap. They struggled over possession of the towel.

"Be careful!" she screamed and they turned on her two dripping laughing faces.

But the laughter left their faces when a gust caught the sail and the boat heeled in a frightening way. Nicholas, now sobered, took charge of the sail. Augusta was at the tiller.

"Where is your compass?" she demanded of Ernest.

Wet tags of hair stood upright on his head. "I'm hungry," he whined. "I'll find my compass when I've had breakfast."

"You may get something out of the hamper," she said, "but I could not let you boys eat with dirty faces."

"Your own face is dirty," Nicholas retorted with a jeering laugh, in which Ernest joined.

Suddenly the boys no longer were the loyal crew. Augusta felt that they were against her. She heard Ernest say, "Compass, my eye!" This crew was ready to mutiny.

She crouched at the gunwale washing her face and hands. She now saw that the boys were eating fruit cake. They were eating greedily, with swigs of cold tea.

"Have some?" Nicholas asked, offering her a slab of cake with nuts and raisins in it.

The boys grinned together like mutineers.

"Thanks," she answered coldly, and ate a chicken sandwich.

The sun now came out gloriously. The lively breeze increased to a moderate wind. Suddenly the boys became a decent crew amenable to orders. "What shall I do?" Nicholas asked when the wind, as though to tease them, changed its course.

"Don't you know?" asked Augusta.

"No."

"But I thought you knew how to manage the sail."

Ernest, peering through the spyglass, asked, "When do we reach Charleston?"

Cautiously Gussie moved to his side and laid her map in front of him. "Can't you understand that first we must reach the American shore, then sell our boat, buy our railway tickets and take train to Charleston?"

Ernest said, "I can't see any shore."

"We shall reach it in time."

"My throat's sore," said Ernest.

Nicholas remarked to Augusta, "We should not have brought this fellow with us. He's always whining and complaining."

"You shut up," said Ernest.

Nicholas shouted back, "If I hadn't this sail to manage, I'd make you sorry."

Ernest began to cry a little. "Gussie," he stammered, "Gussie ..."

Augusta said, "You must not be harsh with him, Nicholas. He's the youngest."

Again the boys turned to her as their captain. But the lake no longer was friendly to them. Its immensity became intimidating. On the lively waves whitecaps appeared. The wind was now quite cold. Gussie wrapped the rug about Ernest's shoulders. She pacified the dove which was getting restless, pecking at the cord which tethered it by the leg.

"I wonder what time it is," said Nicholas. "I wish I had my watch with me."

"I wish I had a hairbrush or comb." Gussie sought to tidy her hair with her fingers.

"I judge," Nicholas had the spyglass to his eye, "that it's about noon."

Ernest snatched the glass from him. "Who said you could have that?" He spoke with temper.

"Boys," said their sister, "we must not quarrel. There's a long journey ahead. There may even be some danger." And she scanned the vast expanse of tumbling waves.

"Danger?" repeated Ernest. "Shall we ever get to Charleston, do you think?"

"If we behave ourselves and don't quarrel," she answered.

"I shall behave," said Ernest. "And I shall even let Nicholas look through my spyglass." He had the effrontery to call it *his* spyglass. He stretched out his hand that held the glass. Nicholas reached out to take it. Between them they dropped it. It struck the gunwale and bounced overboard. No one quite knew how it happened. In trying to save it, Ernest all but fell overboard. Gussie saved him by grasping his hair. He burst into tears as though a terrible disaster had happened. Then he was sick and brought up the fruit cake. He bent over the side of the boat while Gussie held him in her arms. A wave struck the dinghy and then burst over them. They were in water to their knees.

"I'm sorry," said Nicholas. "I'm sorry, Gussie."

Ernest peered into the tumbling greenness. "Did you see where it went?" he quavered.

"It just rolled over and sank," said Nicholas, and repeated, "I'm sorry."

"Never mind," said Ernest. "I still have my compass." He felt in his pocket for the compass. He felt in all his pockets. Raising his eyes, that were wet with tears, to Gussie's gentle face, he quavered, "Do you know where my compass is, Gussie?"

"I'll find it," shouted Nicholas, and began scrabbling among their belongings.

"Mind that sail!" shouted back Augusta.

The boom was beginning to swing ominously, and the sail to flap as though it would tear itself from the mast. "I thought," went on Augusta, "that you knew how to manage the sail." The wind, the noise of the flapping sail, fairly tore the words from her lips, all but drowned the sound of her voice. She repeated, "I thought you understood."

"I don't," he answered.

"You don't know what to do?" she shouted.

"No!" he shouted back and began to cry.

"The sail must be lowered!" she shouted, and began to crawl on hands and knees through the water that stirred uneasily in the bottom of the boat.

The uncontrolled sail set the tiller to swinging wildly, and these appeared suddenly to have complete control of the dinghy. It turned, it wallowed in the green waves. Augusta and Nicholas somehow managed to lower the sail. She lashed the rudder so that it was stable. Now the little boat swung from the crest of one wave to another.

When Ernest saw Nicholas in tears, his own tears dried. He ceased to search for his compass. Casting his eyes over the tumbling waves he asked, "Why has the water turned from blue to green, Gussie?"

"It's the clouds," she answered.

"When do you think we'll see land?" he went on.

"Pretty soon, I guess."

"I'll be glad, won't you?"

"I'm not afraid," she answered stoutly.

That cheered both the small boys. Nicholas said, "I'm hungry."

She gave them dry biscuits, and a fig apiece.

"Lunch," she answered, and opened her mouth wide in a yawn.

"Why are you yawning?" asked Ernest.

"I was on watch all the night."

"Didn't you sleep? Not one little nap?"

"I forget." She spoke crossly.

"More tea, please," they demanded.

She filled the empty bottle from the lake. The green waves strove to submerge both bottle and boat. Through the clouds that now covered the sky they had faint glimpses of the sun. Pale shafts of light from it touched the waves — now nearby — now distant. The lake looked like a strange uncharted ocean.

Presently Ernest found his compass. All three studied it. Augusta exclaimed, shouting to make herself heard, "We are now going east! Nicholas — go to the tiller! Try to change our course!"

But Nicholas was not able to change the helter-skelter course of the dinghy, which slid down one wave, wallowed in the trough, then staggered up the next wave, behaving as though it might at any moment overturn.

Ernest crept close to his sister. "Are you afraid, Gussie?"

She shook her head. "No, not really *afraid*, but I must find the right way. The wind has blown us off our course." She held Ernest tightly by the hand.

He said, "I didn't make much fuss about losing the spyglass, did I?" His forget-me-not-blue eyes, still wet with tears, sought her face for comfort. She thought sorrowfully of that loved possession.

The clouds separated and allowed the sun to shoulder his way between them. The lake appeared to be enjoying a rowdy dance in broad, if chilly, sunlight. Like an accompaniment to this wild ballet of the waves, the wind whistled shrilly and thunder in the distance sounded as muffled drums. The children had nothing to do but watch the weather, and it seemed determined to astonish them.

From the various clouds that, since break of day, gathered and dispersed in the troubled sky, one had emerged as more distinct, more threatening than any other. Now the other clouds moved away from it towards the horizon, leaving a space of a strange greenish colour as a background for it. This cloud took the shape of a man wearing a long cloak, with one arm upraised in a threatening gesture. Not only was the arm raised but, from its gaunt wrist, a hand depended, the forefinger of which pointed downward towards the dinghy.

"Are you afraid, Gussie?" asked Ernest in a tremulous voice. "Is it pointing at us?"

"It's only a springtime cloud," she answered. "What troubles me is that we are off our course."

"When the lake calms," said Nicholas, "we'll put up the sail and I'll take the tiller."

In his shrill child's voice Ernest called out, "Are you afraid, Nicholas?"

"No!"

"Do you wish you were home?"

"No," came back boldly.

"There's something dead in the lake!" screamed Ernest in terror. "It's a drowned baby!"

It was only a large dead fish, pallid and cadaverous, turning over and over in the waves.

Now rain began to fall, pelting down from that menacing cloud in a blinding sheet. So violent it was that it flattened the tops of the rearing waves, took possession of the sky. The dinghy, with its young occupants, seemed to become the object of its vindictiveness. Ernest crouched with his head in Gussie's rain-soaked skirt. Nicholas no longer made any pretence of bravery. He crawled through the water in the bottom of the boat to Gussie's side. Blinded by the downpour, drenched to the skin, they clung together. They did not attempt to speak, but Gussie's slender hands, cold yet comforting, every now and again patted the backs of the boys. The dove sat hunched on her shoulder, its beak sunk on its breast, its wet wings drooping. A very old bird it looked, though it was young.

This deluge of rain appeared to last for a very long time, though it was only a half-hour. It was impossible to guess the time of day. A strange yellowish twilight enveloped sky and lake. The wind had lessened but boisterous waves were white-capped, forming at the horizon a steady line of foam.

Nicholas, ashamed of the tears he had shed, now smiled at Gussie. "I'm hungry," he said.

He actually brought himself to smile. Smiling back she said, "Let's find out what's left in the hamper."

But the contents of the hamper were floating in water. He took from it a piece of pie but it fell apart in his hand. He threw it overboard. At the onslaught of the next wave, the dinghy rocked precariously, the hamper was overturned and its contents floated or were dissolved. Nicholas rescued a cornmeal muffin.

"It's not bad," he said, biting into it. "Have one?" he asked of Ernest.

But the little boy shook his head and then pressed his face against Gussie's side. "I'll never be hungry again," he muttered.

The movement of the clouds showed that another deluge of rain was imminent.

"It would help us to sing a hymn," said Gussie.

Ernest raised his head.

Their young voices were scarcely audible above the uproar of the elements. The boys raised their eyes towards where they hoped God might be lending an ear to them as they sang:

> Eternal Father! strong to save,
> Whose arm hath bound the restless wave,
> Who bidd'st the mighty ocean deep
> Its own appointed limits keep;
> > Oh, hear us when we cry to Thee
> > For those in peril on the sea!

The boys raised their faces, but Gussie sat with her heavy-lidded eyes downcast, her face showing pallid between the mass of dripping hair that hung on either side over her shoulders. She might have been a young creature of the storm, created from the anguished elements.

Scarcely had the singing of the hymn come to an end when the second deluge of rain enveloped them. This they suffered, crouching together in silence, Ernest's face again hidden against Augusta's side. This downpour of rain was briefer than the earlier one but even more penetrating. Any tiniest space left undrenched was now sought out and filled to its limit.

When the rain ceased, which it did reluctantly with a drizzle, the clouds moved westward and the tumbling green lake was revealed. The water in the bottom of the boat moved this way and that, on its surface floating morsels of food, and treasures the children had brought aboard with them. Now the sun shone bright and with warmth in it. Ernest raised his face, strangely mottled in red and white. He raised his tear-drenched eyes to the heavens, and looked askance at the lake.

Tumbling in it was the pallid shape of the large dead fish. "The fish!" he screamed, "the fish!" and threw himself on Gussie.

"It's not the same fish," said Nicholas, his voice sounding hoarse and strange. "It's a bigger one." He peered at it in curiosity.

At the next moment the boat rocked deeply in the trough, the dead fish rose on the wave and was flung with a wriggle into the dinghy.

"Nicholas — put it out!" ordered Gussie, with frightening intensity.

The boy, splashing in the water, caught the fish in his two hands, but its body was so slippery that he dropped it in fright. "It's not dead!" he screamed. "It's living! If you want it put out — do it yourself."

Desperately Gussie disengaged herself from Ernest's clinging arms. She grasped the dead fish and threw it overboard. Caught in the next wave it disappeared.

Searching the sodden edibles in the hamper she found more figs and offered them to the boys. Nicholas eagerly devoured his but Ernest turned his face away. "I shall never eat again," he said.

Again he settled down to cling to Gussie, to hide his face against her. She clasped him but never in all her life had she felt so tired. Pains racked her body. Exhaustion weighed her eyelids. She thought that she had shut her eyes for only a few minutes, but when she opened them again the wind had lessened, the waves somewhat subsided. She saw the taut figure of Nicholas striving to raise the sail. But it resisted, being so wet and, when he had raised it just a little way, it caught the wind, the boom swung wildly outwards, and the boat heeled uncomfortably. They were drifting, buffeted by the boisterous waves.

"I'm starving," Nicholas said in a hoarse voice. "I'm wet to the skin. You look terrible, Gussie. Do you think Ernest is dying?"

"If only I had something warm and dry to wrap him in," she said.

Nicholas said, "Look at the dove! Certainly he is dying."

The dove had resigned himself to the tether by which he was confined. The toes of his little red feet were turned inward and his draggled breast rested on them. His eyes were closed. He ignored the corn that Gussie offered him.

She gathered the last of her courage in a desperate effort to achieve the end of the journey, to reach the beckoning land of America. Her fingers were stiff from cold, so that she could not readily undo the ribbon that held the dove. Even when he was freed he sat drooping.

"Gussie — what are you doing?" cried Nicholas.

"I am sending him home. He will know the way. The direction he takes will show us the way we should go."

Now the sun came through the clouds. The dove sat drooping till the first warmth touched it, then as though new life had inspired it, it raised its wings, two sharply-pointed pinions, skyward. It then in a flutter of energy flew to the top of the mast. This was no quiet perch but rocking as a slender tree in a gale. There the dove sat, staring into the sun, quiet as though carved from alabaster.

The wet shivering children stared up at him entranced.

Suddenly, without warning, he spread his wings and soared upward. Now he was no longer Gussie's dove but a flying bird belonging to sky and lake. He did not falter in the direction he took but sped swiftly on, growing smaller and smaller, till he was no more than a bit of thistledown.

Gussie said, "It's just like I thought. We are drifting back to where we started from."

"Perhaps," Nicholas said, in his new hoarse voice, "we shall see home again."

Augusta stood clinging by one hand to the mast and with the other shading her eyes from the glare of the sun.

XXV

THE RESCUE

Adeline Whiteoak had been awake since sunrise, and that after a restless night. Sunrise had been brilliant. After a few hours of heavy sleep,
induced by a sleeping draught, the fiery blaze of the sunrise struck her
full in the face. Her eyes flying open discovered Philip leaning over her
and her first half-unconscious thought was, "How funny he looks!" for
his face was covered by a yellow stubble, and his eyes were bloodshot.
All came back to her. The nightmare dreams of her few drugged hours
of sleep.

"Don't look so terrified," he said. "At last we have news."

"News?" she repeated, struggling to sit up. "News? For the love of
God — what news?"

He helped her to rise. "Not what you'd like to hear," he said.

She whispered, "Have their bodies been found?"

"No. I think they may still be alive. A young man is here whose boat
they have taken. Tite Sharrow brought him. You'd better come and see
him. Try to control yourself, dearest."

She was pressing her hand against her side to quiet her heart. "Who
is he?"

"A young bank clerk from the town. He owns a small sailing boat which he is just learning to handle. He kept it in a boathouse that he built himself —"

"Are they drowned then?" she whispered through shaking lips.

"We don't know. Come and talk to him."

He led her through the hall that somehow looked strange to her. The young man was in the porch and with him Tite Sharrow.

The young man, fair and thin, took an eager step towards her. "My name," he said, "is Blanchflower. I'm afraid it is my boat your children have taken."

"Blanchflower," repeated Adeline, as though by the repetition of his name she would postpone the dread news he brought. "In Ireland I once knew a man of that name."

"I'm in the Royal Bank in town. I've been saving for years for that boat — it's dreadful to think that it may be the means —"

"You think my children may be on the lake in it?"

"It's not in the boathouse, Mrs. Whiteoak." He looked at her pityingly.

Tite Sharrow spoke up. "I discovered that this gentleman's boat was not in the boathouse, so I went to the town to find out about it."

The bank clerk interrupted, "This lad," he nodded towards Tite, "walked all the way to the town to find me. He must have walked all night. But we had a lift back here. I found that my dinghy was gone. There were small footprints about. I'm afraid ..."

"Could you see any sign of the boat? On the lake, I mean."

"No, Mrs. Whiteoak. And I'm afraid the lake is a bit rough." The young man looked deeply concerned.

Philip said, "The worst is that the young 'uns don't know the first thing about handling a sail."

Tite raised his weary eyes to Philip's face. "Boss," he said, in his low grave voice, "I know a man in Stead who owns a small steam vessel. He takes picnic parties out in it. If I had money to offer him —"

Philip spoke with impatience and terrible anxiety. "You must take me to this man, as soon as possible. Can you ride a fast horse?"

"I can do anything, Boss, if it's in a good cause."

"I must go too!" cried Adeline.

She would not be dissuaded, but must change her clothes.

Tite, serious with the weight of responsibility, set out first to inter-view the owner of the steamship. As he galloped over the country road, sometimes through deep puddles, he had no care for himself or for the horse. His deep engrossing thought was for the rescue of the children. Dark clouds had canopied the sky. Heavy rain threatened. Distant thun-ders sounded across the lake.

Young Isaac Busby came also to Jalna — after an urgent message from Philip. Scarcely had he arrived when the deluge descended. Adeline was in despair, trailing in her long skirts from one room to another, wringing her hands after she had tried to see through the wall of rain that blurred the windows. At noonday it was twilight. Out of the dimness the white form of Augusta's dove appeared. The rain ceased.

The young clerk who owned the dinghy had remained with Adeline. He ran on to the soy grass to investigate, for Bessie had cried out in her excitement at discovering the ghostly shape of the dove. Adeline fol-lowed him.

"Is it Gussie's bird?" she asked, her hand to her throat.

"The maid has gone upstairs to open your daughter's window. The maid thinks that if it is the pet bird," answered young Blanchflower, "it will fly into the house."

The two stood watching the gable where the dove had alighted. Now they saw it slowly, as though wearily, wing its way into Gussie's room. To Adeline it was the final blow. She would have sunk to the ground but Blanchflower supported her. So Philip found them when he came with the news that arrangements had been made to hire the steamship.

"The children are lost — drowned," Adeline was just able to articu-late. "The dove has come back to tell us."

"We must not lose hope," he said, and ran up the two flights of stairs to Gussie's room.

When he came down again he moved more slowly.

"Well?" asked Adeline.

"It's Gussie's dove — looking very draggled. But I believe it's brought good news…. Will you come on the steamship? The owner is having it got ready. Isaac Busby is here on a fast horse."

Young Blanchflower said in an undertone to Philip, "Do you think

Mrs. Whiteoak should accompany us? Supposing we should find the dinghy floating — with no one in it?"

"My wife," Philip returned haughtily, "is not the sort of woman to be left behind."

Two hours later the steamer, fresh-painted and trig for summer service, was moving in erratic fashion about the lake in search of the dinghy with the lost children. There were on board the captain and his crew of two, Philip and Adeline, Wilmott and Isaac Busby, young Blanchflower and Titus Sharrow.

Tite had the sharpest eyesight. He stood in the bow and it was he who first, after hours of search, sighted the dinghy. "I've found it!" he cried. "I've found it! Can't you see?"

But none of the others could as yet see the small boat. They crowded into the bow of the steamship. Adeline stood on a seat, Philip supporting her. Now she discovered the dinghy and the three small half-drowned figures in it. "They're dead!" she screamed, while Philip clasped her tightly. "Don't look," he said. "Don't look."

The engine of the steamer slowed down its speed. As the two boats drew near, Tite leaped overboard. After the splash he could be seen striking out for the dinghy. The steamer stopped.

"Children! Children!" screamed Adeline. "I'm here! Look up!"

Three white little faces were raised towards her. She and the others in the steamship saw Tite clamber over the side of the dinghy.... It was he who lifted the children, one by one, and placed them in extended arms.

Young Blanchflower remarked to Philip, "That half-breed is a wonderful fellow. I've never seen anything more neatly done."

"He shall be well rewarded," said Philip.

"It was remarkable," went on Blanchflower, "how he discovered my boathouse and got the idea that the children had run off with my boat."

"He is an altogether remarkable fellow," said Philip. "Mr. Wilmott can tell you that." But Philip hardly knew what he was saying. His eyes were fixed on the three limp figures, dripping and scarcely conscious. It was he who took them from Tite into his own arms and carried them to the cabin.

"Gussie — Nick — Ernie —" he kept saying. "Papa's here — you're safe. Mamma is here — speak to her." But only moans came from their blue lips. Nicholas was the first to show interest in his rescue. "Tite," he got out, then could not continue. "Yes — yes —" said Philip. "Tite found you. He was the first to sight the dinghy."

Nicholas smiled. "I'm glad you found us," he said.

"How hoarse his voice is!" cried Adeline. "Oh, how miserable he looks!"

"He smiled," said Philip.

Young Blanchflower carried Gussie. To him she appeared beautiful and romantic. He thought, as he crossed the doorsill into the small cabin that smelt of paint and putty, "Why — I might be an old-time bridegroom, carrying his stolen bride over the threshold of his castle!" He was a hopelessly romantic young man.

The little steamship, after this first excursion of her season, turned about and made her way homeward. There were two slippery haircloth sofas in her cabin, and the children wrapped in blankets were laid on these. Ernest caused the greatest anxiety to his parents. In spite of frequent sips of brandy he still continued to shiver. He seemed only half-conscious. Adeline held him in her arms. Philip divided his time between the two older children, chafing their hands and feet, patting their backs reassuringly. On deck, Tite Sharrow squatted in the warm sunshine which now made itself pleasantly felt. A look of extreme peace lay like a veil on his face. For some reason Wilmott avoided him.

The owner of the dinghy, Peter Blanchflower, descended from the steamer into the little craft. Thankful he was to have it restored to him, not damaged — only dirty. He sloshed through the water, in which floated the debris of the children's voyage. He found an empty tin and began to bail out the water. Wilmott, leaning over the rail of the steamer, asked:

"Would you like me to help you?"

"Not unless you want to come, sir."

"Are you sailing back to your boathouse?"

"Yes. The wind is in the right direction. We should arrive some time before the others, who must come from the pier by road. I'd like to have your company, sir."

Climbing with agility over the rail Wilmott too descended into the dinghy. Between them they put the sailing gear in order. Isaac Busby came to look down on their activities. He said to young Blanchflower, "In my opinion you should share equally in the reward with Tite Sharrow."

Blanchflower raised his face which the spring sunlight discovered as particularly candid, unassuming, and attractive. With the sail's rope between his teeth he said, "I have done nothing."

Wilmott said, "I agree. The reward should be shared." Wilmott felt that he would be more comfortable in his own mind if Tite were not given the full reward. To him there was something shady in this rescue, though he could not have told what.

Blanchflower, however, was obdurate, refusing any part in the reward. Tite stood now, at a little distance, listening. A lithe dark figure, his beautiful torso glistening in the sunshine, he listened as though aloof from all these doings.

At about the same time the steamer and the dinghy moved in different directions across the gay springtime lake, the steamer returning to Stead, the dinghy, breeze borne, to the boathouse. Philip called out to Wilmott and Blanchflower an invitation to come to dinner. So, having housed the dinghy and conveyed the news of the rescue to Annabelle, the two set out to walk to Jalna. On the way Blanchflower exclaimed to Wilmott, "I cannot think of a better life than that led by you and the Whiteoaks. When I take my holidays I'd like nothing so well as to come and camp by your river, if I might."

"You'd be very welcome," said Wilmott, who found the young man congenial company. He even confided to him that, some years before, he had written a novel but had never yet mustered the courage to send the manuscript to a publisher. Blanchflower, a confirmed reader of fiction, said with fervour that there was nothing he would enjoy so much as reading the novel.

By the time they reached Jalna they found the family returned, the doctor's gig in front of the door, and the children tucked in bed. They had been given warm bread and milk, though Nicholas had great difficulty in swallowing because of inflamed tonsils. Little Ernest lay in beatific happiness, simply at being able to hold his mother's hand and gaze out of swollen eyes into her solicitous face. He did not notice how pale she was or the blue shadows beneath her eyes. His mind was dazed by the joy of lying safe in her bed, with her beside him. Nicholas was on the sofa in the library, with Nero on the rug beside him and Philip close by. Now and again Philip would say, "All right, old man?" and Nicholas would nod, his eyes filling with tears, his hand reaching towards Philip.

Augusta, having been given a hot bath, a drink of beef broth, was tucked up in bed. She could hear her dove cooing on the gable above. She was content to lie tranquil, unutterably tired, savouring the fact that she and the boys had been rescued from the peril of the lake.

She dozed, but was waked by the consciousness that someone was standing by the bed, looking down at her. It was young Blanchflower standing there with a cup of steaming coffee in his hand.

"Your mother was bringing this to you," he said, "but she looked so weary I asked if I might." And he added, "I have a young sister about your age."

She did not try to hide her weakness from him.

He put a hand behind her shoulders and, raising her a little, held the coffee cup to her lips. She drank.

Never again, in all her life, did any drink taste so delicious. Never again did any young man look so beautiful. She would have liked to kiss his hand. Instead she whispered, "I ran away."

"So did I — once," he said, and tucked the quilt about her. "I ran — to Canada."

"I'm glad," Gussie whispered. When next she opened her eyes he was gone, but, in her fancy, his image had effectually banished the image of Guy Lacey.

XXVI

TITE AND BELLE

A week later Wilmott sat by the writing table in his little sitting room, not writing, but with his head resting on his hand, thinking. He thought of young Blanchflower and how he had read the manuscript of Wilmott's novel, written ten years before, and been enthusiastic about it. Wilmott valued his opinion. Now Adeline Whiteoak had promised, with all her native enthusiasm, to take the manuscript with her to the very den of a publisher in London. She was pleased to do this for her friend, thoroughly resolute about it.

At this moment Wilmott was trying to put out of his consciousness the palpable unhappiness of the mulatto, Belle. She had been broadly smiling, almost exuberantly happy. Now her mobile face expressed foreboding and gloom. Her eyes looked bloodshot, as from wakeful nights and weeping. Yet she should have been happier than ever. Here she was, married to the man she obviously, even slavishly adored. Yes, slavishly — and she a *free* woman — as free as any woman who loved Tite could be. Added to the other causes for her happiness was the fact that the reward offered by Philip Whiteoak had been paid in full to Tite. The half-breed had wanted to keep the cash under the mattress of his bed, and this he had done for the first two nights after possession of it. On the third night, however, Wilmott was woken by an outburst of hysterical crying by Belle. This was no outburst from an undisciplined half-savage creature but a heartbroken cry from a woman's depth of misery.

Wilmott had sprung up and, without knocking, strode into the young couple's room. The room was dark except for a pale moonlight. Tite could be seen clasping Belle to his chest while, with her arms thrown about him, she appeared to be struggling to free herself.

"Now, what is this scene about?" Wilmott had peremptorily demanded.

Belle had completely disappeared beneath the bedclothes but her sobs still shook the bed. Tite had risen and stood, a bronze night-shirted figure, facing Wilmott. They went into the outer room.

"I've stood all of this that I can," Wilmott said. "It's got to stop."

"Belle is ailing, Boss," said Tite.

"Is she expecting a baby?"

Tite spoke reproachfully. "Boss, surely you do not think I would inflict such an inconvenience on you.... No — Belle is ailing because she is too religious. She is all the while accusing herself of sin. She is tormenting herself over fancied sins."

"Have you any inkling as to her fancies?"

"I have none, Boss."

"I will go to her," said Wilmott. "Perhaps she will confide in me."

"I beg of you not to do that, Boss. It will only excite her.... What she needs is a change. My grandmother is very skilful in treating sick folks — with herbs and with good advice. If you think you can get along without us, Boss, I will take Belle to visit my grandmother on the Indian Reserve."

Truly the prospect of being without that dusky pair was very pleasing to Wilmott. He had relished the presence of the pretty mulatto in the house. She was so sweet-tempered, so gay, so solicitous for his comfort. Now how depressing the change! Belle had gone off most dreadfully in her looks — still more in spirits. When the pair drove off in a mud-encrusted old buggy which had appeared as from nowhere, Wilmott had watched their departure with a groan of relief.

Yet how empty, how even desolate seemed the little house! The sound of the river, edging its way among the reeds, was lonely. His mind flew to the days when he and Tite were sufficient to each other for company. Of course he had invitations to dinner, to Jalna, to the rectory, to the Laceys and the Busbys, but still he continued to miss Tite. For one thing he was so accustomed to the physical presence of Tite, his gliding, yet so distinctly masculine movements, his low, gravely modulated voice. Wilmott had taken Tite under his roof when Tite was an almost illiterate stripling. He had found a receptive pupil, so good at his books, so seemingly ambitious, that the two had talked freely of his studying law, of becoming a famous lawyer. But it was just talk. Anyway, what chance was there for a half-breed lawyer in this country? And Tite was not truly ambitious — any more than Wilmott ever had been. The life they lived suited them perfectly. They were perfect companions.

The truth was that Wilmott was jealous of the part Annabelle played in Tite's life. Even her good cooking did not make up for the loss in companionship.

Tite had not said when he and Annabelle would return. Sometimes, during the long rainy week that followed their departure, Wilmott wondered if ever they would come back. There had seemed something so definite, so final in their leave-taking.

On an evening when the rain had ceased and Wilmott, in his punt, was about to push off from the little wharf, the grave, gentle note of Tite's voice sounded directly behind him.

"I'm back, Boss," he said.

Wilmott was dumbfounded. For a moment he was speechless, then he asked, "Where is Belle?"

"She is still at the Reserve, Boss."

"With your grandmother?"

"No, Boss — with my cousin. I've sold her to him."

"You couldn't…. It's against the law."

"Not against the Indian law, Boss."

"Belle will be heartbroken. It's an abominable way to use her."

Tite dropped lightly from the wharf into the punt.

"Boss," he said, "Belle is a slave. She is used to being bought and sold."

"You never think of her feelings. How will this cousin of yours treat her?"

"He will treat her very well. He is a kind man — a widower with three small children. He needs a wife, Boss. We don't."

"The whole affair is unspeakable. Get out of this boat!" Wilmott spoke loudly. He felt that he hated this cruel half-breed who now said:

"Belle is a religious young woman. My cousin is a religious man. I have tried hard to be religious, Boss."

"You're a hypocrite, Tite."

"On the contrary, Boss, I am very sincere. I do the things and think the things that other men would like to do and think. What I like best is to serve you — to think of what you tell me."

"Get out of this boat!" repeated Wilmott.

For answer Tite picked up a fishing rod that lay on the wharf within reach. Also there was a tin of bait. Tite chose a worm and gently put it on the hook. The punt was drifting downstream. Tite dropped the baited line over the side and shortly a fine salmon was drawn in.

"How old is this cousin of yours?" demanded Wilmott.

"He is sixty, Boss."

"What did he pay you?" It was hard for Wilmott to get out the words.

Tite gazed reflectively at the salmon. He said:

"My cousin paid me forty dollars in cash, Boss. He also gave me two acres of land, with a gravel pit on it. He is a well-off Indian, Boss. Belle will be properly looked after. She is lucky to have such a husband."

The gentle scents of early summer rose from the banks of the river. Along its banks marsh marigolds bloomed to the water's edge. Wilmott's anger at Tite faded. It was useless to try to change him. He was as fluid and as stable as the river.

Like a benign shadow he glided about the little house, restoring the order upset by Wilmott. Together they sat down to their evening meal. A slim new moon rose out of the river and shone its silver light on them.

Tite remarked, "It seems to me, Boss, that you and I are not marrying men. We are so happy in the company of each other. A woman is quite *de trop*."

XXVII

ANOTHER VOYAGE

So exhausted were the three runaways when they were brought home, so thankful they were to be there, that they never considered whether retribution for their escapade would befall them, but as they recovered they were expectant of dire punishment. They were quite mistaken. Philip had said to Adeline, "The young 'uns have suffered enough, in my opinion," and she had acquiesced. She herself was so thankful to have them safe that she shrank from anything that would upset that peace of mind.

It was a joyful occasion when the children were able to join the grown-ups at the tea table. Wilmott and Blanchflower also were there — that young man having been accepted into the family circle.

"I see quite a difference in the children," said Wilmott. "I think they've grown." He gave them his smile that had a rare sweetness in it.

Philip looked them over with some complacence. "They've terrific appetites," he said, "yet they all have lost weight. Ernest is positively skinny."

"The sea voyage will restore them. They will come back with roses in their cheeks," said Wilmott.

"Look at Gussie." Philip fixed his brilliant blue gaze on his daughter. "She's as yellow as a crow's foot."

Young Blanchflower gave an admiring glance at Augusta. "It seems to me," he said, "that Miss Gussie's complexion has a delicate ivory quality."

This remark sent the small boys into fits of smothered laughter. Augusta's long lashes were downcast.

"I am at my wits' end," put in Adeline, "to accomplish all I must before we sail. Only think — six people to be outfitted!"

"I only make your party as five," said Wilmott.

"What of my baby?" exclaimed Adeline. "Never again shall I let my children out of my sight."

"But what a care he will be!" said Wilmott.

Philip gave him a wink. "Why, don't you remember how, on the voyage out, I had the entire care of Gussie? Didn't I, Gussie? I did everything — actually everything — for that infant."

The boys again gave way to smothered laughter.

Philip, seeing that they had quite finished their tea, ordered them from the table.

Adeline called to them, "And don't you dare to leave the room!" Turning to Blanchflower she added, "It behooves me to cherish the few children I have left."

His face was full of sympathy. "I did not know ... I'm so sorry," he stammered.

Tears filled her eyes. "It's my poor nerves," she answered. "I can't remember how many I should have."

"They're all four safe," laughed Philip, "and we thank God there are no more of them."

"Our youngest is a lovely child" — her eyes glowed in pride — "he's a blond like his father. We have no red-heads — which shows what a modest woman I am. Ah, but my poor nerves are shattered! You'd never believe how I've changed. Am I not greatly changed, Gussie?"

This was too much for Gussie. She came to her mother's side and gazed down at her in contrition and pity. Tall child as she was, Adeline drew Gussie on to her knee and beamed at those about the table. Wilmott stretched out an arm and drew Nicholas, his favourite, onto his knee. Seeing this, Ernest at once climbed to Philip's lap and helped himself to another scone. Young Blanchflower thought he never had seen a more devoted family.

"I hear," said Adeline, "that Tite Sharrow has come back without Belle, and that they've separated. Is that true, James?"

"I will tell you of that when these young ones have retired," said Wilmott.

"Please tell it now," begged Ernest. "We love gossip."

Philip gave a shout of laughter. "You don't even know what gossip is."

"We hear quite a lot of it," said Nicholas, "but we heard nothing amusing when we were on the lake. Do tell us!"

"No — no." Wilmott pushed him off his knee. Philip looked at his watch. "It's time all three were in bed. Dr. Ramsay says you young 'uns must be in bed by sundown for the next fortnight. So — kiss goodnight all round and off you go."

Augusta stood up straight, then bent to kiss her mother, next Philip, then Wilmott. When she reached Blanchflower she hesitated.

"Go ahead, Gussie — give him a nice kiss," came in Adeline's laughing tones.

The silken mane of Augusta's hair fell over Blanchflower. She just touched his forehead with her lips that still were pale from the ordeal she had suffered.

Back in her own room she thought, "Why, oh why, didn't I give him a nicer kiss! But — if I had — they would have laughed at me."

It was heaven to be safe at home again. It was bliss to wake in the night and to feel the bed steady beneath one. It was bliss to hear the rain beating on the roof and know it could not get at you.

The weeks that followed were crowded with preparations for the journey by land and sea. The three boys had been born in Canada — Augusta in India, but she remembered nothing of the voyage out.

It was thought that the children were not yet strong enough for study. On his part Wilmott relaxed with almost conscious delight in the warmer weather, in the fullness of growth, in the abundance of fish in the stream, in the birdsong that thrilled the woods, and, not least, in the return of Tite as a single man. Rigorously he put from his mind the manner of this achievement.

Of all those affected by this journey, Nero understood least but felt most. He had been told nothing, yet knew all. He knew, for instance, that he was too big to conceal himself in a piece of hand luggage. His hope lay in so closely attaching himself to something that was accompanying the travellers that they would take him unknowingly. When the first trunk was carried down the stairs and set in the hall he placed his woolly body firmly beside it. When other trunks and portmanteaux appeared he investigated each one in turn and gathered them, as it were, under his guardianship. But when members of the family, dressed for travel, came to the hall Nero would raise such pleading eyes to them as might have moved a heart of stone. Yet so occupied were they by their own affairs that they scarcely noticed him. Now and again he would heave a profound sigh. On the last day before departure Tite Sharrow brought a stout leather thong and fixed it to Nero's collar. Tite was strong but he was tired out after he had dragged Nero the wooded way to Wilmott's cottage. It would be months before that loyal Newfoundland would return to Jalna, except to visit the house each day and make sure that all was in order and possibly be given a second dinner by Mrs. Coveyduck.

As for Augusta's dove, it (now definitely *she*) had taken up with pigeons and was building a nest with the masterful assistance of the stout gentleman who previously had paid her such marked attention. Two days before the departure of the family the dove laid an egg which completely occupied her thoughts. It meant more to her than did all the months of devotion Gussie had lavished on her.

The children were now almost completely recovered from the hardships they had endured, yet they were in a degree changed — Augusta most of all. She had grown taller and her child's body had developed new and not so childish curves. The expression of her large eyes, always inclined to be pensive, was now often abstracted, even melancholy. She would appear lost in thought, yet could not possibly have told what she was thinking of. Sometimes her lips would part in a secret smile. She would spread her hands and examine them with interest, but again she would clench them and stalk away like a tragedy actress. Her father's chaffing, her mother's personal remarks, became almost unbearable to her. She wanted to burst into tears. At the same time she was full of gratitude for the magnanimity they had shown toward their runaways. She dreaded the going to sea and the thought of the movement of the ship made her seasick.

The change in Nicholas was noticeable also. He was more adventurous and appeared to have forgotten how disastrously his runaway voyage had turned out. He would boast of the dangers he had endured, swagger a bit in his talk. There was not a corner of the ship that he did not explore. Though he never thought with gratitude of his parents' leniency, he showed it in his willingness to take charge of little Philip, to help him to walk on the deck or to carry him in his arms to visit different parts of the ship. They were favourites in all quarters. When they reached England, Adeline would, she declared, get a proper nurse for him.

There was no physical resemblance between the boys, yet anyone noting their movements, hearing their laughter, would have taken them for brothers. Little Philip longed to do everything Nicholas did, while Nicholas imitated their father, his walk, his speech, his air of a soldier.

On the second morning at sea, Ernest who, in the midst of all this movement of ship, of sea, of passengers, lived rather a lonely life, was wandering along the promenade deck, where ladies reclined in deck chairs, recovering from an encounter with seasickness or simply enjoying good salt air. Ernest took a second look at one of these. She reminded him of someone he had liked long long ago, when he was quite a small boy. Now he felt an experienced traveller, in his belted tunic which reached almost to the knees, his striped stockings, and his buttoned boots.

He trotted to where Augusta stood leaning against the rail. "Gussie," he said, "guess who is on board."

She gave him a dreamy look. "I'm no good at guessing. Tell me," she said.

"Mrs. Sinclair!"

"Did she see you?"

"No. I ran away. Shall we tell her that we were on our way to visit her?"

"For pity's sake — no."

"We could say we just changed our minds."

Augusta bowed her forehead to the rail. "I could die of shame," she said. "Mamma will tell her that we ran away, and were brought back crying our eyes out. I for one will not see the Sinclairs. I will lock myself in my cabin and say I am sick."

"What shall I do?"

"Do what you like."

Ernest felt that Gussie had cast him off, and he seemed to remember having been very kind to her, time and again. He turned and trotted back along the deck.

Lucy Sinclair was sitting where he had left her.

He went close to her and asked, "Do you remember me, Mrs. Sinclair?"

She stared in astonishment, then exclaimed, "Why, it's the little Whiteoak boy! Fancy meeting you here! Are your parents with you?"

"We're all here. All but Gussie."

"Gussie not here? Then where is she?"

"I — I really don't know."

Ernest's mind became a convenient blank but he still gazed in admiration at Lucy Sinclair's beige-coloured foulard coat trimmed with velvet, her hair done in a beautiful chignon.

At this moment Curtis Sinclair appeared, smiling and looking somehow very different from the man Ernest remembered.

"Ah, Curtis," cried his wife, "you have quite deceived this little Whiteoak boy by your Dundreary whiskers."

"Whiteoak," repeated Curtis Sinclair, in bewilderment. "Why — it's Ernest! Are your family on board, my boy?"

"All but Gussie," said Ernest, his clear blue eyes on the whiskers. They made a great difference in the American's appearance, and, to Lucy's mind, a vast improvement. Certainly the disfigurement of his back was less noticeable with a fine fair whisker flowing towards each shoulder. The expression of his mobile face was more assured. His face was fuller. He had the appearance of a gentleman turned out in the height of fashion.

Philip and Adeline, taking a stroll along the deck, now appeared, she leaning on his arm. She gave a cry of delight when she saw the Sinclairs.

"What an auspicious meeting," said Philip, "and what a surprise! Upon my word, Sinclair, you look stunning. Has it taken long to grow them?"

"Not so long," said Curtis Sinclair, caressing his whiskers, "as you might think."

"I hear they are the rage in London," Adeline said. "I really long to discover if they are real."

"Don't deny yourself any pleasure I can give you," smiled Curtis Sinclair.

Lucy Sinclair interrupted with, "You should grow Dundrearys yourself, Captain Whiteoak. You would look really splendid."

"Yellow whiskers," said Adeline. "I can't think of anything less attractive."

"A moustache is good enough for me," said Philip.

Nicholas now came along the deck holding the chubby hand of the youngest Whiteoak. The Sinclairs greeted them affectionately, remarking their growth and good looks. Then Lucy said, "I do wish you had brought Gussie with you. She's such a charming child."

"We did bring her," said Philip. "She's around somewhere."

"But Ernest told me that she was not on board."

Philip stretched out a long arm and caught Ernest by the collar. "What nonsense is this?" His voice was threatening.

"Where is your sister?" demanded Adeline.

Ernest trembled. "She's gone. I guess she fell overboard."

"Overboard!" Adeline's voice was piercing. Those about began to stare.

"Order a lifeboat launched," cried Lucy.

"Perhaps she's in her cabin," Ernest said. "I'll run and see." He ran off. Adeline sped after him. She found the door of Augusta's cabin locked and beat on it, calling her daughter's name.

The door was opened. Augusta stood there. "Mamma," she said, in a shaking voice, "I cannot face the Sinclairs — after what I did — please — please, let me stay here."

"Oh, what a fright this little wretch gave me!" Adeline began to shake him but Gussie begged her to desist. "It was my fault, Mamma. Please don't punish him. Ernest said that only to protect me."

"I should think," said Adeline, "you would be proud of such an adventure. The Sinclairs would be flattered to think you had set out to visit them."

"No — no. It was so — silly," said Gussie. "Please don't tell!"

"Were there ever such children? It's enough to wreck my nerves the things they do!"

Ernest asked, in his gentle voice, "Shall I run up to the deck and tell that Gussie is safe?"

As he was about to pass through the door, Philip entered. Adeline began eagerly, rather incoherently, to talk. Her voice followed Ernest as he ran lightly along the passage. Life had become intensely interesting to him. When he found the Sinclairs still occupying their deck chairs, and Nicholas and the youngest Whiteoak nowhere in sight, he perched on the foot of Lucy's chair, and said, "Gussie might have fallen overboard but I rescued her. She wanted to visit you in Charleston but the lake was rough. So I rescued both her and Nicholas. Please don't tell anybody. I don't want a reward. Gussie's crying because she's afraid I'll tell. I don't really want to be a hero. I just enjoy rescuing my family."

"How did you rescue Gussie?" asked Lucy Sinclair.

"I jumped overboard," he said complacently. "It's a good thing I swim so well. That is twice I have rescued her. But please don't tell."

The Sinclairs, amused and puzzled, promised.

Philip and Adeline now returned. She exclaimed, "That young daughter of mine has *such* a temperament! She's a thorough young flibbertigibbet. I really can't follow her moods." She sank down on her chair.

Lucy Sinclair said, "I think you have a most fascinating family, Mrs. Whiteoak. My husband and I admire them excessively."

"Ah, they're a lively lot," sighed Adeline. "Nicholas is like my family. Ernest and the baby are Whiteoaks. But Gussie, she's like nobody except her own queer self."

At this moment, Gussie, alone in her cabin, again locked the door, opened her portmanteau, and took from it a spyglass. This had been a present from young Blanchflower, just before her sailing. She had told him of the loss of her own, told him without shyness, without a shadow of hinting; and he had told her that, on leaving England, his uncle had presented him with one which lay unused, neglected, and all but forgotten, on a shelf in his clothes cupboard. Would she accept it, he asked, as a goodbye present, a small token of the regard he had for her? She accepted it with modesty but hid it from her family with determination. It was her most treasured possession.

Now she took it out of her portmanteau, and after dusting it with an enormous silk handkerchief that rightly belonged to her father and smelt of his cigars, she went to the open porthole and peered through it.

There came a loud knocking on the door. It was Nicholas, who called out: "Gussie — come! See the last of Canada. Mrs. Sinclair begs you to come."

"I don't think I care to."

"Papa orders you to come! And, look here, the Sinclairs have been told nothing. Come along, do."

Without further hesitation Gussie, now in a mood of daring, followed Nicholas up the stairs to the deck, carrying the spyglass. The sea was a little rough. The coast rose, rocky and dim. Wild and dim were the gulls flying from coast to sea and back again.

"It's getting rough," said Curtis Sinclair and came and stood at Gussie's side.

"I envy you," he said, in his Southern accent.

She could scarcely believe her ears.

"But — why?" she asked, her low sweet voice scarcely audible.

"Because," he smiled, "you are on your way to England for the first time and you own a spyglass."

She offered the spyglass to him but he refused. "No, Miss Gussie, I had rather watch you looking through it. May I say that I admire the picture you make?" He moved away a short distance, then stood looking back.

Gussie's hair was blown from off her face by the strong fresh wind. She held the spyglass to her eyes, gazing, as it were, into her future, and not at the receding coast. For the remainder of the voyage she was dreamy, aloof.

Adeline and Philip were happy to be again in the company of the

Sinclairs. They discovered that they were going to the same hotel in London. The Sinclairs were lively and appeared to be in affluent circumstances.

"Upon my word," Adeline remarked to Philip, "I shall jump for joy when we reach London and I am able to engage a proper nurse for the baby — he's wearing me out."

"He's grown into a little boy," said Philip, "and no baby. The Sinclairs greatly admire him."

"Philip" — Adeline spoke seriously — "where do you suppose all their money comes from? I thought they were ruined when the South was defeated."

"It's cotton" — his eyes shone — "Sinclair's father sent cotton to Manchester. Now Sinclair is coming over to make further arrangements. He advises me to invest in cotton."

"I should love to visit France with them," said she, "but the children cramp all our movements. I had thought Gussie would take part charge of Baby — but no — she moons about with that silly spyglass."

"I shall make some arrangement to please you," said Philip. "I promise you that."

She threw her arms about him and gave him three kisses. After the third she said, "The children would be quite happy with my parents in Ireland. Did I tell you that they are coming to meet us? I had a letter from my mother."

"You didn't tell me," he exclaimed.

"I forgot."

He made the best of it. "That will be nice." He reflected that this would be better than having a visit from them at Jalna. He added firmly, "Please don't tell your father that I expect to make a good deal of money from cotton."

"Indeed, I will not, for he would be sure to want to borrow from you."

It was a smooth and sunny voyage. When the ship docked at Liverpool, there were Adeline's parents to meet them. They would journey with them and the Sinclairs to London on the following day.

Adeline was proud of her parents, proud of the impression they made on the Sinclairs. Indeed they looked little changed since she had last seen them.

The six grown-ups and four children took possession of a large sitting room in the Adelphi Hotel. Lucy Sinclair remarked to Renny Court, Adeline's father, "It is easy to see how dear Mrs. Whiteoak came by her handsome eyes and — her hair."

"The eyes aren't bad," said Renny Court, "but the hair — well, I suppose it's an affliction for a woman."

"I admire it excessively," she returned. "Your daughter is the most strikingly handsome woman I know. Her children are lovely. I envy her them."

"My wife and I are taking the children to Ireland," said Renny Court, "for a long visit."

"What fun!" exclaimed Lucy Sinclair.

THE END

The Jalna Novels by Mazo de la Roche

In Order of Year of Publication	In Order of Year Story Begins
Jalna, 1927	*The Building of Jalna*, 1853
Whiteoaks of Jalna, 1929	*Morning at Jalna*, 1863
Finch's Fortune, 1931	*Mary Wakefield*, 1894
The Master of Jalna, 1933	*Young Renny*, 1906
Young Renny, 1935	*Whiteoak Heritage*, 1918
Whiteoak Harvest, 1936	*The Whiteoak Brothers*, 1923
Whiteoak Heritage, 1940	*Jalna*, 1924
Wakefield's Course, 1941	*Whiteoaks of Jalna*, 1926
The Building of Jalna, 1944	*Finch's Fortune*, 1929
Return to Jalna, 1946	*The Master of Jalna*, 1931
Mary Wakefield, 1949	*Whiteoak Harvest*, 1934
Renny's Daughter, 1951	*Wakefield's Course*, 1939
The Whiteoak Brothers, 1953	*Return to Jalna*, 1943
Variable Winds at Jalna, 1954	*Renny's Daughter*, 1948
Centenary at Jalna, 1958	*Variable Winds at Jalna*, 1950
Morning at Jalna, 1960	*Centenary at Jalna*, 1953

From *Mazo de la Roche: Rich and Famous Writer* by Heather Kirk

International Bestsellers
by Mazo de la Roche
Back in Print!

Jalna
978-1894852234
$24.99

Whiteoaks of Jalna
978-1894852241
$24.95

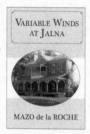

Variable Winds at Jalna
978-1554887934
$24.99

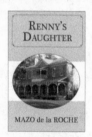

Renny's Daughter
978-1554887927
$24.99

Centenary at Jalna
978-1554889181
$24.99

Mazo de la Roche
Rich and Famous Writer
by Heather Kirk
978-1894852203
$17.95

Mazo de la Roche was once Canada's best-known writer, loved by millions of readers around the world. She created unforgettable characters who come to life for her readers, but she was secretive about her own life. When she dies in 1961, her cousin and lifelong companion. Caroline Clement, burned her diaries, adding to the aura of mystery that already surrounded Mazo.

Available at your favourite bookseller.

www.dundurn.com

What did you think of this book?
Visit www.dundurn.com for reviews, videos, updates, and more!